Praise for John Gilstrap

HOSTAGE ZERO

"Jonathan Grave, my favorite freelance peacemaker, problem-solver, and tough-guy hero, is back—and in particularly fine form. *Hostage Zero* is classic Gilstrap: the people are utterly real, the action's foot-to-the-floor, and the writing's fluid as a well-oiled machine gun.
A tour de force!"
—**Jeffery Deaver**

"This addictively readable thriller marries a breakneck pace to a complex, multilayered plot. . . . A roller-coaster ride of adrenaline-inducing plot twists leads to a riveting and highly satisfying conclusion . . . An absolute must read for thriller fans."
—*Publishers Weekly* (starred review)

NO MERCY

"*No Mercy* grabs hold of you on page one and doesn't let go. Gilstrap's new series is terrific. It will leave you breathless. I can't wait to see what Jonathan Grave is up to next."
—**Harlan Coben**

"The release of a new John Gilstrap novel is always worth celebrating, because he's one of the finest thriller writers on the planet. *No Mercy* showcases his work at its finest—taut, action-packed, and impossible to put down!"
—**Tess Gerritsen**

"A great hero, ⬛⬛⬛⬛⬛⬛⬛⬛⬛ unch of a

"An entertain⬛⬛⬛⬛st-pace⬛⬛⬛⬛⬛⬛⬛⬛⬛revenge."
—*Publishers Weekly*

HOSTAGE ZERO

"No other writer is better able to combine in a single novel both rocket-paced suspense and heartfelt looks at family and the human spirit. And what a pleasure to meet Jonathan Grave, a hero for our time . . . and for all time."
—**Jeffery Deaver**

AT ALL COSTS

"Riveting . . . combines a great plot and realistic, likable characters with look-over-your-shoulder tension.
A page turner."
—*The Kansas City Star*

"Gilstrap builds tension . . . until the last page, a hallmark of great thriller writers. I almost called the paramedics before I finished *At All Costs*."
—*Tulsa World*

"Not to be missed."
—*Rocky Mountain News*

"Gilstrap has ingeniously twisted his simple premise six ways from Sunday."
—*Kirkus Reviews*

NATHAN'S RUN

"Gilstrap pushes every thriller button . . . a nail-biting denouement and strong characters."
—*San Francisco Chronicle*

"Gilstrap has a shot at being the next John Grisham. . . . one of the best books of the year."
—*Rocky Mountain News*

Also by John Gilstrap

FICTION

Hostage Zero

No Mercy

Scott Free

Even Steven

At All Costs

Nathan's Run

NONFICTION

Six Minutes to Freedom (with Kurt Muse)

COLLABORATIONS

Watchlist: A Serial Thriller

THREAT
WARNING

JOHN GILSTRAP

PINNACLE BOOKS
Kensington Publishing Corp.
kensingtonbooks.com

For Joy.

Twenty-nine years and counting.

CHAPTER ONE

Colleen Devlin tried her best to blend in with the commuting crowd, hoping that the long black coat and the stocking cap pulled tight around her ears wouldn't provoke some cop or citizen do-gooder to intervene. After all the training and all the talking, it was finally time to pull the trigger. Literally.

The frigid wind off the Potomac River braced her for what lay ahead, as if by chilling her skin she could likewise chill her nerves. It wasn't that she was afraid of dying—if it came to that, she'd do what she had to do—but rather that she was afraid of failure. Brother Michael had prepared them for the variables of battle, the thousand complications that render the most careful planning useless once the violence begins. If that happened—*when* that happened—she prayed that she would have the resolve and the resourcefulness to adapt. It was about keeping her head.

The Army of God was counting on her. They'd blessed her with their faith, their trust in her abilities. There could be no greater sin than to let them down.

She moved as she imagined a commuter would, her eyes ahead and her stride purposeful, a lone pedestrian on this cold November evening, strolling on the sidewalk, separated from the sea of oncoming headlights by a waist-high Jersey barrier. If it were two hours from now, or two hours ago, the traffic here on the Woodrow Wilson Bridge, one of only two crossings on the Capital Beltway that linked Virginia and Maryland, would have been breezing along at sixty miles an hour, creating a windstorm of its own. Here at six-fifteen, however, the rush-hour traffic moved at barely a crawl, a walker's pace, as the money worshippers left their resource-guzzling offices via their resource-guzzling automobiles to eat dinner with their families in their resource-guzzling homes. Colleen's eyes watered from the cold, distorting the approaching train of headlights into as many shimmering stars, an endless serpent of greed. They were all Users. And they were in for one heck of a surprise.

Colleen's Bushmaster 5.56-millimeter assault rifle felt like raw power, slung muzzle down from her right armpit. She affected a limp to keep it from poking out through the vent of her coat. Loaded with a thirty-round magazine to which a second thirty-round mag was taped for quick re-loading, her most devastating damage would be inflicted in the first fifteen seconds. The first mag would be spent in three-round bursts aimed at the drivers' half of the wind-shields, followed immediately by the second mag, which would be expended in a spray-and-slay raking motion. These shots would be unaimed and random, with the muzzle al-ways a tick or two below horizontal to increase the likeli-hood of scoring hits.

The remaining two mags in the pockets of her well-concealed ballistic vest would be used only in support of her escape. If *that* didn't go well—if capture seemed imminent—she'd . . . well, she wouldn't need more than one bullet for that, would she?

This is what God must feel like, Colleen thought, and then she was instantly sorry for the blasphemy. But it was true. People would live or die at her whim. The ultimate power lay in her hands.

Her Bluetooth earpiece buzzed, startling her. She pressed the CONNECT button. "Yes," she said.

"Are you in position?" It was Brother Stephen. The fact of his call meant that he had taken up position on the opposite end of the bridge, the Maryland end.

Colleen felt her heart rate double. "I am," she said. "It's beautiful."

"I'll see you at the Farm when it's over."

The line went dead. It was time.

Colleen threw open her coat and brought the weapon to her shoulder.

Man, you should have seen the look on the first driver's face.

Jonathan Grave shifted his BMW M6 into neutral to give his clutch leg a rest. "Next time I say yes to tickets," he said, "remind me that I hate traffic."

Next to him, Father Dom D'Angelo shrugged. "I offered to drive."

"You drive a piece of shit." He flashed a smile. "No offense."

Dom laughed. "The diocese looks askance at priests who drive sports cars."

"Surely God wants his representatives in better wheels than a Kia," Jonathan said. "I think I read somewhere that Satan drives a Kia." The car in front moved six feet, and Jonathan eased forward to keep up. "Isn't rush hour supposed to go the other way?"

"I have a theory that rush hours just *are*," Dom said. "There's no why or rationale to them. *Monday Night Football* doesn't help."

The Washington Redskins were scheduled to do battle with the Dallas Cowboys tonight at FedEx Field, and Jonathan had scored a couple of club-level seats. A lifelong 'Skins fan—despite their shameful failures in recent years—Jonathan remained forever hopeful that a winning season was possible. Clearly that wasn't going to happen this year, but games against the Cowboys were like Super Bowls unto themselves. A win against them could counter the humiliation of a four-and-twelve season.

Well, almost.

"If I had to sit in this traffic every day, I think I'd—"

Sharp, staccato hammering drew his attention to his left. The instant he heard it, Jonathan recognized it as automatic-weapons fire. Close range, 5.56-millimeter ammunition—the same NATO round used in every U.S. theater of operation since the 1970s. He reacted reflexively, cupping Dom's neck at the spot where it joined his skull and pushing him toward the floor. "Down!" he shouted.

Dom said something in protest, but Jonathan didn't care. He scanned the horizon for an escape route for the BMW, established that there weren't any, then slapped the transmission into neutral and pulled the parking brake.

To his left, on the opposite span of the bridge, he saw a man die. He saw the spray of powdered glass, followed an instant later by the spray of pulverized brain matter. Then it happened again to a car adjacent to the first one.

"Stay on the floor," Jonathan commanded. Not waiting for an answer, he shouldered open his door and rolled out onto the roadway. One clueless idiot blew his horn at him, clearly unaware that he was part of a mass murder in progress. Jonathan ripped open the zipper to his jacket with his left hand while his right hand found the grip of the customized Colt 1911 .45 that always rode high on his hip, cocked and locked. He drew it.

Across the way, on the southbound span, the shooter continued to unload dozens of bullets into the line of commuters, and on Jonathan's northbound stretch, people were just beginning to catch on. They leaned on their horns and several rammed each other in their haste to get out of the way. Panic blossomed around him, but for now he didn't care. If he could shoot the shooter, the panic would subside on its own. If he could not, then maybe it would be justified.

When there's nowhere for victims to run, a man with a rifle can inflict amazing damage.

This particular shooter was not moving. Jonathan couldn't see him yet, but he could tell from the ripples of gunfire. He weaved through the jammed traffic, scanning the horizon for a target. As he passed a pickup truck, the driver threw his door open and yelled, "Hey! What do you think—"

"Stay out of my way," Jonathan barked. "Get down." What about this situation did people not understand?

As he turned the corner on the far side of a paneled van bearing the logo of a pastry company, Jonathan got his first glimpse of the shooter. He was tall and skinny and draped in one of those flowing black coats that seemed to have become the uniform of murderers. From his bone structure, he could even have been a girl. Jonathan's mind registered that he was young and white, but the glare of headlights made features difficult to discern.

But that didn't matter because the shooter was changing magazines, and he was not especially adept at it. The muzzle of his rifle—a Bushmaster, Jonathan now saw—was pointed harmlessly to the sky as he fumbled the effort to flip his quick-load mag. The shooter would never be more vulnerable.

Jonathan gauged the distance at forty yards, too far for a reliable shot to the head, so he took aim at the center of mass—the shooter's chest—and he squeezed off two rounds.

Colleen had never seen anything so beautiful. It was just as Brother Michael had told her it would be. It was better than any drug. This was power in its rawest form, and as her bullets raked the Users and sent them to Hell, she found herself laughing.

As far as she could tell, every burst of bullets had hit exactly where she'd wanted it to. Puffs of glass and puffs of blood. Her senses took all of it in and it nearly overwhelmed her. Blaring horns and crumpling metal mixed with the pounding thump of her weapon, echoed half a mile away by the hammering of Stephen's gunshots. The tableau of de-struction—the tableau of success—was unlike anything she'd dared to imagine.

The first magazine emptied itself in no time at all, it seemed. She leaned into each burst as she pulled the trigger, bracing herself against the recoil, and each trigger pull drummed the rifle's stock into the soft tissue of her shoulder. After the tenth pull, the receiver locked open, but Colleen was too into it to notice. When the shots didn't come, she nearly fell on her nose.

She'd practiced the first reload dozens of times. Brother Michael had stressed that that would be the moment when soldiers would be most exposed. She'd taped two magazines end-to-end so that when the time came, she'd have only to thumb the mag release, flip the array in her hand, and then reinsert it into the slot. On the range, back at the Farm, she'd learned to do this with her eyes closed. She believed that she might even be able to do it in her sleep. But out here, in the heat of the battle, her hands shook, and she had difficulty finding the slot after she'd made the flip.

She unclipped the Bushmaster from its sling and raised the weapon, pointing it toward the sky. Maybe if she could see the slot, she could get the mag to seat. She took a deep breath. She had to settle herself. She needed to—

Something kicked her in the chest, then kicked her a second time. She staggered back, and as she did, she lost her grip on the rifle. Despite her efforts to grab it, she watched it clatter to the ground.

Somehow, she knew that she'd been shot, and when she looked up, she could see the man who'd done it, very far away, across three lanes of traffic. He stood in a crouch, his hands clasped in front of him. They made eye contact, and the muzzle on the man's pistol flashed again.

Jonathan knew he'd hit his target. First of all, he *always* hit his target—certainly from this range—and second, he saw the bullets hit their marks, dimpling the fabric of the shooter's clothing and causing him to drop his weapon and stagger back a step.

Yet he didn't fall. These were kill shots, yet his target remained standing. Reeling wasn't enough, not after being hit with two .45-caliber slugs. He should have dropped like a sack of bones. That he continued to stand could only mean that he was wearing body armor. As Jonathan shifted his aim for a head shot, the shooter looked up and made eye contact. Jesus, he was only a kid. A teenager. A girl! He hesitated on the trigger just long enough for the shooter to comprehend that she'd been made.

The target flinched as Jonathan squeezed the trigger. The bullet missed its mark by inches, and then the shooter was on the move, running full tilt toward the Virginia side of the bridge. Jonathan followed on his parallel span, plunging headlong into jammed oncoming vehicles while his target emerged into the open in the downstream gap formed by the plug of traffic that she had created.

Cursing himself for his hesitation before, Jonathan would not make the same mistake with a second chance. With the shooter in the open, Jonathan stopped running and readied his aim. This time, there'd be no—

"Freeze!" someone yelled from behind. "Federal officer! Don't move!"

Jonathan froze, even as his mind screamed for him to take the shot. The opportunity lost, he broke his aim and raised his weapon to the sky. He knew all too well that when a federal office yells "Don't move!"—whether FBI, ATF, DEA or any of the other alphabet agencies—the command was to be taken literally. Another trait common to federal officers: they were all very good shots.

"Hold your hands up high, where I can see them," t voice commanded.

A step ahead of you, Jonathan thought. He didn't n The officer would figure it out.

"Drop your weapon!"

Now, here was a potential problem. "No!" Jonathan yelled back. "I'm a good guy, not a bad guy, and this is a three-thousand-dollar pistol. I will not drop it, but I will lay it on the ground." Former Unit member and renowned gunsmith Barry Vance had customized this weapon for him, and he'd be damned if he was going to ruin genuine artistry. Moving slowly and keeping his back to the cop so as not to spook him, Jonathan sank to his knees.

"I said *drop* the weapon," the officer demanded. "Drop it, or I will shoot you."

Jonathan assessed it as a bluff. If this guy hadn't already pulled the trigger, he wasn't going to now that Jonathan was clearly not a threat. That's what he told himself, anyway. The next five seconds proved him to be correct. He gently placed his weapon on the ground and raised his arms again. On the opposite span, panic had begun in earnest. People screamed as realization washed over them.

And the shooter was getting away.

"Get on your face!" the officer yelled. His voice cracked from the strain. "Arms out to the side!"

With his arms still raised, Jonathan pointed the forefingers of both hands toward the opposite span. "The shooter's over there!" he said.

"Now!"

Moron. The cop was so invested in Jonathan as the bad guy that there'd be no reasoning with him. Jonathan did as he was told and lowered his belly to the pavement. Partly to streamline the process, but mostly to steal the officer's thunder, he went ahead and placed his hands behind his back, cuff-ready.

"Don't you move," the officer warned as he approached. "If you so much as blink, I swear to God I'll kill you."

Jonathan listened as the footsteps halted on his right side, ~ar his hips, he figured. This would be the time—at this ~ge—when Jonathan could take the guy out if he'd wanted ~ut the officer would be aware of that, too, making it that ~ more important for Jonathan to be on his best behavior. Most of the friendly-fire incidents that Jonathan had witnessed over his years in the military had been tied one way or another to a bad case of the nerves.

"I see you've done this before," the cop said as he placed his knee in Jonathan's back and gripped his thumbs for control. From the way he fumbled with the cuffs, the guy gave himself away as one who did not do this very often in the field.

"Actually, no," Jonathan grunted through the pressure on his back. "But I've done it enough to others to know the drill."

The cop hesitated. "What, you're going to tell me you're a cop?"

"I'm a lot of things," Jonathan said. "For tonight, though, I'm a private investigator who was seconds away from killing the son of a bitch who shot up the bridge."

"Right," the officer scoffed. "That's not what I saw." He ratcheted the cuffs tighter than they needed to be, then climbed off Jonathan's back and pulled on his wrists to bring him up to his knees. He continued to grasp the chain of the cuffs while he reached into his prisoner's back pocket for his wallet.

Jonathan sighed noisily—a growl, really. "Look, Officer . . ." He waited for the guy to fill in the blank.

"*Agent*," the man corrected. "Special Agent Clark, United States Secret Service."

"Special Agent Clark, then. United States Secret Service. If you got on your radio right now, you might be able to stop a mass murderer before she gets away."

"Why be greedy?" the agent quipped. "I've already got one member of the team in custody. You'll give me the rest in time."

Jonathan bowed his head. Surely the man was being deliberately obtuse. Did he really imagine, even for a moment, that the destruction here could have been wrought by a man with a .45? Jonathan didn't have a lot of respect for cops in general, but he had a particular hard-on for federal agents whose bravado outstripped their abilities. It happened a lot. He resigned himself to losing this battle.

"What in God's name are you doing?" a voice boomed from Jonathan's blind spot. It was Dom D'Angelo.

"Stand away, Father," Clark commanded, clearly noting Dom's collar. "This is none of your concern"

"It absolutely is my concern," Dom insisted. "Not only is that man my friend, he is also my driver for the evening."

"One step closer," Clark warned, "and I'll arrest you, too."

Jonathan stared out into the cold night, blinking his eyes against the wind. There was a killer out there somewhere, getting away while they dicked around with Agent Clark.

It was going to be a very long night.

CHAPTER TWO

Christyne Nasbe enjoyed the cold weather. Having grown up in southern California, she found the four seasons here in Virginia to be invigorating. This year's autumn had been particularly breathtaking, and as Thanksgiving approached next week, the record-breaking cold that was a source of so much griping among her neighbors was a source of unbridled excitement for her.

Not so much for her son, though. At sixteen, Ryan was doing his best to cope with the trials of tenth grade, while trying to abide by his father's instructions to be the man of the house while Dylan—Dad—was deployed. Christyne could tell that Ryan was hurting. Even now, as she glanced across at him in the front passenger seat of the minivan, he had an angry set to his eyes as he listened to his music through the ever-present earbuds. At one level, it was probably hormonal, but she suspected that he mostly missed his dad.

Three years ago, while they were still living on post at Fort Bragg, Dylan decided that Ryan needed to know the true nature of his job in the Army. Christyne hadn't been so sure at the time, and now she felt almost certain that they'd made a mistake. Did a boy really need to know, just a few years after he'd discovered the truth behind Santa Claus, that his father was among the first to get shot at in every violent conflict?

Maybe so. It was getting more and more difficult to explain the lack of uniforms and the presence of long hair and a beard. For all Christyne knew, maybe Ryan had already figured it out for himself—surely boys talked among themselves at school—but Dylan had been disappointed that the proud excitement that he'd expected from his son had never materialized. Ryan had just listened and said nothing. That had always been his way. A born poker player.

In Christyne's mind, breaking the news to their son had marked the dividing line between Happy Ryan and Dark Ryan. Dylan insisted that the link did not exist—in fact, Dylan insisted that Ryan was just being a teenager—but Dylan wasn't around, was he? He didn't see the way Ryan was pulling away from his friends, or how he walked out of the room every time a news report spoke of casualties in Afghanistan or Iraq.

"You're watching me again," Ryan said without looking—a little too loudly because of the earbuds.

"I'm just admiring what a handsome young man you are." He cleared one ear. "What?"

She repeated what she'd said. It was true, too. He'd inherited his father's natural athleticism and his green eyes. To see Ryan was to think of Dylan, and vice versa.

"You're being weird again, Mom," he said.

She smiled. Deep down inside, what child doesn't want to know that he looks good?

Despite the fact that it was only November, many of the merchants in Old Town Alexandria had already put up their Christmas decorations, and the effect was breathtaking. Fayetteville in general, and Fort Bragg in particular, had none of this kind of culture, and the lack of it was a primary motivator for this yearlong sojourn to stay with her sister and her family in Mount Vernon.

Christyne understood that Dylan's job required his full-time commitment. He'd achieved his life's dream—assignment to the First Special Forces Operational Detachment-Delta, the best of the best: Delta Force—and that made him one of the nation's go-to guys whenever something bad happened in the world. He loved his job, and she loved him, and when he needed her to be someplace, nothing would be able to keep her away.

When Dylan was on deployment, though, and she knew that he would be gone for months or years at a time, the closeness of the Fort Bragg community became stifling. Every day, there was a funeral somewhere, or a deployment somewhere else. Every second of every day bore a shroud, a constant reminder that one day Dylan might come home in a body bag. When he was there, it was different—he was her happiness; but when he was at war, all she wanted to do some nights was cry.

She'd moved here in late August, specifically so that Ryan would get an entire year in his new school, and so far it seemed he was adapting well. Her son had turned out to be something of a track star, earning a drawerful of ribbons in sprinting and hurdling. In fact, they were on their way home from such a meet right now, Ryan having finished first in the two-hundred-meter hurdles with a lead of five seconds over his nearest competitor.

"What's with that guy?" Ryan asked, pulling out his earbuds and pointing ahead through the windshield.

She followed his finger to the street corner ahead and saw a teenager in a flowing black coat waving in a frantic effort to flag them down. Them. Their car.

"Do you recognize him?" she asked. He was older than Ryan, but he could have been a senior in his high school, she supposed.

"I think it's a her," Ryan grunted. "But no."

By golly, he was right. It *was* a girl, and she appeared to be in distress. Christyne nudged her blinker and pulled to the curb.

"What are you doing?" Ryan protested.

"Look at her, sweetie. Something's wrong. She needs help." The stranger's face was a mask of angst.

"Do *you* know her?" Ryan was clearly upset by the prospect of picking up a stranger.

The frantic young woman hurried to the van's sliding door and pulled on the handle. When it wouldn't open, she knocked on the window. Three rapid taps on the glass.

"Drive off, Mom," Ryan said. "We don't—"

Christyne pushed the rocker button to unlock the door. She was a child, for God's sake. How could she not offer a hand?

The teenager pulled open the door and peeked in. "I need a ride," she said. "There's a guy up there shooting everybody. Please. We need to get out of here."

Christyne gasped. "*Shooting*? Where?"

"On the bridge, right up there." She pointed toward Maryland. "Please."

"Oh, my God," Christyne said. She beckoned the girl inside. "Yes. Get in."

"Mom!" The way Ryan said it, the word had two syllables.

"Hush," she commanded, drilling him with her maternal death glare. She watched, her pulse pounding, as the newcomer climbed inside and planted herself into the backseat.

"How do we even know that she's telling the truth?" Ryan tried again. "I didn't hear any shooting."

The teenager slammed the door shut, and an instant later, they were moving. "Oh, I'm telling the truth," Colleen Devlin said. She drew a pistol from under her coat and pointed it at Ryan's head. "And if you don't want the shooting to start up again, you'll keep driving and do exactly as I say."

"What's your name?" Colleen asked the terrified youngster in the front seat.

The kid stared straight ahead, his eyes wet and red.

"Don't let the gun scare you," Colleen said. "I won't use it unless you or your mom make me. Now, what's your name?"

Mom said, "His name is Ryan. I'm Christyne. Please don't hurt us."

"Hurt or not hurt, that's up to you," Colleen explained. "But I didn't ask you what his name was. I asked him." She touched the muzzle of her weapon to the base of Ryan's skull. "Let's try again. What's your name?"

He continued to stare straight ahead. "Ryan," he mumbled.

Colleen smiled. "Nice to meet you, Ryan." Brother Michael had trained the Army on intimidation techniques, so Colleen knew how important it was to maintain control of every conversation. Compliance with every command or question was mandatory.

"Why are you doing this?" Christyne asked.

"Because I just shot a bunch of people and I need to get away." At this point, the truth served her better than any lie.

"Where are you taking us?"

"Just keep going straight and follow directions," Colleen said. "Ryan, you're being really quiet."

He turned his head and shot a nervous glance at her pistol. His eyes showed fear, but something else was there, too. Not defiance, exactly, but close to it.

"It's a Glock," Colleen explained, answering what she figured to be the unasked question. "Forty caliber. Devastator hollow points, and in case you don't know, that means there's no fixing the holes it makes in people." Brother Michael had demonstrated the Devastator last summer at the Farm, using a dummy human torso made of ballistic gelatin.

She went on, "And the thing about the Glock is it's got a really sensitive trigger. Nobody here wants me nervous, okay? I say that to you, Ryan, because you know why?"

The boy continued to stare.

"Because you look like you're thinking about being a hero. Even though you probably don't like your mom all the time—what teenager does?—I'm sure you don't want me to blow her brains out."

Christyne gasped at the words and nearly drove off the road.

"Whoa, whoa, whoa!" Colleen said. "Stay in your lane, Christyne. Are you okay?"

"I'm fine," she said. An obvious lie.

"Good. I need you to be okay, and I need you to listen carefully, because this is the kind of thing that could get everybody killed." Colleen paused to make sure she had their attention. "If I were in your position—driving a car with your child at risk—I might think about driving crazy just to attract a cop's attention. Ryan, if I were you, looking at a bad situation and wondering how to fix it, I might think about opening the door and just diving out into traffic. You were thinking about that, weren't you?"

Mother and son looked at each other.

"I thought so," Colleen said. "It's only natural, but you need to know that it would be a huge mistake. See, I just killed a dozen people—maybe more, maybe less, but a *lot* of people. I don't want to kill you, too, but don't think that I wouldn't. I'm even prepared to kill myself if it comes to that."

"You sound desperate," Christyne said.

"Committed," Colleen corrected. "To a cause that's way bigger than any of us. If you do as I say, you'll see tomorrow. I can't guarantee the day after, but you'll be here tomorrow. That's worth not being stupid, isn't it?"

Mother and son conferred with their eyes, and then Christyne spoke for them both. "Yes."

"Thank you," Colleen said. "Do you know how to get to Sixty-Six West?" She was referring to the primary east–west highway across Virginia and beyond.

"Yes."

"Good. So do I. For the time being, that's where we're going."

"What happens after that?" Ryan asked.

Colleen gave him a hard look. "After that is tomorrow. I think you need to look at that as a gift."

CHAPTER THREE

Jonathan hadn't realized that Maryland owned the entire Potomac River. Thus, he was surprised that that state had jurisdiction over his arrest, even though he'd been much closer to the Virginia shore when Agent Clark took him down.

They transported him to the Prince George's County jail, notorious throughout the greater Washington Metropolitan Area as the place where prisoners occasionally died in their cells of blunt trauma that was caused by no one, despite the presence of deputies within shouting distance.

Jonathan hadn't spent much time on the wrong side of prison bars, but by his estimation, this was one tough place. Even more cheerless than other facilities of its kind, the jail was inexcusably filthy, and it reeked of shit and vomit. Jonathan imagined that someone had plugged a toilet, and no one with the power to fix it was inclined to do so. Peeling gray paint absorbed the yellow light cast from the stained and occasionally opaque wire-reinforced overhead light fixtures, casting a pall over the place that made most city morgues seem bright by comparison.

By habit, Jonathan made note of the weaknesses as a rail-thin deputy named Engelhardt walked him through the various security airlocks on the way back to the cellblock. More advanced than some of the third-world rattraps from which he'd liberated a few clients over the years, the PG County jail was nowhere near as advanced as the staff seemed to think it was. With a properly trained team, Jonathan figured he could make a breach and be in and out with precious cargo in under six minutes. Exfiltration would prove to be a bitch once they got clear of the exterior walls, but that was a phase-two issue, and this was strictly an academic exercise.

A breakout here would undoubtedly cost lives, and Jonathan had ironclad rules against harming American law-enforcement personnel.

Engelhardt put him in a cell with three gangbangers likewise accused of murder. Jonathan hadn't been arraigned yet, but he figured that that would be the charge if things went that far. "Thought we'd keep the killers together," Engelhardt mumbled for his own amusement.

What separated Jonathan from his cellies, of course, was the fact that they were guilty. He knew this because when he arrived, the young men were proudly recounting the efficiency with which they'd "capped that mother's ass." People really ought to listen to the lyrics when cops sing the Miranda song.

The arrival of a middle-aged white guy seemed to lighten the mood of the cell. "Fresh meat!" one of the bangers yelled. The others laughed.

Jonathan ignored them. The cell sported four bunks, two each on opposing walls, none of which appeared to have been claimed. The mattresses were still rolled, and the squatty cubes of linens remained untouched. Figuring that the top bunk closest to the toilet constituted the least desirable chunk of real estate, Jonathan targeted that one as his own. Without saying a word, he started to make up the bunk.

A banger grabbed the fabric of Jonathan's shirt and pulled him back. "Yo, asshole, what do you think you're doing? You in our crib, you need our permission."

Jonathan locked eyes and swallowed the flash of anger.

What he saw in the banger's face made his heart bleed. Here was a guy in the prime of his life facing forever in a concrete cage because he killed somebody as part of what likely was a meaningless grudge match. He steadied himself with a deep breath.

"I'm sorry," Jonathan said. "That was rude of me. May I please have that bunk?"

The thug gaped for a moment, then exploded with a laugh. "Hell no, you can't have it."

"Are you using it?"

"I might." The guy was at least three inches taller than Jonathan, and outweighed him by a hundred pounds. Now he was mugging for his buddies.

And Jonathan was getting pissed. "Tell you what," he said. "Why don't you think about it, talk it over with your friends, and then let me know what you decide. Meanwhile, step aside and save us all a lot of heartache." He turned back to the bunk. There were only a couple of ways the rest of this could go, and he didn't anticipate a happy outcome.

The banger made his choice, grabbing Jonathan by the arm and pulling him back again. Hard. Jonathan found himself whirling toward the concrete wall. He had to get his hands up fast to keep from kissing it. By the time he turned, the banger was six inches away, spouting threats and doing that arm-flapping thing that gangbangers do when they get blustery.

Jonathan struck like a snake. He grabbed the guy's balls with his left hand, his larynx with his right, and squeezed. Hard. The banger's knees sagged, allowing Jonathan to pivot him so the wall would take some of the weight.

He noted that the banger's buddies did not rush to lend aid. If they had, Jonathan was ready to handle them; but as it was, he sensed that they were willing to let this assault run its course.

"What's his name?" Jonathan asked the buddies.

"Hey, man, let him go. He can't breathe."

"He's going to be infertile, too. Name, please."

"Dion," one of them said.

"Thank you." He burned his gaze through Dion's skull. "Hi, Dion. My name's Jonathan. My friends call me Digger. You can call me 'sir.'" He squeezed harder with his left hand, and pain shot through Dion like a seizure.

Jonathan let go with both hands and let the banger drop. He didn't look tough anymore. Then again, it's hard to look tough when you're on the floor cradling your junk with both hands, gasping for air. That little whimpering sound didn't help. Nor the piss stain.

Crap. Jonathan looked at his soiled hand as if it might be covered with cockroaches. As he moved to the sink to wash his hands, the banger buddies remained riveted to their spots.

"Here's the thing, guys," Jonathan explained, his tone the very essence of reason. "I tried to be friendly, but you didn't want it that way." He glanced over his shoulder just to make sure they weren't moving on him.

"You never even introduced yourselves," he went on. "Talk about rude." When he finished rinsing, he stepped toward the buddies. As he approached, they stepped back in unison. They jumped in unison, too, when he extended his hand. "Jonathan," he said to the one on the left.

The guy shot a look to his cohort, clearly unsure of what he should do.

"Tell the man your name," the friend said. He rolled his eyes, then reached past him to offer his hand. "I'm Luke," he said.

Jonathan shook his hand.

"This is Jermaine. You already met Dion."

As Jonathan shook Jermaine's hand, he noted that Dion's breathing was returning to normal.

"So, dude, are you like some martial-arts god or something?" Luke asked. His tone dripped admiration.

"I'm just a guy," Jonathan said. "Who happens to be really, really tired, and pretty much up to here with bullshit." He pointed to a spot above his eyebrow.

"But what did you do to him? I never seen Dion drop like that."

Jonathan shrugged. "Just got his attention is all. He'll be fine."

"Man, that was like Spock shit, man. Could you have killed him like that if you'd wanted?"

Jonathan winked. "He'll be fine."

A heavy door opened down the hall and a voice boomed, "Graves! Wake up, you lucky sonofabitch. You're getting sprung." It was Engelhardt, and when he arrived at the cell door, his face turned into a question mark. "What's his problem?" He pointed with his chin to Dion.

Luke gave Jonathan's shoulder a playful slap. "Asshole done got his attention."

Engelhardt didn't care. "Stand back, guys. Your bunky gets to sleep in his own bed tonight."

"Ain't that some shit," Jermaine said, his first words.

Jonathan's posse stepped aside to allow the door to open and Jonathan to pass.

"How'd you get sprung so fast?" Luke asked.

Engelhardt answered for him. "Helps to have friends in high places. That high-and-mighty Secret Service agent who brought you in is sitting in receiving lookin' like he swallowed a bucket of worms."

"This is bullshit," Dion said. Now that a wall of bars separated them again, he seemed to have rediscovered his courage. He still stood funny, though. "You pull that cheap fightin' stuff, and I'm supposed to believe you're innocent?"

Engelhardt had already taken two steps toward leading Jonathan to freedom, and Jonathan nearly let Dion's bravado go unchallenged.

Nearly. In the end, he couldn't do it. He whirled on the bars, and Dion jumped back. "Look, you gangbanging moron, you need to decide if you want to sew your mouth shut or be fitted for a body bag."

Jonathan understood better than most the lives of disaffected youth. At one level, all that differentiated him from these punks was the fact that his father's criminal enterprises had been enormously successful. Money talked. Dion and his friends never had the benefit of Jonathan's fifteen-thousand-dollar-a-year high school education.

These boys had been throwaway strays since the day they were born. Jonathan pitied them the way he pitied everyone who was born into crime. Years ago, he'd founded Resurrection House, a tuition-free residential school for children of incarcerated parents, specifically in hopes of breaking the cycle of misery that began for children when their parents were arrested, and often followed them all the way to their graves in a potter's field beyond their own prison walls.

Jonathan noted a smirk on Engelhardt's face as he led the way back out through the maze of airlocks. "Something funny, Deputy?"

Englehardt bristled. "Keep your tough-guy rap for the inmates," he said. Then he laughed. "But wait till you see the Secret Service dick. You seem to have an interesting way with people."

Jonathan's first impression of Agent Clark when he saw him waiting in the receiving area was that Engelhardt had gotten it wrong—the guy looked like he'd swallowed a bucket of spiders, not worms. Worms would have brought a look of disgust. This guy looked scared.

Jonathan knew exactly what had happened: Dom had placed a call from the Woodrow Wilson Bridge to the J. Edgar Hoover Building on Ninth Street, beginning a ripple of consequences that had led to Clark learning this vivid lesson in Washington politics.

"Good evening, Agent Clark," Jonathan said through a broad smile. "Nice of you to come."

Clark stood, but his face remained as hard as granite. "There are a lot of people dead out there tonight, Mr. Grave," Clark said. "Forgive me if I don't find that funny."

Jonathan glared at the classic inside Washington bullshit. When rocked on your heels, take the offense by being offended. Warfare by sound bite. It was a game Jonathan chose never to play. He shook his head in the most patronizing way he knew how. "I'm going to go home now and read about the murderer who got away because you wouldn't let me shoot her."

That ought to do it.

As Jonathan pushed past, Clark grabbed his elbow. The fact that they were in a police station saved him from a nightmare of facial surgery and jaw wire. "Wait," Clark said.

"If you're not arresting me, you'd better holster that hand," Jonathan growled.

Clark let go. "Look," he said. "I don't know who you are, or how you got the attention of the head of the FBI, but Director Rivers for sure has the attention of Director Miller, and he called me personally to tell me to come here and apologize." He steeled himself with a deep breath. "I apologize."

Most people's features age when they're under stress, but Clark was the exception. He somehow appeared younger. Maybe it was the kid-in-the-principal's-office body language. Whatever it was, Jonathan couldn't bring himself to hammer any more soul out of the man. "Apology accepted."

He started to move past again, and Clark again grabbed his arm. At that moment, the jail's front door opened, and a hot babe in a ski jacket hurried into the over-lit white-walled room. A dark ponytail flopped from under a wool stocking cap. Jonathan could think of no one he'd rather see.

"There's more," Clark said, hanging on to the arm. "I'm supposed to offer you a ride home."

"He's already got a ride," the new arrival said. Then, in response to Clark's confusion, "I'm Gail Bonneville, Mr. Grave's business partner."

Clark looked unsure whether to believe her. Jonathan couldn't have cared less.

"This is the quick-witted Agent Clark of the United States Secret Service," Jonathan explained. "He's the one who put me up in this fine bed-and-breakfast."

Clark reddened.

"Just doing his job, I'm sure," Gail said. "From what I've heard, you showed a lot of courage out there on the bridge, Agent Clark."

Jonathan rolled his eyes. "Let's go home," he said.

Clark cleared his throat and shifted his feet. Clearly, there was more. "The director was very specific," he said. "I am to shake your hand and offer you any other assistance that I can." He offered his hand.

Now Jonathan felt bad for the guy. How much humiliation had Irene Rivers demanded? He accepted the man's hand. "Consider it done. In fact, consider anything else that the director insisted that you do to be done. There really are no hard feelings."

He was pretty sure that was a one-sided statement.

CHAPTER FOUR

Ryan's mind raced. They should be fighting back, shouldn't they? Instead, they were just doing what this bitch with the gun told them to do, driving long into the night—over two hours now—without a word being spoken by anyone.

This Colleen chick was an odd piece of work. Even as she threatened their lives, she managed to sound friendly. Now that the threat was made—and Ryan didn't doubt that she was capable of killing again—she'd stopped talking, except to give Mom occasional driving directions. She spent the quiet time softly humming church songs. Ryan recognized "Amazing Grace"—who didn't know that one?—and several others sounded familiar enough that he could have hummed along if he'd wanted. Ryan didn't consider himself anyone's expert on religion, but he was pretty sure that Heaven was out of reach for murderers and kidnappers. When one person did both, the odds had to be pretty awful.

Colleen had actually spoken Ryan's thoughts when she warned against tumbling out of the car and going for help. That was exactly what he'd been considering. Now, with the dire threat to kill Mom still standing, the moment for action was lost. But maybe only for a little while.

Ryan's dad had told him a thousand times that eighty per-cent of so-called "victims" of violent crime were in fact willing participants who talked themselves into victimhood as a means of rationalizing their fears. They didn't consider life-saving action because it added new risk.

In the abstract, it's easy to think of people who feel fear as cowards, but in real time, when you're the one who's likely to die if the nut job pulls the trigger, fear feels more like a survival skill than cowardice.

Interstate 66 led to Interstate 81, which in turn led to Route 262. After that, he lost track of the route numbers. They drove west, endlessly into the night.

They drove into a future that Ryan imagined held little comfort for the Nasbe family. Their next opportunity to make a difference would arrive when they made their first stop—whether it was at their final destination or at some-place along the way for gas or maybe even a pee break. A dozen ideas churned in Ryan's brain, from the simple to the heroic. Somewhere in the mix of all those options, there had to be one that would work. The trick lay in choosing the right one at the right time.

The trick also lay in Mom's willingness to take a risk. Weapons notwithstanding, two against one presented real advantage; but if one of the two hesitated, none of the rest would matter.

He tried repeatedly to capture his mother's eyes to com-municate that he had a plan, but she seemed to be intention-ally avoiding his glance.

"I need to go to the bathroom," Ryan announced.

The noise seemed to startle the girl with the gun. Then she shrugged. "So go."

Ryan recoiled. "What, on the floor?"

Colleen leaned forward and lifted an empty Evian bottle from the rear center console. "Or here."

He was horrified. "I'm not going to go in a bottle. In front of everybody."

Colleen put the bottle down. "Suit yourself."

"Can't we stop somewhere?"

Colleen laughed. "Could you be more obvious?" She tapped Christyne's headrest with the barrel of her pistol. "How much gas do we have, Mom?"

Christyne cleared her throat, then said, "A little more than half a tank."

Colleen leaned closer to peer over her shoulder. "Looks more like three quarters to me," she said. "A minivan like this, that's got to be fifteen, sixteen gallons. At twenty miles to the gallon and sixty miles an hour, what's that, three gallons an hour? We stop in five hours."

"Five *hours*?" Christyne exclaimed. "Where are we going?"

Colleen said, "Second star to the right, straight on till morning."

Ryan recognized the directions to Peter Pan's Neverland, and had started to look out the windshield again when quick movement from Colleen made him jump. Before he had a chance to react, Ryan was staring down the barrel of the pistol. It looked huge, even in the dark. In his mind, he could almost see the bullet launching into his face.

"Don't ever lie to me again," Colleen warned. "Don't try to trick me, don't try to piss me off. This isn't a game. Do you understand me?"

Ryan nodded. For the first time, the true gravity of what was happening registered in his mind. He was genuinely terrified.

"I need the bottle after all," he said.

Ryan lost track of the turns and the route numbers—and also the time—as the roads became progressively narrower and the night darker. But for the clock on the dash that told him it was one-thirty-three, he would have sworn that it was even later. For the last half hour or more, they hadn't passed a single car. Good thing, too, because Ryan didn't think there would have been room for two vehicles abreast.

The terrain out the window was mountain-steep, and when the headlights weren't splashing over rocks, all he could see were trees. Sometimes—rarely—he caught glimpses of lights shining from buildings way off in the distance, for all he knew maybe miles away, mostly in the valleys far below.

He'd never seen his mom so stressed behind the wheel. The last few miles were all short-radius switchbacks, a far cry from the suburban roads in Mount Vernon, and as the van's transmission screamed for relief, she gripped the steering wheel as if it were a climbing rope. Ryan had considered offering to drive for her, but decided that that would be a bad idea.

Finally, the bitch with the gun told them to turn onto yet another road—paved, but just barely—and then sent them for miles down a lot of nothing, the darkness interrupted only one time by a large house on a hill. At last, they stopped at a heavy-duty gate made of chain link.

"What now?" Mom asked.

"Just wait a second," the kidnapper said.

Two men seemed to condense out of the black night. They wore black clothing and each carried a rifle that looked like the ones soldiers wore in battle on the news. Flanking the van on both sides, they kept the muzzles pointing to the ground as they approached the car, but their fingers stayed precariously near their triggers. The one on the left used his non-trigger hand to make a whirling motion in the air to tell Mom to roll down the window.

As she did, the nut job in the backseat leaned forward to be seen.

The man in the window smiled. "Sister Colleen," he said. "Welcome back. I understand you did some excellent work tonight. We're all very proud." Turning away from the window, he pulled a flashlight from his belt and flashed it twice at the gate.

Within seconds, another black-clad man with a rifle appeared in the wash of the headlights, approaching from the far side. He removed a padlock from a heavy-duty chain and pulled the gates apart. He and the man at the window both stepped out of the way.

"Go ahead," Colleen said, using her pistol to point through the fence opening.

As the minivan eased through, Ryan noted through the side-view mirror that their back bumper had barely cleared the fence before the guards were pulling it closed again.

Outside the wash of the headlights, the darkness that surrounded them was near absolute. This part of the roadway wove through trees, but he sensed that the area was more field than forest. In the dim starlight, he thought he could make out the outlines of buildings, but even that was hard to tell. Some distant windows emitted yellow light, but in each case, the light seemed dim.

By the clock on the dash, it took six minutes to cover the distance from the gate to the sturdy block-and-timber building where so-called Sister Colleen told them to stop. This was one of the buildings with lights on, and now that they were close enough, Ryan could tell from the flickering that they were looking at candlelight. Candlelight and a gun-wielding bitch who thought she was a nun. Oh, this was bound to get interesting.

He shot a glance at his Mom. "No electricity?" he asked. She didn't answer. Maybe it was just that obvious.

"Turn off the lights and the car," said Sister Colleen. Their world went blacker still.

The front door to the house opened, spilling a parallelogram of light across the porch and onto the ground. Two shadows filled the space almost immediately. Both were maybe six feet tall and athletic looking, though Ryan categorized the one on the right as football-athletic, and the one on the left as soccer-athletic. Neither appeared older than twenty. They each carried an old-fashioned oil lamp, the kind with a hurricane globe around the wick and handle on the top—Ryan associated them with movies about old-time railroads—and pistols in holsters on their belts. As they approached, Colleen opened the sliding door, introducing a blast of frigid air.

"Everybody out," she said. "And please don't give us reason to hurt you."

Ryan did as he was told, pausing to grab his coat from the floor and put it on.

"Good idea," Colleen said. "You'll want to have your coats with you. It can get chilly at night."

The one who looked like a football player looked even bigger up close.

"The mission went perfectly," Colleen announced. "This is the Nasbe family."

Football held his lamp high and peered through its shadow for better view. He looked each of them in the eye, and smiled. He exchanged nods with the other lamp bearer. "Perfect indeed," he said. "I am Brother Stephen. This is Brother Zebediah, and you have already met Sister Colleen. Gather closer together." He made a gathering motion with his hands, sort of like a stiff-armed clap, but without actually clapping.

Ryan sidestepped closer to his mom's right.

"I have always believed that honesty is the best policy," Brother Stephen said. He continued to hold the lantern high, and as he spoke, clouds of condensed breath occasionally obscured his face. "You should know that you are prisoners, and that Brother Zebediah and Sister Colleen and I are your jailers."

Christyne's hand gripped Ryan's arm.

"If you behave and do as you are told, your life will be tolerable. If you cause trouble, your life will be hellish, and perhaps unnecessarily short." He paused for effect. "I know you have questions—you'd be foolish not to—but I won't be answering any of them. Consider yourselves fortunate that on a night when so many others died in their cars, you are still alive. Follow me inside now."

Christyne hesitated. Ryan saw tears on her cheeks.

That seemed to please Brother Stephen. "What's your name again?" he asked.

"C-Christyne."

"Do I scare you, C-Christyne?" he reproduced her stammer perfectly.

She nodded.

He gave a little smile and cocked his head. "Good," he said. "It's good to be scared of me. The idea of hurting a pretty lady like you actually turns me on, know what I mean?" He rubbed his crotch.

"That's enough, Brother Stephen," Sister Colleen snapped.

He ignored the rebuke and maintained his eye contact with Christyne. "Be very, *very* afraid of me." He stood, and turned his attention to Ryan. "I'll even let you watch."

Ryan lunged without thinking, and Brother Stephen stopped him with a punch to the center of his chest. Just like that, his breath was driven from his lungs, and he found himself struggling to get it back.

"You a tough guy, little man?" Brother Stephen asked with a grin.

Christyne moved instantly to intervene, pulling Ryan behind her to shelter him with her body. "He didn't mean anything," she said. "We're just both very tired. We're not thinking straight."

"Got your mommy to hide behind, eh, little man?" Brother Stephen mocked.

Ryan had never felt this way. He didn't know what to do. Anger, humiliation, and terror together drove his heart rate to something beyond anything he ever felt on an athletic field.

"Don't say a word, Ryan," Mom said.

"Smartest advice you'll ever hear," said Brother Stephen. "You just do what she says, do what I say, and I won't have to cripple you."

"For crying out loud," Sister Colleen said.

Brother Stephen leaned in closer to the boy, silently emphasizing the five inches in height and eighty pounds in weight that separated them. "But any time you want to go a round with me, you just let me know."

Ryan struggled to find words to say, something cool that might help him resurrect some measure of honor. But he was simply too terrified to make his voice work.

"Inside now," Brother Stephen instructed. "Both of you."

Sister Colleen led the way. The front door opened into the middle of the house, in the center of what appeared in the dim light to be one big room constructed of hewn timbers— like a log cabin, but without the mud crap between the logs. The inside dimensions were smaller than the outside dimensions, though, leading Ryan to believe that there must be additional wings on the sides, accessible, he supposed, through doors that hid in the shadows beyond the lamp light.

An army-style cot, made up with a sleeping bag and pillows, sat along the back wall of the main room, just barely visible along the edge of the flickering light. Ryan thought he saw a sink of sorts, positioned under an old-style hand pump. The remnants of a fire glowed in the bottom of a stone fireplace, just behind and to the right of the cot.

In a flash of understanding, Ryan realized that he'd just reentered the nineteenth century. No electricity, no running water, no heat to speak of. The lack of running water, in fact, explained the vague smell of shit that hung in the air. He wondered if maybe they were in Pennsylvania Dutch country—the Amish, he remembered, from some Harrison Ford movie that his mom had made him watch—but then he remembered that the Amish were all about peace. Whatever these creeps were about, it definitely was *not* peace.

The center of the room was unremarkable, especially in this light, except for a dark rectangle that at first looked like a shadow cast onto the floor, but revealed itself to be an open hatch leading to a stairway to a lower level. Brother Stephen gestured to the stairs with an open hand. Brother Zebediah led the way with his lantern held high. Ryan started to follow, but Brother Stephen's heavy hand around his biceps pulled him to a stop. "You stay back with me, little man."

"Please don't hurt him," Christyne said.

"I'm okay, Mom." Ryan refused to flinch as Brother Stephen's fingers dug deeply into his arm muscle. He watched as his mother disappeared into the space below. Then, when it was his turn, Ryan half expected Brother Stephen to heave him down like a human bowling ball.

The stairway ended at what felt like a concrete floor covered with slime-green carpeting. A worn sofa dominated the back wall, upholstered in a fabric that resembled a moldy chocolate chip cookie. To the left of the sofa, a rectangle of mismatched brick marked the spot where Ryan figured there had once been a door.

"Keep going," Brother Stephen barked.

"To where?" Christyne asked. There in fact seemed to be no place to go.

Brother Zebediah said, "Just follow me."

He led the way across the room to the far wall, the one perpendicular to the back wall, where he stopped and lifted a heavy padlock on its hasp and inserted a key in the bottom. He removed the lock and pulled on the hasp to reveal a doorway that would have been all but invisible to anyone who was not looking for it. Handing his lantern to Christyne, Brother Zebediah said, "You first."

Brother Stephen's grip closed even tighter around Ryan's arm. "You're last," he said.

As Christyne stepped across the threshold, the yellow light of her lantern revealed a squatty room with a ceiling that maybe rose six feet. From outside, Ryan could see furniture, but he couldn't make out what it was.

"There are candles and another lamp in the room," Brother Zebediah said. "But be judicious in their use. They're the only ones you have. When they're gone, the nights will get especially dark for you."

Ryan's stomach flipped. He'd never been a big fan of enclosed spaces.

"Don't be scared," Christyne said, her voice trembling a little. "It's not so bad. There are beds and a sofa. They even have books to read."

"Your turn," Brother Stephen said to Ryan. He gave him a last shove as he crossed the threshold. The door slammed shut immediately. The lock slid into place with a heavy *thock*, and then the Nasbes were alone. It was cold in here—beyond cold, actually—and the stink of an old toilet bloomed strong in the air.

"What the hell is happening, Mom?"

"Watch your language," Christyne said.

Ryan gave her an empty stare. "That was a reflex, right?" he said.

She smiled in spite of herself. "I don't know what's happening," she confessed. She spread her arms for a hug. "At least we're not hurt."

Ryan allowed himself to be embraced, and decided not to tell her just how hideously he expected all of this to turn out.

In the process, he willed himself not to cry.

The hug was an attempt to soothe his fears, but Ryan broke it off as soon as he could. He snatched the lantern out of her hand and turned a slow circle to reveal the details of their new home. In total, the space appeared to be about twelve feet square, and it was crammed with furniture. Immediately to the right of the door, four sagging twin beds had been shoved into the far corner, at what Christyne figured to be the front of the house, each separated from the adjacent bed by a gap of only a couple of inches. A carpet remnant of indeterminate color covered most of the concrete floor. The beds each had two pillows and a bedspread, and appeared to be fitted with sheets underneath.

"Four beds," Ryan said. "Do you think they're expecting more?"

She didn't offer an answer because she knew he really wasn't expecting one.

The rest of the space was crammed with miscellaneous furniture. Moving around among the clutter was a challenge, but Ryan managed okay as he explored their prison.

"Why is it so cold in here?" he mused aloud, zipping up his coat. He paused. "Oh, crap," he said. "This is disgusting." He turned back to face her. "I found our toilet."

Actually, it wasn't a toilet at all. It was a chair with a hole cut in the seat and what looked to be a porcelain pot suspended underneath. "I think that's called a chamber pot," Christyne said. "It's what they used in the days before indoor plumbing when you couldn't make it to the outhouse, or just didn't want to go outside."

"So the poop and pee just sit there?" Ryan asked. This, apparently, was far more horrifying to him than their overall predicament.

"Somebody has to empty it," Christyne explained.

"Nose game," Ryan said, and he quickly touched the tip of his nose with his forefinger. In Nasbe family parlance, the last person to touch their nose in the nose game was "it" and therefore had to perform whatever task was in play.

Christyne let it go.

This time when Ryan looked at her, his expression glowed with anger. "I told you not to pick her up," he said.

While Gail tended the pasta, Jonathan manned the bar. He made Gail's cosmo first, pouring equal parts Grey Goose L'Orange, Cointreau, orange juice, and cranberry juice into a shaker and giving it a vigorous ride. He strained the pink concoction into her favorite martini glass and delivered it over her shoulder.

"Your sissy drink," he said. He kissed the nape of her neck and elicited the shiver he'd hoped for.

Gail scrunched her shoulders and took the drink with both hands. "Sneak up on a girl, will you? That's a good way to get shot."

"I don't scare easy, Sheriff," he said. He walked back to

the bar to make a real martini for himself: two or three glugs of Beefeater and a drizzle of vermouth, definitely shaken (not stirred) with ice, then strained into whatever martini glass happened to be closest. Two olives later, he was done.

He took a sip and became self-actualized. "God, I'm good," he said. He rejoined Gail at the stove and lifted the lid on the marinara. "Smells great."

She hip-nudged him. "You're in my way. Where do you keep your bay leaves?"

"Um. In the bay?"

She sighed. "Unbelievable. How can you have a kitchen this grand and not have bay leaves? How do you make marinara when I'm not here?"

"I pretty much open a jar and call it spaghetti sauce."

Jonathan's home, one block up from the water, started life as a firehouse. He'd bought it a few years ago after the town decided to relocate the fire trucks to newer digs out on the highway. Now he lived on the first two floors, and his company, Security Solutions, was on the third floor, accessible by a separate entrance. Thanks to money passed on to him from his father, who would never again see the outside of a supermax prison, Jonathan could afford the best of everything, from firepower to cooktops. He was even a pretty decent cook. Still, why work to improve a product that was damn near perfect out of the jar?

But this was Gail's treat to him, and he took his role as sous-chef seriously. He even hand-shredded the salad and hand-opened the bottle of Italian dressing. He also lit candles and dimmed the lights in the dining room where they gathered at one end of the table, close enough that their knees touched. Cocktails finished, he opened a favorite Lodali Barbera D'Alba.

Jonathan and Gail's relationship was a complicated one. That's what happens when your first encounter includes a gunfight. She worked for him now as one of his best investigators. Once a member of the FBI's elite Hostage Rescue Team, she could thread a needle at fifty yards with just about any firearm, and if she was afraid of anything, he hadn't yet seen her confronted by it. That was the good part.

Unfortunately, her law degree had somehow melded the Constitution to her DNA, reducing her color spectrum for right and wrong to only black and white: either something was legal or it wasn't. By contrast, Jonathan's color palette for justice was kaleidoscopic. If the ends were justified, the means for achieving them were limited only to the breadth of his imagination and the laws of physics of chemistry. It never occurred to him to question whether a strategy for rescuing a good guy from a batch of bad guys might violate a law or two.

It was a rift that occasionally grew to a chasm.

To give their relationship a chance to flourish, they'd banned work discussions during their off-hours together, adding strategy and tactics to religion and politics on the list of topics that were forbidden in polite company. It made sense in theory, but in practice, their brokered peace occasionally left them with long moments of silence. Tonight was an example.

"So, how terrible was it?" Gail finally asked. "On the bridge, I mean."

Jonathan arched his eyebrows. "I was too caught up in the moment to notice details. A lot of shots fired, a lot of people killed."

"You're lucky you didn't get hurt."

The gin was just beginning to find his bloodstream. He felt a little flushed as he tasted the wine. "I kept my head down," he said. "The shooter's the one who should be counting her blessings. She owes that fed a thank-you card."

"As you owe Wolverine," Gail said. "In fact, you owe her a mention in your will."

Jonathan chuckled. The director of the FBI—Wolverine to Jonathan, thanks to some work he'd done for a Bureau a number of years ago—had covered his tracks on more than a few occasions. "I'm doing better than that," he said. "I'm buying her breakfast tomorrow."

Gail took a sip of her wine. "This is good. Are you going to tell her everything?"

"Lodali's a small vineyard in Tuscany. Everything they touch is great." Saying the words inspired him to take another taste. "I don't see a reason to hold back. There's nothing covert about my presence."

"In a perfect world, it would be nice not to have your name tied to a terrorist attack."

Jonathan recoiled. "Is that nervousness I hear?"

"Of course it is. You tried to kill somebody who'd killed Lord knows how many people. I don't think Fisherman's Cove needs terrorists flooding in to settle the score."

He dismissed the point with a wave—not because it wasn't valid, but because there wasn't much he could do about it. "Wolverine's always been able to keep me out of the news. No reason to think she's lost her touch."

They fell quiet again.

"You know what sort of baffles me about this evening?" Jonathan said to break the silence. "During the time that I was in custody, no one ever once asked me what I had seen out there on the bridge. They were so intent on me being the shooter that it apparently never occurred to them that I might have important details."

"Do you?" Gail asked.

"Probably not. But you'd think they would have asked."

"Would you have answered?"

Jonathan started to answer, then laughed. "Probably not. I was kinda pissed." Another silence as they finished their pasta.

As he refilled the wineglasses, he looked around. "Where's JoeDog?" Normally, the energetic black lab was making her presence well known at this point in a meal.

"I saw her heading off to Kramer's earlier in the day," Gail said. "Must be his turn."

Officially, JoeDog was a stray. She'd appeared at Jonathan's door a few years ago, and while he was her nominal master, she wandered the town on her own, blessed with special dispensation from the leash laws. When she tired of the lazy life of the firehouse, she wandered to the police chief's house—Doug Kramer's house—to mooch off him for a while.

"You know what that means, don't you?" Jonathan said, rising from his chair and holding out his hand for Gail to join him.

She stood and waited to be enlightened.

Jonathan pulled her close and laced his fingers at the small of her back. "It means that we have the bed all to ourselves tonight."

CHAPTER FIVE

This year's school bus driver, Mrs. Pantone, was an absolutist when it came to pickup times. Either you were at the corner at 7:21, or you weren't. If she didn't see you, she didn't even slow down. Once, Aafia had been within twenty yards, running for all she was worth, when the old biddy just sped off without her. Her parents didn't want to believe that such outrageous things could happen in middle school, but it was the truth.

But not today.

Today, Aafia missed the bus because she'd been lazy. She'd been up way too late studying for her science test, and that—let's be honest—was because she'd spent way too much time chatting with her friends online. But given the news of the day, what choice did she have? Merilee Berdan had actually kissed Steve Bayne. On the lips! Sharee Northrup had seen it happen in the hallway between fourth and fifth period. They even did tongues!

So now Maddy Carter was like all pissy because she really likes Steve and now is telling everybody that Merilee is just a slut. Merilee found out about that, and, well, it was hard to break away to study for the science test.

Aafia grabbed a Pop-Tart out of the cupboard next to the fridge as she hurried to the kitchen door, beyond which her way-pissed dad was waiting with the engine already running. It was going to be a long ride to school, filled with lectures of how achievement in school is the only route to achievement in life. She'd hear all about how much her parents had suffered to carve a life for their family here in America, and how her sloth was an insult to Allah himself. Blah, blah, blah.

Merilee and Steve had *kissed*!

Aafia grabbed her coat but didn't take the time to put it on as she rushed out to the carport and slammed the kitchen door behind her. She didn't mean to slam it, but now her mom was going to be pissed that she had, and that was another special moment to look forward to on the far side of the day.

Was it possible that middle school in Pakistan was *that* different from middle school in America? Or were her parents just too old to remember what was important when they were kids?

As she'd expected, the atmosphere inside the minivan was even colder than the Michigan winter as she dumped her stuff on the floor of the front passenger seat and climbed in. She had barely pulled her door closed before they were backing down the driveway.

"I'm sorry, Father," she said in Urdu, hoping to strum a nostalgic string in him.

"English, Aafia," he snapped. "You are an American. Please do not mock me."

So much for nostalgia. In English: "I'm not mocking, Father. I was just . . . I don't know." Like so many others in their town, her father had lost his job at the auto factory almost two years ago, and hadn't been able to get even an interview since. He had long been self-conscious of his accent, but in recent weeks, he'd come to believe that his accent and his dark features were roadblocks to his career. In Pakistan, he had been a supervisory engineer for the automobile company, and in the late 1990s had accepted a transfer here to Michigan to head up an even larger department. That was before Aafia or her brother had even been born.

She didn't understand the details, but after September 11, 2001, things changed for the family. Even though Pakistan was an ally, and even though Aafia and her family were Sufis, a sect of Islam that was far separated from the jihadists who committed those terrible crimes, many white-skinned neighbors either couldn't tell the difference or wouldn't acknowledge it.

Her father told stories of slights and insults at work. For a long time, he tried to ignore them, but after several years—and after children started to arrive—he couldn't take it anymore so he filed suit through the American courts to force people to stop saying those terrible things.

Aafia remembered the day when he won the case in court. Money was paid—she didn't know how much, but apparently it was a lot—and the company was told to mind its manners and make sure that the other workers did the same. On a day when she expected her parents to be happy because they'd won, they turned out to be sad instead. Her father had said then that nothing had really been fixed, and that he feared he might have just made it all worse.

How could that be? Once the courts told people to behave, isn't that what they had to do? Isn't that why we have courts in the first place?

About a year after that, everybody lost their jobs, and nothing had been right at home ever since. To keep busy, and to keep money coming in, her father had accepted a job as a taxicab driver, but that made him sad, even angry sometimes.

"I am a mechanical engineer," he'd said one night at the dinner table last week. "I am very talented at what I do, and now no one will let me do it. Now the only work I can find is to be a servant for strangers." Then he'd started to cry.

Aafia and her brother were sent away from the table at that point, but she believed that her father cried for a long time that night. He and her mother talked and talked and talked. They were still talking when Aafia had fallen asleep.

Her father broke the uncomfortable silence in the car. "You disappoint me with your foolishness. What is happening to you, Aafia? You used to be responsible."

"I try, Father," she said. "I really do. And I am, most of the time. I get all A's."

He started to say something in an angry tone, but then he stopped himself. His features softened. "Yes, you do, don't you? Yes, you do." He looked at her, offered a smile and then returned his eyes to the road.

Aafia didn't know what to do. When you're geared up for a stern lecture, kind words are sort of unnerving. Not wanting to risk undoing whatever good thing had just happened, she chose to remain silent.

"So, this boy," her father said. "This Steve. Do you like him too?"

Her head zipped around, her jaw agape.

"Your brother told me," he clarified. With a gentle smile, he added, "You would be wise not to trust him with many secrets."

"I don't believe he did that."

"Oh, don't be hard on him. He's young, and he loves you. He watches you closely. What's important to you is also important to him. You should feel complimented."

Maybe he'll feel complimented when I kick his butt later, she didn't say.

"So, this Steve," her father pressed. "Tell me about him."

Heat rose in Aafia's cheeks. Was this a new form of punishment? Embarrassing questions for five whole miles? "I don't know what to say."

"Have I met him?"

If she just said no, then maybe the conversation would end. But that would be a lie, and Aafia was not good with lies. "You've seen him in my orchestra," she said. "He plays the bass."

Her father scowled as he searched his memory. "The tall black boy or the shorter white boy?"

Her jaw dropped again. She had no idea that he paid attention to such things. "He's the white boy."

"With the long brown hair. The *dreamy, thick* long brown hair." He laid on that last part with exaggerated passion.

"Father!"

"Handsome boy."

"Father!"

He laughed. Truly, this was a far more effective punishment than any lecture on bad behavior. "And what about his new kissing partner. Merilee, is it? Do I know her?"

"No." She could say that definitively. "She's a cheerleader." She hoped her tone conveyed her level of disapproval.

"And what is wrong with being a cheerleader? Do you not like to cheer?"

Oh, please let this ride end.

"Who would not like to cheer?" he goaded. "Rah, rah, sis-boom-bah."

She laughed in spite of herself. "What was that?"

"Isn't that how one cheers?" He took his hands off the wheel and shook a pair of imaginary pompoms. He repeated his stupid rhyme. "That's it, is it not?"

"Maybe a hundred years ago."

"Then I must have it wrong. I am old, but I am not a hundred. So, what is wrong with Marilee being a cheerleader?"

He wasn't going to let this go, was he? At least they'd breezed through the long traffic light. Getting stopped there could have added five whole minutes to the torture. "There's nothing wrong with it exactly. It's just that those girls can be really mean."

"Is Merilee mean to you?"

The question startled her, made her feel bad. "No," she said.

"So she's a nice cheerleader. That must mean that some cheerleaders are nice, right?"

Aafia rolled her eyes. He was such a parent. Clueless.

"And if she's nice, and she's friends with other cheerleaders, then it only makes sense that the other cheerleaders can be nice, too."

She looked out the side window. If he was going to be this dense, she had nothing else to say to him.

"Aafia, look at me, please." It sounded like a real request, not a demand.

She turned and faced him.

"It's wrong to treat people as if they are a group instead of as an individual. As my daughter, you must know that better than most."

Her face grew hotter as shame nudged embarrassment out of the way. "Yes, Father."

"You're a beautiful girl, Aafia. The handsome boys will kiss you, too."

She rolled her eyes. *He didn't really just say that, did he?*

He went on, "You have to trust me when I tell you that these issues with your friends—the gossip and the giggling and all the rest—will seem so unimportant ten years from now. Crises come and go. But the only thing that lasts forever is education. It is the only important thing, and everything good that happens in your life will flow from your education. Do you understand this?"

Finally, the lecture had arrived. And finally, they were in sight of the school. "I understand, Father. I'll try harder."

They'd arrived with the buses, it turned out. The U-shaped driveway in front of the school was packed with hundreds of students streaming from dozens of buses. That meant her father would be stranded here even longer.

"I'm so sorry, Father."

He made a gentle waving motion with his hand. "You go on inside," he said. "Have a nice day, and try to think of all the gifts that God has given you. Now, give this old man a kiss."

This was the father she'd known before—the one who laughed and teased. He seemed to be trying not to be so angry, and his effort pleased her. She unclasped her seat belt, leaned across the center console and planted a kiss on his cheek.

"I love you, Father," she said, and the words felt strange. It wasn't that she didn't love him; it was just that they rarely talked of such things in their house.

The bitter Michigan air assaulted her cheeks and hands as she hurriedly shrugged into her coat and closed the door behind her. As she joined the stream of classmates making the way to the front door, she cast a look back over her shoulder to see her father inching the minivan through the sea of children as he disappeared between the two ranks of yellow buses.

She was just turning back to face the school when the explosion split the air.

CHAPTER SIX

By morning, Christyne had grown jealous of her son's ability to sleep anywhere and anytime. Within seconds of crashing on the bed, his breath had become rhythmic and even, and as far as she could tell in her hours of wakefulness, he'd never so much as stirred.

Between the unrelenting cold, though, and her crushing sense of guilt for having gotten them into this, sleep was nowhere in her future.

In those quiet hours, she'd reasoned that if their captors had meant them harm, they'd have done them harm. Clearly, they had a plan, and while she had no idea what it might be, it only made sense that if she and Ryan made every effort to get along—to do as they were told, just as they'd been instructed—then their captors would have cause only to treat them well.

Jesus, it was cold. Even with her coat on, and the blankets pulled all the way to her nose, it seemed impossible to get warm. It had to be warmer than freezing, she figured, because the bottled water they'd found was still liquid, but it had to be close.

Until about an hour ago.

The rising sun had just begun to lighten the darkness beyond the tiny windows at ground level, near the ceiling, when she heard the sound of a shovel scraping concrete, a sound that propelled her back to her childhood visits to her grandparents' house on Smith Mountain Lake in Virginia, where coal fueled everything that produced heat, from the stove to the furnace. It wasn't just the timbre and pitch of the scraping that made her think coal; there's a rhythm to coal shoveling that is unique.

The shoveling continued for about twenty minutes, she guessed, and by the time the noise had ceased, the temperature in their little room had risen dramatically. Now, as the sky beyond the windows glowed pink, the heat had driven her out of her covers and caused her to shed her coat, and she was still sweating. She pegged the temperature at maybe eighty degrees now, and rising—high enough to cause Ryan to stir.

He bolted upright with a loud gasp. "Jesus!" he proclaimed. "Why is it so hot?" He stood and shrugged out of his coat. "I'm soaked." His sweater came next, leaving him bare chested. He brought it to his nose and sniffed. "I stink."

"I already knew that," Christyne teased.

Noise outside their cell distracted them both, the unmistakable sound of the lock being removed and the bolt sliding open. An instant later, the door crashed open with enough violence to slam it into the perpendicular wall and a team of men, all wearing black with masks covering everything but their eyes streamed into the room. There were four of them, and they all carried machine guns locked against their shoulders and ready to fire.

Ryan yelled and darted over to his mom.

"Up, up, up!" they yelled, followed by a stream of orders yelled by all of the gunman, some of them contradictory. "Up! On the floor! On your feet! Hands up! Hands on your heads!"

The effect was utterly terrifying. The contradicting orders

froze them in place. As the men yelled louder, Ryan stood with his hands out, as if warding off an angry dog.

Christyne yelled, "Ryan! Put your hands up, for God's sake." She demonstrated by raising her own.

Finally, the message got through and he raised his hands.

The gunman settled down, too, to the extent that only one man now shouted orders. "Both of you step away from your beds."

The gunmen never broke their aim as the Nasbes did as they were told.

The man in charge pointed at Ryan. "You," he said. "Step away from the woman."

The woman? Christyne thought. What an odd way to refer to her.

"Now turn around and face the beds."

As Ryan complied with the order, he shot a look of pure terror to his mother.

"Please don't hurt him," Christyne begged.

The gunman closest to her shouted, "Silence!" and tightened his grip on the gun that was leveled at her forehead.

"Please," she whispered.

"Boy," the boss commanded. "Put your hands behind your back and cross your wrists."

Again he complied, and Christyne started to cry when she saw how badly his hands were shaking. While three gunman held their aim steady, the one doing the talking stepped forward and slipped a loop of plastic over Ryan's wrists and pulled it tight enough to dimple the skin. That done, the gunman produced a three-foot strip of black cloth which he wove elaborately and expertly around the boy's arms, and then pulled tight. Ryan choked back a sob as the man drew his elbows together until they nearly touched behind his back.

"Does that hurt?" the man asked.

"Yes." The pain was obvious in his voice.

"Good. Remember this. Remember the pain." The gunman drove the sole of his black combat boot into the back of Ryan's knees, unlocking them and causing him to drop to a kneeling position.

Ryan struggled for balance, to keep from toppling over onto his face. "What did—"

"SILENCE!" This time, the gunman's voice reverberated in the tiny room.

Ryan fell silent.

"Do not beg," the man warned. "Do not cry, do not say a word or I will hurt you."

The man reached out his hand, and one of the other masked invaders handed him what looked to be a black pillowcase. He shook it open and slipped it over Ryan's head. The edge drooped below the points of his shoulders.

Something broke inside Christyne as she watched them abuse her son. Bound and kneeling, he was so helpless, so vulnerable, even as he kept his posture straight while clearly trying to control his fear through deep, sometimes shaky breaths.

If only she hadn't been so—

The gunman turned to Christyne. He allowed his rifle to hang limply from the strap that attached it to his neck as he walked closer. The other guns remained pointed at Ryan's head.

As he closed to within a few inches of her face—well inside her personal space—she could see even in the dim light that the eyes behind his mask were hooded and creased. This gunman was much older than those they'd dealt with the night before.

"Woman," he said. "Are you frightened of me?"

"Yes."

"As you should be. The whole world should be frightened of me. Do you believe that I am capable of killing your boy?"

Christyne's heart skipped. What did he want to hear? What was the answer that would save her son, and which was the one that would harm him?

"I would like to think that no one is capable of killing a child," she said.

"Ah," he said. His eyes darkened. "A non-answer. Would you care to try again?"

"Yes," she said. "I think you are capable of killing my boy."

"So you must think me to be some kind of monster."

He was building a box for her, a logical trap for which there could never be a correct answer. She nearly begged him to stop, but then she remembered the warning against begging.

"Is that what you think?" the man pressed. "Do you think I am some kind of monster?"

She looked at her feet. "I think the willingness to kill a child is as good a definition of monster as any."

The man chuckled, releasing a blast of cigarette breath. "What would you be willing to do to save his life?"

Something icy formed in her stomach. "Anything," she said. It was simply the truth.

He lightly brushed his gloved hand across her breast. "I want you to think more about that over the next couple of hours."

He turned abruptly. "Take the boy," he said.

Time stopped for Aafia, the events slowing to a crawl that allowed her brain to record the details in exquisite, horrifying detail. She caught the flash out of the corner of her left eye, and it synched perfectly with the bright shadow she saw thrown onto the front wall of the school, far on her right. A giant invisible fist punched the ground under her feet hard enough to make her fall.

Even as her knees were collapsing under her, the closest school bus—still fifty yards distant—seemed to bend for a fraction of a heartbeat before all of the glass exploded in a glittering rain and a fireball consumed everything. The bus itself, now on fire, left the ground, tumbled once in the air along its own axis, and then landed on its side.

She had just fallen to her hands and knees when she saw what could only be their minivan reduced to a fiery ball in the midst of hundreds of pounds of twisted, erupted metal. She knew that her father was dead.

Burning, white-hot shards of steel and aluminum whistled through the air, one of them passing over her head. Three feet ahead of her, and a little to the right, Mr. McMillan, the English teacher, made a terrible coughing sound as something sliced through his belly and spilled his insides out. His face looked blank as he fell nose-first onto the sidewalk.

Aafia pressed herself into the damp grass and curled into a ball, her arms concealing her head, as more pieces of things landed heavily around her.

Ten, fifteen seconds later, when the violence was over, the real nightmare began, driven by a dissonant chorus of moans and screams, combined with the whining roar of fires. When she forced herself to raise her eyes above her forearms, her first thought was that she had been killed after all, and that she had so angered Allah that he'd sent her to hell. So much fire, and so much misery.

All caused by the people who'd murdered her father. Was that even possible?

But she remained very much alive.

Soon, people stopped running away in panic, and started running around in a frenzy. Mostly, they were adults, but there were children among them, too. They ran, and then stopped to kneel, and then they would run again.

When Aafia rose to her feet, she understood. There were many wounded, too many to count. Some sat, dazed looks on their faces, while others lay writhing and still others lay horribly still. And the blood. So, so much blood. Everyone seemed to be covered with it. What spilled from the injured seemed almost magically to transfer itself to the people who came to lend aid.

For the longest time—she had no idea how long—Aafia just stood there on the lawn, watching dumbly as the activity swirled bigger and bigger. Teachers and students continued to flood from the school out into the drive, plus some people she didn't even recognize. As if tugged by the current in a river, Aafia found herself being drawn along, moving closer to the carnage. Somehow, she'd lost her right shoe, one of her favorites—pink with white stripes. Her mother called them her pixie shoes.

Oh, Mama, she thought. "Oh, Father," she said aloud. Who would do such a terrible, horrible thing to him? To all of them?

Of all the terrifying sights, the one she refused to look at was the burning hulk of their little van. She wished she couldn't see the torn bodies and the blood splashes and the scattered body parts.

She needed to do something. She needed to help. Maybe she just needed to cry. She really didn't know. All of it seemed so make-believe, as if she'd stepped into the middle of the worst video-game nightmare imaginable. Why couldn't she do anything? Why, suddenly, did everything around her look to be such an odd color?

A teacher's aide from one of Aafia's classes—she couldn't remember which one now—raced past, but then stopped very abruptly and reached out to her. One hand supported Aafia's arm at the elbow, while the other hand cupped her chin gently at the jawline.

"Oh, honey, you need to sit down," the aide said. "You'll be all right."

And just like that, Aafia was on the ground, staring up into the flawless sky, even though she couldn't remember doing that. Just as she couldn't remember what she had done to cut the inside of her mouth. But sure enough, she tasted blood.

An instant later, the sky was gone, replaced by what looked to be a white plastic ceiling with hardware. The world was filled with a new sound. Could it be a siren? And then a stranger was staring down at her. It was a man, a young one.

He smiled at her. "Hi, sweetheart," he said with a smile that made some of the cold go away. "Can you tell me your name?"

She told him.

"Sweetheart, please stay with me," he said. "I need to know your name."

"Aafia," she said, only this time, she could hear her real voice over the one in her head.

"Can you spell that for me?"

She thought. "I don't think so," she said. But she was such a good speller. Why not now?

"What's your last name, sweetie?" the nice man asked.

"Janwari," she said.

The face turned confused. "Excuse me?"

"That's my name," she said. At least she thought she did. "Aafia Janwari."

The man said, "Oh, shit," and then he went away. Aafia went away, too.

CHAPTER SEVEN

Jonathan met FBI Director Irene Rivers for breakfast at the Maple Inn in Vienna, Virginia. A dive by most standards, it was a favorite hangout for the spooky community that had grown up around CIA headquarters, which sat just six miles north on Route 123—or, as it was called within the incorporated limits of the Town of Vienna, Maple Avenue. Jonathan had lost track of the number of clandestine meetings in the open he'd had here over the years, but combined, his didn't account for one tenth of one percent of the cumulative secrets heard by the restaurant's walls.

Because the food was good and inexpensive, and the beer was cold and plentiful, the Maple Inn's clientele attracted the widest possible demographic, from soccer moms with kids to working folks of every color collar. Most important to Jonathan and the people he met with, the waitstaff knew when to take an order and when to stay away.

After their eggs, sausage, and toast had been delivered, and the pleasantries were out of the way, Jonathan got down to business.

"Thanks for coming to my rescue last night."

She shrugged it off. "The Secret Service has an arrogant

streak that pisses me off," she said. "It feels good to put a thumb in their eye from time to time."

"Will you be able to keep my name out of the press?"

Irene dipped a corner of her toast in the runny yolk of her egg and took a tiny bite. "The Prince George's County Police arrested and released a fellow named Chuck Carr last night," she said. "He was suspected of being one of the bridge shooters."

"And Agent Clark?" Jonathan had already finished his eggs, and had shifted his concentration to making a sandwich with his sausage patty.

"He was never there," Irene said, her face showing disappointment. "That was part of the deal with Ramsey Miller." He was Irene's counterpart at the Secret Service. "Letting the shooter run away was a big enough screw-up that he didn't want the embarrassment."

"So who arrested me? I mean who arrested Chuck Carr?"

"Does that really matter?"

Jonathan thought about that. "No, I suppose it doesn't."

Irene smiled. "Good. So, tell me who you saw on the bridge."

He started from the beginning and went through it all. When he was done, he had Irene's full attention.

"A girl, huh?" she said. "That's a twist. You sure it wasn't a long-haired boy?"

"A long-haired boy with boobs, maybe. My powers of observation are really pretty well-honed. Why?"

She shrugged. "It just runs counter to the profile. These mass-shooting types are always male."

"I think I saw her drop her weapon," Jonathan recalled. "Anything useful from that?"

"Generic Bushmaster, two-two-three caliber, modified for fully automatic fire. What concerns me is the marksmanship. Both of the gunmen—gun *persons*—knew what they were doing, and both were firing the same ammo from the same lot."

"Do you know where they got it?"

"Not yet, but I'm not hopeful that we'll learn a lot from that. Just a gut feeling. These guys feel trained to me."

"Any connection to the mall shootings in Kansas last weekend?" Eight people had been murdered in that incident, with over thirty wounded. When the shooters had been cornered, they'd killed themselves rather than being taken into custody.

"Officially, no. Unofficially, absolutely. They were both invisible teens with jihadist propaganda in their pockets."

"Arab?"

"Not hardly. One of them had red hair. But not all Muslims are Arab."

"Are you thinking terrorist cell?"

Irene's eyes grew wide as she feigned insult. "Good God, Digger. We don't use the T-word for this. The president has made it clear that there will be no domestic terrorist attacks on his watch."

Jonathan chuckled. "What are we calling it, then?"

"The last I heard, they were 'unconnected random acts of violence.'" She used finger quotes for the last part.

"Needs work," Jonathan said. "Way too many syllables."

"Yeah, that's the problem. Too many syllables."

A moment passed in silence before Jonathan said, "You should know that Security Solutions has launched our own investigation into the shootings."

Irene paused in the middle of a sip of coffee. "Please don't do that," she said. "I don't need you exercising your grudge muscles right now."

"It's not about me," Jonathan said. "Of the twelve killed and sixteen wounded on the bridge, three were friends or associates of my investigators."

She scowled. "How is that possible?"

He shrugged. "The Washington Metro Area is really just a small town with a lot of people in it. My folks don't ask stuff like this very often. I can't say no to them. It'll all be pro bono."

"I'm not worried about the money—I wouldn't pay you

anyway. I worry about tainted evidence." She held up her hand before he could respond. "And before you go into denial mode, remember how long we've worked together. I've never seen anyone who can taint evidence like you can."

Jonathan resisted the temptation to point out that a not insignificant amount of the work she was referring to was performed at her request. "This won't be the clandestine side of the shop," he said. "It'll all be by the book."

Irene Rivers was one of very few people on the planet who knew the dark side of Security Solutions. To the rest of the world, it was an investigation firm that worked for some of the most prestigious corporate names in the world.

She wearily closed her eyes. "What can you possibly bring to the table that won't already be brought by a dozen government agencies?"

"Maybe nothing," he said. "Maybe a lot. The only thing I know is that I can't say no to my staff on this one. If I did, they'd just do it anyway. Doing something helps them cope. Makes them feel empowered, I guess."

Irene's phone rang in the pocket of her suit jacket. She issued a deep sigh as she reached for it. "Well, I can't order you not to," she said. "But please show restraint. If we find the not-terrorists who are committing these unconnected random acts of violence, I will shit all over you if so much as a speck of dust is rendered inadmissible because of something done by you or yours."

Into the phone: "Director Rivers."

Jonathan made a show of not listening even as he zoned in on every word. But she didn't speak. Instead, she just listened and her face darkened. "Okay," she said at last. "I can be in the office in a half hour with lights and siren. Assemble the section heads and the SAC in Detroit for a video conference at ten. Meanwhile, get Lee and Jeff on the line. I'll talk to them from the car."

When she pushed the disconnect button, she shot a pained smirk toward Jonathan. "Be sure to watch the news over the next couple of hours," she said. "A jihadist just bombed an elementary school in Detroit."

As Christyne waited for the gunman to return, the temperature in the tiny room soared past sweltering into the range of frightening—easily ninety degrees, if not hotter. The wall on the far side of the room from the door was too hot to touch, leading her to believe that there must not be any insulation at all between the furnace and the concrete block wall. The best she could figure out was that they used the furnace only during the day, and let the fire die at night.

Or, it could be that the heat was a form of torture?

It had been over an hour since they'd taken Ryan, and in that time, she had heard nothing but the drumbeat of her own heart pounding in her ears. Her mind conjured awful things that could be going on, and the imagined images triggered panic. The kind of panic that clouds your thinking and makes you do stupid things.

She wanted to scream, to call out to him. The warnings from the guards made the difference. They demanded silence. Hadn't she already brought enough harm to her family?

What could they be doing to him?

She took a huge breath and tried to settle herself. The panicky thoughts were counterproductive. She was powerless to affect the outcome of this nightmare. What would happen would happen.

If she told herself that often enough, maybe it would bring solace.

For now, all it brought was more fear.

They had her *son*.

After easily ninety minutes of isolation, she heard movement of the lock again. This time, when the door crashed open, she had been anticipating it, and was able not to yell out in fear. The team of gunmen streamed in as before, guns at the ready, all of them trained on her. As four of them stopped six feet away, the fifth one—the man with the threatening eyes—approached another two steps, stopping only when he was face-to-face with Christyne.

"Where is Ryan?" she asked.

"Put your hands behind your back and turn to face the wall."

"Please," she begged. "Is he okay?"

"If you make me hurt you, I will," the gunman said.

Christyne turned and faced the wall, crossing her wrists behind her back as she had seen Ryan do. The plastic loop closed over her wrists tightly enough to restrain her arms, but not tightly enough to hurt. Yet. A moment later, a hood was placed over her head, but to her surprise, it had a mesh front that allowed her to see. Not well, but enough.

"Walk to the door," the gunman commanded.

The line of gunmen parted to allow her to pass, and as she did, they curled in around her to follow. The air approaching the door was easily twenty degrees cooler than the air inside the cell. She nearly asked where they were going, but then decided not to. They would tell her what they wanted her to know when they wanted her to know it.

Ryan was kneeling on the floor immediately outside the room, facing her, surrounded by at least a dozen of the black-clad gunmen, all of whose faces were covered by masks. Ryan's hood had been removed. She could see the desperation in his eyes. His left eye and cheek were swollen and purple. The healthy eye showed an emotion she didn't quite recognize from him. It was as if something inside him had been rewired.

Once she'd been allowed to see, the gunmen slipped the hood back over Ryan's face.

Behind her, the man who'd been doing all the talking said, "It's time now to atone for your sins."

CHAPTER EIGHT

Back in Fisherman's Cove, Jonathan sat at his desk, with the fickle yet adoring JoeDog sleeping flatulently at his feet.

No matter how much he tried to avoid the soul-stealing administrivia that came with running a company, investigative findings had to be reviewed and approved, checks needed to be signed, and the occasional mega-client needed to be stroked. Most of the truly painful boredom was shared by his lead investigator, Gail Bonneville, and his office manager and technology guru, Venice Alexander. (It's pronounced Ven-EE-chay, by the way, and she was known to lose patience with people who blew it more than once.) Even with layers of middle management in place, though, the boss was still the boss, and only so much could be delegated.

On the far wall, Fox News was running with coverage of the jihadist attacks that threatened to "paralyze America." Some outfit that called itself the Army of Allah had released a video of a mother and her half-naked teenage son cowering at the feet of black-clad gunmen. The mother recited a prepared text—a rant about godless heathens and the inevitability of Islam's rule, blah, blah, blah. While they spoke, an Arab translation crawled along the bottom of the screen.

The Army of Allah took responsibility for both the mall and bridge shooting incidents, plus the school bombing this morning. They promised that more violence was on the way. The shootings would continue, in fact, until the United States withdrew from virtually every geopolitical stance it had taken in the last seven decades.

Jonathan knew that the hostages were destined to die, if in fact they hadn't already been killed. In his experience, impossible demands translated to a simple desire to kill. They were photo ops, really, designed to create iconic images of violence that would raise the stakes on terror, and the Army of Allah was doing a hell of a job so far. For the Wilson Bridge Massacre—that seemed to be the sensational moniker with the most legs—that image was the photograph of two ravaged and bloody child seats side by side in the back of a family sedan.

Between the various tableaus of carnage, the talking-head shows ran a loop of experts who seemed united in the belief that Islamist sleeper cells had been activated, and that their existence was evidence that our decade-plus of war had failed to protect us.

One day, Jonathan thought, he'd like to become a talking head so he could go on television and tell all those assholes to shut up.

In fact, he made them do exactly that with the mute button. He had paperwork to do, after all.

His intercom beeped. "Digger, I'm sorry to bother you, but there's something in the lobby you need to attend to." It was Venice Alexander.

"What brand of something?" he asked. Not that it mattered. He'd help polish the furniture if it would rescue him from this tedium.

"A visitor. An Army colonel named Rollins." She spelled it. "He says it's an urgent matter."

Spelling the name was hardly necessary. There were few people drawing breath whom he loathed more than Roleplay Rollins. "What does he want?"

"He won't say." She softened her voice. "But he seems very agitated."

Jonathan thought about telling him to pound sand and disappear, but his curiosity was piqued. "Bring him back to the office, please."

"Into the *cave*?" Venice gasped. It was the corporate term for their highly secure executive suites, and no one from outside the company was ever invited back here. Precious few from *inside* the company were ever invited back here.

"Escort him every step and make sure that Rick searches him for weapons. Be sure he finds the one on his ankle."

Three minutes later, Venice knocked on the door and opened it without waiting. At five-four, with chocolate-brown skin and a flawless complexion, Venice Alexander looked nothing like the computer genius she was. Her face showed utter confusion as she ushered in a graying man in jeans and a polo shirt, whose hair hung nearly to his shoulders, and whose beard made him look like a street panhandler. To those who knew what to look for, he looked exactly like the Delta Force operator that he was.

"Hello, Roleplay," Jonathan said, leaning his butt against the front of his massive desk. Part of the reason for bringing the son of a bitch back here was to let him see just how little his Machiavellian games had affected Jonathan in the long term. JoeDog's tail stopped wagging when she heard the tone in her master's voice.

The visitor shuffled his feet. He clearly knew he was not welcome, and would rather be anywhere else in the world. "Not many call me that anymore," he said.

"Not many people know your true nature anymore," Jonathan countered. Rollins's real first name was Stanley, but in the Unit, everybody got a nickname. The colonel preferred Iceman, and that stuck for a while until he advanced through the ranks and started to put his own career in front of the men he commanded. That was when Jonathan hit on the alliterative Roleplay Rollins, and it stuck like Krazy Glue.

"Are you going to invite me to sit down?" the colonel asked.

"Only if you promise to leave soon."

Venice got squirmy. "I'm going to leave you two alone."

Jonathan stepped forward, beckoning her closer. "No, no, no. I want you here. When you're dealing with Roleplay, witnesses are never a bad thing."

"Oh, for God's sake," Rollins groaned.

"Say what's on your mind," Jonathan said. "Then get the hell out of here."

"Fine," Rollins said. "Boomer Nasbe's family has been kidnapped by terrorists, and we need help getting them home."

Rollins's delivery had the feel of something he'd rehearsed, and it landed with all the force he'd no doubt intended. Boomer had been a rookie member of the Unit at the time Jonathan was leaving, and part of a different squadron, but the organization was small enough that everyone knew everyone else. Jonathan's recollection of the kid was that of a hungry go-getter who could run forever and bench-press nearly three times his body weight. He'd heard through the grapevine that Boomer had pulled off some impressive heroics in Afghanistan.

Jonathan gestured for the sofas and chair over near the fireplace. "Have a seat," he said. "You, too, Venice." Answering Rollins's unasked question, he added, "Think of her as my Miss Annabelle." He referred to the still-sharp, still-impressive eighty-year-old who had been the commander's secretary since the days when the Unit was first formed.

The colonel looked impressed. Miss Annabelle's were tough shoes to fill.

Jonathan left the leather people-eaters to his guests while he took the wooden William and Mary rocker for himself. Years of parachute jumps, bullet wounds, and general abuse had made it difficult for him to get comfortable in soft furniture. Before sitting, he asked if anybody wanted something to drink, but no one did. JoeDog took up the patch of carpet next to the rocker.

"What happened?" Jonathan asked, crossing his legs.

"We don't know, exactly," Rollins said. "Have you been watching the news? They're the family at the feet of the terrorists in the new video."

Jonathan shot a look to Venice, who recognized her cue and stood immediately. "I'll have it set up in the War Room in five minutes," she said, walking toward the door in the office wall that led directly to their high-tech conference room.

"Bring Gail in, too," Jonathan said.

"What about Boxers?"

Jonathan looked at Rollins, and then back. "Make sure he knows the colonel is here, and what the purpose of the meeting is. Leave it to him."

Venice acknowledged the gravity of his tone with a twitch of her eyebrows, and then left them alone.

Without the buffer of a witness, Jonathan felt his hatred returning, and his ears turned hot.

"You can't hold a grudge forever, Dig," Rollins said.

Jonathan raised a forefinger in warning. "You don't want to open that door. Not in here. Not on my turf."

Rollins made a show of looking around. "It's not as if it ruined your life. You seem to be doing okay."

"I was rich the day I was born," Jonathan said. "I give most of it away and I'd still never be able to spend it all. Not in ten lifetimes. It was never about making a living. It was about honor, and you proved you had none."

Rollins did not rise to the bait. "We all have jobs to do. Not all of them are enjoyable. If you had done yours, you'd still be in the Unit."

"I saved three lives that night."

"But to do it, you took five lives that the NCA deemed more important than the ones you saved."

"Don't flatter yourself," Jonathan spat. "Your whim is *not* the National Command Authority. We were in position, we'd taken four days to get there, and they were going to execute those kids."

"I gave an abort order, and you ignored it."

"It was a bogus order. You misunderstood it."

"Jesus, Digger, do you want to go through the whole court-martial again? We can't retry it, but even if we did, the fact will remain that you disobeyed an order."

The door from the hallway flew open with enough force to make a dent in the wall it slammed into, and Boxers stormed into the office. Born as Brian Van de Meulebroeke, Boxers stood closer to seven feet than six, and likely bent the needle on most bathroom scales. When anyone that big moves that fast, you know that damage is going to be done. His eyes showed murder.

"Box, no!" Jonathan shouted as he shot to his feet. Joe-Dog slinked under the coffee table.

Rollins scrambled to rise from the depths of the sofa, but he never had a chance. Boxers closed the distance in five quick strides. He grabbed a fistful of Rollins's shirt in one hand, and his hair with the other, and effortlessly lifted the colonel over the back of the sofa. He heaved him onto the floor with enough force to make two table lamps jump and tumble over.

"What did I tell you last time I saw you?" he shouted.

Rollins landed on his back, his head bouncing off the carpeted floor. He looked stunned. Or maybe terrified.

"Box!" Jonathan yelled. He'd never seen Big Guy this spun up. This homicidal. As he vaulted the back of the sofa to intervene, the conference room door flew open again.

Venice yelled. It wasn't a scream, exactly, but rather a guttural expression of surprise.

Jonathan dove for his friend, catching him by his belt and pulling to restrain him.

Boxers whirled on Jonathan, his fist cocked. He was that far gone. When Jonathan winced—a full-force blow from Big Guy could be fatal—Boxers' eyes changed. Horror replaced rage.

In the hallway, Rick Hare and Charlie Keeling—two of the full-time security guards at Security Solutions—appeared at the door, hands gripping their sidearms. What they saw was clearly not what they'd been expecting.

"Everything okay in here, Mr. G?" Rick asked. His eyes shifted to the various parties, trying to decipher it all.

Jonathan kept Boxers' eye. "You okay?"

Big Guy whirled to Rollins, pointing two fingers like a weapon.

"Look at me, Box," Jonathan said.

"I told him I'd kill him next time I saw him," Boxers said.

The security guards stepped in to take positions around Rollins. With the bad guy identified, they knew who to target.

"And you damn near did," Jonathan said. He smiled and winked.

Venice stood with her hands on her head, her mouth slack. "What is this?"

Jonathan held up a hand for silence as Gail Bonneville arrived in the doorway. Her hand was poised near the Glock on her hip, but then she relaxed. "Oh, there's *got* to be a good story here," she said.

With reinforcements in place, JoeDog felt secure enough to bark. Just once, as if to remind everyone that there was a four-legged killing machine in the room. The absurdity of it made Jonathan chuckle in spite of himself. He directed his attention to the security team. "Thanks, guys. We're all okay here. Just a flash of anger."

Rick Hare looked unconvinced. "You sure, boss?"

Jonathan nodded. "I'm always sure. Not always right, but always sure. How about you, Roleplay? Are you hurt?"

Colonel Rollins eyed Boxers with ill-disguised hatred as he rose to his feet and brushed himself off. The front panel of his shirt was torn at the buttons. "I'm fine," he said.

The guards clearly sensed the tension, but they also understood their order to leave. "We'll be at our posts," Rick said. "Just give a shout if you need something."

Jonathan smiled. "If anyone out there asks what happened, tell them that a bookcase fell over."

Charlie Keeling touched two fingers to his brow as acknowledgment. Gail pulled away from the door to allow
room for them to depart, and then asked Jonathan if she was
to stay or leave.

"I want you here for this," he said. "Let's gather in the
War Room, where we will all keep our hands to ourselves."

Boxers nearly vibrated with anger, but when the tension
left his shoulders, Jonathan knew that he was back with the
program.

As they filed into the War Room, Venice pulled Jonathan
to the side. "I've never seen Boxers like that."

"Did you find the video?"

She clearly wanted more, but knew better than to push.
"Cued up and ready to go," she said.

Tension remained heavy in the air as they filed into the
War Room. Jonathan wasn't sure where the nickname for the
space originated, but given the activities that were often
planned in this space, it was apropos. Detailed in teak and
mahogany and featuring calfskin-soft chairs, the War Room
offered all of the latest in communication and presentation
technology. On the far end, Venice had already retracted the
panels in the wall that housed the 106-inch projection screen,
where the frozen image of the terrified Nasbes stared at
them, frozen in time. He'd already seen it, of course, but it
was time to pay attention.

He asked, "Colonel Rollins, would you like to catch us up
on what you know before we start watching?" By using his
official title, Jonathan hoped to defuse the tension.

Rollins leaned forward and cleared his throat. "The people you're going to see are Christyne Nasbe and her son
Ryan, sixteen. We don't know how they ended up in the custody of terrorists, but we suspect that they were somehow
taken after the Wilson Bridge incident last night. They live
on Bragg when Boomer is home, but they're apparently up
here visiting her sister in Mount Vernon."

"Does Boomer know the family has been taken?"

"He was the one to tell us. He found out purely by

chance. He thought he recognized them despite the masks, and when he tried to establish contact with them, he couldn't. They weren't at the address where they were supposed to be staying, and both of their cell phones were turned off. We did a little checking and discovered that the SIM cards had either been disabled or removed."

Jonathan asked, "Is he just going by the voice?"

"That was the first thing that caught his attention. But then he looked closer. It turns out that the son, Ryan, has a birthmark on his belly. It shows on the video."

Gail asked, "Why are you coming to Security Solutions? A case like this has FBI written all over it."

Rollins hesitated. "I'd rather we discuss this in private, Digger."

Jonathan shook his head. "My team gets to know what I know."

The colonel took a moment to think it through. "Here's the thing," he said at last. "The FBI is a civilian agency. I'm sure they're fine at what they do, but they're pretty damned distracted right now, and we want the Nasbes' safety to be the first and only priority, not just one of many."

Gail started to object, but Rollins held up a hand to signal that he wasn't done yet.

"There's also the Unit connection. The FBI can't know that, and I think it's clear that the kidnappers *don't* know it, or they would have mentioned something about it in the video."

Gail didn't get it. "And why can't the FBI know?"

"Because the FBI is packed with unnamed sources," Rollins answered. "Deep Throat, anyone? What isn't leaked to the press is revealed though congressional hearings. I owe Boomer more than that."

Jonathan nodded to Venice, who pushed the buttons to make the lights dim and the picture come to life.

The setting was all too familiar, although Jonathan wasn't sure that he'd ever seen it staged with multiple hostages. The boy, on the left of the screen, was shirtless and wore what appeared to be blue jeans. The mother wore a nondescript black-on-black outfit that looked oddly stretched out and disheveled.

"Do you see the birthmark?" Rollins asked.

Venice froze the frame.

Rollins pointed from his seat. "Look there on his stomach. Just to the left of his navel. Our left, his right."

Jonathan leaned forward, as if by shortening the distance by five inches he could see the image more clearly.

"I see it," Gail said. "Looks like a little check mark."

"That's it exactly," Rollins said.

Jonathan took it on faith. One of these days, he was going to have to get glasses.

The picture had been framed tightly so that none of the captors' faces showed. In fact all they could see of the captors were legs wearing black pants—Jonathan counted four pairs—and the muzzles of the AKs that were resting against each of the victims' skulls.

Christyne Nasbe spoke for both of them. As she did, Arabic subtitles crawled along the bottom of the frame. "People of America," she began. From the first words, she sounded as if she was reading, but how could that be, with a hood over her face? "We and our satanic government have brought suffering to the peaceful people of Islam for many years. We have murdered tens of thousands of innocent children while they slept in their beds, and we have martyred countless holy warriors as they fight every day only to create a world that will live in peace, free of the sloth and the wickedness brought by our Western ways. We need to realize that we can never win.

"This week, the Army of Allah began a new holy war that will bring you to your knees. They are many thousands strong, and they have already begun their battle, first in Kansas City, and on Monday night in Washington, D.C. This morning, they took the battle to our children, killing our youth as we have killed so many of theirs. The killing will continue until the United States government apologizes to

Islamic people everywhere and withdraws all U.S. forces from the Middle East and Afghanistan. If an announcement to that effect is not made by next Wednesday, one week and one day from today, my son and I will be martyred for everyone to see."

The instant before the image clicked off, the boy's voice said, "Martyred means murdered in English."

CHAPTER NINE

They watched the video three more times before Jonathan asked Venice to freeze it on the image of the huddled captives.

Jonathan turned to the colonel. "I understand that you want me and my team to rescue the Nasbes, but I'm still confused," he said. "This video is going to go viral. Even with their faces blacked out, somebody's going to recognize them. Neighbors are going to call. Distant relatives are going to call. What do my team and I bring to the table that you're not going to get from the authorities?"

Rollins shifted in his chair, recrossing his legs, one over the other. "Two things we need to talk about," he said. "First, we've already reached out to the community at Bragg. We've asked them not to forward any theories on the family's identity, and we're confident that they'll understand. Ditto the immediate family. We've let them know that the best way to bring their loved ones home safely is for them to rally around each other and say nothing."

"Surely someone's going to say something," Gail said.

Jonathan shook his head. "You haven't witnessed the
ommunity built up around the Unit," he said. "They under-

stand the importance of secrecy. Even the kids. Back in the old days, we used to exclude the family from almost everything for fear of word leaking out to the bad guys. But the toll was too great on families." He gestured with his hands as if to say, *ta-da*.

Boxers agreed. "We opened up a lot of the details to the families, and the result was all good—specifically because everyone understood the stakes."

Rollins went on, "I sense that you're looking at the equation from the wrong side. It's not about what you bring. It's about what I bring." He cast another uncomfortable glance at the others in the room.

Jonathan waited him out.

Rollins sighed. "Look, you're not a naïve guy. The new administration has rewritten all the rules. As a guy who's been in the service for more than a few years, I'm more feared by them than trusted. These days, you either toe the line, or you tour a jail cell. The old national security shortcuts just don't exist anymore. But you know how the community works. We look after our own, yet Posse Comitatus forbids the military from engaging in domestic law-enforcement activities. Other laws and executive orders prohibit domestic activity from other intelligence organizations. No eavesdropping without warrants, no questioning without probable cause, no midnight rescues without due process."

"You mean we have to obey the law," Gail said.

Rollins shot a look to Jonathan. "All on the same team?"

Jonathan shrugged. "What can I say? You can remove the girl from the cops, but you can't remove the cop from the girl."

Rollins drilled Gail with his eyes. "With all due respect, some laws are ridiculous. Like the ones that respect terrorists' rights over those of the people they terrorize."

"Oh, I see," Gail said. "All we need is to let the military decide who's good enough for their own constitutional rights."

Jonathan sensed where this was going, and he hurried to

intervene. Gail had never been comfortable with moral gray area in which Jonathan plied his trade, but it made no sense to engage Rollins like this. "No civics lessons, okay?" he said. "I asked him to state his case. We need to let him do that." To Rollins: "Go on."

The colonel shrugged. "The rest should be pretty obvious. The unit has friends in the right places, and they're willing to help us—off the record, of course, and behind the scenes. We need someone to feed the intelligence to, who can then go and bring the family to safety."

Venice cut to the chase. "You want Security Solutions to provide cover for you to break the law."

Rollins smiled for the first time since arriving. "Well, no," he said. "To hell with providing cover. I want you to actually break the law."

Something about the sheer honesty made Jonathan laugh. "What kind of support are you offering?"

"Whatever you need. Any and all intel assets we might have. No hardware, though, and no manpower. There's no way to do that without triggering a congressional hearing."

"How do you provide the soft services without triggering an investigation?" Venice asked.

"Through careful management of resources," Rollins said.

"Who all knows you're here?" Boxers asked.

"I'm not at liberty to answer that."

"How high up the Unit chain?"

"I'm not at liberty to answer that, either."

Boxers growled.

"Here's the thing, Colonel," Jonathan said. "We've still got tread marks on our backs from the last time you threw us under the bus. How do we know you won't do it again?"

Rollins leaned forward in his chair, and his expression became very thoughtful. "I'm sorry," he said. "I'm not making myself clear. I'll be more direct. If this thing blows up— if word leaks out—you are exactly the ones who will take the hit. With all respect, isn't that why people pay you for your services?"

Jonathan noticed Gail's ears turning red so he spoke quickly. "They pay us because we're a hostage recovery team with a perfect record."

"Except outside of the community, nobody knows you have a perfect record. When Daddy Lottabucks's kid gets snatched from spring break, all he knows is that you'll get the job done without the police ever knowing a thing. I bet he's expecting you to take the fall quietly if things go wrong."

"Daddy Lottabucks is paying for the privilege," Boxers said.

"We've got money," Rollins said. "A bunch of the guys pooled our resources, and we were able to pull together sixty thousand. I know that's not what—"

Jonathan held up his hand for silence. "Boomer's a friend," he said. "I don't want your money." His teammates froze at his words. It was a gang poker face.

Rollins smiled, genuinely relieved. "Digger, I appreciate this. I'll inform—"

Jonathan cut him off again. "This meeting never happened, Colonel. We'll do what we do, but we will not keep you in the loop, and we will not accept any help that we don't ask for. If, on the other hand, we ask for help, I expect to get it immediately, and without question."

"But the team was expecting—"

"Nothing," Jonathan interrupted. "Your team should expect nothing because this meeting never happened. I will not answer to you, I will not cover for you, I will not run interference for you."

The colonel leaned back in his chair. He seemed to know there was more coming.

"More than anything," Jonathan went on, "know this. If you cross me, I will hurt you. Badly." He shifted his eyes to Venice. "Please escort the colonel to the door."

* * *

Michael Copley stood on the mezzanine overlooking the shop floor, marveling at the quality of the work his people produced. Thanks to their dedication to him and his mission, they had together raised Appalachian Acoustics to be the source for some of the most sought-after orchestral and choral tools in the world. Lightweight, less expensive than the competition, and easy to assemble by even a single person, his patented acoustic reflectors had become the gold standard.

These one hundred eighty employees were the ones who made it happen every day. Their continuing dedication to him, the company, and their mission stirred emotions that might have been called love if the context were different. They meant that much to him. And he was confident that he meant that much to them.

He heard the approach of his visitor before he saw him. "Hello, Kendig," he said without looking.

Kendig Neen was the sheriff of Maddox County, West Virginia, and out here that still meant something. Tall and stout, with a waxed handlebar mustache and a speaking voice that was made for radio, Kendig *was* the law out here. With the nearest state police barracks nearly fifty miles away, backup was hard to come by, and that meant a freedom to occasionally craft new laws on the fly.

"Morning, Michael," he said. "Have you got a moment?"

"Isn't that an inspiring sight?" Michael said.

"Smells like airplane glue," Kendig said.

Michael gave him a hard look. "You might show some respect. Those people are the reason you have a job, and I'm the reason *they* have a job."

"Will your boardroom work for you?" Kendig pressed. "We really need to talk."

Michael led the way from the mezzanine to the shop floor, and out to the executive wing, as he called it. He realized it didn't look like much, with its Formica tabletop and metal chairs, but it was the best he could afford. For now. If visitors gave the boardroom only a cursory look, they would have seen only the knotty pine paneling and the linoleum floors and assumed it to be cheaply built. You'd have to be an expert, knowing exactly what you were looking for to see that it was a high-tech, soundproofed room.

Kendig started in as soon as the heavy door found its latch. "What were you thinking, putting that mother and her son up on the Internet for everyone to see?"

Michael took his time pulling out a chair and lowering himself into it. It was a common trait of brutes not to be able to see the complexity of the proverbial big picture. "I was thinking about the mission," he said. His voice bore the exaggerated patience of a teacher speaking to a slow child. "We are at war now, Brother Kendig."

"And war requires caution. You put faces on their battle against us. What you did steeled the resolve of every law-enforcement agency in the country. In the *world*. Have you been watching television? Have you heard the kind of resources they're marshalling against us?"

Michael scowled, pretending to be confused. "I've glanced at the television, but I haven't seen anything about us. Are you sure?"

"For God's sake, Michael."

"I've heard some ranting about 'terrorists,' but I haven't heard a word about us. In fact, if I'm not mistaken, if you were to ask any of the new media who 'we' are"—he used finger quotes—"I bet they'd tell you that we were Arabs. Central Asian, maybe; but certainly Islamists. I don't think you'd hear a word about devout patriots from West Virginia."

"But they didn't have to know *anything*!" Kendig insisted.

Michael leaned back and placed his heels on the table. "Now who's being silly?" he said. "Of course they had to know. Knowing is part of the greater ruse. While the authorities are all looking for who we are not, we will attack them with who we are. It's a classic feint."

Kendig sat heavily in the seat adjacent to Michael. "Was it necessary to beat the boy?"

Michael laughed. "Oh, so that's your moral compass? The killing is okay, but you draw the line at a few slaps and punches?"

"I draw the line at cruelty. I draw the line at increased incentive to find us. His hands were bound, for heaven's sake."

Michael waved it away as irrelevant. "Brother Stephen told me that the boy was a threat, a troublemaker. Now he's a frightened boy again. A neutralized threat. No permanent harm was done."

"Brother Stephen is a liability," Kendig said. "I don't like the way he is with the prisoners, and I don't like his attitude around the other soldiers. I think you empower him too much by allowing his shenanigans."

"He is a fine and loyal soldier," Michael said. "He and Sister Colleen will both be honored for their service at the bridge in Washington. That was simply brilliant."

"So why risk the victory with the broadcast? Videos like that can be traced directly back to you."

Michael shook his head. "Impossible."

"It's *not* impossible, Michael. It's inevitable. The feds have uncanny resources to track down Internet broadcasts. Crazy resources that we can't possibly match."

"I have it covered," Michael said. He made a point of keeping his voice modulated and under control. He would not honor shouting with shouting of his own. "Brother Kirkland is quite the computer whiz. He assures me that everything about our transmission will trace back to a computer in Flint, Michigan. When we broadcast again, the signature will trace to Islamabad. We will have to let enough time pass for them to believe we took the family to Pakistan, which will fit perfectly with what they want to believe. That will leave us free to operate even less encumbered by the authorities than we already are."

Kendig stood again. "Do you hear the hubris in your words? You think you're invincible, and that's the kind of attitude that will bring us all down."

Michael sighed. This was all such a waste of time. "I

apologize, Brother Kendig, if I have sprung too big a surprise. I should have been clearer in my communication. But right now, what's done is done. The mission is progressing."

"Is it?" Kendig pressed. "Is it really? Is my mission progressing, or is it only yours? Is it possible that you're having too good a time playing with people's minds?"

Suddenly, Michael felt very real concern. "Tell me, Kendig, what exactly is your mission? Maybe we have in fact grown apart."

"My mission is to set things straight again. To set this country straight again. I'm tired of watching the rich run roughshod over the poor. I'm tired of watching my community swirl down the toilet while places like New York and Washington and Los Angeles thrive in the shade of immorality. My mission is revolution."

Michael smiled. He felt warm again, comforted by hearing his own words recited back to him. "And the revolution begins with small bands of operatives creating havoc. We have succeeded in Washington and Kansas City and Detroit. A strike team leaves tonight and another tomorrow to deal more blows to the Users, and after they are successful, there will be more. The rage against the Islamists will be—pardon me—biblical in proportion." He chuckled at his own cleverness.

Kendig seemed frustrated, as if he didn't feel he was getting his point across effectively. "But the prisoners—"

"Without them, there would be no face," Michael interrupted. "You were right about that. I am, in fact, putting a face on our mission, and that face—those faces, in this case—will unite America in a desire to bring *Islamic* terrorists to their knees. The government will finally do what they should have been doing all along, and while they are focused on the phantom we have created, we will move in to cut the head off the snake."

Kendig cocked his head. "What are you talking about? What snake?"

Michael brought his feet down from the table and leaned

closer. "*The* snake," he said. "The only snake that matters. The United States government."

Kendig cocked his head, intrigued. He lowered himself into a seat again. "What aren't you telling me?"

Michael smiled. "Ah, but I *am* telling you. We fulfilled the GSA contract today, Kendig. Our panels will be installed in time for the president's holiday address."

It was the achievement of a dream.

CHAPTER TEN

With Rollins gone, the atmosphere in the room felt less homicidal.

"Why would they take hostages in the first place?" Jonathan asked his assembled team.

Their chorus of confused looks told him that he hadn't stated his question clearly enough.

He explained, "You're a terrorist group, okay? You're against this or for that, and you do your big nasty. You make a big mark. You've won. Why do you want hostages?"

"To create more terror," Boxers said.

"No," Gail said. "I see his point. They've already scored on a big scale. They've already ruined hundreds of lives. In the showbiz that terrorism has become, imperiling a single family seems like something of an anticlimax."

"But they told us what they were looking for," Venice said. "They told us that their goal is for the United States to abandon its interests in the Middle East and Central Asia."

Jonathan stood and started his classic problem-solving pace around the room. "Something's not adding up for me," he thought aloud. "If we take them at their word, they've already killed dozens of people. They said in the video that the killings would continue until they got their way, but they know they'll never get their way. Even if a complete withdrawal was imminent, a threat like this would cause a delay, just to keep the world from thinking that the U.S. had blinked."

He paused in his stroll to give a long look to the frozen frame of the Nasbes. He kept his finger pointed at them while he turned to face his troops. "With that many people already dead, how do these two rise to the level of bargaining chips? That doesn't make sense to me."

"Maybe you're thinking too hard," Boxers said. "They're terrorists, for God's sake. Do you really think they're parsing every word?"

"Does it matter?" Venice asked, cutting to the chase. "Does the reason they were taken really have anything to do with planning their rescue?"

He gave her the short answer: "No."

Venice turned her attention to her ever-present computer and tapped a dozen keys. "Here's the easy stuff," she began. "The transmission site for this Web broadcast is an address in Flint, Michigan."

"That's the Muslim capital of the U.S.," Boxers said.

"Yes, it is," Venice confirmed.

"The FBI is going to be all over that place," Gail said.

"Already done," Venice said. "According to ICIS, they raided the place about twenty minutes ago." Pronounced *EYE-sis*, the Interstate Crime Information System was a largely unknown outgrowth of the 9-11 attacks, in which data from ongoing investigations were tracked by computer with details made available only to a select few law-enforcement officials with specifically approved federal clearances. And Venice.

"I'm going to guess from the look on your face that they found nothing," Jonathan said.

"Just a frightened college student with something of a gaming obsession. They're going to question him, but nobody thinks he's the guy."

"Any geek worth the tape on his glasses can set up a false routing for Internet transmissions," Gail said.

Venice's eyes flashed. She did not like having her thunder stolen.

Jonathan scowled. "Is the college kid part of the Muslim community?"

Venice tapped some more. "Farouk al-Somebody. You'll have to figure out the pronunciation on your own."

Jonathan declined. "No, that's okay. It's a Muslim name." A thought blossomed in his mind, and as it grew, he waved his forefinger at nobody in particular. "So, riddle me this. If you're a badass terrorist group, and you can reroute your Internet electrons to anyplace in the world you want them to be, why reroute them to the heart of the Muslim community in America?"

"To throw the authorities off the scent," Boxers said. It was the most obvious thing in the world.

"No," Jonathan said. "That's why you reroute the signal in the first place. But if you know for a fact that the feds are going to trace the false location to its source, why wouldn't you tag the signal to a computer in the heart of the Bible Belt? Or to someplace in France? Why the very heart of American Islam?"

"Because that's where their friends are," Boxers pressed. "Dig, you are just thinking way too hard."

But Gail was intrigued. "Where are you going with this?"

"I'm wondering if these bad guys are really Islamic at all," Jonathan said. "I'll tell you for a fact that that kid I eye-balled on the bridge last night was the most Aryan-looking Muslim I've ever seen. The video they posted shows nobody's face, and now they deliberately lead the FBI to the very community you'd think they'd want to protect."

"So, who are the terrorists really?" Venice asked.

"I guess they could be anybody," Jonathan said. "Hate groups are a dime a dozen these days."

Boxers shifted in his chair. Furniture always looked too small for him. "I'm still not following."

"Think about it," Gail said, gaining some momentum in her thinking. "Let's say you're a terrorist group, and you want to pull this sleight of hand where you convince people that the bad guys they've been hunting for the past ten years are still the bad guys. You pull off your shooting sprees and whatever else you're going to do, but you direct attention away."

One of the things Jonathan liked most about Gail was the way she could peel back the onion layers of a mystery and quickly get to its core. A couple of years ago, that tenacious streak had nearly cost him his freedom, back when they were on opposite sides. Intelligence is way more attractive when it's working with you than when it's working against you.

"I've got that part," Boxers said.

Jonathan picked up the thread. "If you *really* want to keep the pressure on—if you *really* want people to get mad at the wrong bad guys, you put a family in front of a camera and make impossible demands."

"I've got it," Venice chimed in. "As the deadline approaches, public anger gets more intense, and the public appetite for alternatives other than violence dries up."

"It'll get like a frenzy," Boxers said, finally getting it. "So, what happens when the deadline expires?"

Gail's face fell. "They'll have to follow through with their threat," she said. "They'll have to kill someone. They could even stretch it out. Kill one of them next week, and the other a week later."

"And they can always grab more," Venice added.

Jonathan didn't verbalize his thought that that might be a good thing. The more frequently a criminal committed a crime, the more likely he was to make a critical error.

"So, what's their end game?" Boxers asked.

Jonathan shrugged. "Terror. Does it need to be more than that?"

"I think so," Gail said. "I mean, it's all well and good to make people think the bad guys are someone other than who they really are, and I suppose it scratches somebody's itch to foment hatred, but don't we have to assume that it's all being done for a reason?"

"Where've you been living the last decade?" Boxers scoffed. "The bombing bastards got no greater goal than killing people."

"I disagree," Gail said. "The jihadists think that they're serving God."

Jonathan waved her off. "I think that's bullshit."

"How else do you get a thirteen-year-old to strap explosives to his chest?"

"Well, okay," Jonathan said with a hesitation. "But that's what the soldiers think. Their leaders—the ones that *we* have to blow up—are cynical assholes."

"Who have the end game of political power," Venice said, throwing her lot to the female camp.

"Okay, so give me a theory," Jonathan said. "What's the Army of Allah's real end game?"

That question brought silence.

CHAPTER ELEVEN

Brother Michael Copley asked, "Are you ready?"

Sister Colleen's heart skipped in her chest and her stomach tumbled. "Yes" was such a simple word, yet somehow she couldn't get her mouth to say it. She settled for a nod.

Brother Michael smiled, a dazzling display of perfectly aligned white teeth framed by perfect dimples. Colleen thought he was the most stunning man she had ever seen. From his green eyes to his spiked blond hair to his muscled physique, he was as fine as any movie star.

"Relax," Brother Michael said. "You are here to be honored, not punished." He turned to Brother Stephen. "What about you?"

Brother Stephen snapped to attention, his deep-set dark eyes locked on a spot on the opposite wall. With his broad, muscled shoulders and his narrow waist, he seemed to Sister Colleen to be the perfect image of a soldier.

"Couldn't be readier, sir," he said.

Brother Michael patted him on the arm. "You can settle down a little, too."

Beyond the white paneled door that separated her from

her destiny, the congregation had been assembling for the last ten minutes. Colleen couldn't yet see them, but she knew who they were. She could see their faces in her mind, and even knew where each of them would sit. They were a young crowd—average age well under thirty—more male than female, but not by a lot.

They numbered around one hundred souls now, and one way or another, they all worked for the church, whether as factory workers, groundskeepers, doctors, or teachers in the school. They all would be dressed plainly, in blacks or whites or blues, because the compound store only stocked plain cloth. Together, they were the Army of God, servants to the Greater Good, united in their opposition to the evil spawned by the Users.

Until last night, Colleen had never witnessed the evil with her own eyes. She'd had no idea that the lights of vehicles could be so bright, or that the very air could smell rancid from the pollutants they pumped into Mother Nature's lungs. It was as sickening as it was exhilarating.

Even now, eighteen hours after the assault had ended, it was difficult to believe that she had been a part in such a momentous victory. But for her efforts—and those of her brothers and sisters throughout the Army of God—the Users would continue their assaults without end. Her mission at the Woodrow Wilson Bridge—a span named for a warmonger and a money worshipper—combined with the brave efforts of her brothers and sisters in Kansas City and Detroit had made clear to the world that being a User meant being at war with the righteous. Within days, in a dozen other cities across the United States, the lesson would be taught again and again.

Those who had died at her hands had perished at the altar of the future, martyrs to a cause they did not yet understand, but would when they found their eternal rest. They died in service to the greater good.

She had not yet shared with anyone that horrible moment when the User on the parallel span of the bridge shot at her.

She thanked God that Brother Michael had had the presence of mind to order them to wear body armor. Without that, Colleen was certain that she would have died.

"It's time," Brother Michael said. There was that smile again. "When you hear me introduce you by name, that will be your cue to enter onto the stage." He looked each of them in the eye and offer them a kind smile. "Be sure to enjoy your moment, children. You have achieved greatness in the Army of God. No one can ever take that from you. Drink in the adulation. You may never feel so special again, so enjoy it for what it is."

Brother Michael disappeared through the doors. The instant he was visible from the other side, all noise among the congregation stopped.

"Good afternoon, brothers and sisters," he said, his voice booming along the twenty-foot-high rafters.

In perfect unison, the congregation replied, "Good afternoon, Brother Michael."

Brother Stephen opened the door a crack to see what was happening.

Colleen pulled on his sleeve and hissed, "Brother Michael said to wait."

Brother Stephen pulled his arm away. "He also said to drink in the adulation. I don't like drinking what I can't see."

His words were rebellious, and therefore sinful, but Colleen was pleased to see him doing what she had been so tempted to do. She pressed in behind him.

Brother Michael stood at the edge of the stage, squarely in the beam of light that flowed from the tall windows above the double doors in the front. He held his hands out in a welcoming motion to all, and they similarly reached their hands out to receive his projected energy.

"I am pleased to say that we have achieved our second milestone in our quest to reeducate the Users," he said.

The congregation erupted in applause and cheers.

Brother Michael gestured for silence, and the congregation quieted. "And I bring sadness from Kansas City. While the mission to the Users' shopping mall was unquestionably successful, Brother Thomas Ezekiel and Sister Elizabeth Marie were both martyred to the cause."

Colleen and Brother Stephen exchanged their silent shock. Neither had heard a word of this. A ripple of distress rumbled through the congregation.

"We will miss them both," Brother Michael went on, "but while we mourn, we must also celebrate. I have heard reports this morning, via the Users' television broadcasts, that our martyred saints killed ten people and wounded many more before their escape became blocked by the police. Brother Thomas Ezekiel and Sister Elizabeth Marie each fulfilled their destiny, and took their own lives."

This time, the applause was spontaneous, loud, and sustained.

Brother Michael shouted above it. "No User's hand touched them. They each remained pure to the end. They entered the kingdom of Heaven with full knowledge that their missions had been accomplished."

More applause.

"Brothers and sisters, this war has finally begun. The age of sin—the age of lust and greed and idolatry and gluttony—will soon end. For many of you in this room, those under twenty-two, this is a moment for which you have trained your entire lives. The time has arrived to disrupt the flow of so-called commerce and to redirect the river of wealth that flows to the Users, and from them into the pockets of heathens and miscreants throughout the world.

"Brothers and sisters, through my eyes and through my soul, the Lord God has laid this awesome and terrible responsibility upon our shoulders. Yours and mine. Together, we will cleanse the world of the blasphemers. We will shake the Users down to their very bone marrow by bleeding them of their precious money. People will be afraid to visit their stores and to travel their roads. In New York City, the second home of the evil whose primary residence is Washington, D.C., the rich will become poor as their precious investments shrink and become worthless."

The congregation erupted in applause again, sustained and rolling, until Brother Michael raised his hands.

"As in every war, ours will be fought with blood. The blood of our brothers and sisters will doubtless commingle on the field of battle with the filthy blood of the Users we kill, but remember that each of us is here on this earth for this reason, and this reason alone. When the time to fight comes, I know that you will each do your part. You will use your training, and you will shoot straight and you will show no mercy."

Brother Michael paused as he let those words sink in. He walked all the way to the front end of the altar.

When he spoke again, his voice was barely a whisper, yet somehow every word resonated. "If it is God's will that you die in this noble struggle, then so be it. But do not believe for a moment that ours is a suicidal struggle. Your duty, when at all possible, is to return here to the compound, to your home. To the Army of God."

He paused again. "I care for you," he said. "Each of you is my brother or my sister, just as you are brothers and sisters to each other. While we lost two of our family in Kansas City, we have two more who have more than fulfilled their mission, and they have returned safely to us. These two heroes, according to Users' news reports, killed twelve gluttons and idolaters, and wounded many, many more."

Brother Stephen looked back at Colleen. He was beaming—filled, she imagined with the same bursting pride that bloomed inside her own chest.

"I think he's about to do it," Brother Stephen said.

Brother Michael's voice crescendoed. "Brothers and sisters, I present to you the first two heroes of the war. I present to you Brother Stephen John and Sister Colleen Erin."

Brother Stephen pushed open the door, and then Colleen found herself somehow on the stage. Surely she had walked, but in the wash of the moment, she couldn't remember doing it.

She had never heard such applause. To a person, the congregation was on its feet, and many of those feet were stamping against the floor. She heard whistles and cheers, and some of the congregants clapped with their hands over their heads.

The cheering was still shaking the walls when Brother Michael stepped behind them both and placed his hands on their shoulders. He leaned in until his lips were inches from their ears and he said, "Smile, give a big wave, and walk off the stage."

There was a firmness to his order that Colleen found startling. Still, an order was an order. She smiled and waved, her hand high over her head, and something about the gesture ignited a new eruption of applause. The noise was still peaking when Brother Stephen led the way back out through the door they'd entered.

When they were alone together in the anteroom, Brother Stephen fell to his knees and threw his hands over his head, his fists balled in triumph. "Oh, my God!" he exclaimed. "Oh, my God, did you *hear* that? We're *heroes*, Sister Colleen. Future generations will talk about us. We'll be legendary."

Colleen held up a cautionary hand. "Be careful. Pride is a sin."

"This isn't pride, Sister. This is fact. Here, let me show you something." He reached into his back pocket and pulled out some folded papers. He started to open them, then hesitated.

"What?"

"I committed another sin to get these."

"What are they?" Colleen knew that it was wrong, but Lord help her, she was intrigued.

"Promise you won't tell."

What could it be? Brother Stephen had always been one to skirt the rules, but not Colleen. She was Miss Straight and Narrow. And she had to know. "Okay, I promise."

Brother Stephen shot a quick glance at the door, then unfolded the pages. "I got these off a computer at the factory."

Colleen gasped. In the hierarchy of forbidden activities, accessing the computers was up there with fraternizing with Users. The punishment was flogging.

"Do you want to see them or not?" Brother Stephen growled.

Colleen nodded.

He unfolded the pages to reveal pictures of a familiar tableau of bloody mayhem. "The Internet is packed with photos of our work last night," he explained. "They're amazing."

Colleen took the stack—there must have been ten pages, each with three pictures apiece, printed in color.

"Everything with bullet holes in the front of the cars is yours," Brother Stephen explained. "Everything with the bullets in the back is mine."

The photos were amazing. "Who took them?" They showed mangled cars, vans, and trucks, riddled with bullets, spattered with blood.

"Everybody," Brother Stephen said. "Cell phones, cameras, everything. All the Users carry something to take pictures with. They just upload them to the Internet."

The images were enthralling, unlike anything Colleen had ever seen before. The third page of the sheaf of papers showed the first picture of a corpse. Brother Michael had told them about the damage that would be inflicted by the .223-caliber ammunition they were firing from their Bushmaster carbines, but until she actually saw the lifeless bodies that they leave behind, there had been no way to fully comprehend it. The bullets cut huge trenches through exposed flesh, and dislodged enormous wedges of skull and brain tissue. Brother Michael's and Brother Kendig's movies and the diagrams proved to be entirely inadequate to describe the carnage.

To her utter shock, Colleen found herself unnerved by the images. This was the mission she'd just been hailed for accomplishing, yet seeing the victory reflected in torn flesh and spattered blood made it feel more like a travesty than a victory. Brother Michael had lectured about the fog of war, and of the emotional trauma brought by taking a human life, but Colleen now realized that an enormous gap existed between the theory of killing and the actuality of it.

She felt emotion building in her throat, but she swallowed it down. She had asked to see these pictures, after all; Brother Stephen had given her the opportunity to say no, so whatever discomfort she felt was of her own making, and she therefore had no rational reason to object.

Then she turned to the sixth page of the photos, and everything changed. The images there showed two toddlers—they may have been twins—dead in their car seats, torn apart by bullets. Something inside of her caught, the way a fish bone catches in your throat. The bullets had entered from the front of their car.

"Now *that's* disgusting," Brother Stephen teased, but his tone was still triumphant. "That's some wild shooting, Sister Colleen. This is the most famous scene out of the whole thing. It's on the television news, in the newspapers, on the Internet, *everywhere.* Not these photos, exactly, because the bodies aren't in them, but those car seats. Man, you've got them pissing in their shoes."

Footsteps approached the door to the anteroom, and Brother Stephen struck like a snake to snatch the papers from Colleen and stuff them down the front of his trousers.

Brother Michael entered. He scowled. "What are you two doing?"

"Nothing, sir," Brother Stephen said, a little too quickly, Colleen thought.

Brother Michael's gaze shifted. "Sister Colleen, do you have something you want to tell me?"

Colleen fought the sudden, inexplicable urge to vomit. "No, Brother Michael," she said.

His scowl deepened. He had an uncanny way of reading people. "You don't look well, Sister Colleen."

"No, sir, I'm fine. Thank you, sir."

He looked back toward Brother Stephen, and then again at Colleen. "A boy and a girl alone in a room on the day they are recognized for valor," he mused aloud. "Forgive me if my suspicious mind gets the better of me. Need I remind you of your celibacy vows?"

Colleen blushed, while Brother Stephen looked as if he'd been slapped. Then they both laughed. It felt good to laugh.

"No, sir," Colleen said. "Not a problem."

"I remember my vows well, Brother Michael," Brother Stephen agreed. "No need to worry about that."

Brother Michael folded his arms and scowled even more deeply. "Well, if not that, then what?"

Colleen caught herself shooting a glance to Brother Stephen, but when she broke it off, Brother Michael had already seen it.

"Interesting dilemma," Brother Michael thought aloud. "If I press you for an answer, you'll likely feel obliged to lie. Lying is a sin, of course, and if I put you in that position, then I will be partly responsible for your eternal torment in Hell." He paused for dramatic effect. "How could I ever live with the guilt?" He winked at Brother Stephen and made a shooing motion with both his hands. "Carry on. Both of you get out of here."

They donned their coats, and as they opened the door onto the bright sunshine, Brother Stephen patted her on the bottom. She whirled on him, but then he pushed past and headed off to join Brother Zebediah and the other boys he hung around with.

Outside, as the frigid air embraced her, Colleen felt herself trembling. A chill had invaded her, and it was not just from the twenty-degree air. It was as if the warmth that flowed through her veins during the rolling applause had turned to something frozen and ugly. Make no mistake: Brother Michael had just authorized carnal relations between her and Brother Stephen. That was the wink; and once authorized, they could not be denied. Certainly, not by her.

She was nineteen now, after all, and she believed that Brother Stephen was twenty—both of them old enough to do their part to populate the Army for the future. And as the offspring of two such heroes, her children would be born into fame. They would be raised with the others in the communal dormitories, but the expectations upon them would be enormous.

Colleen should have felt honored to be coupled with Brother Stephen, but even as a small child, he had been cruel and violent. He preyed on other children under the guise of character-building competition, and the guardians had never interfered.

It had always seemed wrong to her, and while she would never say such a thing aloud lest she invite a flogging, the mother in her could not be denied. Children sometimes just needed to be held, especially when they were small, but after they turned two and they became part of the communal dormitory, such displays of affection were forbidden. To pamper was to encourage weakness, and given the mission at hand, weakness in any form could not be tolerated.

Still, when the younger children became overwhelmed by their schooling and their training, they knew that they could turn to her, and that she would be there for them, not to encourage weakness, but to help them find the pathway to strength when their resolve was sometimes shaken.

Marriage did not exist within the Army because marriage implied ownership of relations. Women between the ages of twenty and thirty were expected to bear children, per the designs of Brother Michael and the Elders, and once weaned, the children became the communal property of everyone. She would lie with Brother Stephen at a time of his choosing, and she would accept his seed, but she prayed that he would at least be gentle.

As Colleen wandered across campus among her fellow soldiers, she became aware that something had changed. She was a killer of innocent children whose crimes consisted of being born to parents who drove along the wrong bridge at

the wrong moment of the wrong day. The images of the ravaged little boy and girl flooded her mind, bringing a rush of
emotion. She gagged. That frigid block of ice that had formed
in her gut seized and doubled in size.

She knew what was coming, and she didn't think she
could stop it. Desperate for some measure of privacy, Colleen dashed twenty yards to a small copse of pine trees,
where she vomited into winter-dead scrub growth that was
clustered at its base. Thankful for the cover provided by the
thick pines, she sat heavily on the frigid mulch and gave in
to the sobs that wracked her body.

CHAPTER TWELVE

"I still don't understand why they did this to you," Christyne said as she fussed yet again at the cut in Ryan's left eyebrow. Upon returning to their sweltering cell, she had had the presence of mind to dangle two of the water bottles out of one of the ventilation windows, suspended by Ryan's shoelaces. Now that one was nearly frozen, she pressed it against his eye.

He yelped and pushed her hand away. "That hurts, Mom."

She persisted, swinging the bottle in the air to avoid his grasp. "You need this to bring the swelling down."

He might be nearly blind from the swelling, but he could still do good interference. "Give it to me, then. I'll do it."

His mom surrendered the block of ice, and he held it against the side of his face, near the cut, but not directly on top of it the way she had done. At least the bleeding had stopped.

"You must have done something to anger them before they did this to you," Christyne pressed. He was pissed that she didn't believe his version of what had happened.

"I didn't do anything," he said again. "Five minutes after they took me out of here, we were upstairs, and one of the guards just hit me. I hadn't said anything. My hands were tied, for God's sake."

Christyne shook her head. "That doesn't make any sense. You must have done something."

That was it. "I did nothing!" Ryan roared, his voice echoing off the walls. "I didn't do a damn thing! They just hit me."

He saw his mom recoil from his words, and he liked that, even though yelling made everything hurt worse. He thought they might have cracked a rib on his left side.

"We have to figure out how to get out of here," he said. "At least I do. Those guys want to kill me."

"There *is* no way out of here," Christyne said, "so don't even talk about it." She started straightening up the cell. Cleaning was her body language for shutting down discussion.

Ryan pulled the ice away from his eye. "Whose side are you on? We *have* to talk about it."

She stopped her work and pointed at him with her forefinger. "Stop," she said. "Right now. Just stop."

"Stop what?"

"You've got that Indiana Jones look in your eye. I want you to stop planning whatever dangerous adventure you've got swimming around that imagination of yours."

He scowled and cocked his head. "You know I'm talking about getting *out* of here, right?"

Mom went to work fluffing a pillow. "I know exactly what you're talking about. It's foolish and you're going to get yourself hurt."

"*Foolish?* You heard what they said up there, right? The part about how they're going to kill us in a week?"

She scoffed, "Nobody's going to kill anyone."

Ryan gaped. "Excuse me? They already killed people on that bridge, and all that other shit they were saying."

She shot him an angry glare. "Watch your mouth."

He didn't back down. "We've been kidnapped by terrorists. Whenever that happens, I get to say 'shit,' okay? Language doesn't count when terrorists are trying to kill you. Isn't that in the Mom Rule Book somewhere?"

She smiled, but he knew she didn't want to.

Ryan pressed on. "So, if they're willing to kill all those people just for the hell of it, what makes you think they wouldn't want to kill us? Especially since they, you know, *said* they were going to kill us?"

She continued to fluff, the conversation over.

"Jesus!" Ryan dropped the ice bottle onto the bed and stood. "Why can't you see this? If there's any way to get out of here, we need to try it."

Mom slammed the pillow to the floor. "Ryan James Nasbe, you are going to stop this, and you're going to stop it right now. This is not one of your video games. I will not have you endangering us both by trying to be a hero. I'm in charge here, and we will do what we're told. Sooner or later, when they get whatever it is they're looking for, they will let us go."

"Fine," he said. "We'll just stay here and die. Why not? I've had a good sixteen years."

"No one is going to die!" Mom barked.

Ryan picked up his ice bottle, walked to his bed, and eased himself onto the spread. The frame cracked ominously. Lying on his back, he closed his eyes, pressed the bottle against his temple, and tried to figure out what was happening.

What was today, Tuesday? He wished they'd let him keep his watch.

They had to get out of here. If Dad were here, he'd be spending every second trying to find a way to make that happen. But Dad wasn't here, was he? No, he was saving the *rest* of the world.

The thought brought instant remorse. It was an honor to serve your country, and as much as it sucked, it was the family's patriotic duty to understand these things. Family, God, and country. That was the patriotic trinity worth dying to defend.

Mom knew this, too, so what was she doing? Why was she being so difficult?

Ryan opened his eyes and shifted his head so he could see could see her. She sat on the edge of her own bed, elbows on her knees, staring at her hands. In a rush of awareness, he got it. He was on his own to get them out of here.

As evening approached, the temperature in their prison cell began to drop again. The wall that had been so impossibly hot was cooling now, and the windows they'd opened were driving a frigid breeze into the space. Without bothering to ask permission, Ryan rose from his bed and closed them. The panes were like smaller versions of the windows they had in his school classrooms, rocking inward on hinges along the bottom edge of the rectangular panels. Where the window frames in school were made of metal, though, these were made of wood.

He took his time pushing the panels shut, examining their feasibility as routes of escape. They were too small for either of them to fit through.

Except maybe. The angle of the tilted pane made it impossible to slide through from below, but how difficult could it be to take a window apart? The hinges were held in by screws, and screws could be turned by just about anything with the right shape. Even a butter knife would do. He'd just have to do something to shrink his head and shoulders.

"Ryan, what are you doing?" Christyne asked.

He pushed the window shut and twisted the latch into place. "I'm getting cold."

"Why don't you put your sweater back on?"

"I will," he said. But not quite yet. After all the sweating he'd done today, it felt good to feel a little cold. "You said they had cards. Want to play rummy?"

Jonathan reassembled his team in the War Room, and from the way they all avoided eye contact, he pretty much knew what was coming before anyone spoke.

"I've been searching all day, and I've got nothing," Venice said. Jonathan heard the frustration in her voice. "Their Internet guy is good. He's covered all their tracks. He's routed that signal through two dozen different countries before landing it at that poor kid's computer in Michigan. If there's a way to trace its origin, I don't know what it is."

Translation: There was no way to trace its origins.

Jonathan turned to Gail. "The bombing in Michigan," he prompted.

She had already opened the speckled theme notebook that had long been her method for tracking cases she worked on. "Sarfraz Janwari," she said. "That was the name of the bomber. Pakistani by birth, and a longtime legal resident of the United States. For years, he worked in the auto industry, but he was laid off twenty months ago when the economy crashed. Thanks to Venice, I was able to access ICIS, and from there hack into the ongoing FBI file."

"Technically, it's not hacking," Venice corrected. "The credentials you're using are all real. They just don't belong to you."

Gail shook her head. "How we stay out of jail is a mystery."

"I told you you'd get used to playing for our team," Jonathan quipped. Not too long ago, Gail Bonneville had been the planet's straightest arrow.

Gail continued, "Mr. Janwari was more or less vaporized in the explosion. Seventeen children and four adults were killed outright, dozens wounded. The dead included his daughter, Aafia, whom he had just dropped off at the school."

"What is it with these jihadist assholes?" Boxers growled. "They murder their own kids."

Gail continued, "Preliminary analysis of the explosives shows the typical terrorist recipe of ANFO derivatives. The Bureau will go through the motions of tracking the components to their sources, but that's always hit-or-miss. On that kind of thing, you're pretty much dependent on witnesses stepping forward, and after incidents like this, the salesman involved is usually not all that anxious to step forward."

Everyone in the room recognized ANFO as the acronym for ammonium nitrate and fuel oil—a homemade explosive that miners had used for years, and was still used by some. Its popularity as a terrorist weapon had much to do with the fact that all the components were obtainable at the local hardware store—the ammonium nitrate as fertilizer and the fuel oil as, well, fuel oil.

"Have they served the search warrant on Janwari's house yet?" Jonathan asked.

"That's ongoing," Gail explained, turning three pages to find her notes on that. "The preliminary results there are interesting, though. Their primary sweep didn't find any bomb makings in the house. The dogs didn't even pick up traces."

"Nitrates are the easiest thing in the world to detect, aren't they?" Boxers asked.

Gail nodded. "Exactly."

"What about Janwari the man?" Venice asked. "Does he fit the profile of a bomber?"

"The media will think so," Gail said, "and that means the pundits and the politicians will think so."

"But not the professionals?"

Gail shrugged. "He certainly looks the part racially, and he was laid off after a long career. Communications in his personnel file show that he believed himself to be discriminated against in the aftermath of nine-eleven. He's Muslim, he lives in Flint, which is the home of some of the most rabid imams, and he's facing financial distress. That makes him a prime candidate for recruitment by radicals."

"Okay, I'm sold," Boxers said.

"As will all the other talking heads be sold."

"What's the other side?" Jonathan asked. "You don't seem moved by any of that."

"I won't say I'm unmoved," Gail said. When she got thoughtful like this, a thing happened with her eyebrows that turned Jonathan on. A lot about Gail turned Jonathan on. "I mean, you can't ignore the obvious completely, but it's all too pat for me."

"As if Osama Bin Laden was about subtext?" Boxers asked.

"He doesn't count," Gail countered. "He's the one who established the baseline for the other clichés to follow. At face value, Janwari could be our guy. What bothers me, first of all, is that he's a Sufi, which is one of the truly peace-loving sects of Islam. As far as I know, there's never been a Sufi terrorist." She looked at Boxers. "And before you say it, yes, I know there's a first time for everything, but it would be a really big jump.

"Next, there's the fact that in all of his known correspondence—even the ones where he was alleging racial discrimination—there's not a single threat to do harm to anyone or anything. But the single factor above all others that makes me doubt that he did this intentionally is the fact that his daughter was there."

She paused for effect. "According to early interviews with school officials all the way back to elementary school, Sarfraz Janwari was the picture of the caring father. He was a regular at PTA meetings, he made most of his daughters' sporting events, and he never missed an orchestra concert when she was playing. In fact, he even chaperoned a couple of the orchestra trips."

"Did he do any of that in the twenty months since he was laid off?" Jonathan asked. "A lot can change with that kind of financial stress."

"Not when it comes to loving your kids," Venice said.

"Couldn't he have assumed that he was doing a good thing by martyring her for the cause?" Boxers asked. "Though I'm not sure what a middle school girl would do with the forty-two virgins."

Jonathan burned him with a glare, and Boxers looked at the table.

"The Janwaris were Sufis," Gail repeated. "They don't buy into that martyrdom crap. They're all about loving children and loving their God."

"Let's assume that Janwari is innocent," Jonatha

"Just for the sake of argument, let's say that somebody planted those explosives in his car, and, I don't know, detonated them remotely or something. Where does that leave us?"

"Obvious shit is obvious for a reason," Boxers said. "If it walks and quacks like a duck, I'll assume it's not a fox."

"Roll with me," Jonathan said. "If some homegrown terror group was trying to frame Islamists for all this killing, what better way is there to seal the deal than having one of them detonate a bomb? At a school, no less."

Venice held up her hand to command the floor. "There's more," she said. "This is just coming in from the wire services. The school where the bomb went off—Gerald Ford Middle School—has the smallest per capita enrollment of Islamic students of any in the area."

Boxers held out his hands, as if to say, *ta-da.*

Venice wasn't finished. "And the four major television networks are reporting that not a single known terrorist organization is stepping forward to claim responsibility for any of the events of the past three days. Not only that, five of the most active groups, including al-Qaeda and Hezbollah, have announced that they had nothing to do with them."

Boxers scoffed, "If al-Qaeda says it, then it must be true."

"Close," Jonathan said. "They have a long history of claiming responsibility when they own it, and they rarely lie about it."

"Honor among murderers?" Venice asked.

"More like good public relations," Jonathan said. "I guess if you kill and own up to it, people are more afraid of you."

"Plus, you don't want to piss off your competition by claiming credit for murders that don't belong to you," Gail said.

That this kind of political calculus—all of it built around ₑ murders of innocent people—actually made sense, made athan despair for the future.

"So let's just make this logical leap," Jonathan said. "Let's at this Army of Allah group is not what it wants us to believe. How does that bring us any closer to finding out where they are?"

Blank faces all around.

"Well, that's the mission," Jonathan said.

"No kidding," Gail replied. "Just how do we do that?"

He turned to Venice. "What spigots do we have running for intelligence?"

"We're monitoring ICIS obsessively," she replied. "And we're monitoring all the news services. I've designed bots to seek out the key words that might mean something, but there's not much more I can do. If they broadcast again, we'll have another shot, but until then, or until we catch a break, we're dead in the water."

Jonathan thought about that, and then turned to Boxers, whose shoulders sagged.

"You're gonna call Roleplay Rollins, aren't you?" the Big Guy guessed.

CHAPTER THIRTEEN

With the furnace extinguished, the night brought the return of frigid temperatures. As Christyne wrapped herself in her coat and pulled the blankets over her head, she tried to settle herself by listening to Ryan's even breaths. At what age, she wondered, did sleep stop coming so easily? As a teenager—as with all teenagers—she'd been able to sleep for fifteen, twenty hours at a time, sometimes sleeping entire weekends away when she was in college. Now, rest felt like a commodity more valuable than gold.

She wished she understood why their captors were being so hard on Ryan. He was only a boy. A frightened, angry boy. Mistreating him would only make him angrier and more frightened. It was the way he was wired. Just like his father.

Christyne told herself that the attitude that made Ryan so difficult as a teenager would also make him a success in life. You never lose if you never give up, right?

These people needed to understand that Ryan was *incapable* of controlling his smart mouth and his occasionally disrespectful glares. He wasn't being difficult; he was being . . . *Ryan*.

It was so dark in here.

How does one measure darkness? she wondered. There were many words for the varying degrees of brightness, why not for darkness? Because "dark" didn't touch the lack of light in their tiny room.

A black velvet cave, she thought. The kind of darkness that gave birth to the scariest childhood fairy tales. In this blackness, every terrible thing seemed possible. No one could protect you because no one could see you. You couldn't even protect yourself.

What was that?

There was a gentle clicking sound, so soft that she never would have heard it if she hadn't been listening so intently to the night. Ryan's breathing continued undisturbed.

Could have been a rat, she supposed, which brought precious little comfort.

No, nighttime creatures didn't stop after a single clicking sound. They'd have made a series of clicking sounds—whatever the clicking sounds might have been.

She sensed movement. This wasn't a noise so much as a feeling, the kind of near-awareness you feel as an airplane slowly changes altitude. In fact, that was it exactly. She felt a pressure change in the room.

"Ryan, is that you?" she whispered. She knew of course that it couldn't be. He hadn't moved.

Another sound. A pop this time, as if wooden furniture were expanding in humidity.

It's nothing, Christyne told herself. It was just her imagination leveraging the most drama out of the thick darkness.

Her eyes strained in their sockets, desperate to see something out there. Anything. Over in the corner by the door, the darkness seemed to have lightened, a vertical shaft of dark gray against pitch black. The door had been opened.

A shadow moved. The shadow of a man.

Realization hit her in a rush and she sat upright in her bed, turning to her left and slapping at the shelf where she knew she'd left the matches for the lamp. *Oh God, oh God, oh God . . .*

"Don't do it, woman," a voice said from the darkness. Christyne recognized the voice as Brother Stephen, the one who had been so terrible to Ryan. "Be silent," he whispered. "Don't make me hurt you."

The shadow moved closer.

Christyne scooted away from the intruder, closer to the head of the bed. "Please stay away," she begged. Her voice came out as a barely audible squeak.

"Shh," Brother Stephen said. "This doesn't need to be difficult." In two more steps, he towered over her, his silhouette a black stain.

"Please don't," she rasped. A new kind of terror enveloped her. She'd seen this man—this boy, really—abuse her son. Now he was—

He sat on the edge of her bed, and the shadow of his hand reached out to her. Settled on her breast. He squeezed too hard, but she sensed it was less an act of torture than inexperience. "All you have to do is be quiet," he said. His other hand fumbled with the front of his trousers.

Christyne started to tremble. Blinding, disabling fear enveloped her like a straitjacket. She knew what was coming, but in her terror, she was unable to do anything to stop it—to do anything to protect herself. "My son," she whispered.

Brother Stephen slid his hand down her stomach. It groped her lap. "Maybe he'll get his turn." His chuckle was even more terrifying than his touch. "A woman like you needs a man like me. I'm going to kiss you now."

His shadow swelled as he came closer and planted his mouth on hers. His tongue pried her lips apart.

"Don't fight me," he whispered.

Christyne shifted in the bed and her hand brushed his exposed, engorged penis. It was wet and slick and her hand jumped as if it had touched a hot stove.

"Big, isn't it?" he hissed. "Go ahead. Feel it. Rub it. Think about all we can—"

A guttural roar filled the room as something massive slammed into her attacker and knocked him to the floor.

* * *

Lying on his left side with all his clothes on—including his coat—Ryan kept his covers up high, all the way to his chin, just to keep warm.

He'd been slipping in and out all night. The bruises on his ribs and his cheek were killing—

He could have sworn he heard the door to their little prison open.

Someone stepped inside. He moved as a shadow, but he kept the door open behind him, and somewhere in the house someone must have left a lamp on, because he cut a silhouette in the darkness.

It was a man, one of the terrorists, but there was no way to tell which one. Until he spoke.

"Don't do it, woman," Brother Stephen said.

Ryan heard clothing rustle, and he heard his mother make a whining sound. She pleaded.

"This doesn't need to be difficult," Brother Stephen said.

With those words, Ryan knew what the intruder was going to do. He knew what rape was. He heard springs squeak as he watched the invading shadow sit on his mother's bed.

She made more frightening sounds, and there was more whispering. Ryan couldn't make out all of it, but he could feel his mother's terror from all the way over here.

She said, "My son," and something about that made Brother Stephen laugh.

Ryan felt his face flush with anger. His heart rate doubled. Tripled. This was the asshole who had beaten the crap out of him when his hands were tied. The man who had promised to kill him if he stepped out of line even one more time.

"I'm going to kiss you now."

That's when something inside him snapped. He tore off his covers and he launched himself at the beefy silhouette, charging full tilt, and aiming high. He had no plan, and no fighting skills, but there was no way he was going to let this asshole get away with what he was trying to do.

As he closed to within the last foot, Ryan tucked his chin in a little and smashed the top part of his forehead into what appeared to be the attacker's temple. Something flashed behind Ryan's eyes on impact and a jolt of pain lit him up from forehead to tailbone. He smelled blood, and then he tasted it. A second later, he felt it streaming down his face, but by then, he was airborne, and as he tumbled, he felt what he somehow knew to be Brother Stephen's jaw nestled in the crook of his elbow. He clamped down on it, turning as they fell. When they hit the floor, Brother Stephen's head hit first, and then Ryan landed on his shoulder and rolled. Something snapped, the sound making him think that he'd broken his shoulder. Except the pain never came.

Everything happened so quickly. Behind him, his mom screamed, but at a whisper level.

He couldn't care about that. He needed to prepare for the counterassault. When Brother Stephen got the opportunity to throw a punch—if he really put all of his strength behind it—he'd separate Ryan's head from his shoulders. He'd already caught a glimpse of the attacker's power while he was holding back. This time, one of them was going to die.

Ryan scrabbled to his feet and found Brother Stephen where he lay on the floor and he fired a savage kick into what he thought was his head, but he really had no idea. The kick landed firmly, though. And Brother Stephen didn't even grunt. He must have been knocked unconscious.

Fire flared to Ryan's right. He whirled to see his mom holding a wooden match high to illuminate the scene. Her face looked pale in the yellow light and tears streaked her face. Her hand shook.

"Are you okay?" Ryan asked.

She just stared at the form on the floor. "He was going . . ." Her voice trailed away.

"I know," Ryan said. He pivoted on his heel and looked around the boxes and crap that surrounded him to find a

lamp. He lifted it off the box closest to his mother's bed—
the one she used as a nightstand—but by the time he got the
globe lifted to expose the wick, the match had burned to a
nub and Christyne had to light another one.

The wick ignited easily, and the light got even brighter as
Ryan lowered the globe, the brightness creating sharply defined, dancing shadows. He swung the lamp to assess the
damage done to Brother Stephen.

"Son of a bitch," Ryan breathed. The attacker lay still on
the floor, his dick and his balls hanging out the front of his
unbuttoned pants. He shot a look back at his mom, working
hard to swallow the anger that welled inside of him. When
she looked away, so did he, sorry for the thoughts that had
entered his mind.

Holding the lantern out in front, Ryan moved closer to
Brother Stephen, and stooped to get closer still. Exposed
junk aside, something wasn't right about the way he was
lying on the floor. He seemed too flat—like a balloon version of himself from which maybe an eighth of the air had
been released. And his head. It was at an odd angle, an inch
or two farther to the side than it should be.

Finally, Ryan saw Brother Stephen's eyes. They both
were open, but the left one just a little more so than the right
one.

"Holy shit, Mom," Ryan breathed. "I think he's dead." He
turned to look at her. "I think I killed him."

Christyne brought her hands to her mouth. "Oh, no. Oh
no, oh no, oh no . . ."

Ryan hurried across the room, pushed the door shut, and
hurried back. "Mom, what are we going to do?" His mind
raced. If those assholes came trooping in here again in the
morning and they found their buddy—their *brother*—dead,
God only knew what would follow. He decided to answer his
own question. "We need to get out of here."

Christyne dismissed it out of hand. "They'll shoot us."

"Mom, they're going to shoot us anyway. They said they
were going to do it before, and now they almost *have* to."

"We need to hide the body," Christyne said.

"But he'll start stinking," Ryan countered. "Especially when they crank that furnace up again in the morning."

"Maybe he's just unconscious," Christyne said.

Ryan rolled his eyes. "Look at his face. Have you ever seen a live person look like that?"

She nodded. "Okay," she conceded. "Okay, he's dead. We need to do something with him."

"We can't put him outside, or people will find him." Ryan looked around. "Maybe we can hide him under all these boxes and crap."

"But what if they come looking for him and find that we hid him?" Christyne thought aloud. "Won't that just make us look that much worse? Anger them that much more?"

"We killed one of their brothers, Mom," Ryan argued. "I think they'll pretty much go off-the-charts pissed when they realize that." He gave her a hard look. "We need to get out of here. We don't have a choice anymore."

She looked across the room. "The door's unlocked," she said. "Could it be as easy as that?"

He shook his head. "If we get that far and get caught, it'll all be over."

Ryan looked up at the ventilation widow, raising the lantern to get a better look.

"There's no way I can fit through that," Christyne said.

"I can," Ryan said. He didn't know how, but he also knew there was no choice. He started stripping off his jacket to make himself smaller.

"Then what?" Christyne asked.

"I'll get help."

It was the best he could do on the fly.

Christyne hesitated, the fear settling deeper into her features. "Suppose they see you?" she asked. "Suppose you get caught?"

He kept stripping the clothes away until he was bare-chested again. Jesus, it was cold. "What difference does it make? They beat the shit out of me just for being here.

Whatever they do if I get caught can't be worse than what they'd do to both of us if we just sit here and wait."

Her eyes narrowed as she studied Ryan's face. "Where are you going to go for help?"

He shrugged. "I don't know. There were those houses out there before we came through the big gate. Maybe they can help."

"Maybe they're part of whatever this is."

"I could break into an empty one, then. All I need is a phone."

She was right. He could see that much in her expression; but it had to be a hard decision to let your son out of your sight. He got that. He also got that there was no other alternative.

Then it dawned on him how disgusting it would be to have a dead guy staring at her while he was gone.

While she continued to think it over, Ryan stooped, grabbed two fistfuls of Brother Stephen's shirt at the shoulder, and started to pull. As soon as the dead man's shoulders cleared the floor, his head lolled at a horrifying angle back and to the side—as if he were staring over his left shoulder at his own butt—removing any doubt that a broken neck had caused his death. Ryan's stomach flipped at the sight, and he redirected his eyes to the side.

In the deep reaches of his brain, he felt a pang of awareness that he had actually killed someone. He also realized that he didn't care. No remorse, no disgust. None of the emotions that he knew were appropriate.

Christyne rose from her bed and scurried four steps to catch up. She stooped and grabbed the assailant's pant legs to help. "Where are we taking him?"

"Grab his ankles, Mom," Ryan said, again shifting his gaze. "You're pulling his pants down more."

Christyne adjusted her grip and lifted the body's legs by his ankles. Together they moved the body to the corner opposite the chamber pot. They covered him with a table, and then stacked some boxes around him.

"It doesn't look like it did before," Ryan observed when they were done.

Christyne planted her fists on her hips and gave him *that look.* "Honey, if they come down here, I think the broken window and missing prisoner will clue them into something being wrong."

"Oh." Ryan felt his ears flush. "I guess so. How long will it take for him to start to stink?" he asked.

"Long enough," Christyne said, but he could tell from her expression that she had no idea. "Don't worry about that. It's time for something to start breaking our way."

A moment passed. They all knew what the next step was, but it was a difficult one to take.

Ryan made the first move, heading back toward Christyne's bed and the ventilation window above it.

"How will you find your way?" asked his mom.

He didn't look back at her as he answered, "Like you said, something's got to start breaking our way." He stood on the bed for a better look at the window. He twisted the latch and pulled the glass panel in. Since it was hinged at the bottom and tilted inward, that panel was the first obstacle to be overcome.

"Blow out the lamp," he said.

As soon as darkness returned, Ryan leaned farther out from the bed, grabbed the panel with both hands, and then dropped all of his weight. It broke with a frighteningly loud crack.

"Oh, my God," Christyne hissed. "Are you okay?"

"I'm fine," he said. "That was the window." He'd snapped it quickly because he knew that if he voiced his intention first, she would have wanted to talk about the alternative options. Screw that. He didn't know what time it was, but he knew that the darkness was his only friend out there, and the more of it he preserved, the better his chances for success.

With the window panel out of the way, the night was visible—a charcoal-gray rectangle against a black foreground. If he looked real hard, Ryan could see shadows.

"Are you sure you can fit through that?" Christyne asked.

Ryan was wondering the same thing. It was a ridiculously tiny hole. "Sure I'm sure," he said.

Christyne grasped his shoulder. "Promise me you won't come back," she said.

He gaped.

She chose her words carefully. "When you make your call for help, promise me that you'll keep going. Promise you won't come back to help."

Ryan felt something snag in his gut. He hadn't thought it through that far, but this wasn't what he was expecting. "I can't just leave you behind," he said. *That's not what Dad would do.*

"You won't be," Christyne countered. "You'll be sending help. Makes no sense for you to walk back into danger."

"How will I know if you're okay?" he asked.

She looked straight at him. "My Ryan doesn't fail."

Tears pressed behind his eyes. He had never heard her say anything like that. He failed all the time.

He needed to say something, but he didn't know which words would be appropriate. And he didn't trust his voice to produce them. In the end, he chose to say nothing.

He turned his back to his mom and faced the window. With a short hop, he was able to reach the window ledge. From there, a simple pull-up brought his face to the opening, where the frigid air assaulted him.

Somewhere out there lay freedom or death. He didn't see a way for it to end anywhere in between.

CHAPTER FOURTEEN

Ryan had no idea that his head was as big as it was. Once his forearms were lodged in the opening of the window, he ducked his chin to fit through, but his nose and the crown of his head formed a wedge that blocked him from moving even an inch.

By rolling his head to the right and pressing down hard with his left cheek against the ledge, he thought there was hope that he might be able to muscle his way through. He might have to leave his ears behind, but he could make it.

Just as he started to worry about how he was going to fit the rest of his body through the opening, somebody—it had to be his mom—grabbed his legs at the knees and lifted them.

"I'll push as you pull," she said.

And that worked. With his head clear, his shoulders slid easily. He elbow-crawled his chest and belly clear, and once he felt his belt line against the ledge, he knew that he was home free. He pulled his legs and feet up, drew them under him, and he was free.

The feeling was overwhelming. It took his breath away.

He didn't realize how crippling the isolation of imprisonment was until he left it behind. He rolled to his stomach and turned back to the window. Before he could even ask, his mom stuffed his clothes through the opening. He pulled them through.

"Stay warm," she said. "And be careful."

The blackness on his mom's side of the window was absolute. As he wrestled back into his clothes, Ryan could see nothing, yet he knew that she was watching him, depending on him. Again, words failed, so he turned away without saying anything.

There was no going back now. He was surprised that the thought brought little angst. What was, was. It was the same mental place he went to during a track meet.

He couldn't count the number of meets he'd won when he'd had no business winning. He wasn't the biggest, and Lord knew he wasn't the strongest, but he was as fast as most, and if you didn't let yourself think about defeat, it was amazing how often you could win.

He needed to get going.

Walking farther away from the house, he tried to make the night shadows jibe with his memories of the drive in on that first night, but the two were not equating for him.

We arrived in the front, he thought. *I must be in the back now.*

Moving even farther away, he navigated a wide circle to his left around the building. He was looking for a long tree-lined driveway leading to an elevated front porch. Once he saw that—or at least what looked like that in the darkness—then he could begin to retrace their route.

As his eyes adjusted to the night, he realized that the lack of a moon was at least partially compensated for by a sky full of stars. The edges of the shadows were surprisingly sharp, he thought, if mottled by the trees, and he realized that he would be visible to others who might have been gazing out at the night.

When he turned the second corner, he saw the porch and the long driveway. Their minivan was gone, though. In fact, there were no vehicles at all. Yellow light flickered in the windows. He had no way of knowing if there were more people inside, or if the place was empty, and he couldn't afford the risk of checking.

His mission was to get help. If he went back to the cabin and got caught, God only knew what would happen to them, but the one thing that was guaranteed was that this opportunity for rescue would evaporate.

And then there'd never be another chance.

He had to keep going. He'd promised he'd keep going.

Dropping to a low-profile crouch, he turned his back on the cabin and moved to the cover of the trees.

His plan—if you could even call it that—was to avoid the roadbed itself because he thought he'd be too visible. Problem was, by staying off the road, he had to walk, climb and crawl through all kinds of weeds and sticks and shit, and in the process he made the noise of an advancing army. After about twenty yards of that, he made the decision to stick to the edge of the roadbed and move slowly. If a vehicle or a person came his way, he'd just have to hope for enough time to drop out of sight.

He had no idea how long he'd been walking down the driveway, but it felt like a long time. Was this the correct way to the fence? He knew they'd spent hours on the road, but he really had no idea how long they'd driven from the front gate to the cabin.

The cold was becoming a problem again, causing him to shove his hands deeply into his coat pockets. His nose ached from it, and when the wind blew, it hurt his eyes. He tried to remember what the local weatherman had said about this cold snap, but Ryan never paid any attention to the news, unless there was a possibility of schools closing.

Is anybody missing me at school? he wondered. Outside of his track team, he didn't know many people. Come to think of it, he didn't know that many on the track team, either. Since most of them had grown up together, there really wasn't a lot of room for newcomers in their cliques.

He and his mom had left their real friends down in North Carolina at Fort Bragg—those were the ones who would notice they were missing, except they'd been missing since summer, when his mom had decided to come north. Other than Aunt Maggie, no one in their circle would care enough to report them missing, and Aunt Maggie was visiting a friend in France.

All the more reason for him to be heading off for help on his own.

As he trudged on, it was hard to tell if the road he was walking on was paved or if it was merely frozen dirt, but as he hunched against the cold and watched the shadows of his feet take step after step, he wished he'd thought to wear warmer socks. The cold came up through the soles of his Nikes as if he were barefoot.

He heard a voice.

His body acted instinctively, without him having to tell it a thing. He dropped to a low crouch and duckwalked quickly to the edge of the roadbed, where he fell to hands and knees along the edge of the tree line.

He heard another voice. Both were male, and neither sounded all that close. Certainly, they didn't sound angry or threatening; just two guys having a conversation about something. Ryan couldn't make out the words, but when one of them laughed, he felt tension drain from his shoulders. They clearly hadn't seen him.

He wondered where they were. The night was so quiet, the air so cold and pure, and the breeze so constant, that they could have been thirty feet away or thirty yards away. Maybe even farther.

But if their sound carried so easily, so would any sound that he made. It was time to be very careful.

From where he lay in the ditch that ran along the raised roadbed, he couldn't tell if the owners of the voices were moving or stationary. He remembered that the guards who

manned the front gate carried guns, and he wanted nothing
to do with any of that.

But he couldn't just stay here. Sooner or later, he was
going to lose the darkness. When that happened, it was all
over.

He needed to move closer. He crawled on his belly at
first—the way he saw soldiers do it in the movies—but that
full-body dragging created way too much noise. He decided
to risk rising to his hands and knees and advancing that way.

Once again, the cold became a real problem. Why hadn't
he thought of bringing gloves?

Yeah, he chastised silently, *next time you get kidnapped,
be sure to dress warmly.*

By being able to place one hand and one knee at a time,
Ryan was able to move far more quietly. He still made noise,
but not that much more than the wind. Besides, the wind was
blowing in his face, away from the people he was approaching, so that should help him be quieter, too.

At least that's what he told himself.

He figured it took five minutes to crawl close enough to
be able to see who was talking. Barely silhouettes in the
darkness, they were tall enough to be adults, though to
Ryan's ears, their voices sounded young. They both wore
bulky coats, and from the roundness of their heads, he assumed they were wearing stocking caps to stay warm. He
envied them those. He also envied them the rifles he could
see slung over their shoulders.

And then there was the good news: Beyond their silhouettes, Ryan could clearly see the outline of a fence. He'd finally made it to the edge of the property.

Now that he'd finally gotten so close, he realized how
flimsy his plan was—or, more accurately, that he didn't have
a plan. Somehow, he was going to get over the fence unseen,
and then somehow, he was going to find a place where he
could make a phone call. That was a lot of somehow.

And all of it depended on these guys moving on. Or
falling asleep. Or getting struck by lightning. For the time

being, Ryan settled on becoming invisible and allowing his breathing to slow down. As the sound of blood thrumming through his ears died away, he could actually hear the words they were saying.

". . . starting a war. Like any war, people are going to be killed."

"But kids. I just don't see how that is anything but wrong."

"It's about the anger. It's about focusing it on all those godless rag heads, and so far, Brother Michael says it's going great."

A long pause followed—long enough for Ryan to wonder if maybe they'd moved along.

Then, "Are *you* willing to go that far?"

"I'm a soldier. If I have to kill, I'll kill. If I have to die, I'll die."

"I don't mean that. That's all of us. I mean kids. You're willing to kill kids?"

A derisive laugh. "Name me one war in the history of wars where kids didn't get killed."

"That's different. It's one thing when a bomb falls in the wrong place, or a stray bullet goes through the wrong wall. I mean, are you willing to *target* kids?"

"I will follow the orders that are given to me." Another pause—a shorter one this time. "Are you saying that you *wouldn't*?"

Ryan heard a distinct change in tone. "N-no, of course not. I'm just saying I'd try to find a different assignment."

"But if you were given an order—"

"I'd do my duty." Another long pause. In Ryan's mind, the guy was getting defensive. "Seriously. I'm just talking here. Don't look at me like I'm a traitor. I'm a loyal servant to the cause, just like you are."

"You make me wonder sometimes, Brother Samuel." The other one said this in a tone that dripped with disapproval. "Questioning leads all too easily to disloyalty. You know this."

"Of course I know it. And Brother James, I'm sorry that I

said anything. I think sometimes that I am not as strong as the others. I worry that when the time comes, I might freeze. I don't want to be one who fails."

Who the hell are these freaks? Ryan wondered. Brother this and Sister that. Killing children? Holy shit.

"We all have doubts," Brother James said. "But I believe that when the time comes, our training will take over and we will do everything that is expected of us. We need to stay focused on the honor, and if we do that, the rest won't matter."

"Do you have your mission yet?" Brother Samuel asked.

Still another pause. "We've been here too long," Brother James said. "You need to walk your route. So do I. Stay warm."

With that, the night grew silent again.

But what did the silence mean? Ryan hoped it meant that they had wandered off, a conclusion rendered more likely by their need to "walk their routes." He thought again of the guards he saw at the gate when they first arrived. First there were just a couple, and then more arrived. It made sense, didn't it, that they would walk the fence line, like sentries in the POW movies?

Only one way to find out.

Ryan rose again to his hands and knees slowly and quietly, and dared to peer into the night. The spot where the guards had been standing was now empty, their cube of space now occupied by the outline of the chain-link fence against the night. The fence was the goal. The first goal, anyway. If he could make it over that, then other options existed for him. If he couldn't, well, only one option remained, he supposed, and that one sucked.

If he tried the fence, he might get out. If he got caught trying, they'd probably kill him outright. That's what the guns were for, right? But if he stayed, they were going to kill him anyway. The fence was the only option.

Even as he inventoried his options, he continued his slow, steady crawl toward the fence. Toward freedom. As he closed to within fifteen yards, and then ten, he fought the urge to hurry. At the ten-yard mark, he realized that the trees were all gone. An unpaved roadway of sorts had been denuded of trees on either side of the fence, presumably to allow the guards to walk their routes, just like Brother What's-his-face had said. He remembered with a shudder how easily he'd been able to make out the details of those guards in the starlight, and now realized that the clarity came from the lack of tree cover. The lack of any cover at all.

Shit. I have to climb the fence in the open.

At the very edge of the tree line, which at this point was more scrub growth than real trees, Ryan leaned out into the cleared space. He pivoted his head first to the left, and then to the right, and there they both were, each about thirty yards away from him, but on opposite sides. They appeared to be moving away, but how could he know without being able to see faces for a reference point?

Time to find out.

Pressing himself flat against the ground, he lizard-crawled across the open space to the base of the fence. He thought to look both ways again, just to be sure, then talked himself out of it. What was it that Dad always said? *In for a penny, in for a pound.*

It wasn't till he actually rose to his knees and touched the fence that he thought about the possibility that it might be electrified. It wasn't.

Ryan slipped his fingers through the chain links and started to climb, telling himself that this was no different than climbing the fence to the athletic field on the days when he beat Coach Jackson to practice. He'd done that half a dozen times, and each time, he'd earned one of those scoldings that was really an expression of veiled admiration.

He didn't expect one of those this time.

The hardest part was to not make any noise. Chain-link fences make a unique tinkling, clattering sound when you climb them. If the guards heard that, it would be over. Good God, there were so many ways for this to be over, and none of them were good.

He refused to look at the guards, fearing that the energy of his glance might somehow make them turn, the way that your eyes are drawn to the girl across the classroom who happens to be staring at you, or the way the teacher knows to call on you the one day out of thirty when you don't have your homework done. Maybe if he didn't summon their glances, things would continue to break his way.

The frigid air registered almost as hot against the exposed skin of his hands and face, and as he scaled higher, the metal chain links felt like they were somehow turning his finger bones brittle.

It took less time than he thought it would to reach the top of the fence, where a Y-shaped frame of barbed wire awaited him, daring to thwart his escape.

Not a chance. He'd already been beaten, and people were already planning his execution. Spiky wire was nothing.

At the top now, he reached up and behind with his right hand to wrap his fist around the wire, taking care to place his palm in a spot between the spikes. That done, he let go of the fence with his other hand and allowed his feet to dangle as he hand-walked upwards and backwards, hand-over-hand until he'd reached the fourth level of wire, which left him dangling free over the cleared aisleway.

A pull-up brought him chin-high to the wire, and then he faced the hard part. Squinting against what he knew was coming, he raised his left leg and hooked the wire with his ankle, where one of the spikes bit deeply into the soft meat in front of his Achilles tendon. Ignoring the pain, he gritted his teeth and hoisted his left leg parallel to the wire. Spikes found his calf and knee and thighs, and he prayed to all things holy that his junk would be spared as he heaved himself with agonizing slowness into the trough formed by the torturous Y. While his scrotum got poked, the point missed the boys, so he called that a victory.

As he lay on his back on this elevated bed of nails, staring at the sky, he paused to collect himself. The dark, negative part of him waited for the sound of gunshots to rip the night, but the rest of him pushed those thoughts away. What was going to happen was going to happen. All he could do was his best; and if his best wasn't good enough, he'd never know it because he'd be dead.

It was time to finish the job.

He rolled to his right, this time clutching his crotch as his belt buckle and parts south passed again through the danger zone. Still in the Y, he was able to get his feet under him enough to duck into a low crouch. He wasn't good with distances, but to his eye, he was ten or twelve feet off the ground—too far just to launch himself into the night.

He turned his hands so they were fingers down, thumbs in, and he carefully nestled his palms into another dead space between the spikes. From there, he pressed his belly against the wire and doubled over, allowing the momentum of his head and upper body to propel him into a somersault that left him dangling by his hands, his shoes maybe five feet off the ground. From there, he let go and dropped to freedom on the far side. He tried to remain limp as he hit the ground, allowing his knees to fold at the impact, and he forced a shoulder roll that left him on his stomach, flat against the ground.

Jesus, he'd made a lot of noise.

Without even thinking, he scrambled for traction with his hands and feet and he darted for the cover of the bushes on his side of the fence. He was still half a stride away when someone yelled, "Who's there?" The voice came from the direction of Brother Samuel, but Ryan couldn't tell for sure that it was his voice.

Powerful flashlights clicked on, and he heard the sound of running feet as the lights bounced in the air and converged at roughly the spot where Ryan had climbed the fence.

He pressed himself flat against the ground, and tried to control his breath, conscious of the telltale cloud he made with every exhalation. His heart pounded hard enough behind his breastbone to actually hurt.

"What's wrong?" Brother James yelled. Ryan recognized that voice.

"Didn't you hear it?"

"Hear what?"

"The fence moved."

"It *moved*? How would it do that?"

"I mean it moved." The night filled with the sound of rattling chain link. "Like that."

The darkness around him lightened as flashlight beams scoured the ground.

"I didn't hear a thing," Brother James said. "Are you sure?"

"I'm sure I heard something."

"Did you see anything?"

"No."

The flashlight beams scoured the ground some more. "I don't see anything out there, either, do you?"

Brother Samuel didn't answer as the lights played on and on.

Ryan didn't know how much longer he could control his breathing. He lungs were screaming. He opened his eyes long enough to see that the lights were near him but not on him, and dared to cover his mouth with his hand and exhale, oh so slowly.

"There's nothing there, Brother Samuel. Maybe it was a deer."

"Maybe we should check with Brother Stephen and have him look in on the prisoners."

Ryan's heart nearly stopped.

"Right," Brother James mocked. "They overpowered him though a locked door."

"I'm just saying that I heard something."

"And I'm just saying that there's nothing out there."

A light swung away from Ryan's woods, and played into the woods on the other side—the area he'd just left.

"What's wrong with you?" Brother James said.

"Maybe it was someone climbing *in*. We're at war now, after all."

"And who would do that?"

"The cops? The FBI? The army? How would I know? But if they found out—"

"Nobody's finding out," Brother James said. Ryan could hear the frustration in his voice. "This is just more of that same problem as before. You have no faith."

"Not true."

"It *is* true. I'm not going to report you—at least not yet—but you're getting paranoid, and the paranoia is making you question all the unquestionables."

"I am not! Maybe I'm a little jumpy—"

"You're a *lot* jumpy," Brother James accused. "Do you or don't you have faith in Brother Michael and his plan?"

"Of course I do. But—"

"No, stop. No buts. If you have faith, there's no room for buts."

The lights returned to Ryan's side of the fence. "I know what I heard," Brother Samuel said.

"I'm not saying you didn't hear anything. Just that you didn't hear an invader. Or an escapee. You heard a deer. Or the wind." One of the lights went out. "Now, turn that thing off before your night vision is ruined for hours."

The light stayed right where it was. Ryan wondered if Brother Samuel was just making a point by defying the order to turn it off. Finally, darkness returned. The boys—Ryan had come to think of them as teenagers, though he didn't know why—said some parting words, and then the night became quiet again.

Ryan lay frozen on the ground—in every sense of the word. Were they really gone, or were they sandbagging, pretending to be gone, and just waiting for him to show himself by moving? If he were them—particularly if he were Brother Samuel, who not only felt sure that he'd heard something, but had something to prove to Brother James—he'd stand there and set a trap for a while. He'd read somewhere, or maybe seen on television, that that was how snipers and countersnipers used to wait each other out during World War I and World War II. The one who lost patience first died.

With his hand cupped to his nose and mouth to disperse the clouds of breath, he forced himself to lie completely still, hoping that the hammering of his heart wasn't audible ten or fifteen yards away.

But how long was long enough? He decided to count to five hundred, metering the rhythm in his head as one one-thousand, two one-thousand, three one-thousand, and on to the end. That would keep him from going too fast.

As he got to a hundred twenty-three one-thousand, he heard Brother James say, "So, can we just say that I was right?"

The sound of his voice made Ryan gasp and his skin nearly stripped itself from his skeleton. Jesus, they *had* been waiting.

"I guess," Brother Samuel said. "I was just so sure."

"Happens sometimes. In ninety minutes, we get relieved, and you can get some sleep."

"Right," Brother Samuel said. "Sorry for the alarm."

This time, Ryan actually heard the footsteps as they walked away. He sent up another prayer of thanks that God had made him so paranoid.

When he could no longer hear the footsteps of the guards, he did a push-up on his frozen hands and brought himself to his knees, his back bent low. They were gone.

But they were also nervous. Brother Samuel in particular would be on a hair trigger, waiting to detect things in the night and shoot them. And Ryan was upwind now, so he needed to be that much more careful about making noise.

He needed to get the hell out of here. Distance was his only weapon.

As Ryan stood and turned his back to the compound, the starlight revealed a lighter strip along the black ground that he presumed to be the extension of the road that he'd been following all along—the road that he hoped was the same one that had brought them here.

It was time to run. It was, after all, the only thing in

school that he was any good at. He needed to find the houses he saw on the way in that had electricity burning in the windows. Where there was electricity, there had to be a phone, right? And where there was a phone, help was only a police-car ride away.

Ryan took off at a jog, a thousand-meter pace, as if he were back on the track team—fast enough to outrun just about anyone if they were going for the distance, but about half the speed of the sprint he was capable of for a short spurt. The cold air filled his lungs and dried him out, making him want to cough, but he knew better than that. No sudden noises.

At least the road was paved. If he'd been on gravel, there'd be way more noise, and if he'd been on dirt, he'd have had to worry about the irregularities of surface, and of an ankle twist or a knee jam. As it was, he could run like this for hours.

It turned out that he only had to go about ten minutes. At first, he thought the specks in the distance were head-lights, triggering another flash of panic; but as he slowed and got closer, he realized that he was seeing the glow of light from inside a building. Closer still, and he saw that the building was a house. A big one, atop a long hill.

Hope bloomed. His mind conjured an image of a family gathered around the television, watching one of the late-night comedy shows. Wouldn't they be surprised as all get out when he showed up at their door and told them his story? He wondered if they had any idea of all that was going on at the compound down the road. It would have been like the Germans who lived down the street from the concentration camps. Surprises like that were the ones that no one wanted.

Except the Germans knew. Most of them, anyway, and the rest were in denial. Isn't that what he saw on *Band of Brothers*? Absolutely. The American commanders made the townspeople go down to the camp and bury the dead.

Suppose these people knew? They'd have to know, wouldn't they?

He stopped dead in the middle of the road. All those terrorists had to live somewhere, didn't they? True, Ryan had barely seen the compound within the fence, but not everyone could live inside there, could they? He couldn't risk it.

But he couldn't stay here in the middle of the road, either. He had to do something.

He retreated back to the wood line on the right-hand side of the road—the side opposite the lit-up house—and he slowed his approach to a cautious tiptoe. From this distance, in the dark, the house looked exactly like Hollywood's version of a mansion, complete with tall pillars out front.

This felt wrong to him. He decided it was not the place to seek help.

He stayed off the road until the lights from the house were no longer visible, and then he dared to start running again on the road. He went a long way, and it took him a long time. He didn't know how far or how long, but from the sting of his legs and the heave of his lungs, he figured it had to be the equivalent of a 5K race. That meant three-point-one miles, or, to the rest of the world, a long way.

How was it possible to run three miles anywhere and not see anything? Even in Fayetteville—which was close to the capital of nowhere—he'd have passed a house or two on a run this long. He supposed it was possible, given the darkness of the night, that he'd passed the very kind of house he was looking for—empty with the lights off—but how could he know?

He craned his neck for a view of the horizon. Still no sign of dawn. He still had time. The plan was still alive.

One day, when all of this was over, Ryan was going to research how it was possible that in West Virginia hills only went up. On the way in on the night they were taken, the entire trip had seemed uphill, and now that he was going the opposite direction on foot, he knew damn well that it was all uphill.

As he crested his current slog, he saw a glimmer of hope. Somewhere in the distance—near or far, he couldn't tell—a tiny light beckoned him. And unlike the lit-up house earlier, this light was far enough away from the compound to give him hope that the people who owned it weren't complicit Nazis, but instead innocent Germans. You know, to keep the metaphor alive.

Still, he had to be careful. Everything was at stake here, including heartbeats and breathing. It behooved him to be careful. He slowed to an old-guy jog, and then to a walk.

Whatever the light was, it wasn't a house this time. It was too small. Like, *really* small. And as he got closer, he noted that a splash of blue had invaded the white light.

He stopped. "Holy shit," he said aloud. Was it even possible? Unless he was hallucinating, that blue spot was an image of a telephone.

Ryan didn't have any coins in his pocket. "Oh, please," he whispered. "Oh please, oh please, oh please." He lifted the phone from its cradle.

Dial tone. *Yes!*

He pressed the receiver to his face and dialed 911. The line clicked with electronic noise, and five seconds later, he heard a voice on the other end.

"Maddox County Sheriff's Office, Technician Phelps. What is your emergency?"

A flood of emotion erupted from deep within Ryan's soul. This was his moment to be brave—to announce to the world that he was here to save his family—yet when the moment arrived, he dissolved into deep, choking sobs.

CHAPTER FIFTEEN

Jonathan snatched up his receiver and brought it to his head. "Yeah." At this hour—Jesus, one-thirty-seven—one syllable was the best he could muster.

"Verify your identity, please, sir," a voice said from the other side.

"Excuse me?"

"Sir, I need you to verify your identity before I can continue."

Jonathan shook his head to rattle the sleep from his synapses. "You called me. Who do you think it is?"

"Sir, we can play these games all night, but it's a waste of time. I have orders to follow." He sounded young.

"Who is this?" Jonathan pressed.

"Sir, it's late for me, too, okay? Must we make this more difficult than necessary? I need to confirm your identity."

Jonathan sat up in his bed and turned the switch on the nightstand lamp. "This is Jonathan Grave," he said.

"Thank you. Next, I need your address and date of birth."

Finally, this was beginning to make sense. He was about to receive intelligence data from someone who had no business giving it to him. He gave the caller both bits of information.

"Excellent," the voice said. "Thank you. And can you verify that you are awake enough to comprehend the information I'm about to give you?"

Jonathan rolled his eyes. "Awake and alert."

"Okay," the young man said. "Because I'm about to deliver information that would send me to prison if it were ever revealed. There's no way I'm going to say this twice, so it's very important that you're ready to copy the details."

Fully awake now, Jonathan swung his feet to the floor and stood. With the phone pressed to his ear, he walked naked to his desk in the far corner, switched on that lamp and sat in his Aeron chair, pen hovering over paper. "I'm ready to copy," he said, and then he pressed a button to record the call.

"I work for the National Security Agency," the young voice said. "In violation of God knows how many laws, we picked up a recording from an American citizen to an American citizen. My boss said I needed to wake you up and relay the information. The only reason I can think of that he didn't call you himself is that he didn't want to be the designated jailee. Personally, sir, before I play you the tape, I need to reiterate that you're a perfect stranger to me, and if I need to throw you under the bus to save my own ass, I'll do it in a heartbeat."

Jonathan laughed. "Don't hold back," he said. "Tell me what you really think."

"I am telling you what I really think," he said. Clearly, his irony sensor had been paralyzed by NSA bureaucracy. "Apparently, you're more important tonight than the entire Constitution, and way more important than my future. Stand by to copy."

Jonathan heard a click and some mechanical noise. Then a voice:

"Maddox County Sheriff's Office, Technician Phelps. What is your emergency?"

Next came a muffled sound he didn't quite recognize until it huffed a little, like a struggling steam engine. The person on the other end of the phone was crying. "Th-this is Ryan Nasbe," the voice said. "Me and my mom were kidnapped."

The rest of the call lasted all of three minutes.

Gail and Venice sat at the teak table in the War Room, looking like rewarmed corpses. Jonathan hadn't given them much time to respond to his call—in fact, the order was "Meet me at the War Room right by-God now."

Gail seemed particularly unprepared. Yesterday's mascara hung like shadows under her eyes, and whatever she'd tried to do with her hair had only made it worse.

Venice just looked tired. Jonathan wondered how she managed to do all that she did on a daily basis. Professionally, she was his administrative and investigative right hand, while on the personal side, she had an eleven-year-old son to wrangle and a high-strung seventy-something-year-old mother to control. Or maybe it was Mama who needed to be wrangled and Roman who needed to be controlled. Either way, she was forever shoving twenty-eight hours of activity into twenty-four-hour days.

"Do we really know where the Nasbes are now?" Gail asked, settling into her usual chair. "And where's Boxers?"

"Big Guy will be here when he's here. We can't wait for him." Boxers didn't appreciate the charms of Fisherman's Cove, preferring the District of Columbia's ready access to bars and babes. Without traffic and with a heavy foot, he'd be here in an hour and a half.

"So where are they?" Venice pressed.

"Maddox County," Jonathan said.

"Maddox County *where*?"

"Don't know. A contact at the NSA called a half hour ago with an intercepted nine-one-one call to the Maddox County Sheriff's Office. Beyond that—"

"Wait," Gail said. "The NSA recorded a call from *inside* the U.S.?" She seemed appalled.

"Don't start," Jonathan warned. "I already had this discussion with Dudley Do-Right of the National Security Agency." He held up a tiny flash drive onto which he'd copied the NSA call. "Venice, please work your magic and bring this up on the speaker system."

Jonathan was an analog man trapped in a digital world. He loved high-tech toys and spent tens if not hundreds of thousands of dollars every year on the best and shiniest gadgets around, but if the toys didn't guide him where he wanted to go or improve upon the flight path of a bullet, he wasn't much interested in learning how they worked. Such was the case with the audiovisual technology of the War Room.

It took Venice less than a minute to bring up the audio. As an added touch, she also brought up a picture of the Nasbe family from happier times, all of them gathered around a Christmas tree and smiling out at them from the projection screen on the far wall.

"Maddox County Sheriff's Office," a voice said, "Technician Phelps. What is your emergency?" Her voice had the practiced drone of an experienced dispatcher.

Knowing what was coming, Jonathan watched Gail as the young voice choked and identified himself as Ryan Nasbe. Just as he'd expected, her eyes reddened at the sound of stress in the boy's voice.

"Th-this is Ryan Nasbe. Me and my mom were kidnapped."

"*Who* is this?" the dispatcher asked. Clearly, kidnappings didn't happen on a regular basis in Maddox County.

"Ryan Nasbe. N-A-S-B-E. I live on Fort Bragg. Well, I used to, but now I live in Mt. Vernon, Virginia, with my Aunt Maggie."

"You're calling from Virginia?"

"No. I don't think so, anyway. I think I'm in West Virginia. That's the direction we drove after we were kidnapped."

"Who kidnapped you?"

The kid's patience evaporated. "How should I know? They're terrorists."

A pause. "Young man, if this is a prank, let me assure you that—"

"It's not a prank!" Ryan yelled. "They kidnapped us in our car after they shot a bunch of people on a bridge. Then they drove us into the middle of nowhere. They're keeping us in a house in the middle of some kind of camp. They're lunatics, calling themselves brother this and sister that. They promised to kill us next week."

"How many of you are there?"

"Two. Me and my mom."

"Where's your father?"

"He's in Afghanistan, I think. He's Special Forces in the Army."

A sigh. "Your father is in Special Forces." The dispatcher spoke disdainfully, clearly doubting his truthfulness.

"If you don't believe me, you can call down to Fort Bragg and ask. Actually, they probably won't answer you, but still, it's true. What difference does any of this make? I need a cop and I need him now."

"Where are you now?"

"I have no idea. Don't you know? Don't you have like caller ID or something?"

The operator fell silent, and the background filled with the sound of muffled voices and some shuffling papers.

The silence lasted long enough for Ryan Nasbe to say, "Are you still there?"

"You said your name is Ryan Nasbe, is that correct?"

"Yes, ma'am."

"Okay, Ryan, I have your address. You're at a pay phone, is that right?"

"Yes, ma'am."

"I need you to stay exactly where you are. We'll have someone there in a few minutes."

"I can't just wait here. Somebody might drive by and see me."

"Then step off to the side of the road. Hide in the trees. Our car will turn on the emergency lights, so you'll know it's safe to come out. Can you do that for me?"

Ryan's voice broke. "Yes, ma'am. Ma'am?"

"Yes?"

"I'm really scared."

"I know you are, Ryan. This will be over soon."

"Please hurry."

"We'll get there as fast as we can."

"Okay," Ryan said. "I'm going to hang up now."

"Okay, sweetie. This will all be over very soon."

The line went dead.

Gail's features folded into a deep scowl. "That's odd," she said.

She had Jonathan's attention.

"Why did she let him hang up like that? She should have kept him on the line, keeping him calm and just keeping track of him in general."

"He said he was scared," Jonathan said. "He's going off to hide in the woods."

"And that's kind of odd, too. It would be one thing if the boy had suggested that on his own, and then he hung up on the dispatcher, but this was her idea."

Jonathan didn't get what she was driving at. "She wanted him to stay safe, out of sight."

Gail shrugged. "Well, it's just different than the way any dispatcher I've ever known would handle it."

"I've got something weirder than that," Venice announced. She'd been typing on her ubiquitous keyboard. "ICIS has nothing on it."

Gail sat forward in her seat.

Jonathan said, "Isn't it a little early? The phone call isn't yet two hours old."

"ICIS triggers when a call is dispatched," Gail explained.

Venice closed the loop. "Which means that if there's no tracking, the call was never put into the system."

"Maybe instead of dispatching it," Jonathan said, "the call taker just looked over her shoulder and told some deputy to go pick him up."

"It's not about dispatching, Dig," Gail explained. "It's about opening the file. Two hours into a missing persons case, there'd be something. There'd have to be."

"Even for a case that happens in the middle of Nowhere, West Virginia?"

Venice started to say yes—he could tell by her body language—but she stopped herself and held up a finger instead. She tapped her computer keys. "There it is," she said. "Maddox County Sheriff's Office. Let's give them a call, shall we?"

CHAPTER SIXTEEN

Ryan didn't just hide in the trees, he hid *way back* in the trees, far enough off the road that he was completely invisible. With all the leaves missing, that meant twenty or thirty yards off the parking lot.

Now that he wasn't moving, the nighttime noises seemed louder to him, but because his ordeal was about to end, they seemed less frightening. Fear, he realized, had the same effect on you as heavy exercise. It was exhausting. Hope—which he guessed was the right word for the opposite of fear—brought lightness. It felt good to rescue someone you loved.

He was surprised how quickly the police car got there. The guy must have either been around the corner or driven a million miles an hour. Ryan saw him first as approaching headlights. It could have been anyone, and that twisty feeling returned to his gut. But when the blue light bar painted the night, he nearly cheered out loud.

He started to run out of his hiding place, but just as he was rising, he thought better of it. This was a time to be very, very careful.

Let's see what the cop does.

After the light bar came on, and the vehicle stopped, Ryan saw the interior light come on, and then a guy in regular clothes stepped out of the driver's door and stood. It was hard to tell at this distance, but he looked big as he stepped around the front of the vehicle, shielding his eyes from his own lights. When the lights were behind him—when he was looking in Ryan's general direction—he stopped and planted his fists on his hips, like the Jolly Green Giant in a suit.

"Ryan Nasbe?" he whisper-yelled. "Are you here?"

That was it. The man knew his name and he drove a police car. That was all Ryan needed. He rose to his full height and held up his hand, as if being called on in class. "Right here," he said. He spoke in his normal voice, but in the silence of the night, it sounded more like a shout.

The cop's gaze came closer, but he still didn't see. "You can come out now, son."

Noise didn't matter anymore. Ryan allowed his feet to drag through the dried leaves, and he didn't cringe a bit when his foot broke a stick. It was difficult to fight the desire to run, but he worried that it would look, you know, too babyish.

"Are you Ryan?" the cop asked. He spoke in regular tones, too, and absent the whisper, his voice sounded like one that should do movie trailers. It had that deep, gravelly quality.

"Yes, sir." He kept his stride even as he walked a direct line toward the man.

"Well, you are a man of your word, Mr. Ryan Nasbe," the cop said. "You said you were going to be in the woods, and you are, by God, *in the woods*." He leaned on those last words, and then laughed as if he'd told himself a joke.

As Ryan closed to within a few yards, the cop raised his hand, and a bright flashlight beam nailed him in the eyes. He recoiled and raised his hands as shields. "Jesus, Mister."

The light shifted down a little. Concentrating more on his chest than his face. "Sorry about that. I just wanted to see what you look like." He held out a friendly hand. "Kendig Neen," he said. "I'm the sheriff of Maddox County."

Ryan hesitated, though he didn't know why. His warning radar had picked up something that wasn't right. "How come you're not in a uniform?" he asked.

He laughed again. "You're lucky I'm not in pajamas," he said. "You know what time it is? Cops have to sleep, too, you know. I got the call, and these were the best duds I could find. That okay with you?"

Ryan found himself nodding without really intending to. "Sure," he said. He accepted the handshake.

"I'm glad to hear it." Everything about Sheriff Neen was big, so it shouldn't have been a surprise that his handshake hurt. It just went on a little too long. "You've got to be freezing. Let's get in the car and have a chat."

"We need to get my mom," Ryan said. "She's in a basement just down this road." He dislodged his hand from the sheriff's grip so he could point with it.

"Yet another reason to get in the car," the sheriff said.

Venice rested the phone on its cradle. "Well, there you go," she said. "No such call ever happened."

Jonathan wished he was surprised, but he'd been listening to her end of the conversation. "That's it? Just didn't happen?"

"Exactly. You heard me on the phone with her. I had to soft-pedal a little around the whole illegal eavesdropping thing, but I asked her about a missing-person report, and she said that they'd received no such report. Those were her words, actually. 'We've received no such report.'"

Jonathan scowled. "Theories?"

"How sure are you that it's the right Maddox County?" Gail asked. "Are there any others within a reasonable drive of Alexandria?"

It took Venice ten seconds and a few keystrokes to do the

Google search. "No other Maddox County in the whole U.S. of A," she proclaimed.

"And we're all sure we heard the operator answer, 'Maddox County,' right?" Jonathan asked.

They both nodded, and Venice added, "I'll go so far as to say I think I just talked to the same lady that Ryan did." She checked her notes. "Her name is Phelps." She tapped her keyboard again, but this time it appeared to be a more complicated challenge, eating up the better part of a whole minute. "Stacy Phelps," Venice announced. "Average grades in high school, no college. She—"

Beyond the glass windows of the War Room, the door to the cave burst open and Boxers strode into the outer office. He wore a long black topcoat over a black turtleneck with a black watch cap pulled down to his eyebrows. No one said anything until he rounded the corner and stormed into the War Room.

"God *damn*, this had better be good," he said.

"What's with the outfit?" Jonathan teased. "We interrupt you in the middle of a burglary?"

Gail and Venice both chuckled.

"Snigger away," Boxers said. He peeled off the overcoat and revealed a tailored black suit. He looked very Hollywood—or at least like the man who ate Hollywood. "I was on a date."

The words hung in the air like a cloud.

"What are those looks?" Boxers asked, noting their expressions of . . . shock? "I go on dates just like everyone else."

Jonathan let it go. "We intercepted a call from the Nasbe boy," he explained. It took a few minutes to catch him up on the essentials. "Venice was about to give us details on the dispatcher who took the call."

With that, the floor returned to Venice. She squinted as she read from her computer screen, scrolling and clicking with the mouse as she summarized. "Stacy Phelps attended John F. Kennedy Elementary School in Maddox County, followed by Oliver Wendell Holmes Intermediate School and then graduated seven years ago from Maddox County High School."

She paused as she clicked and typed and switched to a new database. "Looks like she worked at McDonald's for a couple of years. No, wait, that was in high school. Right, and then six months after high school she started work for the sheriff's department at eight twenty-five an hour. She started as an assistant clerk, then progressed to clerk, and then senior clerk."

Jonathan smiled as Venice clicked through to another page. This was Venice self-actualized. She loved nothing more than tickling restricted databases and then showing off by spouting ridiculous levels of detail. He'd let her run for a little longer, but if she didn't get on point soon, he was going to have to interrupt.

She continued, "Three years ago, she was promoted to dispatcher, at which she's making fifteen thirty-eight an hour." Venice looked up. "Pretty good career track in just a couple of years."

"Are you going to get to anything useful?" Boxers asked. His bullshit tolerance was considerably smaller than Jonathan's, and given the circumstances, his reservoir was about empty. "Tonight, I mean. You know, within the next hour or two."

Venice pretended not to hear. "She has a completely clean criminal record. Not even a moving violation, which is actually kind of creepy." An otherwise law-abiding, straight-shooting model citizen, Venice Alexander was by anyone's estimation, a speed demon. Wrapped in Glow Bird—the name she'd given to her butt-ugly blaze-orange Miata—her right foot turned to solid lead when she got on the road.

After a few more taps, Venice continued her monologue. "She lives in the Nathan Bedford Forrest Mobile Home Park, where she pays . . ."

Jonathan knew to wait for it.

". . . three twenty-five a month in rent."

"That's all?" Gail gasped.

"We're talking rural West Virginia," Venice said.

"But I come from rural Indiana, and—"

"You ever been to rural West Virginia?" Boxers asked with a smirk. "There is no rural like rural West Virginia." To Venice: "We're talking coal country?"

She nodded. Then scowled. "Only coal is not the big industry there." She used her finger to follow the words on the screen, the way other people might read a newspaper. "Apparently, the mines in Maddox County are pretty much played out. The big corporate taxpayer there now is Appalachian Acoustics. They make acoustic shells, those things that go up behind orchestras and choruses to direct the sound out to the audience."

Boxers looked to Jonathan. "Are you seeing the relevance to any of this?"

"Intel is intel, Box. It's like ammunition—I've never wished that I had less."

The look Venice gave to the Big Guy would have been more complete if she'd stuck out her tongue, but she restrained herself. "They employ nearly two hundred workers in a factory there that makes . . ." She strained to read further on the page. "Wow. A hundred million a year."

Jonathan's jaw dropped. "On acoustic shells? A product I'd never heard of until right now?"

"Despite your love of concert halls," Gail joked.

"They're a big company," Venice said, reading on. "International, in fact, with exports to just about everywhere. And they supply to the federal government. Their brochure says even the White House uses their products."

"I'm a little lost myself," Gail confessed. "Why is all this demographic data important to us?"

Venice started to answer, then deferred to her boss. "Go ahead," she said. "You tell her."

"Leverage," Jonathan explained. "We don't get to play with warrants and court orders, so we need to be persuasive in other ways. The more we know about the community, the more we can strategize about leverage."

THREAT WARNING   145

"Who are we leveraging?" Gail asked.

"Whoever we need to. We know for a fact that the Nasbe family has been taken to someplace called Maddox County, West Virginia, and we know that a call for help is being covered up. I think that Ms. Stacy . . ." He looked to Venice.

"Phelps," she prompted.

"I think that Stacy Phelps is a good place to start. Why would a law-abiding public servant pretend that a call never happened?"

Gail's eyes narrowed. "And we're going to extract that information from her through *leverage*"—she used finger-quotes—"without any legal authority to do so."

Jonathan shrugged. "That's as good a summary as any."

"That means blackmail?" she asked.

"Persuasion," Jonathan countered. "Whatever it takes."

She didn't like it. "I thought we made it a point not to tangle with domestic law-enforcement agencies. I thought you thought that was the ultimate recipe for disaster."

"I still feel that way. Up to but excluding the point where the law enforcers become a part of the problem. Besides, Stacy Phelps isn't a cop. She's a dispatcher."

"Who works for cops," Gail said. "You really think that we can mess with one without messing with the other?"

Boxers asked, "Maybe her bosses have no idea what she's doing. If that were the case, then we'd be doing the Maddox County Sheriff's Department a favor by ferreting out someone who's covering up a crime."

"Then let's call the sheriff's office and tell them what we know. Why not let them handle it?"

"First, there's the source of our information," Jonathan said. "That's one hundred percent off the table."

"And then there's the fact that the sheriff's office might be in on it," Venice added.

Jonathan was impressed. Venice rarely weighed in on conspiracy theories.

She saw it in his expression. "Don't give me that look. I'm not as Pollyanna as you think I am."

Jonathan and Boxers laughed. "Oh, yes, you are," they said in unison, making them laugh again.

Venice's eyes returned to her screen, and her brow furrowed. One day, Jonathan figured that practicality would trump vanity and she'd get some glasses. Such words would never pass his lips, however.

"Now this is interesting," Venice said. "I did a data search on the Nathan Bedford Forrest Mobile Home Park. That is one tough neighborhood. They could have their own police substation for all the calls that run out there."

"Can I go home?" Boxers said. "If we're going to chat, I've got other stuff to do. If we're going to go to Maddox County and kick some ass, I'll stay."

Jonathan asked Venice, "How far is this place?"

She tapped. "As the crow flies, three hundred twenty miles. Throw in the mountain roads, and I'd guess an eight- or nine-hour drive."

As he'd figured. "Too far to drive. Take too long. Box, find us a way to get in by air, and do all the planning you need to make that happen. Make sure you work with Venice to make any arrangements we need for landing zones and such.

"Ven, keep researching the area. If it looks interesting or relevant, make a note of it, and send it all to me electronically. It'll give me something to read on the flight. Also, I need you to get us some wheels. Usual methods. Find us a place to set up a CP, too." He knew that she would understand the abbreviation for command post.

Jonathan looked at Gail. "You come with me to the armory and we'll load up the Batmobile."

"What are we bringing?" Boxers asked, clearly annoyed that he wasn't involved in the arms selection.

"A little bit of everything," Jonathan said. "I have no idea what we're looking at on the far side of this thing. I'll plan for the worst."

"How big a 'worst' are you talking about?"

Jonathan's shoulders sagged. "Would you like me to let you see it before we load it up?"

"I think that's a good idea," Boxers said. "You know, since I'm the one who's likely to be carrying it all."

"Plan for a heavy load."

"I'll get us a chopper with horsepower to spare." Boxers knew as much about mission planning as any five logisticians in the business.

Jonathan checked his watch. "I show that it's zero-three-twenty-five. I want to be airborne by oh-six-hundred. Everybody good with that?"

He asked it as if there were a choice.

CHAPTER SEVENTEEN

The cop—Sheriff Neen—drove way too slowly for Ryan's taste. His mom was about to die, for God's sake, and this guy hadn't even turned on his lights and siren. He just, you know, *drove*. He even stopped at stop signs.

"This isn't the way," Ryan said. "I came straight down that road there."

"All in good time, son," Neen replied. He had a mustache that looked like something out of cowboy times, a big bushy thing that covered his entire lip and curled up at the ends. "This isn't the big city. I can't just call a SWAT team and have them go charging in. It's just me and some deputies—sleeping deputies at that—and before I go charging anywhere, I want to make sure I know what I'm getting into. Now, tell me about this kidnapping you say happened."

That I say happened? Ryan didn't like the sound of that. Who would make up something like this? He told the story about driving through Old Town Alexandria, and the long, harrowing ride out to here. Then he talked about being beaten up and having to stand there while his mom read stupid lies.

"I couldn't see through my hood," he concluded, "but I assume they must have had a camera there, or else why would they have her do that? Maybe it's up on the Internet or something."

In the dark, he could see the sheriff's head nodding—not as if he was saying yes, but as if he were thinking about things.

"What's wrong?" Ryan asked.

"That is really some story," the sheriff said.

His stomach fell. "You believe me, don't you?"

The man's silhouette turned in the dark. "Would you believe it if you had just heard it from someone?"

"Yes!" Ryan yelled loudly enough for his voice to crack. "Here." He released himself from his seat belt and pulled his coat, his shirt, and his sweater over his head as a single unit. "Look at these bruises." He tried to hold his ribs up in a way that they would be visible in the dim light of the car.

Neen seemed startled, and then chuckled. "Put your clothes on, son," he said. "I'm not saying you're lying, I'm just saying it doesn't all add up for me. I'll get someone to look at the bruises later."

"It has to add up," Ryan said. A growing panic made him speak louder and faster than he wanted to. "It's true. I have to rescue my mom."

The sheriff piloted his car toward civilization. Ryan could see the sky lightening, but it didn't look like dawn. "So why didn't you bring your mother with you?" he asked.

"I couldn't. She wouldn't fit through the window."

"So this prison they put you in—"

"It wasn't a prison, it was a room in a basement."

"A guest room."

"No, not a guest room! It had locks on the doors, and they beat me up! Why won't you believe me?"

"Don't shout at me, son."

"I'm not your son, dammit! How can I not shout when you won't even believe me?"

The sheriff's stern look polished itself to something frightening. "I'd watch that mouth of yours, unless you want another beating."

What was wrong with this guy? Was everybody in this town crazy, or just stupid? Maybe a little of both. Ryan wanted to scream that to Neen, but he held back. One way or the other, he needed this idiot's help, and pissing him off would accomplish nothing.

Instead, Ryan said, "I'm sorry. I'm just really, really scared right now. If people come down there and find . . ." He hesitated to avoid mentioning the dead body, and covered with, ". . . that I'm missing, they're going to go ape sh . . . they're going to be angry. God only knows what they'll do then."

"These people who captured you," Neen said. "What do you know about them?"

"I know they're weird. They call everybody brother and sister, and they like to wear hoods. They've got lots of guns. They shot up a bridge on the night they took us. Killed a lot of people. I think they're all about killing people. I think they're terrorists."

The sheriff turned onto a better-paved road. "For all these guns and all this violence, they just let you climb out a window and escape?"

"They didn't *let* me do anything," Ryan said. "I snuck out."

"How?"

"What do you mean, how?" He sensed that the sheriff knew he was holding back, but Ryan didn't want to give up the business about killing Brother Stephen. Sure, it was an accident, and it was the truth, but the truth hadn't been working for him so far with this guy.

The road led to the end of what appeared to be a long driveway. The sheriff gunned the engine and they started climbing the hill. "I mean, how does it happen, when you're in a locked room, that there's an open window in the first place? And while we're at it, with armed guards all around, how do you grow a set big enough to escape in the middle of the night?"

"I told you that we were being held prisoner. My mom still is."

"And how did you get past the guard?" Up ahead, at the top of the hill, a mansion loomed large. Built of white stone with tall white pillars in the front, this looked a lot like the White House. It looked a lot like the house he'd skirted when he was first running away. Could it be the same one after all this driving?

And how had he missed the guards the first time around? They wore black uniforms and carried rifles.

They were the same uniforms and rifles he'd seen in the compound.

Something dissolved in Ryan's gut, and tears rushed to his eyes.

"Might as well tell me now, son," Neen said.

Panic shot like electricity up Ryan's spine as he scoured his universe for options that did not exist. If he tried to fight the sheriff, he'd never have a chance. The guy was huge. If he tried to run, they'd just shoot him down. If he—

"Ryan Nasbe," Neen said, "I'm afraid that your bad day is about to get a lot worse."

Please, God, protect Ryan. Let him find safety. Let him send help. Please.

Christyne wasn't much into prayer. With a husband who made his living in perpetual harm's way, prayer grew exhausting after a while. And having watched far too many flag-draped caskets being wept over by wives and children who no doubt prayed for their loved ones' safe returns, she'd grown a kind of fatalistic outer shell about God and His plans for people. If He wanted them to live, they'd live; if He wanted otherwise, otherwise would happen.

She never admitted her fatalism aloud, of course—especially not among the other Unit wives, who often were fiercely religious—but it brought her an odd sense of peace to entrust all of it to God without her presumptuous interference. Who was Christyne Nasbe to presume that she could know more about the Grand Plan than the divine architect Himself? By placing the fate of her family in His hands, she freed herself to live her life in the present, prepared to accept the good or bad that the future might hold for her while embracing her powerlessness to influence any of it.

When it came to Ryan, though—her frustrating, attitude-filled, beautiful, flawless Ryan—none of that rationalization meant anything.

She needed God's intervention, and she needed it now.

It felt as if he'd been gone for hours. Surely there had been enough time for him to find help. Enough time for him to find safety. It had to be true simply because the alternative was unthinkable.

Here in the dark and the cold, surrounded by the pall of death, Christyne told herself again that it had been right to let Ryan go for help. She told herself that she wouldn't have been able to stop him no matter what she did.

How would she ever know whether she'd made the right decision? How can anyone plan for something like this? Later, when all this was over and either they were free or their bodies were discovered somewhere, people would judge for themselves whether she'd been a good mom or a bad one.

She could almost hear the questions she'd be asked by the morning television hosts: Why didn't you stay at Fort Bragg, where you have friends to support you and your child? Do you think it was wise to let a sixteen-year-old wander out into the night by himself? Wouldn't it have been better for the two of you to stay together? How does it feel to have killed a man so young, one who was barely older than your own son?

She could hear the questions because they were always the questions that were asked after the fact. In today's news media, everything bad that happened to children was always the fault of the parent. That her husband was in the military would only cause them to question that more closely.

Boomer, where are you?

This was never the way it was supposed to have been. Christyne was never supposed to have been the crisis decision maker. She'd married a warrior, for God's sake. One of the most elite in the world. He was supposed to protect her. That's what she'd thought when they first married, but that was before the reality hit her. In military families, the trained protector was forever protecting someone else. On the home front, crisis control rested squarely on the shoulders of the spouses, everything from broken bones to broken hearts, leaking water heaters to car repair.

Why, then, shouldn't it fall to her to deal with carjackings and kidnappings? One day, when all of this—

Something moved outside the door to her cell.

The door burst open, and people flooded into the tiny space. At first they were invisible in the darkness, but then the darkness erupted in white as brilliant flashlights found her eyes and gouged her retinas.

"Take her," someone said.

Something hit her hard on her cheek. It ignited a flash of purple.

CHAPTER EIGHTEEN

As the whisper-quiet AgustaWestland helicopter flared to land, Jonathan looked at his watch. Six-fifty-eight. From the ground, darkness still ruled, but on their approach, he noted the redness of the horizon, a harbinger of a beautiful day that would arrive far too soon.

He rode in the back of the chopper, with Gail on his right, and as Boxers went through the shutdown procedures, she shot him a look.

"He really *is* good, isn't he?" It was her first time on an op with them, and she seemed genuinely surprised by the professionalism.

Jonathan took the comment more seriously than he probably should have. "Do yourself a favor," he said. "Never doubt the Big Guy." His words came out sharply, almost angrily. He'd come to think of it as Boxers' curse: Big Guy's size and abrasive manner projected oafishness to some people, a general lack of intelligence. They could not have been more wrong. In Jonathan's experience his good friend was a brilliant technician and tactician who happened to be larger than most monuments. Fearless and intensely loyal, Boxers had pulled Jonathan's ass out of the fire—both literally and figuratively—too many times to count.

"I need to go get us some wheels," Jonathan said when it was quiet enough to be heard.

Boxers gave a splayed five-finger bye-bye wave over his shoulder, like something an infant might do. "Go," he said. "Gunslinger and I can take care of things here until you get back." Gunslinger had become Gail's radio moniker after she shot down a helicopter a few months ago using only a rifle. She had rejected two previous handles that Boxers had tried to inflict on her: G-Girl and Triple-A, for anti-aircraft artillery.

"It shouldn't take me too long," Jonathan said. Like his colleagues, he wore woodland camouflage clothing, in part for its utilitarian use in blending with the surroundings, but also to blend in socially. This was deer-hunting season, and as in any rural community, half of the people they encountered today were likely to be wearing woodland camouflage clothing.

Jonathan slung his rucksack over his shoulders, glanced at his GPS to reaffirm his bearings, and then started off on his hike.

As a rule, Jonathan avoided stealing from innocents during missions. Not only did it offend his sense of right and wrong, it also added an unnecessary element of risk. Given all the moving parts in play during an 0300 mission, he didn't want to risk it all coming apart because a local cop noticed a vehicle from a hot sheet.

Sometimes, though, it couldn't be avoided.

By massaging her databases and scouring satellite images, and in general working the magic she was famous for, Venice had been able to find them the perfect command post—a dilapidated old house on the grounds of an abandoned mine—but it was way in the boonies. The nearest car listed for sale was fifteen miles away. If they'd had the luxury of time, Venice would have pored through the local classified ads for an appropriate vehicle and worked out a delivery plan using cash and messengers.

Unfortunately, time was the commodity in shortest supply, so that meant thievery.

Jonathan hiked at a brisk pace through the thinning forest, covering the mile and a quarter in a little over a half hour. According to the maps and the imagery, nothing but woods lay between him and this morning's target, so he could afford to make some noise. As he closed to within a hundred yards or so, he slowed and took the time to survey his surroundings.

A house lay ahead, on the far side of what Jonathan estimated to be six acres of open field. To call it a farm was overstating it, but rows of decaying cornstalks testified to at least a little income from selling produce. Lowering himself to one knee at the edge of the tree line, Jonathan unslung his ruck and pulled binoculars from a side pocket.

A porch light was on, as was a light somewhere in the house, but on the far side. They seemed dim from this distance, making him wonder if the illumination had less to do with someone being up and around than the proverbial light in the window, left on all night to keep the boogeyman at bay.

The target for this mission was the white Dodge crew-cab pickup truck parked in front of the house. He watched the place for a full minute, looking for signs of movement that would make things more difficult. Seeing none, he set off across the field.

Daylight had arrived, though it was still quite dim. Like any Special Forces operative, he hated the daylight. It leveled the playing field too much.

He strolled upright through the dried, sagging cornstalks, making some effort to be stealthy, but not breaking his back over it. He had to assume that whoever lived in the house was awake, and if they looked out the window he wanted to appear to be a wandering hunter with nothing to hide. He figured that he'd be less likely to get shot at this way than if they saw him skulking about.

He covered the distance without incident, walking right up

to the pickup, apparently without being seen. From here it would either be easy or get really complicated. He moved to the driver's door and pulled the latch. It opened. Good start.

Jonathan lifted the Velcro flap from a pouch on his belt and withdrew his Leatherman tool. All he had to do was break the steering-wheel lock, strip the ignition keyway, and then he could be on the road with his stolen vehicle.

His butt had just hit the cushion when a small voice said, "Who are you?"

Startled the crap out of him. He whirled to see a little girl with dark hair standing eight feet away, wrapped in a bulky flannel robe over flannel pajamas and threadbare pink slippers. She had an odd look about her that Jonathan recognized in the dark as the telltale signs of Down syndrome.

"Hi," he said. He felt his cheeks blushing, partly because he felt embarrassed to have been caught, but also because of the shame he felt for automatically assessing whether or not the girl was armed and posing a threat.

"Are you the repo man?"

"Excuse me?"

"She asked if you are the repo man," said another voice. This one belonged to a tall young woman dressed similarly to the little girl. She also held a twelve-gauge over-and-under shotgun. It dangled by her side, her finger close to the trigger. "They said they'd be coming for the truck, and Jilly's been obsessing about it ever since. That's Jilly, by the way."

Jonathan forced a smile, his mind spinning at a thousand miles an hour for his next move. Could it really be as simple as telling her that he was here to repossess her vehicle and drive off?

"Well?" the woman pressed. "Answer her. Are you the repo man?"

"Are you going to shoot me if I say yes?"

"No, I'm going to shoot you if you say you're a burglar. If you say you're the repo man, I'm going to ask for your ID, and then I'm going to be without a truck, which means that even if I got a job offer and an opportunity to pay back your boss's precious money, I wouldn't be able to take it." Her voice had none of the twang that Jonathan associated with this part of the world. If anything, she sounded like Yankee elite. He thought he saw tears in her eyes.

Jonathan rose from the seat, keeping his .45 angled away from the woman so she wouldn't see it and panic. "How long ago did you lose your job?" he asked. It was a stall more than anything else, a way to bide time as he thought of a way out of this.

"Three years," she said. "I used to work for Appalachian Acoustics until they got their new asshole owner and he put in all his own people."

"Michael Copley is an asshole," Jilly said.

"That's enough out of you," the woman scolded.

"Sorry, Mama."

"So, are you or aren't you?" the woman pushed.

"What are the chances that I can convince you to put that weapon down?" Jonathan asked.

She scowled. "My *weapon*? What are you, a cop?"

"If I say yes, are you going to shoot me?"

"Seems to be your fixation," she said.

"I get that way with armed people."

"Most people say gun," she said. "You said weapon. My husband's in the Army, and the only people I know who talk that way are his buddies and cops."

Suddenly, Jonathan found himself caring more. "Is he on deployment?" he asked. "Your husband, I mean."

"*Again*," she said, leaning heavily on the word. "To Iraq. *Again*. I thought this new guy in Washington was supposed to get us out by now."

"Wars are complicated things," Jonathan said. "When is he due back?"

"What's it to you?"

Jonathan shrugged with one shoulder. "Let's just say I have a soft spot for active-duty personnel."

"There it is again," the woman said. "You all sound alike. Who are you?"

"Well, I'm not the repo man. How's that for a start?"

She lifted the gun to hold it in both hands, but with the barrel still pointed harmlessly. "Not so good," she said. "Jilly, come over here by me."

The little girl looked confused.

"Now, Jilly."

Suddenly frightened, Jilly scampered over to her mom.

"Suppose you tell me why you're in my truck, if you're not the repo man."

Over the years, Jonathan had honed an ice-melting smile that by itself had defused many a volatile situation. He used that now. "I came here to steal it," he said.

The double barrels pivoted closer.

"The weapon is not necessary, ma'am. I swear to you. You don't want your daughter to see you kill a man anyway. Not over a car. Besides, I'm not going to steal it anymore."

The woman gave a wry chuckle as she jiggled the shotgun a little. "I could have told you that."

"Fair enough. Fact is I'm going to help you."

She hardened her stance. "I don't need your help."

Jonathan held her gaze. "I think you do. How much do you owe on the truck?"

"That's none of your business."

Jonathan shrugged. "In a different circumstance, I'd agree, but let's be honest here. It's a cold morning, and you were worried enough about having your truck repossessed that you stayed up all night with a shotgun. All things considered, I'd argue that privacy is not your first priority. Come on, tell me. How much do you owe?"

She snorted a derisive laugh. "What, are you going to buy it?"

"Yes," Jonathan said.

Her face went blank. "Yes, what?"

"Yes, I'm going to buy your truck."

"It's not for sale."

Jonathan just stood, giving her time to hear the ridiculousness of her own words.

"If I let you buy it, what am I supposed to do? I'll be stranded out here."

Jonathan cocked his head. "What was your plan when you thought I was the repo man?"

"I didn't have one. That's why I was going to try and talk him out of it."

"With a shotgun? Who did you plan to have take care of Jilly while you were in prison?"

She threw an uncomfortable glance at her daughter, but said nothing.

Jonathan took the opportunity to further drive his point home. "Wouldn't it be better to greet the repo man with a wad of cash than a twelve gauge?"

The woman clearly didn't know what to do. "So, what, you expect me just to take a check from you? Even if it was good, without the truck—"

"I said cash," Jonathan interrupted. "You know, folding money."

Her shoulders sagged in disbelief. "You just happen to have twenty-two thousand eight hundred and fifty dollars on you?"

"As a matter of fact, I do."

"Then why not just buy a car of your own?"

"That's what I'm trying to do," he said. He was being deliberately obtuse now.

"I mean—"

"I know what you mean. Thing is, there are no dealerships out here."

The woman scowled as a thought crossed her mind. "Where are you from? How did you get here?"

This was why it was better to work at night—why it was always a bad idea to engage in chitchat.

Jilly sneezed and hugged herself tightly. "Mommy, I'm cold."

"Me, too, honey."

"Let's go inside, then," Jonathan suggested.

The woman coughed out another laugh. "Excuse me?"

"It's warm inside," he said.

"You really expect me to invite a strange man into my house?"

Jonathan polished his smile. "There's a lot going on right now that I didn't expect, but it's happening anyway. What are your choices?" He counted the options on his fingers. "One, you can shoot me, but for the sake of argument, let's stipulate that you're not going to do that. Two, you can just take my money and let me drive off in your truck, but it doesn't look like that's happening, either. Three, you can go inside and just leave me out here, in which case I'll just take the truck. Four, we can all continue to stand out here together and freeze, but that's just plain stupid. That leaves the most logical choice, which would have us all go in together. You have the shotgun, after all."

Again, she stared as she tried to wade through it all. In the east, the sun had fully bloomed.

"Look," Jonathan said. "I know we met awkwardly, but I really am one of the good guys. Either take my money for the truck and let me drive off, or let's all go inside. It makes no sense for Jilly to be shivering like that."

"So, I'm just supposed to trust you. The stranger who was about to steal my car."

"I'll introduce myself, then. I'm Leon Harris." He considered reaching out to offer his hand, but worried that it might come off as aggressive. "Look. I'm going to step away from the truck now, and when I do, you're going to see a holstered pistol on my thigh. Don't freak out."

She didn't freak out, exactly, but the business end of the shotgun lined up closer to his chest. She'd still miss if she fired, but Jonathan didn't think she knew that.

"Put it on the floor," she commanded.

He pushed the truck's door closed. "I can't do that," he said. "First of all, it's an expensive weapon, and second, it's modified to have really sensitive parts. It's not a weapon that other people should handle."

Her eyes remained locked on the weapon.

"Ma'am, I know that this is stressful and confusing, and to be honest with you, there's a lot of it that I can't explain. What I want you to understand—and the reason why I didn't just continue to hide my weapon from you—is that if doing you harm were on my agenda, I'd be doing it, and with all respect, there's nothing you could do to stop me."

"I could shoot you."

"And I could shoot *you*." He said this in the most reasonable tone. "Or, we could shoot each other, but if it came to that, I one-hundred-percent guarantee that I would still be standing here unharmed when the smoke cleared. My point, though, is the very opposite of any of that. I have no intention of harming you or your daughter."

She lowered the muzzle to the ground. "Susan Shockley," she said. "Call me Sam. Or call me idiot, because that's what I probably am for doing this." She turned and put her hand on Jilly's shoulder. "Come on, sweetie. Let's get you warm."

Jonathan wasn't quite sure what they'd decided to do here.

"Come on, Mr. Harris," Sam said. "Do you like coffee?"

They sat in the kitchen at a rectangular table that might have been hand-hewn from local hardwoods. At the far end, closest to the window that provided a sweeping view of the fields at the rear of the house, a place was set with nice china, complete with crystal stemware. Sam did not sit there, and she did not offer the place to Jonathan. She must have sensed his trustworthiness, because she'd returned the shotgun to its rack over the fireplace in the adjacent family room, where Jilly sat on an overstuffed chair, wrapped in her blanket and watching cartoons.

While his hostess moved through the ritual of brewing the coffee, Jonathan set his ruck on the floor and opened the top flap. On missions like this, it always paid to have cash on hand, the more the better. He counted out thirty thousand dollars in banded stacks of Franklins and set the money on the table.

Sam saw it as she was about to pour coffee into mugs, and she froze. "You were serious?" she said.

"A deal's a deal," Jonathan said. "My word is my bond. I can do platitudes and clichés all day."

Steam rose lazily from the mugs. "Sugar's on the table," Sam said, pointing with her forehead to the bowl in front of him. "I've got milk if you need it."

"No thanks," Jonathan said. Ordinarily, he did drink his coffee with cream, but he didn't want her waiting on him. For today, black would do just fine.

Sam took the seat across from Jonathan, and as she settled in, he pushed the stack of bills over to her. She made no effort to touch them. "What are you *really* about, Mr. Harris? Is that even your real name?"

"It's real enough," he hedged. "And what I'm really about is a very important matter that I can't discuss."

"Where did you come from?"

Jonathan sighed. "Tell you what," he said. "Rather than you asking a lot of questions that I can't answer, let's just stop at me being on the side of the angels."

"Did you rob a bank or something? That's a lot of money. It's a *whole* lot of cash."

"I don't use credit cards for my work," Jonathan said, again with the smile. "And most of what I need to buy costs a lot of money."

Sam looked at the stack of bills more closely. She picked up one of the packets and riffled it, perhaps checking to see if it was real. "This looks like thirty thousand dollars."

"That *is* thirty thousand dollars."

"I don't owe that much on the truck."

Jonathan twitched a shoulder. "Keep the change. For the inconvenience."

Sam scowled deeply. "That's almost six thousand dollars in change. I can't do that."

"Sure you can. I want you to have it. Surely you can use

it. If you're upside down on the car, then you must be upside down on other debts as well. Apply the excess to those."

Sam placed the packet on top of the stack and leaned heavily on her forearms. "This is crazy. Why are you doing this?"

The real answer—the true answer—was that he felt sorry for her. That preserved place setting at the end of the table was testament to the sad, brave story that was being lived every day in tens of thousands of households around the world. Spouses and children waiting for their husbands and fathers to return from war. It pained Jonathan that this particular warrior would return to poverty, perhaps with only a few short months before his next deployment. Jonathan could afford to pay off every debt owed by thousands of such families, and this particular one happened to be within reach.

But he'd share none of that with this young mother, lest his altruism come off as creepy. Instead, he explained, "I need to buy time. I need you to feel fairly compensated so that you don't pick up a phone and call the police as soon as I leave."

Sam considered that. He could see that her defenses were weakening. "This must mean that you're intending to use the truck for a crime. I don't want to be any part of that."

"It doesn't mean that at all. If someone comes and asks, tell them that you sold the vehicle to a stranger who offered you full price. If push comes to shove, you'll have the record from the paid-off repo guy that he got his money. The paper trail will work for you."

"Until you get caught and testify against me."

Generally, it wasn't this difficult to give a generous gift. "I never said that I was going to do anything illegal. You assumed that I was, and I gave you a good cover. Hypothetically, though, if lawbreaking were on my mind, the last thing I would do is throw you under the bus."

Sam clearly had no idea what she should do.

"Think about it, Sam," Jonathan said, closing the deal. "Is there really much choice to be made here?"

Turns out there wasn't.

CHAPTER NINETEEN

The faded sign, no doubt handmade with what appeared to be a child's wood-burning kit, had been nailed to a tree, and likely would have been invisible if they'd arrived in the dark. The sign read NATHAN BEDFORD FOREST MOBILE HOME PARK. A cluster of rural-style mailboxes teetered underneath it.

"Aren't there supposed to be two Rs in Forrest?" Gail asked, leaning forward in the backseat, so that her head was between Boxers and Jonathan, who occupied the driver and shotgun seats respectively.

Jonathan chuckled. "I guess it depends on whether you're talking about the person or a place."

Boxers asked, "What person?"

"Nathan Bedford Forrest," Gail said. "Father of the Ku Klux Klan."

"Charming guy to name a neighborhood after," the Big Guy grunted.

He piloted the big Dodge down a narrow wooded road until it opened up on a cluster of sad, aged house trailers, probably dating back to the 1960s. Jonathan could almost smell the mildew from all the way out here. He counted seven units altogether. Despite their weatherworn appearance, most appeared to be well cared for. Each of the mobile homes sat on what appeared to be a half acre of land, and showed the remnants of gardens out front. Two had already put up Christmas decorations, the most elaborate of which involved red foil and a wreath on the door.

"Which one belongs to Stacy Phelps?" Gail asked.

Jonathan said, "I've got the address one one seven, but I don't see any house numbers." He relayed the question into his radio, and Venice answered right away. "All the way to the end on the right," he repeated. "By the way, Mother Hen, anything on ICIS about our borrowed vehicle?"

"Not yet," she said. "I'll keep monitoring and let you know."

Jonathan had considered dropping the Dodge off somewhere and stealing a second vehicle, but he'd gotten a good vibe from Sam.

"So how are we working this?" Gail wanted to know. "Are we just going to knock on her door?"

"That's my vote," Jonathan said. "Box?"

Boxers shrugged. "It's a little boring, but it'll do. I think we should kill the phone first."

"Agreed." Jonathan turned to Gail. "I'm going to badge her when she answers the door, but I want you to do the talking."

Gail made a motorboat sound in her throat. "I hate it when you use the badge," she said.

Jonathan and Boxers exchanged looks, but they didn't comment. Their FBI credentials weren't as false as most of their kind. Fact was, the Bureau occasionally found itself in positions where they shouldn't be, with a requirement to go where they shouldn't go. When those occasions arose, Security Solutions was always on the short list of contractors to clean up the mess, and the creds came in handy. In return, the people who counted at Bureau headquarters agreed to look the other way when Jonathan needed them for his own purposes. It wasn't as if they had a lot of options, after all.

No one relished the idea of Jonathan Grave speaking in open court about the things he knew.

The ultimate irony, of course, was that Gail had actually been a sworn agent of the FBI, but she had no credentials, and refused to allow Jonathan to have some made up for her.

Boxers parked the Dodge out front of Stacy Phelps's mobile home, its bumper nearly touching the trunk of her eight-year-old Celica, blocking her ability to drive away. All three climbed out together, but Jonathan and Gail hung around the vehicle while Boxers went around back.

Thirty seconds later, the bud in Jonathan's right ear delivered Boxers' report that the phones had been disabled. He'd hang around back there to cover the black side of the building, just in case.

The steps to the stoop were too narrow to accommodate both of them, so Jonathan led the way and rapped on the door. He did it heavily, using the heel of his fist rather than his knuckles. When you're pretending to be a law enforcement officer, the last thing you worry about is stealth. For them, it's all about intimidation, and it begins with the knock on the door.

When the door remained unanswered thirty seconds later, he pounded again. A moment later, he heard movement, and then two locks slid and the door opened a crack, revealing the sleep-puffed face of a woman in her twenties. "Who do you think—"

Jonathan held his badge in the open door crack. "Special Agent Harris, FBI," he said. "Are you Stacy Phelps?"

Stacy's anger morphed to confusion. Maybe to fear. "I'm Stacy Phelps. What's wrong?"

"May we come in?" Jonathan asked.

"Why?" she asked. Then, as an afterthought: "We?"

Jonathan pivoted his body so that she could see Gail at the bottom of the stairs. "That's Special Agent Nichols."

Gail gave a curt nod, but otherwise didn't move. She had her game face on. "You don't look like an FBI agent," Stacy said.

Jonathan acknowledged his woodland cammies with a glance. "Never judge a book by its cover," he said. "Out here, all respect, might as well wear a target on your chest as wear a necktie. I'd really rather talk inside."

Stacy stepped aside and left room for the two of them to enter. "I'd offer you some coffee," she said, "but I don't have any made. I work nights and I was sleeping."

"Yes, ma'am," Gail said. "We know you do."

Stacy paled. She had an undernourished, overworked look to her—long, stringy black hair that needed a wash—and why wouldn't it after a long night at work? What Jonathan noticed most were the dark circles under her eyes. They didn't impress him as the transient variety that would go away with a night's sleep.

"Y-you know I work nights?" she stammered. "Why would the FBI be interested in knowing my work schedule?"

Rule one of negotiations: Control the conversation by asking all the questions. Gail said, "You received a phone call during your last shift from a young man who reported a kidnapping. Do you remember that?"

Stacy physically reeled at the question. Her eyes grew wide and her mouth dropped a little. Her lips seemed to want to say something, but no words came out.

"Let's sit down, Stacy," Jonathan offered, gesturing to her living room with its sofa and two chairs. They no doubt had been sold as a set, all three of them sharing identical beige fabric that reminded Jonathan of an old sport coat in his closet back home.

He led the way and she followed, with Gail bringing up the rear. She chose the sofa and seemed startled when Gail joined her on the adjacent cushion.

Jonathan said, "In answering Agent Nichols's questions, please remember that it's a felony to lie to a federal officer. If you do that, I won't hesitate to put you in handcuffs and take you out of here." Since he was playing the bad cop—another gambit that always worked, despite the cliché—he figured he might as well get into character early.

"We have no interest in arresting you, Stacy," Gail said. "But Agent Harris is right. We'll do what we have to do. Now about that phone call."

"Who told you?" Stacy looked as if she was living her worst nightmare. Exactly as Jonathan had hoped.

"You need to ask less and answer more," Gail said. "A young man named Ryan Nasbe called at roughly one-twelve this morning asking to be rescued. Do you remember that?"

Stacy's head twitched.

"Please answer verbally for me," Gail said.

"Yes," she said. "I remember."

"Thank you. What came of that call?"

Stacy broke gaze and shifted in her seat. This was a woman who should never play poker. "What do you mean, what came of it?"

"Is this the way it's going to be, Stacy?" Jonathan said. "You're going to make us re-ask every question so that you can buy time to make up a lie?"

Terror. "No, I swear. I'm not doing that."

"Stacy, look at me," Gail said. "Just tell us what happened."

"I-I don't want any trouble."

"Of course you don't. Neither do we. All we want to do is gather information. There's nothing wrong with that, is there?"

"I-I suppose not."

"There's no trouble to be caused by the truth, is there?" Gail pressed. "The truth will set you free."

"And a lie will get your butt thrown in jail," Jonathan said, drawing an impatient look from Gail. Okay, maybe he was laying it on a little thick.

"What happened after you received that call?" Gail asked. She gently touched Stacy's knee to draw attention away from Jonathan and signal that she was trustworthy.

Stacy's lip trembled. Her hands, too. Tears balanced on her lids as her eyes searched the room for something to look at other than her visitors.

"Stacy?"

She bolted to her feet, startling them both. Jonathan's hand moved toward his .45. Right away, though, it was obvious she meant no harm. She just couldn't sit. "I knew this would happen," Stacy said. "I am so sorry that I ever got involved in any of it."

Gail shot a quick look to Jonathan that said, *Now this is interesting.*

"Please sit down, Stacy," Gail said. "You make us nervous when you jump up like that."

"I knew it, knew it, *knew* it."

"Knew what, Stacy?" The rule book said it was important to use the other person's name as often as possible in a negotiation. It was a trick that salesmen have known since the beginning of time. "Tell us what you knew."

"What do you think?" she spat. She brought her hands to her head, her fingers lost in her twisted hair. "I knew that someone would catch on."

"Catch on to what?"

"What do you think? To the Army."

Gail checked silently with Jonathan to see if any of this made sense to him. It didn't.

"Sit, Stacy," Gail said, more forcefully this time. It was the command you'd use for a dog. "Sit, settle down, and start from the beginning."

Stacy just stood there, her right hand in her hair, the other on her hip, staring out the front window. Jonathan recognized it as a posture of angst. She was trying to decide between doing right or wrong. Gail started to say something, but Jonathan raised a hand. They needed to give her a minute.

Her right hand dropped to her hip. "Screw it," Stacy said. "Fine. This is long overdue anyway."

As she started back to the sofa, she froze in her tracks and craned her neck. "There's a huge man in my backyard," she said. "He's armed."

"He's with us," Jonathan said. He pressed the transmit

button that was located just out of sight up his left sleeve—
his non-gun hand. "We're secure here, Big Guy. You can
come in."

"You're *secure*?" Stacy repeated. She seemed aghast.
"Secure from what?"

"Focus, Stacy," Gail said. "Come. Sit. Start from the beginning. What is it that is coming apart?"

Stacy retook her seat next to Gail. Exactly per the plan,
she was hopelessly confused. None of her world made sense
right now, and confusion always played to the benefit of in-
terrogators.

"You said something about the Army. Are you talking
about the United States Army?"

"The Army of God. It's a nutso group of paramilitary
types here in the county. They're like all the groups you hear
about in the news. I don't know that they do any harm, but
they're just creepy. Every now and then, one of the soldiers—that's what they call themselves—tries to get away.
Not often, but occasionally."

Boxers entered the home without knocking, and effectively filled the opening. Stacy drew an inch or two closer to
Gail, who again put a reassuring hand on her leg. "Really,
he's okay," Gail said. "So what happens when they try to get
away?"

"If they call us, we're instructed to tell the sheriff right
away."

Gail produced her speckled composition notebook from a
pouch pocket in her cammies and opened it. "What is the
sheriff's name?"

"Neen. Kendig Neen." She brought her hands to her face.
"Oh, God, I'm going to be in so much trouble for this."

"And what does Sheriff Neen do with the information?"

Stacy wiped away a tear. "It's not as if he reports to me,
you know? I mean, it's the other way around."

"I understand."

"I don't know the details. All I know is I tell him, and
then the problem seems to go away."

Jonathan leaned in closer. "What does 'go away' mean?"

The longer the interview went, the smaller Stacy seemed to become. "I mean that I just never hear any more about them. The problem just . . . goes away." Clearly, it was the only way she knew to phrase it.

"Does that mean that the children also went away?" Gail asked.

Stacy's eyes darted up. "Oh, they weren't all children. In fact, this is the first one who was a child. That's why I thought it was so, well, sad."

Jonathan was confused. "You mean to tell me that you get calls from adults seeking help from a kidnapping, and you routinely do nothing to stop it?"

"No, no. Not at all. Not children and not kidnapping. Just people who want to get away and need help doing it."

Boxers growled, "And you just hang them out to dry." He had a way of making the floor move with his voice when he was pissed.

"It's not like that," Stacy said. Her voice showed deep frustration at not being able to get her point across. "They're all adults over there. Or adults with children. It's like a closed community. As far as I know, no one's kept against their will. It's just that sometimes, I guess, people want to be somewhere else.

"When we get the call, we turn it over to Sheriff Neen, who himself is pretty active in the Army—or at least he seems to be. He goes out and I guess he talks to them, and then there's no problem anymore. It's like an internal matter. A family matter."

Gail said, "But in last night's call, Ryan Nasbe said specifically that he and his mother had been kidnapped. He also said that his kidnappers had killed those people on the bridge in Virginia. Surely you heard about that."

Stacy wiped her eyes again.

"Didn't you think for a minute to call the police or something?"

"We *are* the police, ma'am. Out here, we're all there is."

"The front of every phone book lists the number for the FBI," Jonathan said.

Her whole body seemed to sag now. "I'm a dispatcher, Agent Harris. I'm not a sworn officer. I do what I'm told, and in this case, I was told to tell Sheriff Neen and forget about it." She turned to Gail. "And how do you know so much about this call, anyway?"

Gail ignored her. "Where do we find Sheriff Neen?"

Stacy squinted as she looked at the clock on the far wall. Red marks on the side of her nose testified to glasses that she had neglected to put on. "I imagine he's still at home asleep. He usually gets into the office around nine."

"And where's the headquarters for this Army of God?"

"The headquarters or the compound?"

Jonathan waited for it.

"Well, they're different places," Stacy explained. "The man in charge of the Army is Michael Copley, and the—"

"He owns a factory here," Jonathan interrupted, recalling the reference from Sam Shockley.

"Appalachian Acoustics, right. He runs everything there, or so I'm told. So I guess the headquarters would be at his house. His castle, really. The place is huge. But the compound itself is all the way at the end of Hooper Road. Do you know Hooper Road?"

"I'm sure we can find it," Gail said.

"Maybe not," Stacy corrected. "I don't think it's on any map. Anyway, the camp—or the compound, or whatever you call it—is huge. Must be a hundred acres. Maybe even more."

"And that land is owned by this Copley guy, too?" Jonathan asked. Venice would verify all of it later, but he was curious what Stacy would say.

"I guess he owns it." She shrugged. "I never really thought about it. He owns an awful lot out here. Anyway, there must be a couple of miles of fencing around it, and there are armed guards."

That got all of their attentions. "*How* armed?" Boxers asked.

"Pretty darned armed. Rifles and such. Or so I'm told."

"And that didn't impress you as odd?" Gail asked.

"Everything about them impresses me as odd," Stacy said. "Start with the fact that they think they're an army. As if we need another one of those. You hear shooting and stuff from up there all the time. Sheriff Neen says they have one of the best target ranges he's ever seen. Him and the deputies shoot up there all the time."

"And the soldiers?" Jonathan pressed. "Do they shoot up there, too?"

"I imagine. Why else have a range?"

"What are they arming up against?"

"I have no idea. Maybe just to keep people out. I've never heard them make any threats or anything. Plus, they've got those government contracts, so they can't be but so far out there."

Jonathan raised a hand to seek clarification. "Appalachian Acoustics has the contracts, right? Not the Army of God."

Stacy nodded. "Right. Not that there's a lot of difference. Most of the employees—maybe all of them—are members of the Army and they live on the campgrounds. It's like the old days when the mines provided housing and the company store."

Jonathan remembered Sam Shockley mentioning that she had recently been laid off from the factory. "Has the Army of God always run the factory?"

"They've always been involved, as far as I know, but not like they are now. Lots of folks in this area lost their jobs when Copley decided to bring everything in-house."

"Is the factory on the compound?" Boxers asked.

"Might as well be. There might be a fence or a road or something separating them, but for all intents and purposes they're on the same property."

"Have you ever been up there?" Gail asked.

"Good heavens, no. That is one secure place. More fences, more guns. I think it has to do with their government contracts."

Or their paranoia, Jonathan didn't say. "What exactly are they contracted to do for the government?"

Another annoying shrug. "Make stuff, I guess. Whatever stuff they make. What does any of this have to do with the phone call from the boy? Is he somebody special?"

Jonathan said, "He is now."

CHAPTER TWENTY

Ryan tried to find a comfortable position in the straight-back wood-and-leather chair, but it wasn't possible. It was a dining room chair—the kind you'd find only in a very rich man's house. The chair back was framed in wood, but with a black leather panel that ran down the length of his spine. They'd run his arms through the openings on either side of the panel, and then fastened metal handcuffs to his wrists way too tightly. The only way for him to take the pressure off the bones of his wrists was to shove his arms all the way through the openings, up to the bends in his elbows. To do that, though, meant pressing his forearms through some very narrow spaces. Sure, he was skinny, but there was a limit.

Even as the sheriff pulled up to the front of the house to drop him off, Ryan had sensed that trouble was on the way. First, there'd been the way the sheriff had been acting all during their ride, after he'd picked him up; but the real fear didn't hit him until he saw the guards dressed in black on the front porch.

He was tired of guards dressed in black. Apparently, everybody in West Virginia was a terrorist.

When Sheriff Neen looked at him, Ryan sensed that he even felt a little apologetic.

"Why are you doing this?" Ryan had asked.

"It's a new world, son," he'd said. "And it appears that you just got sucked up into it."

He'd allowed himself to be cuffed without a fight, partly out of sheer exhaustion, but mostly out of a hopeless sense that he'd been rendered powerless.

So here he sat trussed like a Thanksgiving turkey in the middle of some rich guy's dining room, sucked up into a steaming pile of bad news, while on the other side of closed doors on the opposite side of the house, two men yelled at each other.

Ryan couldn't make out the words, but there wasn't a doubt in his mind that whatever was being said, the anger was about him.

Michael Copley's mind reeled at the multiple layers of incompetence. Kendig Neen sat comfortably in the leather club chair next to the fireplace in Brother Michael's office, his legs crossed while he casually fingered the waxed edge of his mustache.

The son of a jackal didn't even have the decency to show remorse. "What do you have to say for yourself?" Copley challenged.

Neen seemed to ponder that, and then said, "You're welcome?"

Copley felt his ears redden. Neen had always worn an arrogant streak, but this was too much. "Excuse me?" He sharpened his tone to sound as menacing as he could.

Neen cleared his throat and said more loudly, "You're welcome. You know, for bringing the boy back in safely and stopping this publicity hunt of yours from turning into a disaster."

Copley felt himself breathing heavily. "You arrogant prick," he said. "He's a boy, and he escaped from the prison *you* set up, after getting past the guards that *you* trained."

"Which in both cases never should have existed in the first place."

"We're at *war*, Brother Kendig," Copley bellowed.

"On two fronts," Neen bellowed back, matching the tone exactly. "One of which should never have been opened."

"That is not for you to decide! The Board of Elders decided that now was the time—"

"I'm on the Board of Elders, remember?" Neen said. He'd modulated his voice back to the late-night-DJ tone that suited him so well. "And with few yet notable exceptions, the elders are your lapdogs. If you asked them to stick needles in their eyes, three quarters of them would do it without questioning the wisdom of blindness."

Brother Michael took a deep breath to yell, but settled himself. Spiking his blood pressure would help no one and change nothing. "We've had this discussion before, Brother Kendig. That you disagree with the opinion of the majority does not grant you authority to disregard their decision."

"Which is why I established a prison room on the compound and why I trained a contingent of guards."

"Yet their performance was abysmal."

"I don't know that that's true," Neen said. "I mean, clearly, something went wrong if the boy was able to get away, but I have no idea yet what that something might have been. I'm told that the guard who was supposed to be on duty—Brother Stephen—is in fact missing."

"Where—"

"I don't know where. But Brother Michael, you have to understand that this is yet another case where you refuse to acknowledge that actions have consequences."

Copley scoffed, "Certainly it's plain that investing in guard training has the consequence of incompetence."

"And what about the panic you instilled in that family by making them read a statement to the world that they would be executed? Do you think maybe that increased their desire to get out, and therefore made them take chances that they otherwise never would?"

"We needed symbols—"

"To hell with the symbols, Michael," Neen blurted.

The words hit Copley like a hammer. "How dare you?"

Neen laughed. "How dare *you*? Don't you think that the trail of dead bodies across the country is enough of a symbol? Do you really think that we need the image of a mother and her child to make people any more frightened than they already are?"

"You pretend to know the entire plan, Brother Kendig," Copley said. "You do not. All of this plays an important role."

"I know more than you think I do. I know that the importance of the GSA contract for your company reaches far beyond the revenue that it will generate. We're *this close*, Brother Michael, to accomplishing all that we've fought so long to achieve. We can bring the disunited states of America back to its roots. We can tear it away from the money grubbers and the Users."

"It's not that we *can*, Brother Kendig. It's that we *will*."

Neen gave a little wave to concede the point. "Fine. Absolutely. We *will* succeed. Just as you said. But we can do it without the grandstanding for the cameras."

Copley eased himself into the chair opposite the one occupied by Neen. "I heard the recording, Brother Kendig," he said. "I know who this boy's father is. He's one of the very people who is bringing so much misery to the world." He leaned back in his chair and crossed his ankles as he interlaced his fingers across his chest. "His father is a U.S. soldier. Special Forces."

Neen became suspicious, cocking his head to the side. "What's your point?"

"He is the point on the sword," Copley said. "He leads the fighting that creates all the evil. We have an opportunity to show the world that no one is safe. Not even their most elite warriors."

Neen waited for the rest.

"Think of the spectacle. We can hold a public trial and stream it to the world."

"No," Neen said. "God, no, Michael, you can't go there. You can't even think that way."

Was that weakness he saw in the sheriff's face? Fear on the countenance of Kendig Neen?

"This is what I was talking about," Neen said. His voice grew louder. "This is the hubris that will be our undoing."

"You're out of your mind," Copley fired back. "This is what will make the Movement famous throughout the world."

"As the stupidest thing done in a generation. Have you forgotten nine-eleven?"

"Don't patronize me, Brother Kendig. That was a botched effort by a bunch of amateur—"

"It rallied three hundred million people to go to war!" Neen boomed. "The greatest mistake those jihadists made was to deliver a symbol to the media. The symbol becomes manipulated and what is righteous becomes evil."

Copley smiled. "And that is exactly the point, is it not? They think that we are those very jihadists."

"But sooner or later, you're going to have to reveal the truth. After the world rallies behind us—once the government is exposed in all its weakness, and they realize that it is safe to rise up against the true evildoers in Washington—this business of harming a soldier's family will be all that people remember."

Copley sighed. How could a man so smart be so naïve? "What you're missing, Kendig, is that—"

A knock on the door interrupted them. It was louder than it should have been and more rapid than normal. That spoke of a problem, Copley thought. "Come," he said.

The door opened to reveal Brother Duane—one of the elders—towering in the frame next to Sister Colleen, whose red eyes betrayed the fact that she had been crying.

"What is it?" Copley asked.

"I'm afraid we have some terrible news," Brother Duane said.

A door slammed down the hall, and Ryan heard the sound of heavy feet in the hallway. They were coming toward him, and they were many. His heart rate spiked as he did his best to straighten himself in his seat, but his arms remained pinioned behind him and threaded through the chair.

They appeared in the archway as a group—Ryan counted seven of them—and all but the sheriff who'd brought him here wore the same heavy black boots as the men who stormed their prison room. This time, though, there were no masks. Among them, he recognized the bitch they'd picked up in the car a hundred years ago. Or maybe it was only a day.

They formed a kind of wedge in the space that separated the dining room from the hallway, anchored in the middle by a thirtysomething blond man who looked angrier than anyone Ryan had ever seen. If the wedge were an arrowhead, the angry man would have been the point. The others were angry, too; but that anchor guy was scary.

If Ryan wasn't mistaken, the only girl in the group—her name was Cathleen, wasn't it? No, but something like that—looked less angry than the others. In fact, she mostly looked scared.

The man said, "You're a murderer."

"I'm not," Ryan said. "That asshole attacked my mother."

The man closed the distance that separated them in four long strides. He was still moving when he unleashed a wicked open-handed smack across Ryan's face. He smelled blood instantly, and within seconds, streams were flowing from both nostrils.

"You will not use that language in my house!" the man bellowed.

"That's what he is," Ryan said. He wanted to sound defiant, but he ended up having to cough blood from his throat.

He needed to spit, but he knew that would be trouble. If you're not allowed to say "asshole," then spitting blood on the carpet was a non-starter. "He was trying to rape her," he said.

Maybe the next slap hurt more because it landed with more force. Or maybe it just landed in exactly the same spot. Either way, it made a purple strobe flash behind his eyes as something bounced around inside his head.

Maybe it knocked him out, because the next thing Ryan knew, he was sideways on the floor, carpet against his face. He was vaguely aware that the carpet was for sure stained now.

". . . kill him," someone said. Ryan thought it was the sheriff, and his tone sounded more like a warning than a suggestion. Anyway, it didn't scare him.

"No one fouls the name of a brave warrior in my presence."

"Get him up, for heaven's sake," the sheriff said.

Hands were on him, pulling and lifting, and a lightning bolt of pain shot through Ryan's right arm, from wrist to elbow, launching a howl that to him sounded like it was coming from someone else.

"Look what you did," the sheriff said. "You broke his arm."

Oh, shit, Ryan thought. *They broke my arm?* Then his head cleared. *Oh, shit. They broke my arm!*

"Ow!" he yelled. Then he shrieked it as they continued to lift him, still tied to the chair. As he shifted in his seat, the bones shifted under the skin and it felt like they were tearing off his arm like a drumstick. "Stop! Stop! Oh, God, please stop!"

Things flashed behind his eyes again, but this time he didn't think it was because he was being hit. He thought it was just the pain. He'd felt pain before, but this was something new. This was Technicolor pain, sharper and brighter than anything he'd felt before, like the difference between

Dorothy in Kansas and Dorothy in Oz. *And what a weird analogy*, he thought.

But they kept manhandling him. Finally, he just screamed—as close to the sound of the scared-shitless lady in a horror movie as he could get without cutting his balls off.

"Stop!" a new voice boomed. "Take the handcuffs off. My God, I'm going to get sick if I watch his arm bend any more."

My arm is bending? He screamed again.

They lowered him back to the floor, and they must have really bent it because there was another flash of light, and an instant later, he was back in the chair with both hands free, except his right one was propped on a pillow that had been placed on his lap. The arm didn't look right at all. His hand and his wrist were already swelling, and his forearm looked funny under the fabric of his clothes. The lines weren't straight anymore.

Someone was holding him in the chair by his shoulders.

"Are you awake now?" the sheriff asked. The big man had taken a knee in front of Ryan, and was looking him in the eyes. "I think he's okay now," he said over his shoulders to the others who had gathered around.

Ryan had expected at least a small look of sympathy from the gathered terrorists, but he got nothing of the sort. If anything, they looked even more pissed than before. They all stared, but none of them seemed to know what they wanted.

The sensible part of Ryan—the one that desperately wanted the pain to stop, and to just be left alone—knew that this was the time to be quiet, but the other part of him—the one that was pissed off and humiliated—overruled.

"I wasn't lying," he said. It wasn't until he tried to talk that he realized that blood had actually dried in the back of his mouth, leaving a kind of crust back there. "Your guy— Brother Stephen, I think was his name—attacked my mother."

"It's true," the girl with the K-name said.

The point man—Ryan assumed him to be the leader since

he was the guy who owned this big house—shot an angry look at her. "You were there?" he asked.

"I was there when they found his body," she said. She looked at the floor. "He was . . . *exposed*."

"That's not proof," Point Man scoffed. "They could have done that to him to make it look like he was trying to attack."

What, like I'm going to pull out some guy's dick? Ryan thought.

"I think that's a stretch, Brother Michael," the sheriff said.

So the leader's name was Brother Michael.

The comment drew another angry glare.

"Don't look at me that way," the sheriff said. "How likely do you think it is that they would really do that? Why would they?"

"So that they could escape," Brother Michael said.

"And why would Brother Stephen have been in their room to allow that to happen?"

Owned you, dude, Ryan didn't say. He winced against a twitch of pain in his arm.

Brother Michael's face went blank, but then he came back. "Even if that were true, that doesn't grant permission for prisoners to execute their guards."

"I didn't execute anyone," Ryan said. The words were out before he could stop them. Once launched, what was the sense of pulling back? "I couldn't even see what I was doing. I just launched on him and tackled him. I guess I grabbed him around the neck and twisted it. We hit the ground, and when I got up, he didn't. It was kind of an accident."

Brother Michael seemed to swell for a moment. Clearly, Ryan had said the wrong thing, but for the life of him, he didn't know what it could have been.

"Where's my mother?" Ryan asked.

"You will pay," Brother Michael said in a tone so soft that Ryan could barely hear him. He leaned close, so that only inches separated their noses.

Ryan broke first, shifting his eyes to stare at a point on the floor.

"Look at me," Brother Michael said. He placed his hand on the boy's bad arm, right on the break, and he squeezed.

Ryan howled as a spike of pain rocketed not just through his arm, but somehow through his whole body.

"Brother Michael!" Sheriff Neen boomed.

He squeezed tighter. "With God as my witness, you will pay dearly."

The sheriff stepped in front of Brother Michael, breaking his grip on Ryan's arm, but not before the bones moved and the agony topped a new height.

"Stop this!" Neen boomed.

But Brother Michael's eyes never left Ryan. It was as if he'd gone to a crazy place in his mind. He lunged for the boy again, but Neen restrained him.

"Get him out of here," the sheriff commanded to the room.

"Where do we take him?"

"Somewhere other than here," Neen barked. "This is out of control. Take him to the basement. No windows this time, and I want guards posted at the doors around the clock."

A crowd moved closer.

"Don't touch me," Ryan said. "Please, God, don't touch me. I'll come along." Oh so gently, he slipped his left forearm under his right to splint the break, and then he stood. Movement was excruciating, and he thought he might pass out. His legs got wobbly, and some of the color drained from his vision.

When a hand grabbed him under his good arm, the touch was surprisingly gentle. It was K-girl again. "We'll just take it slow," she said.

CHAPTER TWENTY-ONE

They left Stacy Phelps quivering in her slippers over a threat to throw her in jail for obstruction of justice if she breathed a word of what they'd discussed. They also dropped a hint that they were actively listening and watching everything she did. Given their inside knowledge of Ryan Nasbe's phone call, she was primed to believe every word.

Back at the command post, Boxers fired up the audio-video satellite link and brought Venice into the loop on what they had learned. She, then, started tickling electrons in cyberspace to get them something to go on.

"No Army of God has any charity status within the IRS," she reported. "But they do have status as a private school."

"What does that mean?" Jonathan asked.

"Which of those words didn't make sense to you?"

"No one likes a smart-ass, Ms. Alexander."

"Says the pot to the kettle," Venice teased. "Among other things, it means that there are children there. But when I dig a little deeper, I can't find anyone ever graduating from it. And before you ask, that means that it's an odd kind of school. Who'd want to enroll their kids in a school that has no record of advancement? And I mean *no* record. We don't even know who the attendees are. Of course, we don't know who the parents are, either."

Gail raised her hand, as if this were a classroom. "Not necessarily as unusual as you might think," she said. Until that moment, Jonathan had forgotten that Gail was involved with the Branch Davidian raid in Waco back in the day. She had street cred when it came to cults and nut-job militias. "They establish a school so that the government can't use truancy as an excuse to shut them down. They don't register their children for the record because they don't have to. For a lot of these groups, the driving goal is to remain invisible all the time."

"So why no graduation?" Boxers prompted.

Gail offered a one-shoulder shrug. "I can't say for sure, but we investigated a Utah group that made it a point of faith never to leave the compound where they lived and bred. We're talking two or three generations here that had never been beyond the fence."

Boxers gaped. "You're shitting me. Who would agree to that?"

Venice wondered, "Is it that much different from any exclusive and devout religious sect? If it's not physically isolating, it can certainly be intellectually isolating."

"This is irrelevant," Jonathan said. "I doubt that they've got the Nasbes in the school with everyone else. What we need is to find out where they do have them, and then get them out."

Venice said, "I took the liberty of asking Lee Burns to retask SkysEye to give us a picture, but he warns that it's going to take longer than normal. He happens to be swamped, but he'll get us a link as soon as he can."

Jonathan said, "Did you emphasize—"

"—that a life is in the balance, yes. I didn't, however, mention the link to your friend Boomer. You didn't give me permission, and I know that it's sensitive."

"Maybe you should," Boxers said.

Jonathan shook his head. "No, if Lee could do it, he would. Add Boomer to the mix, and it just adds guilt."

"So, what are our options?" Boxers asked, clearly disagreeing. "Slinging a little guilt seems like a way better option than knocking on doors. 'Excuse me,'" he mocked, "'but are you harboring any kidnapped families? We'd like ever so much to have them back.'"

"There's always another way," Jonathan said.

"What about Rollins?" Gail asked.

"Absolutely not," Boxers said. "I'm not gonna be beholding to him for nothin'."

"Seems like a way better option than knocking on doors," she countered with a smirk. "What is the big problem between you all anyway?"

"No," Jonathan said, effectively shutting down the issue. "We're not discussing that. Not here. Not now." He steadied himself with a big breath. "Ven, you've got Rollins's card. Get him on the horn."

Venice didn't hesitate as she disappeared off screen to work a different phone.

Boxers seemed to expand with anger.

"Dig—"

"Mission first, Box," he said. "Everything is second to the mission. The Nasbes need every resource we can muster. Period. Ven?"

"I'm patching him through now," she said. Then, almost at a whisper: "It's like he was waiting for us." There was a click, then: "You're on with Digger and the team, Colonel."

"Is the line secure?" Rollins asked.

"Encrypted," Venice said. "That's why I placed the call. We're scrambling it."

Which meant, Jonathan knew, that anyone who had access to the right technology, and wanted the information badly enough would be able to listen to and understand anything they wanted to.

"This is your op, Grave," the colonel said. "Tell me what you need."

It took Jonathan all of ten minutes to do just that.

Christyne was in a place beyond fear, beyond terror or despair. She was terrified for herself, and she was terrified for Ryan. Clearly, he had been caught, and no one would tell her what had been done with him. No one would tell her anything about anything, in fact. After the smash and grab in her little cell of a room in the basement, she'd lost consciousness.

When she awoke, she was blind, although she was fairly certain it was from something wrapped around her eyes, rather than the actual loss of her sight. Her eyes felt glued down, and when she squinted, she could feel the stickiness on her cheeks, too. In her mind, she'd been bound with duct tape, but how could she know for sure?

Her arms had been bound, as well—behind her, and so tightly that her hands were numb. Her feet were likewise tied together, as were her knees. The net effect was a near-total paralysis that had quickly morphed into an ache and then a screaming pain in her shoulders, hips, neck, and knees. She believed that she was lying on her left side, but even that was not a certainty. Such was the disorientation that comes from having no visual reference to key off of.

The surface on which she lay was hard, but not especially cold, and from time to time, when she heard a door open or close, the sound seemed to echo, leading her to believe that she was in a big room, or maybe just one with a tall ceiling. If the thought weren't so absurd, she might have guessed that she was inside a church.

Wherever they'd deposited her, they'd made sure that her head was unsupported, and that her body was under constant strain. If they were going to kill her, she wished they'd just hurry up and get it over with. She supposed those are the thoughts of every torture victim.

The door opened again, seemingly far away, and this time it remained open for a long time—long enough for the cold air from outside to roll to her, triggering a chill. When the door finally closed, the room returned to silence again.

Then there were footsteps.

They sounded heavy, so she assumed them to belong to a man. Clearly, they were approaching her, each tick of sound just slightly louder than the one that preceded it. He said nothing as he approached, and his gait seemed abnormally slow, as if he were intentionally trying to intimidate her. It was working.

When the footsteps finally stopped, they seemed very close. When he remained silent, Christyne wondered if it was a test of wills to see who would speak first. "Who's there?" she asked.

"You killed one of my soldiers," the man said.

Christyne said nothing. She'd heard this tone only a few times in her life, and it was always tied to impending violence. She sensed that nothing she said could take the edge off his anger.

"Do you have anything to say for yourself?" he asked.

"Where is Ryan? Where is my son?"

The man let out a roar, an animal sound of pure anger or perhaps anguish. It shook the room, and continued to echo for a full second when he had finished. "Is that really all you have to offer?" he shouted. "Is that really all you have to say after you murder one of my best men? You want to know what became of the man who murdered him?"

"He didn't murder him!" Christyne cried. Something inside her seemed to have broken, and her own anguish poured out in her words. "Your soldier was attacking me. Ryan protected me. He didn't intend to kill that young man. Ryan couldn't hurt a soul. Please don't hurt him."

Silence returned, and then the footsteps started approaching her again. They were smaller steps this time, and as he got very near to her, she thought perhaps that she could see a shadow fall across her eyes.

"So it *was* he who killed him," the man said. "Thank you for verifying that."

"No," she said quickly. "That's not what I meant." Her heart and her brain both raced to find a way to undo the damage. How could she have been so stupid? "I didn't mean that he was the one who killed him."

"But that's what you said."

"I know. I—" Words were gone now, replaced with blind fear and guilt and shame. She heard herself sobbing, trying to beg for mercy, but all that came out was noise.

"That's all right," the man said. His tone took a softer edge to it. "It wouldn't have mattered in the end. Dead is dead, and someone has to pay."

"Not Ryan," Christyne begged. "No, please, please not Ryan. He's just a boy."

"Not anymore," the man said. He place something heavy and wet on the floor near her. It made a dull thump as it hit.

"What?" Christyne begged. "Oh, my God, what is that?" Jesus, was that blood she smelled?

"We'd have killed him anyway," the voice said.

She gasped. *This isn't possible. Please, God, don't let this be possible.*

"I thought you might like to have a chat with him."

"What? What did you do? Oh, my God, what did you do?"

"I brought your son's head to visit you. I thought you two had some things to discuss."

Christyne Nasbe screamed until her throat was raw.

Jonathan and his team killed the next three hours poring over commercial-grade satellite maps of the Army of God compound. The photos were fuzzy at best, but by overlaying them with tax maps and a few ancient permits to tap into public water supplies, they were able to get enough of a rough layout to know that a random assault was out of the question with just the three of them. If they had the three of them times ten, it would still be out of the question without good intelligence on where the Nasbes were being held.

As Sam Shockley had indicated, the compound was huge, and a continuous fence showed clearly through the blur of the substandard imagery. There appeared to be several dozen buildings arranged in a pattern that suggested streets or pathways between them. According to utility company records, the compound had no electrical service on site; but Venice had been able to leverage Yellow Pages leads to tap into the sales records of local vendors who delivered gasoline, diesel, and propane to the compound. The amounts and frequency told Jonathan that the propane was likely used for cooking and the gasoline for fueling vehicles. They would have consumed fifty or maybe a hundred times those quantities if they were powering an electrical plant.

"Looks to me like we got some kind of cult working here," Boxers said, reviewing the data. "They don't appreciate the last hundred fifty years of progress."

"They're also dispatching death squads around the country," Jonathan said. "What is it about the Stone Age that terrorists admire so much?"

Gail looked very concerned by it all. "You make light, Jon, but if the people in there are as armed as we've been told, we're going to need help." Her eyes bored into him. "You're going to hate to hear this, but we're going to have to call in the FBI for this. At a minimum, the West Virginia State Police."

Boxers watched his boss expectantly, not agreeing, but not arguing, either.

"That's the worst thing we can do," Jonathan said. He kept his tone dismissive and authoritative. "We'd expose Security Solutions, we'd go to jail, and all the evidence they gathered would be thrown out because it was tainted by the fact that we violated laws to obtain it. Everybody loses."

"I don't accept that," Gail said. "There has to be a way around. There has to be something other than a suicide mission."

"Whoa, Sheriff," Boxers said. He alternately used her former title as a term of endearment or as a weapon. This time it sounded like the latter. "We don't do suicide missions."

"Are you looking at the same data as I am?" she said, pointing at the map.

"I am," he said. He looked at Jonathan, who looked away to let the Big Guy do a little verbal roaming. "Here's the thing. Once Digger and me start something, we finish it."

"All I'm saying—"

"Let him finish, Gail," Jonathan said sharply.

She looked wounded. Maybe betrayed. Jonathan had never spoken to her like that before.

"All you're saying is surrender before we engage," Boxers said. "You're looking at failure as the only option. That's not the way Digger and I do things. We plan the mission and the extraction as best as we can, and we execute. We've never failed. Not once. One of the reasons for that is that we don't accept that any other outcome is possible."

Gail was stunned. She made a puffing sound that might have been a derisive laugh, and said, "So, you engage in self-delusion."

Boxers started to say something, and then deferred to his boss with a simple glance.

"We engage realities," Jonathan said. "We don't have the luxury of reinforcements, and we don't have the responsibility for arrests. All we have to do is take the good guys from the bad guys. Nothing else matters."

"Even if it means dying."

Jonathan chose his next words carefully. Gail had been a shooter on the FBI's Hostage Rescue Team, and she'd seen her share of firefights both as a sworn officer and as a member of Security Solutions, but she'd never been part of an 0300 mission with Boxers and him, and for the first time, he wondered if she might have become more a liability than an asset.

"Dying doesn't happen to us if we stack the odds enough in our favor, and we get our heads in the right place."

She rolled her eyes.

"Don't do that," Jonathan said. "Please don't do that. We're a couple of hours away from going hot on this op, and I will not tolerate doubt."

"You won't *tolerate* it?" At what point in her life had she started seeking permission from Jonathan Grave?

"That's what I said. Gail, you're damn good at what you do. I've seen you perform in the shit, and I admire the hell out of you, but those times were all reactive. Someone took a shot at you, and you fired back. Tonight might not work that way. The reason why Box and I are still alive is because we don't hesitate to do what needs to be done in support of the mission, and the mission is always one hundred percent about getting the PC home whole and healthy."

He allowed the weight of his words to settle, knowing that she would recognize PC as the acronym for precious cargo, the universal term for hostages needing rescue.

"The quickest way to die is to hesitate," he went on. "Microseconds matter. If the bad guy tickles his trigger before you do, his bullet leaves the muzzle first. After that, nobody has an edge. I need you to tell me that you can shoot first, or I've got to leave you behind."

Gail didn't know what to say. In her world—you know, where the grass is green and the water wet—what Jonathan described was murder. For him, the elements of the law didn't matter because he saw a world that was divided into good and evil, and he could compartmentalize the illegality into irrelevance.

Back when she first met him in the hills of Pennsylvania, just hours before the ground would be littered with blood and bodies, and the world would seem to be on fire, Jonathan had told her with an utterly straight face that he was on the side of the angels. She'd taken such a corny line as prima facie evidence that he was mentally disturbed. Then she witnessed his skills as a warrior, and his warmth and mercy as a human being, and she realized that he was merely stating the truth. That was the moment when she first thought she might be in love with him.

"I won't let you down," she said. She didn't have a clue how she would pull it off, but if it came to a choice between shooting a bad guy in cold blood or letting Jonathan die, the bad guy wouldn't have a chance.

"Has your assistant sent you the satellite images we pulled down?" Rollins asked over the satellite link.

On the screen, Jonathan could see Venice's jaw lock. She was nobody's assistant, and he halfway expected her to tear into the colonel. He admired that she restrained herself. "It's coming up now," she said. "While we wait, can I get you some coffee, or maybe take your shirts to the laundry?"

The team at the CP roared with laughter while Rollins remained silent. Jonathan assumed that he didn't get the joke.

Overall, the image on their computer screen was more or less identical to the one they'd been studying, but with ridiculously greater detail. The trees had been digitally removed by top-secret software, revealing a level of nuance that was at least two generations of sophistication beyond anything Jonathan had seen previously. He said, "Wow," and then was surprised that he'd spoken aloud.

"Wow is right," Rollins said. "See what happens when you leave the Community? I want you to know that we just spent about fifty million taxpayer dollars to get you these pictures. If I wanted to, I could zoom in and count freckles. In a shoot-out, we can mark individual GIs and opfor and track them in real time. We can take any one of them—or more than one of them—and convert the image to ground-level view and beam it to whoever we want. If we've got a shooter in a window waiting for a target, he can watch the computer image of the guy approaching in his left eye while he aims through the scope with his right. He'll have range and windage data dialed into his scope and be able to meet the bad guy with a bullet as soon as he steps into the target window. This shit's amazing technology."

Amazing didn't touch it, Jonathan thought. This was the stuff of science fiction. Rollins's willingness to share it openly with Jonathan's team—and risk a significant prison sentence to do it—told Jonathan that he'd been too distrustful of his former colleague.

The satellite imagery mostly confirmed what they'd already put together, although the compound had roughly twice the number of buildings that Jonathan had estimated.

"Before we get to the audio," Rollins said, "I want to point out a few major features that you're looking at." An orange dot appeared in the middle of the screen. "Do you see my cursor?"

Jonathan said, "Yep."

The cursor moved, and so did the picture. It paused on a spot, flashed once, and then the image grew rapidly, as if they were falling toward the ground, to reveal the head and shoulders of a man standing near a fence. The image flashed again, and the virtual camera swung down to a ground-level view of a man in his twenties dressed in black with an M16 assault rifle slung across his chest. From there, the camera pivoted to reveal individual features on the man's face. You couldn't count the pores in his skin, but you could certainly pick him out of a lineup.

"These are *satellite* images?" Venice asked. Her tone spoke of pure admiration.

"Yes, ma'am," Rollins said. "And please don't ask me for details. You folks are the first people without compartmentalized clearances ever to see this."

Jonathan understood the significance. These guards were well-equipped. "They've got the right toys," he said. "Do we know if they know how to use them?"

"You need to assume they do," Rollins replied. "There appears to be a shooting range there at the facility. I figure why have a range but to teach people how to shoot? I can show it to you if you'd like."

Jonathan shook his head. "Later."

"How many of these guards are there?" Boxers asked.

"I count six, but you're free to do your own analysis. I can only send you a static picture, but it's fully functional. You can zoom in or out as you wish. But first, I want you to really study this guy. Each of the sentries wears the same kit as far as I can tell, and to me it looks like they're not wearing any body armor. Or if they are, it's light and under their coats."

Jonathan nodded and pointed to the screen. "I don't see any reloads, either."

"Look closer," Rollins said. "They've got their mags taped together, 'Nam-style."

Jonathan saw it. Back in the day, soldiers taped ammo mags more or less end-to-end to make for quick reloading during a firefight. The theory was that they would merely flip the empty mag and reinsert the other end to keep the volume of fire intense. In practice, it created more problems than it solved. First of all, the ammo in the bottom mag was always exposed to the elements. In a jungle environment, that meant mud and spiders and assorted junk that would foul the action of the already-cantankerous M16, and in cold weather like this it meant potential accumulations of ice. Plus, in a combat environment, when adrenaline is flowing like a river, flipping a mag is no easy trick with nervous hands.

It did look kinda cool, however, when the guys in the movies did it, and wherever guys are involved, the coolness factor is a very important consideration.

Jonathan noted all of it. The two mags still gave them sixty rounds apiece—a little over three seconds per mag on full-auto, plenty of bullets to create a very bad day—but most inexperienced warriors wasted the first sixty rounds on either the sky or the ground just a few yards in front of their feet. The real takeaway from this photo was the lack of body armor. Jonathan's team would not make a similar mistake. It would be heavy and limit mobility, but he'd already had enough holes blown into him, thank you very much. After the last incident in Pennsylvania, he'd made a promise to himself to keep all of his blood confined to its assigned vessels from now on.

He said, "Okay, Colonel, while you've got the controls, give us a tour of this compound." He figured it was what Rollins was dying to do anyway.

The virtual camera resumed its bird's-eye view again and the ground fell away. From above, they viewed twenty-three well-constructed buildings of various sizes. Frame built and brick veneered, this was a community designed to last. The largest of the buildings—Jonathan guesstimated it to measure thirty by fifty feet—sat in the middle of the occupied acreage and was served by a straight access road that appeared to lead directly from the main gate. Jonathan's money said that the central structure was the church or common meeting hall. Most of the other buildings could well have been houses, maybe fifteen hundred square feet each, and they were arranged in a sharply defined grid pattern, reminding Jonathan of the residential areas of suburbia everywhere.

"Any idea of how many people in total live here?" Jonathan asked.

"Hard to say," Rollins replied. "A couple dozen, certainly; maybe a couple hundred. Watching the place in real time, we see lots of movement, but there's no way to tell without more detailed analysis whether we're seeing different folks or the same dozen or so over and over. There are a couple of features of this place that I think you need to concentrate on."

The image shifted to reveal a wood-frame building that could only be a school, built in the classic old style, complete with a tiny steeple out front.

"If I took you to a ground-level view on this one, you'd actually see the word 'School' over the door," Rollins explained. "I show you this because of what it implies regarding children on-site. I want to make it extraordinarily clear to you, Digger, that dead children are not part of the package. I will not authorize that."

Jonathan exchanged glances with Boxers. "Last time I checked, you're not authorizing any of this. We're not in the habit of killing children."

Rollins cleared his throat. "I heard about an op in Colombia a while back that left a lot of blood on the ground. Rumor has it in the community that you might have had something to do with that."

"Move on," Jonathan said. There had in fact been such an op, but the children hadn't been killed by the good guys. Either way, he didn't owe an explanation to Roleplay Rollins.

The colonel got the hint. The picture moved again, this time swinging in for a close-up of the main building.

"I figure that to be the church and meeting hall," Jonathan said.

"Agreed," Rollins confirmed. "But it's got an interesting feature. Here, look at this."

The image flashed, and then there were looking at an infrared scan of the same building. In IR imagery, warmth is white and cold is dark. Here, the main building looked like a negative image of itself.

"Look how cold that building is."

"Maybe it's unoccupied," Gail offered.

"Maybe, but that wouldn't explain it being *this* cold."

Jonathan had seen images like this before, and he didn't like where his imagination was taking him. "You think it's armored, don't you?"

"That's exactly what I think," Rollins confirmed.

Gail scowled. "I don't get it," she and Venice said together.

Jonathan explained, "No matter how cold the weather a nice day like this, the radiant heat of the sun raises the face temperature of buildings—brick in particular.

layer of steel behind it, though, or build it out of reinforced concrete, and it stays relatively cool. This heat signature at this time of day tells me that the brick façade is covering up some heavy-duty shielding."

"Which means they're expecting an assault," Boxers said.

Jonathan closed the loop: "And none of that is good news for us."

Over the link, Venice said, "So you're telling me that you're raiding a fortress?"

Jonathan looked to Boxers, then shrugged. "Well, it's not going to be a walk in the park, but I think calling it a fortress might be overstating it. Think of that assembly hall as the castle keep—the place to administer the Kool-Aid if all else fails. Colonel, have you analyzed the other buildings?"

"In a cursory sort of way, yes. This appears to be the only one reinforced like this. I like your analogy to the castle keep. I think that's probably pretty accurate."

"So we need to try to engage them outside of that," Boxers said. "If they retreat to the keep, then we'll have an interesting day."

"Suppose that's where they keeping the Nasbes?" Gail asked. "Isn't that the most sensible place?"

Jonathan said, "Not necessarily. They clearly think they're out of reach or else they wouldn't be so aggressive with their communications to the world. If they don't feel endangered, then there's no reason to be on high alert."

"Didn't all of that change when Ryan escaped?" Gail asked.

Jonathan sighed. "Maybe."

"Maybe not," Rollins said. "We've got a cell phone intercept. I need to set the scene a little bit for you. Tell you where the voices are coming from." Papers rustled on the other end of the phone. "Okay, you're going to hear two voices, both of them picked up from encrypted telephone conversations. I leaned on a friend at the NSA to program a computer to monitor every telephone conversation coming out of Maddox County, West Virginia, looking for certain key words that we thought were important."

Gail's mind reeled. If the *New York Times* ever got wind of this, the jail time would be the least of their worries.

Jonathan placed his hand on hers and brought his lips close to her ear. "Remember the end game," he whispered.

Rollins continued, "The first voice you hear—the one that wants to just kill the captives and dispose of the bodies outright—comes from a cell phone that traces to a location outside the compound. I can send you a map if you want, but I don't think the location itself is in play. Because we're dealing with cell phones, we can only get within so many yards of the signal, but our friends at Fort Meade narrowed it down to a residential street that happens to be where Sheriff Kendig Neen resides. We printed the signal against a known recording, and we came up with a four-nines reliability quotient."

"Four-nines" meant ninety-nine point nine-nine percent likelihood that the voice belonged to the person they suspected.

"The other voice—and there are only two in this recording—traces back to a location where there happens to be only one structure within a half-mile radius. Watch your screen."

The picture moved rapidly and then the camera settled onto a familiar sight.

"That's the home of Michael Copley," Jonathan said.

"So you've been busy," Rollins said. "You're exactly right. I'll run the recording now. It's truncated at the beginning because it takes a few seconds for the computer software to kick in. Okay, here we go."

Jonathan listened to more movement, and then the quality of the sound changed to the characteristic scratchiness of a telephone recording. As promised, this one picked up in the middle of an ongoing discussion.

". . . we decided this. You keep walking out to the edge

like this, and it's going to fall away. If you're going to kill them, do it and be done with it." The voice had a buttery baritone quality that would have been appropriate for a radio broadcaster. "The rest is just unnecessary. It's getting disgusting. It's one thing to execute, but it's another to torture and maim. Did you see what you did to the kid's arm?"

"This is not your call to make," the second voice—the one belonging to Michael Copley—said. "They killed one of my soldiers. They need to pay."

"I don't disagree, Brother Michael. Say the word and I'll take care of it myself. But you need to do it quietly. This Internet broadcasting stuff is just going to bring trouble to all of us."

"The world needs to know that we cannot be fought," Copley said.

"The world doesn't even know who the hell we are," Neen protested. "And the less they know, the better off we're going to be."

"They *killed* Brother Stephen. *Killed* him."

Neen sighed audibly. "And we will punish in kind. We can do it publicly within the community, but I'm begging you not to turn this into a show on the Internet. I begged you last time, and now I'm begging you again. It's too much of a risk. It will anger people, and they will be all that more determined to identify us and bring us down."

Copley laughed. "Given what we have done, and what we are about to do, I believe that horse has long left the barn."

"Think of the data trail, then. Why take the additional risk when we don't need to?"

"Because the world needs to know."

"No, they don't!" Neen railed. "Brother Michael, we have our cause, and our cause is just. We're wreaking terror, and the blame is being cast on the Muslim heathens. All that we've worked for and all that we've built is finally coming to fruition. With all respect, sir, this grandstanding is putting that at risk. Forgive me for saying so, but that's irresponsible."

"Don't lecture me, Sheriff." Copley's tone darkened.

"I'm not lecturing you, Brother Michael. I'm trying to understand what you're doing. I thought we agreed when I dropped him off that he was too valuable to kill. His father is a commando, for heaven's sake. Surely we can use that to our benefit."

"Indeed we will," Copley said.

Neen paused long enough that Jonathan wondered if the recording had ended. Finally, the sheriff said, "What are you telling me?"

"Be at the house at seven," Copley said. "I'll reveal the plan to all of the elders then."

"Can we discuss the wisdom of the execution at the meeting?"

"If you still believe that there's anything to discuss at the conclusion of the meeting, then you are free to bring up whatever you wish."

The audio clicked again and Rollins's voice returned. "That's all of it," he said.

Boxers asked, "How long ago was this recorded?"

"Less than a half hour. Call it twenty, twenty-five minutes."

"What else do you have for us?" Jonathan asked.

"Nothing of note," Rollins said. "But we'll keep listening. If we get anything, we'll let you know."

"Thanks, Colonel," Jonathan said.

Venice recognized the thank-you for the signal that it was and she dumped Rollins's call. The team was on its own again.

Venice said, "I'm going to put this on a disk and have Dom deliver it to Wolverine. She needs to know."

"She won't be able to act on it," Jonathan cautioned.

Boxers added, "And if she does, she'll have to throw us under the bus."

"She needs to know," Venice said again.

CHAPTER TWENTY-TWO

Ryan couldn't stop shivering.

He was sick of pain and cold and darkness. He didn't know how much more he could take. From what he saw in the brief seconds when he'd had a chance to survey the place in the light spilled from the hallway, it was a concrete storage room, maybe ten feet square. There was stuff in there, but he hadn't taken the time to really note what it was. It looked like stuff you'd find in any attic, stacked haphazardly and precariously, but leaving enough room on the concrete floor for him to plant his butt and nurse his arm.

Part of him was glad he couldn't see. He'd seen broken bones before—on himself, even, when he'd broken the opposite arm in a skateboarding accident—and they were gross. Seeing the way the bones bent only made it hurt more, and more pain was one thing that he definitely did not need in his life.

One of his captors had been thoughtful enough to let him bring the pillow with him when they paraded him downstairs to his new prison. In fact, it was Colleen, K-girl's real name. Except here, she was Sister Colleen.

Sitting Indian-style with his legs crossed and the pillow

on his lap was about his only option to keep the pain under control. Problem was, the awkward posture put a lot of strain on his shoulders and neck, which were beginning to ache.

What was he going to do now?

He rested his forehead on his good hand, which itself was propped against his thigh, and he tried not to cry. How the *hell* could a trip home from a track meet have ended with this much trouble, this much hopelessness?

Brother Michael was a nutcase. There'd be no reasoning with him. Even if reasoning with him was possible, what would he bargain over? Ryan didn't even know why he was here. He didn't know what he'd done wrong.

Except killing that guy, but that was after.

Maybe this was just pure random bad luck, in which case Ryan wanted nothing to do with it. Maybe this was God working his mysterious ways, just as his mom always liked to talk about.

Tell you what, God. Keep your mysterious ways. How about getting off your ass and coughing up a solution?

Certainly, their first plan to get out of here had been a miserable failure.

If you can't trust the cops to do the right thing, he wondered what was left.

Whose responsibility is it to watch after the cops, anyway? If they're the enemy, then who else is there?

Maybe his dad was coming to get him right now. Maybe they were fueling up the Little Bird helicopters at this very moment, and they were waiting to swoop down and take everybody out. That's what the Unit did for perfect strangers, right? Was it too much to ask for a little of the same consideration for family?

No, it wasn't too much to ask.

But it was too much to answer.

The fact was that Ryan and Christyne Nasbe were flat-ass out of options. This prison he was in now was impenetrable and inescapable. And even if there was a chance that lightning would strike the guards whose shadows he could almost see walking around in the strip of light that infiltrated in under the door, what was he supposed to do with a broken wing?

Jesus, it hurt. Reaching over with his left hand to explore his wounded right, he could feel how his fingers had swollen to the size of sausages. His wrist had swollen, too, making the cuff of his jacket and his sweater way too tight, but it was so freaking cold in here that he didn't want to take them off.

His eyes began to sting as he thought through the stink pile that his life had become, and he felt his lip tremble. There had to be a way out of here. There had to be a way for him to be more than a simple victim.

His breath caught in his throat.

"Don't cry," he whispered aloud. He didn't want to give them that kind of satisfaction.

Movement outside his door brought his eyes up and put him on full alert. He heard the sound that could only be that of a padlock being manipulated in its hasp.

He tried to prepare himself for a fight, but his wounded arm simply would not let him.

The lock slid clear, and then the horizontal seam of light was joined by a vertical cousin. Someone was entering his space.

"Just stop it," a voice said. It was Colleen. "I'm going to do this."

"They said to leave him alone," another voice said.

"This is the right thing to do," Colleen said.

"I'm not covering for you."

"I didn't ask you to," she said, and then she entered his little space. The light behind her in the hallway was dim, but it still made Ryan squint. "Hi, Ryan," she said. Her arms were filled with items that he couldn't quite make out.

"What do you want?" Ryan asked.

"My name is Sister Colleen," she said. "I'm here to splint your arm."

Ryan drew himself up tighter. "That's okay, I'm fine."

"You're not fine," Colleen countered. "Your arm is broken and it needs to be splinted. It'll make it feel better."

"What do you care?"

She moved to his side and set a gym bag on the ground. When she opened it, he saw gauze and scissors and a piece of wood. Suddenly, he was back in Cub Scouts playing with first-aid stuff.

Colleen didn't look at him as she said, "Brother Michael shouldn't have treated you like that. That was wrong."

Ryan couldn't help but chuckle. "Aren't you the one who killed a bunch of people in their cars?"

She shook her head. "That was different," she said. "They were the enemy. You're our guest."

Holy shit, did she just say guest? He opted to keep his mouth shut.

"I know you think we're bad people," Colleen said, spreading out her gear like a surgeon would spread out his instruments. "But we're not. This is what happens when you go to war."

"War?" He'd blurted out the question before he could stop himself. "Who are you at war with?"

"The Users," she said.

The word rang a bell as one she'd used earlier.

Colleen leaned forward to get a better look at his arm, then shouted over her shoulder, "Turn on the light."

The voice from the hall said, "Brother Michael said no."

"Then rat me out later," Colleen said. "Right now I need light."

It probably took ten seconds, but ultimately, an overhead lightbulb jumped to life, bathing them in incandescent white light. As he'd suspected, his wrist and hand—the only parts he could see—were purple and swollen, the discoloration extending all the way to his knuckles on his first two fingers. The angulation of the bones wasn't as disgusting as he'd feared, but that probably had as much to do with the bulk of his clothes as the actual arrangement of his anatomy.

"I know what I'm doing," Colleen said. "I've treated injuries here on the compound for years. You can relax."

Instinctively, Ryan protected his arm and scooched backward on his butt.

"Really, I'm not here to hurt you."

"No, you're just here to kidnap me."

Colleen paused as she considered those words. "Different things," she said. As if that was an explanation. She picked up a pair of scissors, the kind you only see in doctors' offices, on which one of the jaws is blunted so it doesn't cut flesh. "We need to get your coat and sweater off."

He tried to move farther away, but he was up against a hard stop of stuff. "I'm really fine the way I am."

She cocked her head in a look of feigned patience. "Do you know what can happen if a broken bone is not mended?"

"Yeah," Ryan said. "It stays broken."

Colleen rolled her eyes. "Well, that, yes. Of course. But that's the very best case. The worst case is that you move the wrong way and a bone end pinches a blood vessel or maybe punctures one. They you either bleed to death or you get gangrene and they have to cut off the arm. The alternative would be to die. Which one of those do you like?"

He didn't know what to say. He offered his arm.

She slid the blunted side of the jaws under the cuff of his sleeve, and with a gentleness that surprised him, she moved an inch at a time, pinching a bit of fabric and then snipping it, going through all the layers simultaneously. "If I hurt you, let me know."

"Sister Colleen," Ryan said, tasting the phrase. "Are you a nun or something?"

When she shook her head, he caught a flash of fiery red hair from under the scarf she wore. "No, I am not a nun. I am, however, a child of God."

"Aren't we all?"

He'd meant it as a throwaway line, a space-taker, but Colleen didn't know that. "Not all of us," she said. "Not the Users."

Colleen's thumb found a sensitive spot on his arm and he jumped. "Ow!"

She stopped cutting and pulled the scissors hand away. "I'm sorry," she said. She looked like she meant it.

"That's okay. Hit a nerve or something, I guess." As the flesh of his arm was exposed, he discovered a sense of relief. His arm was swollen, and the area from the middle of his forearm to his wrist looked like it had been bruised, but it didn't look as bad as it hurt. He'd been expecting something L-shaped, but it was nothing like that. As the scissors passed his elbow, Colleen gently placed his forearm back on the pillow, and then used both hands to cut his clothes away to the shoulder.

"You have good muscles," she said, stroking his biceps.

The words startled him. Her touch inexplicably turned him on. "Um, thanks. A few weeks in a cast should take care of that, though." As soon as the sarcasm escaped his mouth, he wished that he could bring it back. She was being nice to him, for God's sake. You know, *after* she'd kidnapped him and threatened to kill him.

"Who are the Users?" he asked, hoping to change the subject.

"They're most of the world. They're the people who take all of God's gifts for their own and give nothing back. They live for money and not for goodness. They forget about Him and refuse to pay Him His due."

Colleen put the scissors down and returned her attention to his forearm. Reaching into her bag, she produced a padded board splint, much like the ones he'd seen in Coach Jackson's first-aid kit.

"I'm going to put this under your arm for support," she explained. "Then we'll tie your arm to the board with some gauze wrapping, and then we'll put your arm in a sling. It will mend faster if it's immobilized."

"But it's going to hurt," Ryan said, cutting to the chase.

"Well . . . yes. I'll have to move your arm a little, and I guess that has the potential to hurt."

Potential turned to reality. The site of the break shot new lightning bolts as she slid the board into place, but in five seconds, it was over.

"Now, that wasn't so bad, was it?" Colleen asked.

"Says the chick with two good arms." He said it with a smile. *Jesus*, he thought. How perverted could he be, getting a woody from the lady who's hurting him? *Well, she did say I have good muscles.*

"Am I a User?" Ryan asked.

"Probably." Colleen opened a white paper container that was marked KLING WRAP and revealed a cylinder of gauze. "Judging from your car and your clothes—and your mouth sometimes—I'd say there was a very good chance that you are a User."

"What does that mean, though? User, I mean."

"Can you hold your arm up for me?" Colleen asked. She demonstrated what she needed by raising his wounded forearm, using the splint.

Ryan slid his left hand into the spot where her hands were.

"Good," she said. "Just like that." Her fingers seemed to work automatically as she unraveled the Kling Wrap, binding his arm to the board. She carefully avoided the site of the break, leaving that part of his skin unbound.

"You *have* done this before," Ryan said. "Thank you."

Colleen kept her eyes on her work as she smiled. "You're welcome. Here at the compound, we have to learn to do many things. I've even delivered a few babies."

Ryan recoiled at the thought. "Eew. Really?"

She laughed at his horror. "What's wrong with delivering babies?"

"They're gross and slimy. Why not just call an ambulance? Or drive them to the hospital?"

Colleen shook her head. "Oh, no. Outsiders are Users. That's no way to bring a new life into the world. We don't want those hands to be the first to touch one of our infants."

"There it is again," Ryan said. "Users. I asked you before

and you didn't tell me. Is that some kind of secret word to you people?"

"You wouldn't understand," Colleen said. By the time she rolled out the last of the Kling Wrap, the end of his arm looked like a giant Q-tip. It felt better, too. "It would be like explaining sin to a sinner. It's difficult for people to understand what they are."

"Try me."

Colleen stopped working on his arm, and sat back to look him in the eye. "What prayer do you say before you eat a meal?"

He scowled. "What, you mean like grace?"

"I suppose." Clearly, it wasn't exactly what she meant, but her expression showed that it served her point.

"I don't," Ryan said. "Except, you know, sometimes at Christmas or Thanksgiving. It's kind of part of the tradition."

"So even when you say it, you don't really mean it. It's something you have to do to get to the food."

"So that makes me a User? A User and a sinner are sort of the same?"

"We are all sinners, Ryan. Do you work for your money?"

He coughed out a laugh. "What money? Yeah, I work some during the summer, flipping burgers or stocking shelves somewhere. But I don't make shit." The disapproving glare told him that dropping the S-bomb was a mistake. "Sorry. Another sin for the list."

"You're not getting it," Colleen said. "Of whatever money you get working whatever job you have, how much do you give to the poor?"

"I *am* the poor. I don't have anything to give."

"You have everything to give. Every day you get paid, you have money to give. Every time you put shoes on, you have shoes to give. You have clothes, and food and possessions that in one year's time will cease to have use to you, yet you continue to accumulate more."

Oh, man, he wasn't getting this at all. "So anybody who has anything is a User? Is your enemy?"

Colleen rolled her eyes in that special way people do that really got his blood boiling. "Yes, you're obviously one of them."

"One of *who*?" He shouted that and, in the process, did something to make his arm bite him and he grunted against the pain.

"This is why it's useless to try to communicate with anyone outside of the community. You refuse to see things as they are."

"I don't even know what we're talking about."

Colleen settled herself as if preparing to explain the obvious to a dimwitted child. "It's not about owning *anything*," she said. "It's about wanting to own *everything*, and never being willing to give anything back. You'll destroy other people, you'll destroy other countries, you'll destroy the earth itself, if that's what it takes."

Ryan felt like he'd entered the play of his life in the middle of the second act. "I'm sixteen," he said, chuckling at the absurdity. "Even if I *wanted* to do some of those things, I couldn't. Give me a break."

"There it is again," she said.

The second guard appeared in the doorway. "I told you it was a waste of time," he said.

"Who are you?" Ryan said. He'd learned the hard way that when these nut jobs formed a crowd, life got difficult.

"I'm one you should be fearing," he said. The guy was older and bigger than Ryan, but not by much on either count. "Brother Stephen was a friend of mine."

"Then you should keep better friends," Ryan blurted before his filter could slide into place. "He tried to rape my mother. What would you do?"

The guy smiled. "I guess I might have waited my turn."

"Stop it!" Colleen commanded. She put a hand on Ryan's shoulder as she spoke, as if to reassure him that this new guy was out of line. "This is Brother Zebediah. And sometimes he doesn't know when to keep his mouth shut."

"The fact is," said Brother Zebediah, "it's not about *you*.

Nothing in this world is about *you*. Nothing is about anyone. We live or die together on this planet, and you Users are so intent on owning the world and its resources for your own gain that you kill indiscriminately. Not just with guns, but with power. It's time to return the power to where it belongs."

"To you," Ryan said, still trying to wrap his head around it all. "And you do it by killing others. Killing to stop killing. Am I getting it right now?"

The expression in Sister Colleen's face hovered somewhere between hurt and disappointment, yet Ryan still didn't have a clue why. She stood abruptly and threw a tightly rolled ball of tan fabric onto his lap.

"That's a triangular bandage," she said. "I think you should tie a knot in it and put it around your neck as a sling. Try to keep your hand higher than your elbow if you can."

Clearly, she was done, and even more clearly, she was angry. She turned to the door.

"What did I say?" Ryan asked after her.

Colleen said nothing. She stormed out past Brother Zebediah, who followed her and slammed the door. He was still refitting the padlock when someone flipped a switch and Ryan's world returned to blackness.

CHAPTER TWENTY-THREE

"At least we know that Ryan is in Copley's house," Venice said. "That's important data."

"I disagree," Jonathan said. "All we know is that Neen dropped him off there. Other than that, we've got only conjecture."

"And what about the mom, Christyne?" Gail asked. "Nobody even mentioned her."

"Baby steps," Jonathan advised. "Explore the lead you've got, and hope that the others fall into place."

"By sheer dumb luck?" she asked with a chuckle.

"In a perfect world, no," Jonathan said. Her negative tone was beginning to wear on him. "But if the best I can catch is pure dumb luck, then I'll take it."

Boxers said, "I recognize that look, Dig. What's the plan?"

Jonathan looked at his watch. "We know that the meeting of the elders—whatever the hell that means—takes place a little over five hours from now, at seven."

Venice said, "Digger, do you agree that the conversation we eavesdropped on said that the meet was going to happen in Copley's house?"

"I do," he said.

"Good," Venice said. "Because when he built the place twelve years ago, he used an architect and a professional engineer. And wouldn't you know it? He had the decency to file all the plans at the assessments office at the courthouse."

Jonathan grinned, yet again amazed by Venice's capabilities to ferret out information. "Are you telling me you have drawings?"

He could hear the smile in her voice when she said, "I've got floor plans, electrical, HVAC, sewerage, you name it."

Gail scowled, as if to say, *Is that even possible?*

"Only a fool bets against Venice," Jonathan said.

"This is unbelievable!" Venice howled from Fisherman's Cove. "Copley likes to buy his furniture from a place called Colony House in Falls Church. I can send you purchase orders, if you'd like."

Jonathan assured her that that would not be necessary.

It took a few minutes for the floor plans and other architectural drawings to transfer, but once they did, the first stage of their plan became obvious. Jonathan discussed it with his team, spending the better part of an hour working through the details and the possible complications—of which there were too many to count—but when they were done, everybody had a job to do.

They'd changed into black, despite the brightness of the day.

Camouflage was a particularly difficult challenge in the wintertime, given the absence of leaves on the trees. Throw in the fact that every breath you took launched a cloud of condensation into the air, and blaze orange was as good a color as any to stay invisible.

Rather than trying to blend in with their surroundings, then, Jonathan's team had opted to blend in with their adversaries. They'd still make every effort to remain invisible, but on the off chance that they were spotted, they hoped that the spotters might see armed people in black and assume that they were friendlies. It was a high-risk bet, but sometimes you just had to play the hand you were dealt.

They drove from the command post to a side road near the Copley house, but far enough away to remain undetected. Following their GPS, they hiked a quarter-mile due west to the fence line. From there, it would be another quarter mile to the house itself.

Contrary to Jonathan's conservative survival plan, they forwent the heavy body armor that he generally would have insisted upon—ditto the Kevlar helmets—in order to match the kit worn by the resident guards. Jonathan also left behind the twelve-gauge Mossberg shotgun that he would normally have worn slung under his armpit, and the bandolier of ammunition that went along with it. You never knew what kind of spotters they had deployed, and that kind of accoutrement was just too easily identified.

There was a limit, though, to the extent Jonathan would go to blend in. They would each carry their M4 carbines, which looked enough like the M16s used by the staff to pass a cursory glance, but he insisted that each of them carry a full load of ten extra mags of ammunition, for a total of three hundred rounds. It bulked them up on their web gear, but ammunition was the one thing he would never scrimp on. They each carried a sidearm, as well. Jonathan had his Colt 1911 .45, Boxers his Beretta nine millimeter, and Gail her Glock .40. Sidearms were the most personal of weapons. The smart warrior carried the one with which he was most comfortable. Gail's years in the FBI had made the Glock .40 second nature to her.

Jonathan also insisted on night vision. The violent side of his world was inescapably tied to the night, and the ability to navigate where others were blind was the single greatest playing-field leveler. Each of them, then, carried a rucksack that contained night vision, glow sticks, a couple of general-purpose charges with initiators, plus a supply of Pop-Tarts—a high-sugar and high-carb source of emergency food in case their PCs hadn't been fed in a while.

The hike through the woods was entirely uneventful. They walked cautiously, trying to make as little noise as possible in the dried leaves and underbrush, but daytime stealth was different from nighttime stealth. The trick was to look as natural as possible while still trying to remain undetected.

They spread out, too, keeping fifty yards between them both laterally and longitudinally. Boxers led, with Jonathan bringing up the rear. They kept in contact with each other and with Venice—"Mother Hen"—via encrypted radio.

"Hey, Scorpion," Venice said through Jonathan's left earbud. "I've got more good news for you. The house has got security cameras, and they beam their signals to a security company via the Internet."

Jonathan pressed the transmit button in the center of his chest. "How is that *good* news?"

He could hear the pride when she said, "Because I own the Internet. I'm working right now to record empty fields of view. If you can give me a half hour, I'll be able to loop the recordings and route the fake images to the transmitters."

Amazing, Jonathan thought. "What are their fields of view?"

"Assuming that they use only one company to monitor, it appears that only the house itself—the perimeter and the interior—are monitored."

"The fence line?"

"Absolutely."

"Mother Hen, you're my hero," Jonathan said. He knew that Venice would take it as the high praise that he had intended.

Ten minutes later, Jonathan, Boxers, and Gail all arrived at the fence that surrounded Michael Copley's sprawling home. The fence was nothing special—chain link, but of a gauge more suitable to a secure military facility than, say, a swimming pool. A Y-shaped bed of barbed wire capped the fence. If the links proved too tough to cut—and Jonathan guessed that they would—those same links would be that much easier to climb, and provide that much more stable a platform to take out the barbed wire with a pair of snips.

"Sure is a lot of sunshine out here," Boxers grumped as they hunkered together in some bushes at the base of a very significant oak tree.

Jonathan looked at his watch. It was almost four o'clock. "Not for long. Give it another hour."

"Bullshit," Boxers said. "I'll give Mother Hen the thirty minutes she needs to cover my ass, and then I'm going to work."

Watching Jonathan and Boxers interact with each other—the lighthearted banter in the face of impending danger—Gail realized that she didn't belong here. She would never be a full-fledged member of the team. These two men shared so much history—so much past pleasure and pain—that she couldn't hope to become a part of it.

Everything about this operation felt alien to her. In her ordered world, formerly defined by the rule of law, planning meant everything. You didn't make a move without a piece of paper telling you it was approved, and you didn't fire a shot unless you were one-hundred-twenty-percent sure that it was defensible in court.

Even the sole focus on the rescue of the precious cargo was unique to her experience. During her days with the FBI Hostage Rescue Team, the primary goal hadn't truly been the liberation of the hostages. Rather, it had been to lawfully ensure that the bad guys did not get away, and that the legal case you built against them would withstand the scrutiny of the bad guys' legal defense team. They worked very, very hard to make sure that the hostages remained unharmed, but at the end of the day, it was a better career move to convict a kidnapper for murdering a hostage than it was to reunite a hostage with his family and then have his assailant walk on a technicality.

Gail was surprised by how rapidly her heart was hammering in her chest. She didn't dare contribute to her colleagues' banter for fear that her voice would tremble in the process.

She told herself to settle down. This wasn't the first time

that she'd strayed outside the law while in Jonathan's employ. That trend had started on the mountaintop in Pennsylvania, and then continued into the wilds of Alaska some months later. She'd approved illegal wiretaps and photographs that never should have been taken, but those were mere violations of civil rights. She'd killed, but that had always been in self-defense. Jonathan was right to question her ability to kill prophylactically. That skill—to kill in order to eliminate an enemy before he could kill you—was perhaps the single most important factor that separated what police did from what soldiers did.

Studies had been written about it, in fact. Several decades ago, during America's War on Drugs, the Drug Enforcement Administration had enlisted the aid of Navy SEALs for the interdiction of seaborne drug trafficking. The planners had envisioned the SEALs as a legal force multiplier that would chase down bad guys, place them under arrest, and recover countless millions of dollars in drugs.

In practice, the plan had proven disastrous. The SEALs chased down the boats easily enough, and they recovered the millions of dollars in drugs, but more often than not, there were no people left to arrest. If a bad guy had a gun, he was killed, consistent with the SEALs' long-standing training.

It made sense when Gail thought about it. What was the point in having a conversation with a guy who wants to kill you?

If only prosecutors were that sensible.

The lesson learned from SEAL exercise was that training trumped intentions. When you invest millions of dollars in creating a warrior, that's what you get. You don't get a cop.

Now, Gail worried that the opposite was true. Could she be the warrior she needed to be when the time came to pull the trigger? And if not, then who would take her place?

Finally, an easy answer: No one would take her place. If she froze, the mission would come unzipped; and if that happened, everyone might die.

She could do this, she told herself. All it took was a total commitment to—

"We've got a guard coming," Boxers' voice said in her ear.

Gail shot her gaze first to the Big Guy, and then followed his eyeline into the woods, where a black-clad sentry was wandering into view.

"No guns," Jonathan whispered. As he spoke, he drew his KA-BAR knife from its scabbard on his left shoulder. The finely honed edge flashed white against the flat black finish of the blade. Gail shifted her eyes and saw Boxers mimic the move.

Her own knife remained in its sheath on her belt. Another training deficit. She reached out to Jonathan and touched his arm.

He glanced at her briefly, then shook his head and pursed his lips in a silent *shh*.

"Let him go unless he poses a threat." Jonathan's whisper was barely audible over the radio.

Gail settled more deeply behind the bush that provided her concealment, her heart hammering Verdi's "Anvil Chorus." To her right, Jonathan and Boxers both looked like coiled snakes, every muscle tensed, their knives ready to separate the guard's soul from his body.

The foliage confounded any clear view of the man as he approached, but to Gail's eye he could have been the very sentry they'd seen in Rollins's satellite photo. Tall and lean, he appeared to be young. He wore his M16 casually, dangling by a sling from his shoulder. He was nowhere near ready to confront an intruder. He had the complacent, bored look of a man who'd been walking the same route for far too long while seeing far too little action. Gail thought ruefully that she could probably jump out at him and yell, "Boo!" and he'd be half a mile away before he ever got his hand to his weapon.

This was all good news.

As the sentry approached within a few yards of their hiding place, Gail looked at Jonathan, whose eyes never left his prey. He remained perfectly still, nothing moving but his eyes as the young man passed the tree that shielded them, and then continued to wander down the line and around the corner. The danger had come and passed in a little over a minute. When the guard was out of sight, Jonathan's shoulders finally relaxed.

"That was encouraging," Boxers said, sliding his KA-BAR back into its scabbard. "I like clueless guards."

Jonathan raised his eyebrows as he slid his own knife into its sheath. "I make it a point not to underestimate anybody with an automatic weapon."

"Actually, I thought I was overestimating," Boxers countered with a smile.

"Are you guys safe and clear now?" Venice asked over the radio.

Jonathan touched the transmit button. "Affirm," he said. "Wasn't even close."

Really? Gail thought. What does close look like if that wasn't it?

"You sounded pretty tight on the radio," Venice said. "Are you sure?"

"Does it matter?" Emotionally, Venice had the most difficult job on the team. Hers was a world of impressions and anticipation, while the team on the ground had the benefit—for good or ill—of real-time knowledge. It never hurt to shield her from certain realities.

Venice said, "I've got all the footage I need for the broadcast loop. Are you ready to go?"

It was the statement they'd been waiting for—the statement Gail had been dreading. Was she ready to go?

"Are you spinning the recording?" Jonathan asked.

"All the monitoring company will see is uninterrupted boredom," she reported. "But understand that I'm going to need to record again. We're going to have to show nighttime approaching. Otherwise the monitors will see something wrong. Then, once it gets dark, I'll need another half hour of darkness to make the loop."

"Shit," Jonathan cursed off the air. He hadn't considered that.

"I'll give you plenty of notice," Venice assured. "I'll also be monitoring the live feed, so I'll be able to tell you if danger approaches."

"Are we set?" Jonathan asked his team.

Boxers was already on his feet, walking toward the fence.

Gail nodded, but apparently, it wasn't convincing.

"This is fish-or-cut-bait time, Gail," he said softly.

She nodded more aggressively this time. "Let's go," she said.

They chose a spot along the fence in the rear sector of the estate where trees pressed in close and drooped over the barbed wire. Jonathan judged this to be a spot where the cuts they needed to make would be less likely to be spotted.

Boxers climbed the fence with a dexterity that Gail would have found impressive from anyone, but particularly given his size. Maybe it helped that by just standing at its base, he was already three-quarters of the way to the top. He planted the toe of one boot in the wire mesh of the fence and reached with one hand to raise himself high enough that the barbed wire was at face height. He'd already drawn the snips with his other hand.

"I hate this part," he said. He placed the jaws of the snips around the wire, then hunched one shoulder to protect his neck, and looked away and down. "In three," he said. "Two, one."

There was a snapping sound, and then the wire sagged. He repeated the procedure for the four lines of wire on their side of the fence, and then he leaned across and dispatched the four lines on the far side. That done, Boxers continued up and over the side.

"You okay, Big Guy?" Jonathan asked. "You look a little winded."

"Winded my ass," Boxers replied. "When you get your little razor butt over here, we'll arm wrestle and see who wins."

It had been a long time since Gail had climbed a fence, and she was proud of herself for doing it with her dignity intact. When they were all assembled on the other side, she said to Jonathan, "What happens when the sentry notices the cut wire?"

He shrugged and forced a smile. "That's another one of those moments where we pray for luck to be on our side."

The lucky breaks were beginning to stack pretty high.

They spread out to recon the mansion from the outside. Sooner or later, they were going to have to enter the house, and before committing to that kind of risk, they needed to learn as much about the place as they could. Jonathan and Boxers split the duties to view the front and sides, each of them taking positions on either side of the long driveway, and Gail was relegated to watching the rear and reporting on what she saw.

Despite the risk of losing the Nasbes in the next hour or two, Jonathan decided to wait till nightfall to approach the mansion. The ability to function at night was such a huge force multiplier that it was worth the risk. Easy to say, he supposed, until he found out that the bad guys had harmed the family while they were waiting things out.

Jonathan worked his way into a thicket of evergreens in the southeast corner of the front yard, where he could see a good bit of the driveway and the front door of the residence. He imagined that Boxers had a similar view on the opposite side of the driveway.

Moving slowly and quietly, Jonathan settled into his hidey-hole and oh-so-carefully slipped out of his ruck. Reaching into a side pocket, he found his digital monocular, and brought it to his eye. With the digital boosting, he could dial in to sixty-power, but at that magnification, even his heartbeat made the image dance. He settled for twelve-power.

Two sentries stood guard on the front porch, flanking the front door. Both wore sidearms—they looked like Glocks, but both of them stood with arms akimbo, their hands resting on the pistol grips, making positive ID impossible. If they had access to long guns, those weapons were out of sight.

Jonathan pressed the mike button on his vest. "I'm in position and I count two bad guys at the front door."

Boxers' voice popped in his earbud. "I'm in position and I confirm two at the front door. I don't see any others."

"The black side is clear," Gail said. In their parlance, front was white, back was black, left was green, and right was red.

"Mother Hen, how do you copy?" Jonathan asked.

"Clear as crystal," Venice said. "The live feed shows the one sentry on patrol still, but he seems to be taking a break, and sticking close to the fence line. He's not a problem for now."

"Copy that," Jonathan said. "Mother Hen, I want you to prompt us for a sit rep every fifteen minutes while we're spread this far apart. Otherwise, let's keep the channel clear unless there's something to report."

Surveying the mansion, Jonathan noticed nothing special. It was a big old place, built in the style of old plantation houses, complete with pillars in the front that would please Scarlett O'Hara if she saw them. The drawings they'd studied showed it to be about ten thousand square feet on the main two levels, plus basement space underneath.

Pulling the monocular away from his eye, he pulled the floor plan from his pocket and studied it some more. If there was one thing he'd learned the hard way it was that any floor plan that was older than five years—this one was dated thirty years ago—was as reliable as an unwound watch. All the parts would be there, you just never knew how accurate the arrangement would be. He remembered one prison rescue back in the day when all of their intelligence data told them that there would be wide-open space after turning a corner, but when they got there, he encountered a reinforced concrete wall. They'd managed a work-around, but that one nearly cost them the mission.

Still, the drawings provided a sense of scale. And important landmarks such as stairways and utility lines normally remained constant even after major renovations. As long as he could—

In the distance, a thick *crack* split the air. Clearly a gunshot, it sounded far away, but had the unique qualities of one particular weapon.

"Scorpion, Big Guy," Boxers' voice said in his ear. "Did that sound like a Barrett to you?"

Yes, it did. Just like that, this mission took on a new tenor.

Michael Copley tucked the recoil pad of the massive Barrett .50-caliber sniper rifle into the soft notch of his shoulder, rested his hand atop the stock, and his cheek atop the back of his hand. Through his ten-power scope, he wasn't sure he would recognize the true nature of his target if he hadn't designed it himself. He certainly would not have recognized the finer points of the design.

The Model 9000 Symphonic Reflector—the gold standard in acoustic reflectors—sat firmly in its frame, fifteen hundred yards away, fixed in the braces that he'd designed specifically for outdoor use. It wouldn't do, after all, to ruin the very performances these were designed to augment by blowing over in a wind. Sturdy yet lightweight; high quality yet inexpensive. That's what made Appalachian Acoustics so popular.

Certainly, that's what had sold these units to the federal government. When the United States Navy Band played a concert, every note was worthy of being heard, as was every word spoken by dignitaries and heads of state. Indoors or outdoors, the Model 9000 worked better than any other on the market.

Presently, the panel on the opposite hilltop was positioned as if the concert were being delivered away from Copley, and his scope was thus showing him the back side of the panels. His sight picture, then, was the Appalachian Acoustics logo, printed over and over in a pattern that appeared random, but in fact was anything but.

At this range, every environmental factor mattered, from the slightest breeze to the moisture content of the air. As far as the latter was concerned, thank God for the cold winter. At this temperature, the atmosphere was bone dry.

He'd entered the air temperature, windage, and ammunition data into his handheld ballistics computer, and the results were as astounding as they always were. While the target was stationary, he nonetheless had to compensate for the ten-mile-per-hour breeze and the impossibly long distance. His computer told him to correct for 260 inches of drop and a lot of drift. In a sport where half-seconds of angle resulted in huge misses, this business of sighting in his scope became ridiculously important. When the time came to take his real shot, there'd be no room for trial and error.

"The spotter is safe," said Brother Franklin from his right. "Fire when ready." A member of the Board of Elders, Brother Franklin was one of the original founders of the Army of God, and the second-best sniper in the group, next to Michael himself. Both had trained for years.

Trained for this one shot.

Copley ran the numbers in his head, and found the appropriate mark on the logo. He placed that spot in the very lower rightmost arc of his sight picture. He took a deep breath, let half of it go, and then caressed the trigger.

The firing pin engaged, and the weapon erupted, launching its massive, 660-grain bullet at 2,800 feet per second. As the shell casing flew from the receiver, the muzzle brake and floating barrel took most of the recoil, or the kick might have broken bones. It would take over a second and a half for the half-inch-diameter bullet to traverse its nearly 1,500-yard trajectory. He'd just brought his scope back to the sight picture when he saw the panel move.

He'd hit his spot precisely; but it wouldn't be time to smile until he knew he'd hit the true target, which was beyond the panel, and out of his sight. A few seconds later, one of the children from the compound rose from behind the rock that shielded him and waved a white flag over his head.

"Dead center," Brother Franklin said. "White means perfect shot." He lay next to Michael on his stomach on the ground, peering through the eyepiece of a digital spotting scope. "Great job, Brother Michael." Truly, it was a shot that the best snipers in the world would have trouble making.

"One more," Brother Michael said. He again settled the reticle into the most unlikely part of the scope and launched another bullet.

The boy with the flag dove for cover after the bullet hit, and then sheepishly raised the white flag again.

"Perfect," Brother Franklin said. He couldn't help but laugh, and then he patted Michael on the shoulder. "It was a mean thing to do to the boy, but it was perfect. Two in a row is a trend," he said.

Copley lifted his cheek from the weapon, and then pushed himself up to a kneeling position. "This is one amazing weapon," he said.

"But hardly practical," Franklin countered. "What does it weigh? Twenty-five pounds?"

"Twenty-eight and a half, empty," Copley said. "Not my first choice for close quarters."

Copley left the weapon on the ground and stood, brushing dirt from the front of his clothes. Franklin joined him. Together, they walked to the flat rock where they'd placed their backpacks and a thermos of coffee. Copley poured into Franklin's cup first, and then into his own.

"It has cream and sugar," Copley said. "I hope that suits."

"In this weather, all that matters is that it's hot," Franklin replied.

They sipped in silence for nearly a minute. Finally, Copley said, "I had dual purposes for bringing you here, Brother Franklin."

"I figured as much," the other man said. "You rarely have only one thing on your mind."

Copley smiled at what he perceived to be a compliment. "Even more so now that the war has begun," he said. "I want you to speak freely."

Franklin half nodded, half shrugged.

"What do you think of the video we put out on the Internet?"

"You mean of the User family? Wasn't that the plan from the beginning?"

"A question is not an answer to a question," Copley admonished.

Franklin's whole body shrugged. "I think it's what we needed to do. What's the sense of having assets if you're not willing to exploit them?"

"Did you feel that the recording and airing of the video were the evidence of hubris on my part?"

Franklin looked uncomfortable.

"Again, I ask you to speak freely."

He took his time. "I don't know how to answer you," Franklin said. "Hubris means pride, and I suppose that pride is a sin, yet, you have every reason to be proud of what we are accomplishing."

"Was it the right thing to do, in your opinion?"

"It was an important thing to do. The necessary thing to do. The entire point was to portray ourselves as a Muslim offshoot. That's a main strategy."

Copley found himself smiling at the words he'd wanted to hear.

"If you don't mind me asking, why do you ask the question?"

"Brother Kendig," Copley said. In its own way, that was a complete answer.

Franklin took a sip of his coffee and gave a conciliatory nod. "Well, yes. Brother Kendig has always been . . . careful. Is he the one who accused you of hubris?"

"On more than one occasion." Copley paused to consider his next question. "What do you think of the good Sheriff Neen?"

There was that uneasy look again. "I think that he's been a friend of mine for many years."

Copley sat on the flat rock, ignoring the aching cold that

seeped through his trousers and into his spine. "Do you think he is an asset to our mission, or a hindrance?"

Franklin joined his commander on the rock. "You ask me to speak frankly, and then you ask a question about loyalty. In time of war, the underlying accusation carries a death sentence."

"For good cause," Copley said.

Franklin took his time assembling his words. "I've known you for many years, Brother Michael. For as many years as we have both known Brother Kendig. If you're harboring paranoid thoughts that he is somehow against what we are doing, then I respectfully—"

"Not *against* us," Michael said, raising his hand to interrupt. "Just not entirely *with* us."

"Two ways of saying the same thing, sir. The entire community has trained long and hard for this war. For those who are under twenty, they have trained their entire lives. Much of that training came from Brother Kendig. Without him, we would not be empowered as we are now."

"But people change, do they not?"

Franklin considered that. "Of course they do. We all change. Our hair turns gray with time, and we get winded sooner during physical training. But I don't believe that we change fundamentally. I believe that who we are remains who we are. That means Kendig is a talented soldier and loyal to the cause."

"Yet he disrespects me," Copley mused aloud. None of this was what he'd expected to hear. Brother Franklin's words, in fact, made him wonder if a conspiracy of sorts might be in play.

"If you say, then it must be so. But if you're seeking my counsel as an elder, then my advice to you is to think carefully about the space that separates disagreement from disloyalty." He paused, obviously hesitant to state the rest. "One could argue that if a person holds an opinion deeply and firmly enough, disagreement could be judged the highest degree of loyalty. Sir."

In an academic setting such lofty statements would have more meaning for Copley than they did right now. For a team to function healthily, dissent was wrong. He was surprised that Franklin didn't already know this.

"What are your thoughts on the execution?" Copley asked.

Franklin's answer came without pause. "I think that you have no choice. They killed a soldier."

"The boy maintains that he was protecting his mother from rape," Copley baited. "I cannot say that such a crime is beyond the reach of Brother Stephen."

"And had he lived, he would have been appropriately punished," Franklin said. "As it is, that opportunity for justice was denied."

"Exactly," Copley said. "And do you agree that the execution should be broadcast live on the Internet?"

Franklin's body seemed to stiffen with the question. "Is that important?"

"Our goal is to rend the fabric of what the Users believe is comfort in their lives. Could there be anything more unsettling?"

Franklin hesitated. "Nothing I can think of."

Copley didn't like the noncommittal answer. "I said you can speak freely."

A deep breath, followed by a settling sigh. "I worry about cause and effect," he said. "Actions have consequences. It's one thing to watch the news and hear and see reports of the mayhem the Army is sowing. But if you present the public with the spectacle of an execution, I fear that instead of justice, they will see only cruelty."

"You fear," Copley said. He was sick to death of that word. "Is cowardice in battle likewise not a crime?"

Franklin stood. "You told me to speak freely."

Copley felt a wave of anger approaching, but he pushed it down. "Yes, I did," he said. He stood as well and pointed with his chin to the rifle. "Are you up to more spotting?"

"I am," Franklin said. As they covered the distance to the weapon, he said, "Please, Brother Michael. If I offended—"

Copley waved him off. "You're fine," he said. "Everything's fine."

The two men moved almost in unison as they lowered themselves to their bellies on the ground in front of their respective toys. Copley positioned himself at the gunstock and wriggled a bit as he settled into a comfortable position on the ground.

"Be aware on the left," Franklin said. "It looks like one of Mrs. Shockley's cows has wandered out of the pasture."

"Is it likely to wander into my field of fire?" Shooting was a head game, and he didn't appreciate the interruption.

"Probably not. Not unless you shoot wild. She ranges at twenty-one fifty yards and three hundred twenty feet from the target."

Copley reacquired the acoustic panel and ran the previous ballistic calculations through his head. "Is the cow moving or standing still?"

"Looks like she's grazing."

Without saying a word, Copley pivoted the Barrett to the left, adjusted in his head for the new range, and squeezed the trigger. Again. And again. The massive weapon bucked with each round, the pressure wave at the muzzle blasting dirt and leaves.

Two point two seconds later—long before the sound of the gunshots could arrive on the opposite hill—the cow erupted in a pink cloud, one of its hind legs spinning away and landing ten or fifteen feet from the rest of the carcass.

Copley smiled. He lifted his cheek from the butt stock and craned his neck to look over his shoulder at Franklin, whose face was a mask of disbelief.

"You didn't even aim," Franklin said.

"Of course I aimed. I just did it quickly." He rose to his knees and hefted the Barrett from the ground. "But a shot like that tells you that it's time to stop for the day."

He walked back to the flat rock to begin the process of cleaning the weapon and returning it to its padded case, leaving Franklin to pick up the sandbags and other clutter from their shooting perch. Arriving at the rock, he gently placed the weapon butt-down on the flat surface. He removed the five-cartridge magazine and cleared the breach.

"Franklin?" he said without looking.

"Yes, sir?"

He liked the "sir." That's what happened when you made people nervous. "Can I count on you to make things happen tonight?"

"Of course," he said. Then, after a beat: "What things are you talking about?"

"I want the entire compound assembled for the executions, and I want it on a live Internet feed. Route it as we did before."

A long moment passed in silence. Copley turned to see Franklin just standing there. "Brother Franklin?"

He seemed startled. "Yes, sir," he said. "I'll see to it. What time?"

"Eight-ish? After the trial."

Franklin clearly wanted to object, but he swallowed his words. "Both of them, sir?"

"One at a time, of course. What do you think would make the best drama for television, a mother watching her son die first, or the other way around?"

There was that look again.

"I *can* count on you, can't I, Brother Franklin?" The action of the Barrett made a loud *clack* as it slid closed.

"Always, Brother Michael."

"Then who do you think we should send to God first, the woman or the boy?"

Franklin searched a long time for the right words. "I'm sure that any decision you make will be the right one, Brother Michael."

That unsettled, appalled look would soon be shared by the entire world, Copley thought.

CHAPTER TWENTY-FOUR

Nothing happened at the mansion for an hour and a half. Literally nothing. The sentries didn't change, and no one left or arrived. From this distance, with the equipment they had available, there was no way to monitor what might be going on inside, but Jonathan's instincts told him that they were in a lull.

It was possible that they'd missed their precious cargo completely, but thoughts like that were self-defeating, so he pushed them away. If they'd blown the mission, they'd blown it. For the time being, until he had data to the contrary, this was their plan.

As the sun dropped, it took the temperature with it, and under a new moon without a cloud anywhere, they were staring down the maw of double awfulness: frigid temperatures and a bright starlit sky.

He'd switched to night vision about fifteen minutes ago, and the view was like green daylight. Once Venice had the coverage she needed and she'd successfully overridden the video feed, they would move into the house and liberate their precious cargo.

"Cars coming," Boxers said into his earbud. The sudden noise startled him.

"A bunch of cars," Venice corrected. "I thought nothing was supposed to happen till seven."

"Damn bad guys didn't read the playbook," Boxers mocked. "What're you thinking, Scorpion?"

Jonathan answered with a question. "Mother Hen, do you have enough to cover an entry now?"

"I could use more," she said.

"With all this activity out in the front yard, we're missing the perfect opportunity to enter through the back," Boxers said. "Distracted guards are my favorite kind."

"Understood," Jonathan said. "We wait till Mother says it's okay to go." He shared Boxers' urge to move, but he stifled it. You had to take a longer view of these things. The video loop was as much about their escape as their entry, and he was rolling the dice that five minutes wouldn't make a lot of difference one way or the other.

Jonathan counted seven cars in total. Most were pickup trucks or SUVs, but there were a couple of beat-up sedans in the mix as well. The headlights flared his night vision, so he flipped the goggles out of the way. In the starlight, though, while he could see people moving, he couldn't get enough detail for a hard count.

"Big Guy, how many people do you see?"

"I don't have the angle for that," he said.

"I want you to know that I'm feeling very left out back here," Gail said.

"We'll be there soon enough," Jonathan promised. "How are we coming, Mother?"

When she didn't bother to reply, he knew that she was lost in concentration. A minute later, she said, "Okay, team. Go."

Three minutes later, they'd all gathered in the rear of the mansion. They reviewed the plan one more time, and when

Jonathan was satisfied that everyone knew what to do, they moved toward the house. Having studied the architectural plans, they'd decided to make their entry through a door that led to a back hallway near the kitchen. Stealth mattered tonight, and that meant subtlety.

For now.

The first order of business, then, was to find the electrical service and wire it with explosives. If the moment came when they wanted darkness, they would want it right by-God now, and detonating cord with a wireless initiator would do the trick.

They found the meter on the black side, in the corner nearest the red side. Gail and Jonathan took defensive positions, their backs to the building, rifles at the ready, while Boxers set the charges.

When the Big Guy was done, he turned and gave a thumbs-up. "Let's go in," he said.

The three of them moved in a deep crouch to stay below the level of the windows as they made their way along the back of the house to the door they'd selected as the point of entry.

"How sure are we that there are no alarms?" Boxers asked into the radio.

Venice answered, "I've deactivated all the alarms for now. Windows, doors, the whole nine yards. Besides, who keeps the intruder alarm on when people are arriving for a meeting?"

That was good enough for Jonathan. He stooped to his haunches and unslung his ruck. While he and Boxers were cross-trained in everything—except for flying aircraft, which was the Big Guy's exclusive purview—their job functions broke down roughly along the levels of violence required. Boxers was the breaker of things and the blaster of holes.

Jonathan found the fiber-optic cable he'd been looking for in its designated pocket in his ruck. Just to make sure there wasn't a crowd of people waiting on the other side of the door, he used the point of his KA-BAR to dimple the weather stripping at the base of the door and threaded the spaghetti-size cable into the space beyond.

Turning his head, he noted that both members of his team were watching him work. "Don't look at *me*," he said. "Look out for bad guys."

"And if we see them?" Gail asked.

"Try not to shoot."

The cable he threaded under the door contained both a camera and a transmitter, tuned to his PDA. He flipped his NVGs out of the way, cupped his hands around the screen to shield the light wash, and took a tour of the room beyond. It took the better part of a minute for him to fuss with the exposure enough to get a clear picture of the dark space.

"Looks empty to me," he said. "All I see is a lot of closed doors. There's light at the far end of the hallway, but I don't see any people."

Now for the burglar stuff. Jonathan kept his lock set in a leather pouch about the size of a very thin pack of cigarettes. He thumbed the cover flap out of the way and found the Y-shaped tension bar and the rake, a three-inch steel rod with a serpentine squiggle at the end. He put rotation pressure on the keyway of the dead bolt, and then dragged the rake along the top and the bottom to dislodge the pin tumblers. In short order, all of the pins moved, and the lock turned. It took even less time to pick the knob lock.

The door floated inward.

"Peeping Tom *and* burglar," Gail whispered with an admiring smile. She adjusted her M4 in its sling. "Let's go."

Jonathan put a hand on her chest. "You're out here for external security," he said. "We need eyes outside, and Big Guy and I have done this together a lot of times." He sensed that he'd just hurt her feelings, but he didn't care. Not now. If there was fallout, they could deal with it later.

She said, "Keep in close contact, okay?"

"Deal," Jonathan said. He turned to Boxers. "You ready?"

"Oh, my, yes," he said.

Because of their relative sizes, it always made sense for Jonathan to lead on any entry. He pushed the door open, took two steps inside, and dropped to a deep crouch, his M4 trained on the hallway ahead. The last thing he wanted at this point was a gun battle—that would almost surely cause the Nasbes to be killed. Two seconds later, Boxers was in and the door was pushed closed again.

This was where it got tough. Absent any useful intel, Jonathan and Boxers had become little more than well-armed burglars. They would have to feel their way into this new environment, using the ancient floor plans as a template, but anticipating that everything about them was wrong. They didn't know where the bad guys were, and, even more critically, they didn't know where the good guys were—assuming that they were here at all.

Their advantage had been whittled to nothing more than superior marksmanship.

For the better part of a minute, they stayed frozen in the hallway, listening and watching. With buds in both ears—the right one for the radio traffic and the left to monitor any audio feeds they might get—it could be difficult sometimes to pick up distant conversations. You had to adjust to the ambient noise, and then react as much to background anomalies as to actual sounds themselves.

In this case, he heard the people arriving in the front of the house, but their conversations were an indiscernible rumble.

"Can we at least get some cover?" Boxers whispered over the radio. In superquiet environments like this, the radio was the most efficient way to communicate. The mikes they used could pick up the faintest whispers, yet still be decipherable in the middle of a firefight.

"I think we need to split up," Jonathan whispered.

"And I think one of us just had an aneurism," Boxers replied, "because I could have sworn that I just heard my boss suggest that we split up. That ain't happening."

"We've got to. We've got to search the house, and we need to find out what's going on at this meeting. Together we make too big a footprint. Separately, we can stay out of sight easier."

Boxers made the growling noise that usually meant surrender. "Promise no shooting without me," he said.

"Not if I can avoid it. You stay on this level with the guests. I'm searching for the basement."

Boxers didn't like it, but he didn't argue. "Shout if you need me, hear?" he said.

Jonathan crossed his heart. "Got it. And no killing people just because you're bored."

The second door on the left led to the basement. Boxers was with him step-for-step until that moment, and then, after they parted with a knuckle knock for luck, Jonathan was on his own.

The stairs were finished with lush carpets, and the walls on either side were decorated with artwork that Jonathan could not have cared less about. He noted with interest what appeared to be drops of blood on the walls. When he touched one, it smeared, and he became even more convinced that he was in the right place.

He descended along the side of the risers for the same reason every teenager who ever returned home after curfew did: the farther you stay from the center of any board, the less likely it is for it to squeak. He chose the left side so that his right hand—his preferred shooting hand—could remain on the grip of his M4.

He moved slowly, taking one step at a time, pausing between each to listen for any noise that might indicate trouble.

Patience was a great asset to soldiers and burglars alike, and perhaps the single most distinguishing trait that separated professionals from amateurs. The slowness was agonizing; the temptation to just get it over with overwhelming.

It took every bit of five minutes for Jonathan to reach the carpeted floor. Now he knew that the floor plans were a waste of paper and electrons. The place was fully furnished down here, complete with a pool table, a bar, and a big-screen television. A man cave. And it was entirely unoccupied.

It also took up only about a quarter of the total footprint of the house, maybe less. That meant that there was more to the place than what he could see.

A vertical seam of light on the far side of the room solved the riddle. As he closed to within a few feet, he clearly saw the outline of a double door in the wall. Lowering himself to his knees, he once again used fiber optics to peer into his future.

The image on his PDA showed a brightly lit area of utilitarian construction. An unremarkable off-white hallway rose from an unremarkable tile floor. Distances were difficult to judge, but every ten feet or so, the walls gave way to closed doors. He'd seen this sort of unimaginative décor in countless office spaces throughout the world.

The good news was that he didn't see any people in the camera's field of view. But *someone* had left the lights on.

Hoping to find the means to open the door, he used the flat of his palms and rubbed the door from knee to shoulder height. Sooner or later he'd find a knob. When he couldn't find it after a minute or so, he flipped his NVGs out of the way and opted to use the muzzle light from his M4. Within seconds, the bright white disk of light revealed not a knob but a D-ring that had been recessed into the wall. If there was an alarm system, he couldn't see it.

Didn't mean it wasn't there, though. He winced in anticipation as he turned the ring. While Venice could easily disable even a sophisticated system from sounding the alarm at the off-site headquarters, she was powerless to silence local alarms that were tied directly to the sensors.

Holding his breath, he pressed the door open, and . . .

Nothing. The mission gremlins remained on his side. He

slipped inside and closed the door behind him. He pressed his transmit button and whispered, "Radio check." He would have been inaudible to someone standing two feet away.

Venice answered, "A little crinkly, but I've got you."

"I'm in the basement."

"Copy. Take care of yourself."

The first order of business was to establish a forward operating base for himself here in the bowels of enemy headquarters. If the conversations they'd monitored were still operative, he had more than an hour to kill before anything interesting happened, and standing in the middle of the hallway for that amount of time was a nonstarter.

He decided to start in one of the offices. First, though, he owed his team some intel. "Mother Hen, Scorpion," he said.

"Right here."

"I've got a total of eight rooms on either side of the first hall, directly inside the doorway. They're pretty heavy construction, and they've got some heavy locks." In Jonathan's experience, people used big locks to secure against big fears—the kind of fears that posed big threats to people like him. In his mind, he could see Venice back in Fisherman's Cove typing like crazy to document what he was telling her.

"More in a minute," he said.

Neither of the first rooms on the right or the left bore padlocks, so he targeted those first. The one on the left was locked at the knob; the one on the right was not, so he chose the locked one. There was no way in the world he was going to hang out in an unlocked room, and if the room on the right was supposed to remain unlocked, so be it.

Using his picks, he gained entry in seconds. He was in somebody's office. The computer and the file cabinets were a dead giveaway. He locked the door behind him and keyed his mike. "Radio check."

"Not as strong as before," Venice said, "but I've got you."

"Continuing, then," Jonathan said. "The hallway on my side terminates in a right-angle turn to the north. I can't see around the corners, but it looks to me as if this area is designed either as secure office space or secure storage. I'm about to step out to surveil the area now."

He didn't wait for a response. Stepping back into the hall-way, he turned left and eased quietly down the hall. He moved at a crouch, his M4 up to his shoulder and ready.

The bright light was his greatest immediate hazard. At least they were overhead fluorescents. The shadows thrown by fluorescents were far less prominent than their incandescent cousins.

Jonathan heard voices as he approached the turn, and stopped. If they were approaching him, he was screwed; the mission would come to a violent end right now. As it was, the voices seemed stationary, neither getting closer nor farther away.

With his M4 dangling parallel to his body via its sling, Jonathan moved at an excruciatingly slow pace to the end of the hallway at the turn. He pulled a rubber-handled dental mirror from a pocket in his sleeve—the analog equivalent of fiber optics—and used it to take a look down the perpendicular hallway. He advanced it with the lens pointing toward the floor to guard against an unintentional flash of light, or an errant reflection fairy on the wall.

What he saw made his stomach flip. Two young people, late teens, early twenties—a boy and a girl—stood about halfway down the hall, flanking a heavy door. They both wore holstered sidearms and appeared heavily engaged in a whispered argument, the text of which he couldn't hear. The girl was the one standing farthest from him, and she was turned so he could see her face.

When he realized that he recognized her, he nearly gasped. That was the shooter from the bridge.

In his ear, Boxers whispered, "Okay, we're pegging the weird-o-meter up here. They're changing into robes. Think Klansmen without the hoods."

Jonathan withdrew his mirror, replaced it in his pocket, and quietly unslung his ruck and placed it on the floor. They needed to be able to watch what was happening in that hall-way.

"This is a trial," Boxers whispered. "But the defendants aren't present, and there's not a lot of doubt how it's going to go."

"You're talking a lot," Venice said. "Are you under enough cover?"

There was a pause. Then Boxers tapped his microphone to say yes.

Jonathan found the wireless camera and transmitter he was looking for in the left-side pocket. He splayed the flexible wire legs that served as a tripod, and he placed it on the floor, using the point of his finger to move it past the angle of the turn. About the size of his thumbnail and black, it would be visible to anyone who looked at it, but if you didn't know what you were looking at, it could easily be written off as an insect. In fact, he'd had a few of these babies stomped on over the years.

"I've got your signal," Venice said in his ear without him asking. "I see two people standing in a hallway. They've made no indication that they've seen you."

Jonathan acknowledged with a tap to his transmit button. What he needed was a way to peek inside that room they were guarding. If the Nasbes were there, and they were to-gether, he'd pull Boxers in, snatch them both, and make a running getaway. But he couldn't do that with the guards there.

With nothing better to do, he headed back to his make-shift FOB to wait out the next event, whatever that might be.

While he did that, Venice polled them for situation re-ports. Boxers replied by breaking squelch, and Gail said that she was bored.

Boring was good, Jonathan thought. But he doubted that it would stay that way for long.

CHAPTER TWENTY-FIVE

The pain in Ryan's arm had dulled to a low, constant throb, punctuated by occasional jolts of agony when he gave in to the urge to test if it still hurt to move his fingers or wrist. It was a stupid thing to do—it *always* hurt, and why wouldn't it since the bones were broken?—but he couldn't resist. It was like testing the wet-paint sign, only with high-voltage paint.

The splint and the sling definitely helped. He supposed that he should feel more grateful to Sister Colleen than he did. She showed him kindness that no one else showed, after all, and she liked his muscles. But even if she blew him, there'd be no getting around the fact that she was a flaming nut job.

He refused to believe that they were really going to kill him. That thing with Brother Stephen had been an accident, after all. Wasn't a broken arm punishment enough? Besides, why go through all the effort to splint his arm if they were just going to murder him anyway?

He tried not to think about what might have happened to his mom through all of this. If they knew about Brother Stephen, then they had to have done something about her.

He tried telling himself that it couldn't be any worse than what Brother Stephen had been trying to do, but he knew that wasn't true. He'd seen movies, and he'd read books. He knew all about how awful people could be to each other.

For the life of him, though, he couldn't begin to understand why it was happening to them.

He pushed it all away, because the only way to keep the panic at bay was to keep yourself from thinking about it. Besides, he had a far more pressing matter to address. With difficulty, he rose to his knees, and then to his feet. He walked through the dark to the seam of light he knew to be the door, and knocked on it with his left hand.

"Hey!" he yelled. "I need to go to the bathroom."

"What do you want?" a male voice yelled, startling Jonathan out of an empty place in his head. He shifted his eyes to the remote image and saw that the sentries at the door down the hall had both turned to face it.

"Well, hold it," the guard said again.

Jonathan couldn't hear what was being said from the other side of the door, but the phrase "hold it" could only mean that the prisoner was asking to use the restroom.

The female guard—the shooter from the bridge—sagged her shoulders and said something that Jonathan couldn't hear, but looked like an argument in favor of bladder maintenance. She held out her hand, and her partner gave her a key.

"Looks like they're opening the door," Venice reported from her screen. By giving the updates to the rest of the team, she saved Jonathan possible exposure by being overheard.

The door down the hall opened, and out stepped the young man Jonathan recognized from his picture to be Ryan Nasbe. He was smaller than Jonathan had been expecting, and he carried himself as if he was in pain, sort of hunched at the shoulders, consistent with the broken arm that Kendig Neen had alluded to in his telephone conversation.

The male guard led the way down the hall, directly toward Jonathan's camera. He looked young, fit, and strong—exactly the opposite of what Jonathan would have liked. He was big enough to block the camera's view of Ryan until he passed the lens, and that's when Jonathan got his first solid look at the boy's arm.

"It's definitely Ryan Nasbe," Venice reported. "And his arm is heavily bandaged. Looks like it might be broken."

"Do you need me, Boss?" Boxers asked, his whisper barely audible.

"Negative," he whispered.

"I'm on my way," the Big Guy said.

"Scorpion says negative," Venice said. "He'll call if he needs you."

"We need to take him *now*," Boxers insisted. "These guys up here just sentenced him to death. Him and his mother both."

All of them were past the camera now, but Jonathan could hear them in the hallway outside his door.

"Hold your position, Big Guy," Venice said. "Scorpion is very exposed. You'll have no cover."

A door on the opposite side opened. "Make it fast," the male guard said.

Jonathan considered firing up another camera so he could peer under his door into the hallway, but decided that it would take too long and risk making too much noise.

"Can you at least close the door?" Ryan's voice sounded young for sixteen, but Jonathan liked the attitude he heard. He was more impatient than whining.

"Just do what you need to do and get it over with."

Jonathan realized now that the unlocked door he'd encountered was the bathroom for this level.

"For heaven's sake," the female said. "There are no windows in there. Let him go to the bathroom in peace."

A cell phone rang.

"I swear to God, kid. If you step out of line—if you lock

the door or even think an ugly thought, I'm going to bend that break backwards."

The door closed.

The cell phone's third ring was cut short. "This is Brother Zebediah."

Boxers said, "Scorpion, I know you can't respond, but listen to me." He was speaking a little louder now, less guarded. That must mean he was no longer directly in harm's way. "I urge you in the strongest possible terms to take him now if you have a shot."

Zebediah said into his phone, "I understand. Yes, sir. Right now."

Jonathan drew his KA-BAR knife from its scabbard on his shoulder. It would take only seconds. At this distance, he could be in the hallway and have both guards bleeding to death in less than three seconds, well before they would be able to process that they were under attack. One slash each across the throat, and they'd fall like big bricks. He'd have Ryan, and they'd be out of here, and then they could sweep in and rescue Christyne.

Brother Zebediah closed his phone—Jonathan could hear the snap of the plastic—and said, "It's time."

"Both of them?"

"Both of them. Now."

Jonathan glanced back at the screen of his PDA. *Both of them.* Christyne Nasbe wasn't here. They'd left the door Ryan had been imprisoned behind open and unguarded. If she were here, someone would be guarding her.

"One is better than none," Boxers said in his ear, as if reading his thoughts.

Ryan had never realized just how useless his left hand was to him until he tried manipulating himself to pee. You had the zipper, the underwear and finally the business parts. For a while there, the smart money said that he'd end up letting fly while still inside his trousers, but in the end, he got everything where it needed to be, but without much time to spare.

Then, when he was done, there was the whole matter of reassembling himself. On a different day, it would have been funny. He was smiling, in fact, when he opened the door again and addressed his captors. "Wow, do I feel bet—"

Something clearly had changed. Brother Zebediah looked way angrier than before, and Sister Colleen looked as if she might cry.

Ryan stopped and took a step backward. "What?"

They grabbed him.

The boy yelled, "Ow!" and there was a scuffle on the other side of the door. "My arm! What did I do? Please!"

Jonathan's fist tightened on the knife handle. The screams were excruciating to hear.

There was more scuffling, and something hit the door to Jonathan's room hard. He imagined that it was a person, and because it wasn't accompanied by a shriek of pain, he figured it had to be one of the guards.

"Stop fighting," Brother Zebediah commanded. "You're coming with us one way or the other."

"I'm not fighting you!" Ryan yelled. "You're hurting me!"

That last part sounded farther away. A moment later, the door at the end of the hallway opened and closed, and then Jonathan was bathed again in silence.

He keyed his mike. "They're coming toward you, Big Guy. Do *not* take them here. PC-Two is not accounted for. We'll let PC-One lead us there."

"For all we know, PC-Two is already dead," Boxers said. Then his voice dropped again to a barely perceptible whisper. "I see them. Shit, there's only two guards."

"Gunslinger here," Gail said over the radio. "I'm flooded

with guards out here, white side. Soldiers. Whatever. I count fifteen, and many are armed with rifles. I concur with Scorpion. We need to let them go."

"But I can take them."

"Stand down, Big Guy," Jonathan said.

Boxers hissed, "This is a mistake."

"Stand. Down," Jonathan said forcefully. "It's my mistake to make."

He wondered if the Nasbes would disagree.

Outside, Gail had positioned herself in the trees out front, roughly in the position that Jonathan had held earlier. Once the team was inside, it made sense for her to reposition herself to where the action was. And as the parade of people took to their cars, she realized that it was time to reposition yet again.

She'd been listening to the communications, so she knew that they were taking Ryan Nasbe to his execution. The presence of all the cars indicated that they had to drive to the place of execution, and that meant that she had to follow them or lose them.

She needed to get to the truck. That meant running faster and farther than she had in a very long time, but only after she'd backed away far enough from the house that she could afford to make some noise. She gave it about twenty yards—long enough that she heard the sound of engines starting—and then she started to jog. Having arrived in the daytime, yet leaving at night, she had to guess at her directions until she fished her GPS out of a pouch pocket in her pants. It confirmed that she was right.

Tree branches slashed at her as she sprinted through the night, and bushes conspired to trip her. But for the night vision, it would have been impossible. As it was, her rucksack, with all of its equipment and bulk was making it nearly impossible.

She keyed her mike. "I'm following them in the car. Be

advised I'm shedding my ruck in the woods." As she shrugged out of the straps and let the pack fall to the ground, she punched a button on the GPS to mark the spot so they could come back and get it later, if that's what they decided to do. Forty pounds lighter now, she was still burdened with her rifle, sidearm and ammunition, yet she still felt light enough to float away.

Between clatter of her equipment and the racket raised by plowing through the underbrush, she knew she was making way too much noise, but she didn't know another way.

A voice yelled from the dark, "Hey! Stop."

At the very same instant, Venice said in her ear, "Gunslinger, there's a sentry on the live feed. He's very near you."

Gail's heart skipped, but she kept moving.

"Stop!" the voice yelled again. "Stop or I'll shoot you."

"He's gaining," Venice said. "And the cars are loading."

Jonathan's voice crackled in her ear: "Turn and shoot, Gunslinger."

"I swear to God, I will shoot you!" the pursuer yelled.

Gail slid to a halt and turned. The sentry was indeed close, maybe twenty feet away. In the green glow of the night vision, he looked young, but it was hard to assign an age. Early twenties, maybe.

"Who are you and what are you doing here?" the sentry asked. His voice cracked, the fear obvious. He held his rifle at chest height, the stock tucked under his armpit. Either he hadn't been trained, or the training hadn't stuck.

Gail said nothing.

"Cars are rolling," Venice said.

"What's Gunslinger doing?"

"Looks like she's talking. The guard has her at gunpoint."

"I said, who are you?" the sentry pressed.

"Gunslinger, Big Guy and I are on the way," Jonathan said. "We're clear of the house."

Gail searched her brain for alternatives. Things were unraveling quickly.

The sentry stopped. "What . . . holy shit, you've got a gun!" He shouldered his weapon.

That was it. As Gail dropped to a knee, the sudden movement must have startled the sentry because he fired a wild shot as she swung her M4 up to her shoulder. She fired three times, hitting him twice in the chest and once in the head, the third bullet drilling him after he was dead.

"Shots fired! Shots fired!" she heard in her ear. She thought it was Jonathan, but wasn't sure. She wasn't sure of anything other than the fact that she'd just killed a young man in cold blood.

The voice in her ear said, "Gunslinger, sit rep."

He lay so still. Such was the awesome power of a bullet that it could end everything in a fraction of a second, snuffing a life that had barely begun.

"Gunslinger! Answer up."

Venice said, "She's not moving, but appears to be okay."

"Gunslinger, Gunslinger. Can you hear me?" Now the stress in the voice—it was definitely Jonathan's—was obvious. She could hear the impact of his running footsteps in his words.

Her body felt leaden, paralyzed. By any reasonable standard, she had just committed murder. Jonathan would tell her otherwise—that the larger cause justified the sacrifice— but that wouldn't change the facts. She knew the elements of the law, and if presented with these facts—an armed trespasser kills the owner of the trespassed property—the most junior prosecutor in the most backward jurisdiction in the country would walk away with a conviction without even breaking a sweat.

"Gail! Are you all right?"

She slapped her transmit button. "I'm fine. He's dead."

And Ryan Nasbe would die if she didn't get her ass in gear and do something. There'd be plenty of time to beat herself up later. The sentry would be dead forever, after all.

She took off at a run again, her GPS taking her directly to

the spot where they'd cut the wire. She scaled the fence, vaulted to the other side, and then headed for the truck.

"Mother Hen, this is Gail." She couldn't bring herself to use her Gunslinger handle. Not now. "Are the cars all gone?"

"Negative, but I saw the Nasbe boy get loaded into a white pickup truck. He appears to be hurting badly. His truck has left."

"Any obvious response to the gunshots?" Jonathan asked.

"Nothing I can see," Venice said.

"Gunslinger, hold your position at the vehicle. We'll be with you in three minutes."

I don't have three minutes, she didn't say. In fact, she didn't say anything. She had a job to do. Doing it right, she decided, meant not waiting for anyone.

She found the truck right where they'd left it along the side of the narrow road, its doors unlocked, keys in the ignition.

"Gunslinger, Scorpion. Did you copy?"

She hesitated for an instant, and then pressed the transmit button. "I copied," she said. "But I'm not waiting. They're leaving now. I'm following. I'll report back what I find."

The engine turned on the first crank, and two seconds later, she was on her way to somewhere.

CHAPTER TWENTY-SIX

"How's that plan working for you now, Boss?" Boxers poked as they arrived at their parking spot to find the truck gone. His chest heaved for air.

"Well, what do you expect?" Jonathan poked back. "As slow as you run, they could've gotten to Ohio before you got to the fence." In addition to the limitations brought by size and girth, Boxers had adopted a titanium rod for a femur after some unpleasantness while in the employ of Uncle Sam.

Without discussing a plan, they started walking down the road in the direction of the Dodge's skid marks. "God had to make you fast to compensate for bein' so small."

Jonathan laughed.

They kept to the middle of the road as they walked because it was faster. On a bright night like this, out in the open, it was in many ways easier to see without night vision than with it, so Jonathan lifted the lenses out of the way. He'd have done it a minute ago, but Boxers beat him to it, and it was never a good idea to let the Big Guy think that you were imitating him.

"So, do you think she bolted on us?" Boxers asked. His tone was light, but Jonathan knew it was a serious question.

"No, she's following them."

They walked in silence. Their years together had imbued Jonathan with the ability to read his friend's mind. He knew what was coming, and he knew that Boxers was twitchy as hell just thinking the thoughts.

"Hey, Boss, I've got a question for you," he said at last.

Jonathan glanced over at him.

"It's about Gail."

"What about her?"

Boxers cleared his throat, readjusted his M4 against his vest. "Look, I know you two are close. I think you think that other people don't know, but it's pretty obvious—"

"Get to the question, Box."

"Yeah, well." He cleared his throat again. "Do you think she's really up to all this?"

"Which 'all this' are you talking about?" Jonathan knew the answer, but there was something enticing about prolonging the discomfort.

"Look, I know she's great at door crashing, and she can track down evidence like nobody's business."

"But?"

Another throat clearing. "Well, she's, you know, a cop."

"Not anymore."

"I mean in her blood," Boxers said. "I mean at the same level where you and I are soldiers. First and last."

"You're asking if she's trustworthy? If she'll do her job?"

"If she'll do her job without hesitating."

Jonathan craned his neck to look at the Big Guy. "She killed the sentry a few minutes ago."

"Well," Boxers hedged.

"She killed him. Shot him dead."

It was Boxers' turn to look incredulous. "Were you listening to the same radio traffic I was?"

"She shot him."

"Right. About thirty seconds after you would have."

"We weren't there," Jonathan said. "It's not for us to judge."

"Oh, really? Seems to me that I'm one of the first to get drilled if she screws up."

Jonathan felt his blood pressure rising. "Careful, Box."

"Careful about what? I'm not talking about Gail the person, I'm talking about Gail the operative."

Jonathan let silence reign for a minute or more. "I have the same concerns, okay?" he said, finally. "Warrants and probable cause are part of her DNA, and that's a potential hazard to us. Is that what you wanted to hear?"

"Don't treat me like I'm the bad guy here, Dig. We live and die as a team. This ain't personal. Not toward anyone."

Jonathan let it go.

"They've headed into the compound," Gail announced on the radio. "The whole parade of cars went in there."

Jonathan keyed his mike. "Where are you?"

"On my way to pick you up."

Eight minutes later, they were outside the gate where Gail had seen the tail end of the motorcade disappear into the night. They sat in the Dodge, engine and lights off, watching.

"These guys love their fences," Boxers said. As before, this one was chain link with barbed wire.

All three of them peered through digitally enhanced night optics. Jonathan concentrated on the construction of the gate leading to the interior of the compound. "Did you see them open the gate?" he asked Gail.

"It was already open when I got here," she said. "Looked to me like it opened outward."

"As any well-designed security gate should," Jonathan mused aloud. He was becoming more impressed with the sophistication of the operation up here, and being impressed was not good. "Any blockades or blocks on the far side?"

"None that I saw. Traffic was flowing through at the time, though, so if they had any, they would have been down or disabled."

Of course they would, Jonathan thought. It had been a stupid question.

"I count three sentries at the gate ," Boxers said. He looked at his watch. "It's ten till eight. How do you want to handle this?"

"Without a lot of subtlety," he said. Then he gave them the details.

Christyne no longer felt human. Consumed by grief and crushed under the weight of total exhaustion, she felt drained not only of energy and will, but of life. When the hands finally fell upon her and sat her up, she barely felt them.

"Stand for us," a female voice said.

She stood. If they'd told her to fly, she'd have flown.

They supported her—braced her, really—as the bonds on her ankles and knees were sheared.

"Spread your feet apart, please," the female said. "We need you to find your balance." Clearly to someone else, she said, "Get the blindfold off."

More manhandling. This time, everything was made more complicated by Christyne's hair, which apparently was tangled in whatever they were removing from her eyes.

"She's tall," a second voice said. This one was male, and he seemed to be explaining his difficulty in removing the tape from her eyes. It was definitely tape. She could tell by the tearing sound.

They'd killed her son. These terrible, terrible people had killed the sweetest boy in the world, and Christyne had done nothing to stop them. Nothing they could do from this point on—literally *nothing*, including burning her at the stake—

could possibly hurt more than that. And all because of . . . *what*?

What had she done—what could anyone do—to justify this level of cruelty?

The last strip of tape pulled painfully at her eyebrows and eyelashes. She yelped, but no one cared. When she opened her eyes, she tried to focus anywhere else, but there was no fighting the temptation to see that which she dreaded seeing. Almost involuntarily, she shifted her eyes to the floor, where she fully expected to see Ryan's remains.

Instead, she saw only a blood smear. On an altar, it seemed. Truly, this terrible place was a church. What level of blasphemy must that speak to?

"How can you do this to us?" she asked the woman who stood closest to her.

"I don't expect you to understand," the woman said.

"Do not speak to her!" a voice boomed from the back of the room. Christyne jumped at the noise, but so did her captor, whose eyes snapped away from Christyne's face and down to the business of removing the rest of her bonds. The man who had just boomed his command stood in the middle of the center aisle, his hands on his hips. He wore a black robe that covered his entire body, from shoulders to floor.

When her hands were free, Christyne brought them around to the front, and she was aghast at how much they had swollen.

"You there," the robed man said. "Stand tall."

The words triggered a memory in Christyne how Ryan would have popped off to someone who had spoken to him like that. God bless Ryan, ever prideful. Forever dead. Christyne started to cry.

And she stood tall.

"Take off your clothes," the man said.

"No way," Ryan said. "I'm not taking off my clothes for you, you perv."

Even as he said the words, though, he was already shrugging out of what was left of his sweater and shirt. "Why are we doing this?" he asked.

"Soon enough, it will be very clear," Brother Zebediah said. They'd driven back into the compound, but stopped at a different little house from the one in which he and his mom had been imprisoned. It was the same design, but this one looked more lived-in than theirs. It had well-worn furniture, and there appeared to be books on the shelves along the walls. It was hard to tell in the dim light of the kerosene lamps.

"Where is my mother?" he asked. "Is she all right? She had nothing to do with the killing."

Brother Zebediah remained focused on the wall just beyond Ryan. He and Sister Colleen appeared none too comfortable with their assigned duties. They both made a show of not watching him while in fact they watched him carefully.

Bare-chested now, he sat on the sofa to unlace his shoes. His hands were trembling, and tears spilled from his lids. This was wrong. This was so terribly, terribly wrong. If he hadn't messed up his escape, they'd be away from this godawful place. Instead, he'd made everything worse.

With the laces undone, he pulled his Nikes off with his opposite feet. Trembling miserably, he stood and unfastened his jeans, letting them drop as a puddle of fabric to the floor. Cold and exposed, he stood there before his captors in his boxers and socks, covering himself as best he could, his left arm supporting his throbbing right.

"Good thing I wore clean underwear," he joked. Anything to preserve a little dignity.

"Those, too," Sister Colleen said.

CHAPTER TWENTY-SEVEN

Gail drove the Dodge pickup to the front gate with Jonathan in the shotgun seat and Boxers coiled out of sight in the flatbed. She pulled to a stop just outside the gate. The wheels had barely stopped turning when Jonathan had his door open and was stepping out.

A sentry hit them in the eyes with a supernova of a flashlight beam. "Stay in the vehicle, please," the sentry said.

"Get that thing out of my face," Jonathan barked. He'd learned long ago that the right tone of voice caused people to obey. It was instinctive.

The light dropped away. The guard approached him, while another walked up to Gail's door.

"You know the protocol," Jonathan's sentry said. "You stay—"

"Now," Jonathan said. In unison, he and Gail leveled their sidearms at the foreheads of their respective prey. In the same instant, Boxers rose to his full height in the flatbed and leveled his M4 at the startled guard on the far side of the fence.

"Don't move!" Boxers yelled. The command carried the tacit promise to kill if he was not obeyed.

"Listen to the man," Jonathan said to his guard. "You twitch, you die. Gunslinger?"

"He's frozen," she said.

He didn't bother to ask Boxers. The absence of a gunshot spoke for itself.

"Thank you," Jonathan said to the guard closest to him. Like sentries everywhere, this one was a kid, maybe twenty-three. His eyes were one-hundred-percent focused on the muzzle of Jonathan's .45. "What's your name, son?" He kept his tone commanding yet understanding.

"You shouldn't be here," the kid said.

"Well, sometimes shit happens. I asked your name."

"Put your hands down!" Boxers yelled to his guy on the other side of the fence. "Just let 'em dangle, and don't move."

Jonathan's kid darted his eyes up to the sound.

"Look at me, son," Jonathan said. "What's your name?"

"I am Brother Jonah."

"Gunslinger?"

"Mine is Brother James," Gail said.

"Lots of brothers and sisters," Jonathan said. "Must be a big family." He gave a rueful smile that was intended to intimidate. The kid took a step back. "Don't bolt on me, Brother Jonah. You have a very good chance of living tonight. That's not so true of your colleagues. You should count your blessings."

Brother Jonah nodded. "I do, sir. Every day." He seemed to be stating a fact, not being flippant.

"Here's what I want you to do," Jonathan said. He talked him through the process of taking two giant steps back and then lying face down on the ground so that Jonathan could zip-tie his hands behind his back, and his ankles together.

They repeated the procedure for the guard on Gail's side, and then together Jonathan and Gail approached the guard on the far side of the gate, taking care to leave a clear fire lane for Boxers' rifle if it came to that.

"And what's your name, son?" Jonathan asked. Taking a

look at the guard's face, he had to suppress a laugh. Standing there in the wash of the pickup's lights, with Boxers' muzzle light bathing his face, the kid gave a whole new meaning to the expression "deer caught in the headlights."

"I am Brother David," he said. "Please don't shoot me."

"Don't make me and I won't," Jonathan said. "That's a promise. Now, I want you to approach very slowly and unlock the gate."

"The man out there says he'll shoot me if I move."

"Not now. Not that I'm here."

"Does he know that?"

Jonathan sighed. "Big Guy!" he called, louder than a whisper, but not quite a shout. "Tell Brother David that it's okay to move."

"As long as he's careful, he'll be okay," Boxers replied. From behind the lights, and filtered through his fear, he must have sounded like the voice of God to the kid.

"You heard him," Jonathan said. "Move smartly, please."

Brother David did as he was told. He produced a key from the pocket of his coat, slipped it into the massive padlock, and slipped the loop out of the hasp.

"Throw that away," Jonathan said. "Into the woods."

He heaved the heavy lock in an underhand arc that made it disappear into the night. After that, they zipped him up like the others, disarmed him, and dragged him to safety on the far side of the gate's swing arc. He laid the guard face-first in the mulch, and then planted his knee between his shoulder blades.

"I haven't hurt you yet, have I?" Jonathan asked.

Brother David shook his head. "No, sir. Well, your knee hurts some, sir."

"I guess I'm making a point," Jonathan said. "You need to know that I am capable of hurting you a great deal. Do believe that, son?"

His emphatic nod looked more like a spasm.

"Okay, then the way to avoid pain is to answer one question."

"Yes, sir."

"And if you lie to me, I will come back here and cripple you."

"They're assembling in the parade field, sir," Brother David said. "That's where the executions will happen."

They made Christyne strip naked before they gave her a white gown to wear. Gown overstated it, actually; it was more like a muumuu, with slots for her head and her arms. Sleeveless and stark white, the cover reached to her ankles. A cluster of people watched her—men, mostly, but a couple of women, as well. Christyne wondered if the women were there just to keep the men from hurting her. One of the women, herself dressed in black garb with her face covered in the manner of an Arab peasant, actually helped her don the simple garment, holding the openings wide so that it would slide easily over her body.

"She is ready," the dresser said.

Christyne realized that the garment wasn't a gown or a muumuu. It was a burial shroud.

Her stomach knotted, and she started to cry. "Why are you doing this?" she whispered to her dresser. Part of her believed that after nonviolent physical contact as mundane as helping another person dress, there might be a vein of kindness to be tapped.

"Very well," said the man from the aisle. "Tie her hands. It's time to proceed."

Christyne felt panic boil in her core. She tried to focus on options she might have, but nothing materialized for her. All she saw was bleakness and death. This was the payback for showing kindness to a girl on a cold winter night. How could that possibly be right?

If it's possible to tie someone's hands gently, that's what they did. Christyne stood unmoving. She didn't fight and she didn't squirm. They took her arms one at a time, brought them behind her back, and wrapped them with what felt like nylon rope, smooth against her skin.

What would Boomer do? she thought. He probably had nowhere near the superhuman capabilities that she had dreamed up for him as she imagined his exploits overseas. He'd be devastated when he heard about what happened to his family. When he did, the people responsible for this misery had better plan for short futures.

Boomer had his faults and he had his weaknesses, but his sense of loyalty was second to none. Ditto his sense of vengeance.

She just wished that she would be around to see it all unfold.

When Ryan's face crystallized in her mind, it arrived without preamble or even active thought. She saw him climbing out the window of their terrible little cell and looking back at her, wishing that there were a way to take her along.

He'd always been a protective boy. A happy boy, but with his dark side. When she realized that she was already thinking of him in the past tense, misery washed over her and she began to cry.

Outside, a motor cranked and caught. An instant later, the night burned white.

The man in the aisle reached behind his neck and lifted a hood over his face, covering everything but his eyes. He looked like an executioner.

"Bring her to me," he said.

In the distance, the horizon erupted in light.

"What the hell is that?" Jonathan said, pointing.

"Looks like they found themselves a generator," Boxers said from behind the wheel. He'd relieved Gail of her driving duties for a lot of reasons, but mostly because Boxers *always* drove. He was extremely good at it, and he got a little whiny when someone else was behind the wheel. Throw in the lack of legroom in the crew cab's backseat, and it only made sense.

"Scorpion, this is Mother Hen. Be advised, the Web page is up and broadcasting. At this point, all I see is an empty stage, but something clearly is about to happen. The tracer now shows that the transmission is originating in Islamabad."

"Which means nothing," Jonathan radioed back. This explained the blast of light in the distance. "Definitely a generator," he said to the team.

"I think we should take that away from them," Boxers said.

"Mother Hen, Scorpion. Is there any chance we can get support from SkysEye? A little satellite imagery would go a long way."

"I've spoken to the powers that be, and I'm told they're moving heaven and earth, but that it's a major retasking. He is not hopeful."

A new voice boomed on the channel, "The generator is located on the northern perimeter of the parade ground. In front but slightly to the east of the stairs leading to the main assembly hall."

"Who the hell is that?" Boxers asked the truck, not on the radio.

Jonathan smiled. He recognized the voice of the scared kid from last night's wake-up call. "He's a friend from the NSA," Jonathan said.

"A friend from the NSA," Boxers mocked. "I believe they call that an oxymoron."

The role of American intelligence services in special operations has always been tenuous, at best. The intel you received from State was generally skewed toward pacifism, and that from the CIA tended toward hawkishness. Jonathan had learned to depend most heavily on intel from the Defense Intelligence Agency, which had a tactical bent. DIA was about the good guys kicking the bad guys' asses.

The stuff from NSA was always . . . careful. That

with the rod up his ass was still hanging in there made Jonathan proud.

"Who is that on the channel?" Venice said, pouncing on the interruption.

"Let it go, Mother Hen," Jonathan said. He turned in his seat and asked Gail, "How long do you need to take out the generator?"

"Once we find it, it'll be the absolute distance divided by two thousand feet per second."

Boxers asked, "Is the plan changing?"

"Nope. The plan is to get the Nasbes out alive," Jonathan replied. "No matter what the cost."

"That sounds like a goal, not a plan," Gail said from the back.

"It's the best I can do. Rescue, evade, and adapt, and not necessarily in that order." Even as he said the words, he heard their emptiness, and he dialed back. "Once you take out the generator, we'll have darkness on our side. We'll also have the element of surprise."

"Scorpion, Mother Hen. I've got video of Christyne Nasbe being led out of the main building—the assembly hall, or church, or whatever. It's now designated Building Alpha. She's in some kind of ceremonial garb, looks like nothing underneath. Barefoot. Nothing good can possibly come from this. How close are you to being in position?"

Boxers' foot leaned more heavily on the accelerator.

The sudden noise and light startled Ryan. He wondered where it was coming from when the whole town—or whatever you call this place—had no electricity, but then he recognized the unique sound of a generator, probably like the ne that Coach Jackson brought in for track practices after rk.

After they'd made him strip naked, Sister Colleen had d him pull this piece-of-shit tunic over his head—he refused to think of it as a dress—and thread his arms through the corresponding holes.

As far as he could tell, this was all about humiliation and discomfort. The former was obvious, but the latter, the discomfort, was all about making sure that he stayed cold all the time. His bare feet felt like ice blocks against the floor, despite the heat from the wood stove, and the rest was breezy as hell.

"Why are you doing this?" When they didn't answer—*again*—he promised himself never to ask the question again.

When he was finally ensconced in his ridiculous outfit, two guards took turns holding him at gunpoint while the other walked to a closet and donned black KKK robes with a weird facial twist to the hoods. They looked like Arab terrorists. The fact that their faces were covered told him that there was going to be another ceremony of some sort, maybe for another television camera, and the fact that he was wearing this . . . thing, told him that it was not going to go well for him.

Just as they finished dressing, the door to the house opened, and another eight of these masked nut jobs streamed into the room. Ryan felt panic swelling in his gut. They were here to kill him. All doubt that it was anything else evaporated. It's what they promised from the very beginning, but now they had a reason because he'd killed Brother What's-his-name.

Stephen. His name was Stephen, and you should always think well of the dead. Even when the dead guy was an asshole.

"Is the condemned prepared?" asked one of the masked guys in the front of the crowd.

"He is," said Brother Zebediah.

The condemned? Ryan's mind shouted. *What the hell?* Knowing in your gut and hearing with your ears were two entirely different things.

A hand clasped the bare flesh of his biceps on his left side—his good side—and Ryan jerked it away. "Quit touching me!" he yelled, and he started to run. He didn't know where he was going, but he by God knew where he *wasn't* going, at least not without a fight, even if it just meant an extended game of tag through the living room.

The game stopped, though, when Sister Colleen punched him in his arm, right at the spot where it was broken—the spot where she'd worked so hard to help him mend. The bones inside moved against each other at the impact, igniting a sharp, mind-splitting, electrical pain that rocketed through his arm, and up into his neck and shoulders. The spike of agony made him see stars, and his knees sagged.

When Sister Colleen grabbed him under his armpit, she said very softly in his ear, "Don't make us tie this arm behind your back, Ryan. Die with dignity."

CHAPTER TWENTY-EIGHT

As they opened the doors to the church, the cold air hit Christyne like a wall. Fear and frigid temperatures combined to trigger a spasm of trembling. The bright lights blinded her. She drew to a stop just short of the doorjamb, but hands fell on her, squeezing her biceps and nearly lifting her off her feet.

"Keep going," the female voice said quietly in her ear, the sound muffled by the veil that wrapped her face. "It will be over soon."

Christyne looked at her. "What will be over soon?" Even though she knew, she wanted some kind of acknowledgment that she was about to die.

A crowd had gathered in the night. She could feel them as much as see them, a terrible malignant energy that sickened her as she watched their covered heads and robed bodies undulate in the artificially lit night. When they saw her, the crowd erupted with jeering. Fists pumped the air. Somewhere out there, a ripple of gunfire tore at the air. She saw the flashes of light. Women in the crowd ululated. It was as if by walking through the doors into the night, she'd passed into a different part of the world. It was as if someone had brought the Middle East to West Virginia.

"Killer!" someone yelled. Or was it "Kill her"?

Others picked up the chant, and as the noise grew, she realized that either interpretation meant the same for her.

The hands tightened around her arms as she was half guided, half pushed out the door. She found herself standing on a kind of stage in the front of the building. Maybe it was just the porch, but if that was the case, it was a big one. As she approached the front edge, the crowd surged forward, hands reaching for her. One hand grabbed her ankle and she kicked it away. Two of her robed guards hurried to take a position between her and the crowd, as if to provide personal security.

Off to her left, the generator that was responsible for half the noise and all of the light churned away, pumping exhaust fumes into the night.

Once her guards were positioned on either side, another commotion arose from the crowd on the far right, the other side of the stage. More gunshots filled the night. More ululating.

Christyne watched heads turn, and people stand on tiptoes. They craned their necks to see who or what was approaching, and as they did, she scanned the crowd and the night for some way to get away. Even if she were able to shake free of her captors, the crowd would tear her apart as soon as she entered it. This was a frenzied herd of animals, and she was the red meat that would soon be thrown out to keep them sated.

There had to be a way.

Boomer would find a way.

No, she thought, Boomer would never have allowed himself to be taken in the first place.

"Killer!" the crowd yelled. They started chanting it again, and as they did, she was surprised to see so many looking away from her.

She bent forward to see what they saw. It couldn't be.

There was Ryan, dressed identically to her, looking small and bent as he was ushered up some stairs to the same platform as she, but separated by twenty feet.

"Ryan!" she cried.

His head snapped up. "Mom!"

"Kill them both!" someone yelled. "Avenge Brother Stephen!"

Now they had a new chant: "Avenge Brother Stephen! Avenge Brother Stephen . . . !"

"I love you!" Christyne yelled.

True to form, he looked embarrassed and cast his eyes downward.

These people are all crazy, Ryan thought. It sounded like a friggin' football game, with people shouting and chanting. Then the idiots with the machine guns, firing them into the air.

He'd picked up a couple of extra guards as soon as he stepped outside the house into the cold, and they formed a kind of flying wedge to escort him through the mob. There had to be two hundred people out here. At first, he moved as if he were invisible, with everyone's attention distracted by something toward the front of the crowd. He didn't look up to see, because he was too busy trying to keep track of where he placed his bare feet on the freezing ground. When everyone else in the world is wearing heavy boots, you become keenly aware of your feet.

Then they started to recognize him. He didn't know how they even knew what he looked like, but he heard his name muttered nearby. Then the same voice shouted, "That's Ryan!"

The focus of the crowd turned. They pushed and shoved, trying to get closer to him, their hands reaching out to grab him as if he were some kind of rock star in hell. Everyone wanted a piece of him, and every bit of jostling launched new pain through his arm. Through his whole upper body now.

As he approached a set of stairs, he tried to settle himself. As Sister Colleen had told him, he was going to die with dignity.

Someone yelled, "Killer!" and then all hell broke loose. More shouting and gunshots, and that weird warbling sound he'd heard on the news from Arab countries when they get all spun up.

"Keep walking," Brother Zebediah said to him. "Don't slow down." There was fear in his voice, as if his reading of the crowd was as dire as Ryan's.

He had no idea where they were going. For the longest time. All he could see were his own feet and the ass of the guard in front of him. There were occasional flashes of hooded faces, too, but they freaked him out so much that he didn't want to look at them.

Finally, he was at the foot of some stairs, and hands were lifting him to help him climb. He yelled in pain, but no one seemed to care.

The stairs led him to a stage, and when he got there, the crowd really went wild.

He saw the man in black robes holding a knife. It was a long, ugly thing with a tarnished blade and an edge sharp enough to see from here. And somehow, Ryan knew it was for him. His body stiffened and he thought about running.

"Remember what I said," Sister Colleen said.

"To hell with dignity," Ryan spat. His words brought an agonizing squeeze that triggered the purple flashes again.

"Ryan!"

He recognized that voice. He looked up, and there she was, dressed to die, just like he was. The crowd yelled, "Avenge Brother Stephen! Avenge Brother Stephen!" over and over again, yet somehow over the din, he was able to hear his mom say, "I love you!"

His sense of shame overwhelmed him. He'd failed them both, and now they were going to die.

* * *

"Oh, Lord, Scorpion," Venice moaned over the radio. "Both Ryan and Christyne are on the stage now. Can you see them?"

"Not yet, but we're close," Jonathan said.

"Hurry! A man with a hood covering his face is wielding a knife, and the crowd is cheering. He's making a speech."

"What's he saying?"

"There's no audio."

Of course not, Jonathan thought. They were trying to convince the world that whatever this was, was unfolding from the Middle East. An audio track would kill the illusion. This Brother Michael guy knew what he was doing.

One hundred yards ahead, the crowd, dressed all in black, moved less like humans than a swarm of bees on a tree branch. Too many to count, they surged and ebbed at random. Whatever was going on had them fired up big-time. Even with the windows up, Jonathan could hear the cheering plainly.

"What do you want me to do, boss?" Boxers asked. "I can ram the crowd, but the bodies'll probably disable the vehicle. That'd suck."

Yes, it would, Jonathan thought. "We stick with the plan. Get Gunslinger in close enough to where she can make the shot on the generator. We need darkness."

Which meant that they dare not draw attention to themselves too early.

"The angle's gonna be a problem," Boxers mused aloud. "All those people. Unless the generator is on a damn scaffold, it's gonna be hard to get a shot." While he spoke, his foot got heavier on the accelerator.

"Slow down," Jonathan warned. "We get made too early, we're screwed."

"Scorpion, Scorpion. Mother Hen. Oh, my God, you have to hurry. Something awful is happening!"

* * *

Michael Copley stepped forward to the edge of the assembly hall's massive porch, and he held aloft the knife that would change the future. How fitting that it was a butcher knife. The crowd—this flock that adored him, to whom he was more beloved than their own blood—cheered at the sight of it, because they thought they understood what it meant. They thought exactly what he'd intended them to think, and the response was a thunderous cheer.

With the blade raised high, he allowed the cheering to peak, and then he raised his other hand for silence. They obeyed.

Aware of the camera, he wished that he could remove this ridiculous mask and face the world who watched from afar so that they would know the identity of the man who would soon bring true justice. That was not possible, of course, because the world needed to continue to think that they were who they were not. The world needed to continue to believe that the Army of God was the Army of Allah—the Islamic enemy that they wanted so badly to hate. That was, after all, what the computer experts would determine when they saw that this signal was beaming from Pakistan.

As he addressed the crowd, his voice boomed. This was oratory of the old school, and his disciples would know exactly how to react. They had been in training, after all, for twenty years, the last decade made so much easier by the fortuitous disasters in New York, Washington, and Shanksville, Pennsylvania.

Thus, when he released his own carnage in Kansas City, Washington, Detroit and now in Maddox County, West Virginia, the states of America would truly unite in their natural hatred of Islam, and with their attentions distracted, he could fulfill his ultimate goal.

"Brothers and sisters," he yelled, "God bless us all."

"God bless us all," they answered in unison.

"We warned them, did we not? We gave our demands, and

they did not listen. We made a promise, yet they did not believe. And here we are on this night to fulfill that promise."

The crowd cheered louder, and he let them go for a while. The world didn't need to know what they were saying. They didn't need to know the reason for the executions; they needed only to watch a mother and her son die in each other's presence.

Copley looked over his right shoulder to Brother Franklin. "Bring me the boy."

Ryan saw the man coming for him, and he panicked. "Please don't," he said, and he dug his frozen bare heels into the unyielding concrete of the porch deck. He pushed back, trying to run, and someone squeezed his arm again. He yelled. He screamed. Like an animal caught in a trap.

"No! Please. I'm sorry! Please don't hurt me any more!" He heard the words leaving his mouth, and he knew that he was giving the crowd exactly what they wanted to hear, but he couldn't stop himself.

The big man's hand extended from the sleeve of his robe like a snake emerging from its hole, and it grabbed Ryan by the back of his neck. The hand had a ring with a red stone on the finger.

"Please!" Ryan sobbed. He wanted to run. He wanted to disappear. He wanted to fight back, but it just hurt too much, and there were too many of them. "I'll do anything. I swear to God, I'll do anything."

Across the stage, he heard his mom screaming for him.

The man's hand clamped hard around the back of Ryan's neck, and he shifted behind the boy to more easily escort him to the anointed spot at the front of the stage.

Ryan allowed his legs to fold under him like a petulant two-year-old, and for an instant, he was free. Using his left hand for leverage, his feet found traction and he started to run.

Then it became unthinkable.

* * *

"Now, Scorpion!" Venice yelled into her mike. Never the calmest one under pressure, this was the sound of panic.

"Stop," Jonathan commanded, and Boxers stepped on the brakes. They couldn't plow through the crowd. Even discounting the useless carnage, there was no way for them to make it even halfway through the throngs. And if they did, what then? They'd be at every form of disadvantage, with no chance for escape.

"What are we doing?" Gail asked. Her voice wasn't as stressed as Venice's, but it was close.

Jonathan opened his door. "We're adapting. Gunslinger, take your shot from here. Whatever shot you can get. Then take the truck and drive around back of Building Alpha. We'll meet you there."

"We will?" Boxers said. "That's a plan?"

"That, or you stay with Gunslinger."

He didn't wait for an answer. He was already on his way to the back of the crowd when Boxers got his door open.

Christyne was screaming. No words, just the guttural, animal sound of panic and pain and fury. She saw the panic in her baby's eyes and the pain wracking his body. She lunged and kicked to get away, to help him, but whoever had her by her bound wrists held her fast. He was unyielding.

"Let go of me!" she shrieked. "Ryan!"

Her captor's grip tightened, and new hands found her arms and her shoulders. She whipped her head around to the hand at her shoulder and she bit it. Hard. Her teeth pierced flesh, and the taste of blood filled her mouth. A new scream—this one of sheer agony—filled the night, and Christyne felt fulfilled.

Someone hit her in her left kidney, and the pain was exquisite. She bit harder, and she twisted her head, the way a dog would with a chew toy. If they were going to hurt her little boy, and they were going to hurt her, then by God she was going to hurt them back.

Across the stage, Ryan dropped from view. Had he gotten away?

That glimmer of hope made her falter, and at the same instant that another punch landed in the same kidney, and her legs buckled from the blow, the person whose arm she'd ruined let her fall.

Agony flowed as a wave through her back and abdomen, and when Christyne spit blood, she wasn't sure that all of it belonged to the man she'd bitten.

Ryan shrieked.

It was remarkably like the sound he made as a three-year-old, when his Big Wheel dumped him onto the concrete outside their home in Fayetteville. There was blood that day, too, and a cut whose ghost was lost in the bristly fuzz that sprouted from his chin. It was a sound that no mother could ever forget, and her response to it was so hardwired that she felt sick to her stomach the instant she heard it.

Then she saw why.

As they lifted him by his arm, she saw the bones shift under the shredding bonds that held them to his splint. He howled.

"Stop it!" she shouted. "You're hurting him!"

But the crowd loved it. They cheered as if it were a sporting event. "Kill them both! Kill them both!"

They brought him to the front of the stage and kicked the back of his knees. They hit hard against the concrete.

"Brother Zebediah!" the leader called. "Step forward."

A different robed figure, one of the ones who had man-handled Ryan, stepped forward, and the leader handed him the ugly knife with the shiny edge.

Ryan tried to stand.

Jonathan strode into the crowd as if he belonged. He approached from the rear, and instantly he wished he were a taller man. From back here, even with the action on the stage, he could barely see over the hooded mob.

The sick bastards were yelling, "Kill them both! Kill them both!"

As a cheer rose, Jonathan snapped his head up and saw them lifting Ryan Nasbe by his broken arm. Even over the cacophony of the crowd, he could hear the boy's shrieks of agony. But they were nothing compared to the animal howls of his restrained mother.

"Excuse us," Jonathan said as he elbowed through the crowd.

Someone said, "Hey," and pushed back, but Jonathan merely caromed off another spectator and kept focused on the action up front. Dressed as he was, more or less in the uniform of this zoo's own security forces, he seemed to be of little concern. Besides, they all had something far more interesting to watch.

"Scorpion, Mother Hen," Venice said on the radio. "Do you see this? If you've got a shot, now would be the time."

But that was the problem. He didn't have a shot.

Jonathan switched his radio selector from PTT—push-to-talk—to VOX, voice-activated transmission. From here on out, until he switched back, everything he said would be transmitted over the radio. "Big Guy?"

"No shot yet," Boxers said.

"My angle's bad, too," Gail said. "With the M4 at this range, I'm fifty-fifty to hit the kid."

"Then take out the goddamn generator then. Give me *something*."

They kicked Ryan's knees again. This had all become an exercise in pain.

Whatever they'd just done to his arm had screwed him up big-time. The pain enveloped his entire body, from his waist to his neck. When his knees slammed into the concrete, they screamed, too, but there comes a point where a little more pain stops mattering.

In front of him, the masked crowd cheered. He could feel their hatred, taste their desire to hurt him. This was it. This was the end.

And he was too wiped out to do anything about it.

The asshole leader in the black gown called, "Brother Zebediah!" and another asshole in a black gown stepped forward. The leader handed Brother Zebediah the knife. The crowd somehow grew even louder. "You do it," the leader said.

Brother Zebediah said, "Thank you, Brother Michael."

The executioner held the knife up for the crowd to cheer. Ryan felt a hand on his head, and suddenly it felt as if someone were using his hair to pull his scalp off his skull. He tried to stand against the strain, but someone planted his foot in the crook of his knee, effectively nailing him to the floor.

Brother Zebediah pulled back and down on his fistful of hair, and Ryan found himself staring at the sky.

His mother screamed.

The knife flashed against the blinding, artificial light. He saw it shift in the executioner's hand and he saw it come down.

Blood sprayed everywhere.

And then it was dark.

"I've got him," Jonathan said into his mike.

The shot materialized because some tall guy turned to say something to the shorter guy next to him, opening a V-shaped window that exposed the executioners. Jonathan was still seventy-five feet away, but once he saw them pull the kid's head back, he knew that all options had expired.

He planted his feet, whipped his M4 to his shoulder, and snap-shot two rounds. The first one reduced the executioner's head to a bloody mist, and he dropped out of sight. The second took out someone else on the stage who'd had the bad luck to stand directly behind a killer. The knife dropped out of view.

Immediately in front of him, the kid who'd turned his head to talk dropped like a stone, too, knocked senseless by the muzzle blast and the ballistic crack of the bullets passing within two inches of his ear.

Without hesitating, Jonathan shifted his aim two degrees to the right to take out the man who was standing on Ryan's knees, but just as he felt the trigger break, Gail's burst of gunfire found the generator and the world went dark. The status change startled him just enough to make him twitch, so he had no idea if he'd made the shot or not.

It takes a human being about a second to register a frightening incident with a physical twitch, and another two seconds to process its meaning. In a crowd, reactions are slower because of so many conflicting inputs. Against experienced warriors, you've got about six seconds to complete an assault without counterassault. With an inexperienced cadre that is caught completely off-guard, call it ten seconds. That's the window of opportunity for true shock and awe.

After that, the calmer, more experienced troops will start gathering their wits and organizing their comrades. Ten or fifteen seconds after that, you've got a good old-fashioned firefight on your hands.

"NVGs," Jonathan commanded as he flipped his night-vision goggles back over his eyes. The world turned the luminescent green that was natural to him as a sunny day.

Panic swirled around him. People yelled and pushed, stumbling over themselves and each other to get to safety. They buffeted Jonathan, but they were nowhere on his radar. He had his sights on the people on the stage, where the panic was every bit as alive as it was on the ground.

"How you doin', Big Guy?" he asked.

"I'm right behind you, but I think the crowd is catching on."

Just as the words left his mouth, someone yelled, "That's them! Gun!"

This was bad news of the first order.

CHAPTER TWENTY-NINE

Jonathan ignored the provocative words and kept his eyes on the stage. That was his mission. PC-One and PC-Two were both still in his field of vision.

"Big Guy, how much trouble are we in?"

"Too much. They see us. They're pointing."

"Take care of it," he said. Up on the stage, PC-Two—Christyne—lunged for her son, but her guards restrained her. One of them produced a pistol from under his garment, and Jonathan shot him. Then, for good measure, he shot the other guard, too.

The yelling got louder.

Someone blindsided him from the left, throwing a punch that landed mostly on Jonathan's ear. The blow knocked him off balance and skewed his NVGs. The follow-up punch knocked him to the ground. He fell on his ruck, and as he switched his grip on his rifle to repel the threat, three three-round bursts of automatic weapons fire split the night. The attacker and several revelers near him dropped instantly, and the crowd stampeded. Jonathan cast a glance to his left and was entirely unsurprised to Boxers standing there in a shooter's crouch, rifle still pressed to his shoulder.

Jonathan found his feet and refocused on the stage.

He figured they were fifteen seconds into their assault, and the enemy had already figured out the plan and calculated the stakes. The man whom Jonathan had tried to shoot when the lights went out was in fact still alive, and he'd grabbed Ryan Nasbe over one shoulder and under the other, and was using him as a shield as he hurried toward the end of the stage. The guy's situational awareness was perfect, keeping the boy at exactly the right angle to prevent him from being shot.

"Big Guy, PC-Two is yours." Jonathan hated people who hurt children.

When Christyne saw the sheet of blood down the front of Ryan's shroud, she knew beyond doubt that he was dead. Her scream froze in her throat as her heart froze in her chest. This was too much. It was too horrible, too—

The last thing she saw as the world went dark was a look of utter confusion on her son's face.

She lunged to help him as he disappeared into the darkness, but her captors held strong. To her right, a captor yelled, "Weapons out!" and then he made a sound that was half cough, half bark, and he fell heavily on the floor. The instant she heard a gunshot, something hot and wet splashed her, and the guard on her left dropped to the ground. She was free.

In the silver unreality of the starlight, she could make out the developing pandemonium as people on the stage scrambled for cover. Ryan was in the melee somewhere, but she didn't know where. He yelled again in pain. Such a recognizable sound, it rose above everything else. Everyone else.

Guns materialized out of nowhere, and people waved them about. More shots rang out, and the two people closest to her fell dead. Across the stage, she saw others fall as well.

She needed to get to Ryan. Once a center of attention, she now seemed irrelevant to the crowd, as they swarmed in panic. Everyone wanted off the porch now. Some raced inside the assembly hall, but most scattered into the night.

Where was her son? Where was her boy? Just seconds ago, he'd been *right there*, and now, there was no sign of him. She started that direction, but then her way was blocked by the most enormous person she'd ever seen. Tall and wide and dressed in black, his body dripped with weaponry, and his face was covered with a night-vision array.

"Christyne Nasbe," he said. "I'm a friend of Boomer's and we're here to take you home. Stay with me."

With that, he hooked her neck with his arm, pushed her to the floor, and opened fire on the crowd nearest them. People screamed and bodies dropped.

"Ryan!" she yelled—grunted, really, under the weight of what felt like the man's knee in her back. "I have to get—"

"He's being taken care of," the big man said. "He's in good hands. So are you."

He rose to a crouch and wrapped his left arm under her shoulder. The hardware around his chest scraped her frozen flesh and she yelped against the pain, but there would be no wriggling from this man's grasp. When he stood, her feet left the floor.

Wherever he was going, she was going, too.

Jonathan killed anyone he saw brandishing a weapon. Running was fine, cowering was fine. Standing like a deer in the headlights was fine, too, and he saw a lot of all three strategies amid the panic he had created.

The others made their choices and paid the price. He liked to think that their example showed others what not to do. The fewer the guns, the greater his advantage.

He'd lost track of his precious cargo in all the confusion. He saw the man carrying Ryan step down off the left-hand side of the stage, but then the crowd swallowed them. Burdened as he was with a human shield, though, the bad guy couldn't have gotten far. With a compass point to head for, Jonathan pressed forward.

When he heard Boxers telling Christyne through his open mike that Ryan was in good hands, he resisted the urge to correct him. He would be, soon enough.

"Ryan Nasbe!" Jonathan bellowed to the night. "Ryan Nasbe, shout out! I'm here to take you home!"

The people nearest him jumped at the sound of his voice and two of them made threatening gestures, planting their feet for a fight. Jonathan assessed the hazard as low. "Take off, boys," he said. "You don't want to die tonight."

They backed away.

"Ryan!"

Jonathan continued striding into the crowd. With enough weapons, and a certain bearing, people readily get out of your way. They comply with your commands. It's the reason why SWAT teams wear scary-looking clothes. Dispelling violence—or creating it—is as much a psychological exercise as it is a physical one, and Jonathan had The Walk down to a science. People parted from his path as if he were equipped with a railroad cowcatcher.

"Ryan Nasbe! Shout out, son!"

In his mind, Jonathan tried to calculate how many targets were out here. If someone told him the crowd numbered two hundred, he would not have been shocked. He was just gratified that they were mostly in retreat. That couldn't last, though. Sooner or later, someone in charge was going to rally them.

"Ryan! I'm here to help you! I'm here to take you home!"

Then, from Building Alpha's green side, ahead and to the left, he heard the words he'd been waiting for: "I'm over here!"

At about a hundred fifty-five pounds, Ryan wasn't the heaviest kid on the planet, but from the way this guy picked him up and used him as a shield, you'd've thought he weighed nothing at all. Ryan tried yelling and he tried kicking, but nothing he did loosened the man's grip, and everything he did made his broken arm scream.

The whole world was screaming, in fact, literally and figuratively. Through the blast of noise, above the din of the shouting and the gunfire, he heard his mother crying out for him. He cried out to answer her, but he didn't think that his voice cut through enough to be heard.

"This isn't my fault!" Ryan yelled, begging his captor for mercy. "I didn't do this."

"Shut up," the man said.

"Where are we going?"

"I said shut up!" His grip tightened around Ryan's chest enough that he had a hard time breathing.

They'd just reached the corner of the building and turned right to head toward the back of the house when he heard a voice yell, "Ryan Nasbe! Shout out! I'm here to take you home!"

His captor must have heard it, too, because his grip turned pythonlike, squeezing so tightly that Ryan couldn't move air in or out.

This is bullshit, he thought. This was *the* moment. He'd already messed up his first chance to get away; he wasn't going to let something as transient and insignificant as pain ruin his second shot at freedom.

Live or die, this was the time.

Kicking his legs at the air and tossing his head and his good arm, he wriggled like a grounded fish, making himself impossible to hold on to.

"Stop that!" the man commanded as he stopped and grabbed him with both arms in a futile effort to control him.

Ryan heard his name called out a second time, just as he felt his captor losing his grip.

"I'm over here!" he shouted. His voice broke with the effort and rose an octave, but man, was it loud. "On the side of the building! Over here!"

As he slipped through, his captor lost his grip on everything but the boy's bad arm. "Shut up, kid." He tried lifting him by the arm again.

Ryan howled. "The left side of the building!"

Up ahead, at the edge of the shadow, he saw the silhouette of what could only be his dad. He had the night vision and the vest, and he had a rifle at his shoulder.

"Here!" Ryan yelled as he fell to the ground.

Gail's bursts of gunfire had brought instant darkness and panic. From back here, from this elevation, she witnessed the pandemonium. People were running everywhere. The NVGs erased a lot of detail, but muzzle flashes popped right out. From their location, and from the results—bad guys falling down—she figured that her team must be winning.

When she saw Boxers bolt onto the stage and cover PC-Two, she knew it was time for her to get back to work.

She slid on her butt down the windshield onto the hood, and from there darted around to the driver's door. She slammed it shut, adjusted the seat—nothing last driven by the Big Guy could be driven by anyone else without adjustment—and dropped the transmission into gear.

The plan was simple. The guys would seek primary shelter inside the armored walls of Building Alpha, but only long enough for her to drive around to the back, and then they'd get the hell out of there.

How they were going to do that without being torn apart by superior numbers was a little fuzzy, but a plan is a plan. In dynamic situations like this, plans were little more than fantasies, anyway—pictures in your head of how things would go if everyone else played their parts perfectly.

She hit the gas hard to get ahead of the wave of fleeing Klansmen, or whatever the hell they were, and pointed the nose of the truck down the red side of the building.

She was too late. She hadn't yet driven fifty feet before the leading elements of the fleeing terrorists caught up with her.

She hit the brakes hard to keep from running over one of them, and that proved to be her big mistake.

"It's one of the shooters!" someone yelled, and then they swarmed the vehicle. In an instant, they were everywhere. Two of them climbed onto the hood, and God only knows how many climbed onto the flatbed. They stomped at the hood and the windshield, rocking the vehicle violently on all axes of motion.

"Gunslinger's in trouble," she said on the net. "They've got me in my vehicle."

She stomped on the gas again. The wheels spun in the gravel, and as the truck slid sideways, the attackers on the hood and the roof went flying. But the additional two thousand pounds of humanity in the flatbed made the truck sluggish to respond.

Gail dropped the transmission from Drive to Low for the extra torque, and it helped for a second or two.

In her ear, Boxers' voice said, "PC-Two is in hand, we're going to Alpha."

Then the glass in her door erupted in on her, showering her with ragged beads that bloodied the side of her head. Someone pulled her NVGs from her head.

Hands reached through the opening and grabbed the wheel, cranking it hard to the left.

She pressed harder on the gas, but with the wheels turned so acutely, the rest was inevitable.

The centrifugal force flipped the vehicle to its side. Just before she lost her grip on the wheel and was thrown across the cab into the inside of the passenger door, she radioed, "They've got me."

CHAPTER THIRTY

Jonathan saw the man torturing the boy, but there was too much movement for a clear shot.

"Gunslinger's in trouble. They've got me in my vehicle."

Jonathan's heart skipped. He threw a glance over his right shoulder, to where Gail had to be, but all he saw was the crowd of bad guys.

"PC-Two is in hand," he heard Boxers say. "We're going to Alpha."

When he looked back down the green side, the torturer had let the kid drop and was already disappearing around the corner to the black side of Alpha. His distraction with Gail had let his moment to shoot evaporate.

"They've got me."

Jonathan cursed under his breath.

And he turned his back on Gail. He had a job to do. This mission was first and foremost about the Nasbes. Once he had them secure, he could start worrying about the team. This wasn't the way it was supposed to go.

With his weapon pressed against his shoulder, he made his way down the side of the building to the boy. "Ryan Nasbe," he said.

The kid looked confused. "You're not my dad."

"No, I'm not," Jonathan said. "But I sure could use his assistance right now. Can you walk?"

He was already rising to his feet. "My arm's broken."

"Then I promise I won't make you walk on your hands. Stick very, very close to me."

In his ear, her heard all kinds of commotion as people grabbed Gail and pulled her out of the pickup. It filled the airwaves.

"Who are you?" Ryan asked.

The distraction of Gail's capture unnerved him. It would unnerve all of them. He switched his radio to push-to-talk. "Big Guy and Mother Hen, switch to channel two and PTT. Mother Hen, continue to monitor channel one. Hang tough, Gunslinger. We'll come and get you soon." The words hurt his stomach. Gail was on her own.

"Are you talking to me?" Ryan asked.

Jonathan placed a protective arm around the kid. "Scorpion on channel two. PC-One in hand, on our way to Alpha."

The words had barely cleared throat when he heard intense gunfire from inside the building.

"We've got bad guys in Alpha," Boxers said on channel two. Another burst of gunfire followed his words.

To Jonathan's ear, they all sounded like rifles. Five-five-six millimeter, if he wasn't mistaken, and some were set on full-auto.

"I'm coming in on the green side," Jonathan said. "How does it look there?"

"I'm looking forward to you telling me when you get here," Boxers said. Translation: *Hurry the hell up.*

"What's going on?" Ryan asked.

"The beginning of a long night," Jonathan said. "I need you to do exactly what I tell you, in exactly the way I tell you to do it."

Ryan nodded.

Behind them and to the right, the crowd was catching on. They needed to get inside now.

Jonathan moved to the green-side door and tried the knob. Thank God it was unlocked. If he'd had to blow it to gain entrance, there'd have been no way to lock it behind him. He pushed Ryan flat against the wall. "Crouch down," he said, and the kid did exactly as he was told.

Jonathan cracked the door. It was thick and heavy, true to its suspected role as the castle keep. He peeked in. It appeared to be an anteroom of some sort, not unlike the vestry in St. Katherine's Church, where he'd spent hours of his youth as an altar boy. It was empty.

"Come on," he said to Ryan, training his weapon down the side of the building now, in case any of the panicking mob saw them and decided to take action.

PC-One reacted instantly, slipping through the opening and into the room. Jonathan followed and pushed the door closed. It moved with the kind of momentum that would take a hand off if it got caught in the jamb. On the inside, Jonathan used the heavy metal lever to slide steel pins into the sides of the jamb with a resonant *thunk*.

"What was that?" Ryan asked, reminding Jonathan that in the zero-light environment, the kid was literally blind.

Beyond the interior door, a battle raged.

The anteroom provided no decent cover. Jonathan escorted Ryan to the exterior corner. "Stay here," he instructed. "No matter what, stay right here."

Ryan nodded.

"Say it," Jonathan said. In stressful moments, people are many times more likely to remember something they're told if they say it aloud.

"I'll stay here."

"No matter what."

"No matter what. Can I have a gun?"

"No." He didn't have time for this. Boxers needed—

"A knife, then," Ryan said. "I'm not letting them take me again. I'm not letting them cut off my head."

Something in the words resonated with Jonathan. There

was a desperation to them, but also a visceral commitment. And the kid had a point. At Resurrection House, Jonathan told the children that if someone tries to snatch them, they should fight to the death.

How was this different?

He lifted the trouser flap near his right calf, and produced a .38-caliber snub-nose revolver. It was his last-resort back-up weapon. He placed it in Ryan's hand.

"Tell me you're left handed," he said.

"Okay, I'm left handed."

Jonathan caught the tone. "But you're not, are you?"

"No."

"Consistent with the rest of the night," he said.

"Scorpion, Big Guy," Boxers shouted in his ear above the chatter of gunfire. "Sit rep? I sure could use some company."

Jonathan kept his focus on Ryan. "You don't have to cock it," he instructed. "Just point it and shoot. You'll have to pull the trigger kind of hard. You have five shots."

"If they get to me, I'll only need one," he said.

That one stunned him. He clamped his hand around the gun. "Listen to me, Ryan. I made a deal to bring you and your mom home safely. If you shoot yourself, I swear to God, I'll kill you."

Even in the artificial light, he saw the boy smile. He got the irony.

Now it was time to join the war.

Gail understood that the promise to come get her was an empty one. This vehicle was their only way out. Without it, the entire mission was doomed. Looking back, she realized that it had been doomed from the beginning. The whole thing had been driven by too much testosterone and bravado, and not nearly enough thought.

Yet, she'd gone along, and here she was. Having wit-nessed what they'd tried to do to that little boy, she could only imagine what they had in store for her. She wasn't going to give them that chance.

It was useless to resist as the mob rolled the pickup truck all the way onto its roof so that they could drag her out through the broken windows. She closed her eyes as she passed through the shards, and once her face was clear, her gear kept her pretty well protected from the rest of the wreckage. Her only hope was they would be so distracted by manhandling her that they wouldn't notice in the dim light that the tactical holster on her thigh was empty.

They stood her up and pushed her backwards against the side of the vehicle. Hands started to paw at her. She fired her Glock from her hip, and the attacker closest to her dropped. Perhaps the noise was lost in the gunfire coming from the church, but the remaining attackers did not react until she fired again. And again. As two more attackers fell, the others caught on. Most backed away a few steps, some ran. Two raised their rifles. She shot them both, one in the forehead, one on the point of her jaw.

Startled, the rest of the crowd dove for cover. She knew they wouldn't stay down for long, and from what she could see, most of them were armed; they just hadn't yet set themselves to fight. She emptied her Glock at the assembled crowd as she scooted away, not so much aiming as peppering them. The intent was to keep their faces in the frozen ground long enough for her to get out.

When the slide locked back, she dropped the empty mag and slapped in a new one on the run. She slid the pistol back into its holster and switched her hands to the M4 dangling from its sling.

Nothing in her FBI training had ever addressed full-out retreat like this, but she instinctively knew to run in a zigzag and to keep low. She thought she heard firing behind her, but she didn't turn to verify. All that mattered was that she hadn't yet been hit. As long as that was the case, she was fine.

Her only hope at this point was to get to the black side of

the church. From there, she'd at least have some cover. After that, well . . .

When she got to the red-black corner, Gail hook-slid on her butt and rolled to her stomach with her weapon poised on her shoulder. Even without night vision, she could make out a cluster of five or six of them running after her. When they saw her go to ground, two dropped to their knees and brought weapons to their shoulders. The others assumed standing firing positions.

She saw muzzle flashes and she opened up on them. They all dropped, though she wasn't at all sure that she'd hit any of them. Moving with speed she hadn't mustered in a very long time, she belly-crawled to the shelter of the back wall, where she switched to a left-handed grip and peered back around the corner at the troops she'd just shot at.

She felt a huge relief as she saw them all running away.

The first indication she had that anyone was behind her was when something heavy smashed into the back of her head.

Jonathan pressed his mike button and said, "I'm entering from a door on the green side."

"About damn time," Boxers replied. "If it's the door I think it is, you'll be able to hook left a few feet and enfilade these assholes. They're all hunkering under pews and shooting like girls. I'm at the green-white corner. When you're ready, I'll lay down covering fire for you."

Jonathan inched the door open enough to slither out on his belly and pushed it closed again. It was indeed a church, and it was lighted by a massive, three-tiered candlestick chandelier, which cast a bizarre, dancing light in Jonathan's night vision. "Ready," he said.

The second syllable had barely left his mouth when Boxers opened up from Jonathan's right. The M4's muzzle flashes nearly whited out Jonathan's NVGs.

To his left, he saw chunks of wood flying from the wooden pews, and he knew precisely where the bad guys were. He pivoted to his left, rose to a crouch, and with his weapon up and ready, he advanced down the side aisle until he was even with the rows Boxers was targeting.

There they were. He didn't have time to count, but it looked like eight or ten of them. They all wore the stupid caftans, and each of them was armed with some form of rifle, not that they were doing them any good at the moment. They looked more like they were trying to melt into the floor.

They looked so frightened that Jonathan decided to give them a single chance at survival. He said into his radio, "Cease fire."

Boxers' fusillade ceased as quickly as it had started.

In the silence that followed, Jonathan bellowed, "Nobody move! Stay down or I will kill you."

Instinctively, he supposed, two of the shooters raised up. Jonathan stitched the wood above their heads with a three-round burst, and they dropped again.

"Down means down, assholes!" His tone was equal parts madman and drill instructor, specially cultivated for moments just like this. "Flat on the ground, arms out, fingers splayed. That's the only way you survive."

He sensed movement to his right from the white-green corner, and a quick glance confirmed that Boxers has risen to give him better cover.

"Everybody over there good, Big Guy?"

"One of us is bruised up and scared shitless, but—" He cut off his words and shifted his aim toward the back wall. "Guns!"

Boxers opened up at the back wall, where a black-clad figure pivoted and fell.

Jonathan dropped to a knee and brought his own weapon to bear on the shadows.

"Goddamn idiots!" Boxers boomed.

Where there was one gunman, there almost always was

another. Jonathan held his aim, scanning the altar for a target to shoot. In the enhanced artificial light, he looked for curves where there should be straight lines and straight lines where there should be curves. And he looked for movement.

He saw it on the right-hand side of the altar, someone emerging from the shadows, and he swung his aim on it to take it out. He was half a pound from trigger break when he realized that the emerging target was Gail.

"Hold your fire!" he yelled. "It's Gunslinger."

She moved awkwardly, sidestepping out just a few feet into the open. Her weapon was gone, and he thought he could see a smear of blood in her hair.

Then he saw the pistol pointed at her head from behind the curtains that framed the altar.

"Take them, brothers and sisters!" a voice yelled from behind the curtain. "They won't shoot as long as—"

Boxers' rifle shot severed the man's hand at the wrist, and the pistol dropped harmlessly to the floor. It hadn't yet bounced when Jonathan raked the man's location with bullets. Gail dropped out of sight.

In those two seconds of bedlam, mass insanity was born.

It started with a single voice launching a guttural yell from the cowering fighters huddled among the line of pews. It was the sound of raw emotion, and in two seconds, it had metastasized to the entire room.

"This can't be good," Jonathan said.

It wasn't.

As the chorus of voices rose from all corners, he shot a look to Boxers. The Big Guy seemed hopeful for a fight.

He got his wish.

As the ear-shattering eruption of noise crescendoed, robed gunmen seemed to materialize out of ether. One second, the church seemed mostly empty, and the next, it was filled with target silhouettes, each one standing, and each one brandishing a rifle of some sort.

Jonathan eliminated the most immediate threat by unleashing the remainder of his M4's magazine—twenty-one steel-jacketed rounds—down the length of the gunmen to whom he'd tried to show mercy. The bullets left the muzzle of his rifle in seven three-round bursts, and the bad guys were so well aligned that individual bullets had to be taking out multiple targets as they passed through one person into the people standing behind him. He did it all from his knee, and in less than five seconds, the bodies were everywhere.

With that threat neutralized, he shifted his aim to the rest of the cavernous room. He saw one gunman in the far right-hand corner—the red-black corner—but even as his finger tightened on the trigger, he saw blood spray from his shoulders, and he dropped, dead on the spot from a burst delivered by Boxers.

As quickly as the sound had peaked, the room was now silent, save for the moans of the wounded. Jonathan yelled, "Big Guy?"

"Fully satisfied," Boxers yelled back.

"And PC-Two?"

"Still scared, still okay."

"Gunslinger?"

Gail sat up on the stage, her legs crossed, and pressed her hand against her bleeding head. "I'm fine," she said.

Jonathan started his check of the room and the wounded. The issue at this point was not to provide them with medical assistance—they'd lost that courtesy when they opened fire en masse—but rather to disarm them to make sure that they could pose no further threat.

The numbers were astounding. Jonathan counted eighteen dead and seven wounded, all of whom would likely be dead before the sun rose. With the gift of marksmanship came the curse of accuracy. While he surveyed the carnage from the green-side aisle, Boxers shadowed him from the red side. When they were done, they'd collected an impressive arsenal of weapons.

They met in the middle, near the altar, where a Klansman lay with his head unzipped and his brain excised. Jonathan said, "I think we're clear." He walked a few steps to Gail, and stooped to assess her head wound. "Are you okay? Here, let me take a look."

She pulled away. "I'm fine."

"Let me see anyway," he said. He pulled his NVGs out of the way for a better look. The candlelight wasn't nearly bright enough, but he didn't dare give the enemy outside a white-light target. He thought he saw a one-inch gash, maybe worthy of a couple of stitches, maybe not. "I think you'll be fine," he said.

"I already told you that," Gail replied. She surveyed the carnage, really taking it in for the first time. "What's with these people? That was like a mass suicide."

"I write it off to zealotry," Jonathan said.

Christyne Nasbe stood from behind the pew where Boxers had taken shelter. "Where's Ryan?"

Boxers pointed his forefinger as if it were a gun. "You stay down."

"Shut up!" she shouted. "Where's my son?"

CHAPTER THIRTY-ONE

Kendig Neen found himself overwhelmed. As faithful soldiers of the Army swarmed him, looking for leadership and a plan, he was desperately looking for Brother Michael. Unbelievably, several soldiers had reported seeing him and Brother Franklin running away after Brother Franklin bolted from the stage using the Nasbe boy as his shield.

With Michael and Franklin both gone, Kendig was in charge, if only because of his position on the Board of Elders. He'd sidelined himself from the main event of the execution after Brother Michael berated him for showing cowardice.

Oh, the irony.

With a veritable war being fought inside the assembly hall, he needed to form a counterassault, and he needed to form it quickly. As the soldiers of the Army of God fled for their lives, he stood in the open, his arms extended, trying to stop them and bring order to chaos.

Some stopped, most didn't. Of those who did, the majority were members of his security unit. Virtually everyone who had gathered for the execution was armed, so firepower would not be a problem.

He felt pleased that they'd only lost a few minutes to chaos. "Gather 'round me, brothers and sisters," he shouted above the din. Those who heard—those who *admitted* that they'd heard—stopped and formed up around him.

"Everybody settle down!" he called. "Who has hard data?"

"Brother Zebediah is dead," someone said.

"Brother Neil and Sister Sonia Mary," someone else said.

Kendig waved off that information. "I don't need a casualty report. I need to know how many people we're facing and where they are."

"There must be many in the assembly hall," someone said. "Listen to the gunfire in there."

"That's speculation," Kendig said. "I want fact. I want to hear from people who have *seen* things with their own eyes, and who can report *fact.*"

A young lady—Kendig always had difficulty with names—stepped forward. "I saw a very large man take one of the prisoners inside the assembly hall."

"I saw Brother Franklin running away with the boy. With Ryan," someone else said.

The phrase *running away* triggered a disturbed murmur through the crowd.

"Where's Brother Michael?" a soldier asked.

Kendig ignored the question. He needed to motivate these young men and women for action, and if they perceived that the top leadership had run for their lives, nothing good would follow. "What's going on in the assembly hall?" he asked. "Who are the Users shooting at?"

"Brother Benjamin was in there preparing for services after the executions."

"How many people did he have with him?"

"Twenty. Maybe twenty-five."

"Did anyone see the assault force?" Kendig asked. With as many as twenty-five soldiers inside, maybe this whole incident could go away quickly.

"I saw that one big soldier," someone said.

"Huge," someone else corrected.

"I think I also saw someone running after Brother Franklin."

Kendig turned his gaze toward the soldier who spoke of Brother Franklin. "So of course you hurried to help him."

The soldier looked at his feet.

The crowd around him continued to grow, and as it did, a plan began to form in his mind. Two against many was impossible odds. If he could just—

"Brother Kendig!" someone yelled from the night. The tone was frantic.

As one, the gathering crowd turned toward the voice. A clot of soldiers emerged from the night, still dressed in their ceremonial robes. Two appeared to be spattered with blood. "She killed four of us," one of them said hurriedly. Kendig thought he remembered the young soldier's name to be Brother Kurt. "We tried to stop her, but she fought us."

"A woman fought *all* of you?"

"We were in the process of disarming her when she got shots off."

Kendig couldn't believe this. "All of you are armed," he said. "Why didn't you shoot back?"

"We tried, Brother Kendig. We really tried. I think she got away into the assembly hall."

As if to punctuate his point, the shooting in the assembly hall crescendoed.

"We did strip her of this, though," Brother Kurt said. He handed Kendig a portable radio.

Ryan had never heard so much noise. It rolled on and on, individual gunshots combining to form a continuous pounding. As he pressed himself into the corner and tried his best to dissolve into the floor he jumped at the sound of what could only be bullets sailing through the wall that separated him from the shooting. In the oppressive darkness, where his only sensory input was the bedlam of shooting and the stench of gunpowder, he found himself screaming, as if adding a human element to the cacophony would take the edge off so much death.

And then it was over. Just like that, silence became more oppressive than the sound of battle. The silence came so abruptly that he wondered whether he'd gone deaf.

He heard movement out there beyond the door, but it didn't sound violent. It didn't even sound urgent. Just voices talking about things.

Suddenly the darkness of his room—and the loneliness of it—became unbearable. He'd been alone enough. He'd been scared and victimized enough. Now it was time for him to *do* something. He had no idea what that something might be, but by golly, he was going to do it. His hand tightened on the grip of his revolver.

"Where's Ryan?"

Jesus, was that his mom?

"You stay down!" boomed a voice.

"Shut up! Where's my son?"

Ryan coughed out a laugh before he could stop it. That was definitely his mom's voice; but it was attached to an entirely different brain.

He decided that whether the good guys had won or lost, he was going to be with his mother. He stood and made his way to the door. He pushed it open.

"Oh, my God," he heard as soon as he stepped clear of the jamb. "Ryan!"

He turned to his right, and there she was, dressed in the stupid white gown, her arms tied behind her. She ran toward him. She didn't walk quickly, or jog; she *ran*.

As she closed the distance between them, he instinctively turned to present his left side, shielding his right.

"Oh my God, oh my God, oh my God, I thought you were dead," she said.

She was still five yards away, when Scorpion stepped forward and held out his hand to stop her.

"Whoa, whoa, whoa," Scorpion said. He drew an ugly knife from somewhere over his left shoulder and made a swirling motion with his fingers for Christyne to turn around. The rope from her wrists fell away without resistance, and now she was ready to hug her son.

"The arm, Mom!" Ryan said, but he knew that she knew, and he knew that there'd be no stopping the assault of kisses.

She grabbed his face in both hands. "Oh, my sweet baby, I've been so scared. You're so beautiful." She kissed him again.

Embarrassed, Ryan shot a glance at the other men in the room, and he saw that they were embarrassed, too. "Mom."

"I don't care," she said. "You're alive. We're both alive."

She threw her arms around him, and somehow, it didn't hurt.

Emotion bubbled out of nowhere. One second he was embarrassed by all the mommy shit, and the next, he was completely absorbed by it. He wrapped his good arm around her, gun still gripped in his fist, and he buried his face in the crook where her neck met her shoulder.

Wracking sobs came from a place in his gut that hadn't been tapped since he was a kid. Shame and sadness and anger all flowed in an unnerving tsunami of emotion that startled him. And as his tears poured out of him, his mom rubbed his back, just as she'd done when he was a little boy.

"Shh," she said in his ear. "We're fine. We'll be fine. Shh."

He closed his eyes, and he tried to transport to a different time. A better time.

For two seconds—maybe three—it worked.

Then reality returned.

Jonathan was a sucker for a tearful reunion. That was, after all, why he did what he did. But while the Nasbe family enjoyed their moment, he still had a war to fight.

"Close those shutters!" he commanded. True to its role as the castle keep, heavy wooden shutters framed the assembly hall windows. To Jonathan's eye, they were thick enough to stop all but the most powerful conventional firearms. Four-inch-wide slots had been cut vertically and horizontally to accommodate gun barrels in the event of a firefight. They ran from about four feet off the floor to six feet. When closed, they formed paired crosses over every window, as if to further blaspheme.

Father Dom would not approve, Jonathan thought.

His earpiece popped and a deep baritone voice said, "Whoever you are, we need to talk."

Jonathan shot a glance to Boxers, who shrugged. A glance toward Gail told him how the bad guys had gotten a radio. He unplugged the earphone jack so Gail could hear, and he pressed his mike button. "You may call me Scorpion," he said.

A derisive laugh. "Tough name," the voice said. "Scary name."

"That's him!" Ryan yelled, pushing away from his mother. "That's the sheriff, the guy that picked me up. I forget his name."

Jonathan hadn't. "Well, hello, Kendig," he said.

Kendig recoiled at the sound of his name.

"How does he know you?" Brother Kurt asked.

"He doesn't," Kendig snapped. "That boy—that Ryan—is in there. He must have—"

"Are you in danger, sir?" Jonathan asked over the radio. "I'm sorry we let you down."

Kendig felt himself going pale. To the group around him, he said, "He's playing a bluff." He fumbled the delivery, though. He sounded too defensive, even to himself.

"Try to run, Kendig," Jonathan said. "Signal that you're out of the line of fire and we'll open up to keep their heads down."

He keyed his mike. "Nice try, Scorpion. Nobody out here is buying it."

"Oh, my God!" Jonathan exclaimed. "I didn't know people could hear you. I, uh . . . I'm sorry."

Kendig looked to his assembled troops. Some of them were in fact buying it. "He's trying to undermine my authority," he said. "Brother Kurt, Brother Absalom, assemble your soldiers. Prepare them to assault the assembly hall." Into the radio, he said, "Whoever you are, this is your one opportunity to surrender. In ten minutes, that opportunity expires."

When he lifted his thumb from the transmit button, he saw that neither of his commanders had moved. "Assemble your soldiers," he said again.

Brother Kurt shifted uncomfortably on his feet. "Where did these invaders come from, Brother Kendig?" As he asked the question, his hand shifted on the grip of his rifle.

Kendig made himself swell larger and took a step closer to the young man. "Assemble your soldiers," he growled. That deep baritone was a tool he'd perfected over the years. "Or I will shoot you right here and right now for mutiny."

"What the hell kind of gambit was that?" Boxers yelled from across the giant room as he slammed another set of shutters and slid their blocking bar into place.

"Son of a bitch wanted to chat," Jonathan explained, working on his own set of shutters. "So I chatted. I figured he had people nearby, and it wouldn't hurt to throw some psy-ops into the mix." He pointed to Gail. "Gunslinger, check the back of the altar. Make sure every door is locked and blocked. We may be here for a while."

As his ears recovered from the firefight, the moans of the wounded became more distinct.

He eased by the Nasbes to block the windows of the vestry. As he reentered the sanctuary—what else do you call a big room with an altar?—he saw Christyne Nasbe approaching the cluster of Klansmen he'd shot behind the pews.

"Whoa," he said. "Stay away from them."

"My God, there are so many," she gasped. "They're suffering."

"They're dangerous," Jonathan countered. "All wounded animals are dangerous. Wounded animals who know how to shoot even more so. Stay away from them."

"But they're bleeding. Can't you help them?"

Boxers said, "Let 'em bleed long enough and they won't need help."

Leave it to Big Guy to take it one step too far.

"What happens next?" Ryan asked.

Jonathan answered by walking to the stacked firearms and ammunition, and coming back with two M16s and two belts of spare magazines. "What happens next is, it gets interesting," he said. "How about giving me back that peashooter and taking this instead? Give that left arm of yours a workout."

The kid took it, but he wasn't happy about it.

"You want to shoot it out with them?" Christyne gasped. The horror was evident in both her tone and her body language. "They'll kill us."

"Bet you thought you were dead ten minutes ago, didn't you?" Boxer said. His voice rolled through the rafters of the sanctuary.

"But there must be a hundred people out there."

Jonathan held out a rifle for her. "But there's five of us." He said it with his most charming smile.

"That means we have to shoot twenty apiece," Ryan said.

"Well," Jonathan said, "some of them will run away." He was trying to keep it as light as he could, because the reality of their situation was at best dire.

"Generally speaking, we prefer to plan a little more carefully," Gail said from up at the altar. "But the whole execution thing put us on a fast track." To Jonathan, she said, "Everything's battened down back there."

"Are you really a friend of my dad's?" Ryan asked.

Christyne brightened. "You know Boomer?"

"We worked together for a while," Jonathan said.

"So you're in the Army?"

Jonathan gave a coy smile. "We worked together for a while."

"Hey, Boss," Boxers said from the red side wall. "I think you, me, and Gunslinger need to powwow."

Gail heard for herself and walked that way.

To the Nasbes, Jonathan said, "You guys go on with your reunion. Stay away from the wounded, and if you see anything scary, yell out right away."

With that, he walked across the sanctuary to join his colleagues. "What's up?" As if he didn't know.

"You realize our position is untenable, right?" Boxers asked, getting right to it.

Jonathan inhaled loudly. These sorts of standoffs never worked out well for the people behind the barricade. Even with the reinforced walls, the good guys were still only one RPG round or even a bonfire away from dying in place or being overrun. "I'm open to any and all ideas," he said.

"Well, let's take surrender off the table first," Boxers said. "It's not in my nature."

"Nor in mine," Jonathan agreed. "Besides, their judicial system here sucks."

"We have the wounded," Gail said. "They should give us at least a little leverage, don't you think?"

"I wouldn't count on it," Jonathan said. "They're taught to kill themselves rather than submit. If that's their worldview, the wounded are just collateral damage."

"I agree," Boxers said. "So they're coming. What do you think? Good old-fashioned frontal assault?"

Jonathan shrugged. "If I were them, I'd run a feint attack on one side to buy time to set charges on the doors. Blow them, they're inside and we're dead."

Gail looked horrified. "You know, playing with you guys is nowhere near as fun as I had hoped."

Boxers said, "So, we each take a side and stick to our posts no matter what. Is that it?"

Jonathan shrugged. "The best I can come up with. We'll keep the Nasbes together on the green side. I'll take white. Big Guy, you're red. Gunslinger—"

"Black," she said. "I got it. And when we get home, I'm getting a new handle."

"All right," Boxers said, heading to his post. "We'll have us a good old-fashioned gunfight." He'd never sounded more self-actualized.

Jonathan headed off to give the Nasbes their assignments. He gave them a crash course in how to work their weapons, and then took them into the vestry and planted them in front of their assigned windows.

"Keep your selector on single fire," he told them for the second time. "If you see someone with a gun, shoot. If they fall down, move to the next target. If they don't, shoot them again. Questions?"

Each of their faces was like a giant blank oval.

"Okay, good. I'll be in the front. If you need anything, just shout out." The muzzle of Christyne's rifle had started to drift in toward Jonathan, so he reached out and gently pushed it to the side. "And try to remember to keep your weapon pointed outside."

"But the windows on the other side of the shutters are closed," Ryan said.

"They're glass," Jonathan said. "They'll go away once the shooting starts."

This wasn't the way an 0300 mission was supposed to go. If they came out the back end of this thing alive, he was going to owe Boomer one hell of an explanation.

CHAPTER THIRTY-TWO

Kendig's ten-minute deadline was overly ambitious, but he'd known that when he'd first issued it. It would take longer than that to get the Army fully outfitted and ready to fight. Ultimately, as the deadline came and went, that would further unnerve the Users who had commandeered the assembly hall.

The silence from inside the building seemed to have unsettled the soldiers in his Army as they moved farther and farther back from the building. There'd been no more suggestion of mutiny since Brother Kurt's outburst, but the invader's radio ruse had had some impact. Outside the Army's security force, Kendig hadn't had a lot of contact with the rank and file because there'd been no need. He was on the Board of Elders, and as such served an executive role; but living off the compound as he did, he didn't get much opportunity to interact in routine matters.

All of that translated to not a lot of personal loyalty.

The ranks had thinned considerably. Some of his soldiers had been martyred, but he suspected that even more had fled. Those who remained—he figured it to be a force of eighty, maybe eighty-five—were terrified.

The assault that lay ahead fell far outside any training that the cadre of soldiers had received. Their training had always focused on specialized two- or three-person disruption teams who focused on their particular missions. The idea of a mass assault had never been addressed.

But now it was necessary.

Once Sister Colleen returned from Brother Michael's house with his equipment, they'd be ready to begin. He'd allowed her to take his sheriff's vehicle, so it shouldn't take long.

As that thought was passing through his mind, he saw lights moving to his right, and he turned to see his Ford sedan pulling onto the grass from the driveway and heading straight toward him. When it stopped, he was shocked to see four people climb out. He walked over to join them, and as he closed to within a few yards, he recognized the sentry staff from the front gate.

"I found them tied up in the trees," Sister Colleen explained as she opened the tailgate and pulled out two cases that looked not unlike electric guitar cases, but which in fact contained Barrett M82A3 fifty-caliber sniper rifles.

Kendig lost interest in the sentries and turned his attention to the rifles. "Only two?"

"The other two are missing," Colleen explained.

Kendig scowled. "You checked the armory rooms in the basement?"

"That's where I found these."

"And the ammunition?"

Sister Colleen pointed to the two cans on the car deck. "That's them. Green and silver tips, right?"

Kendig smiled. The heavy walls of the assembly hall made a conventional assault virtually impossible, but these Raufoss MK 211 explosive penetrator rounds would make quick work of it all. Tipped with an RDX explosive mixture, the Raufoss round left the barrel at twenty-eight hundred feet per second, but on impact with armor would launch a tungsten spike at four thousand feet per second to punch a three-quarter-inch hole. As the penetrator continued through the hole, it would spew zirconium particles, which would then ignite like a high-velocity sparkler. What wasn't dismembered by the penetrator or blown apart by the high-order detonation of the RDX would likely be incinerated in the long-burning cloud of zirconium.

It was a heck of a bullet.

As he started to load ten-round magazines, he said to Sister Colleen, "Please find Brother Kurt and Brother Absalom and tell them I need to see them."

The narrow view allowed by the slots in the shutters rendered Jonathan's NVGs useless. He wore them rocked back on his head and pressed his monocular against his eye. His first impression was that there were a lot of them out there, followed by a more depressing realization that they were becoming organized. What had once been a crowd of people swarming in their panic had settled down to something that resembled organized units.

"Big Guy," Jonathan called. "What do you see?"

"I got nothing over here."

"Gunslinger?" When he got no response, he called again. This time, she responded. "Right here."

"Do you see any activity?"

"Nothing back here."

"Hey, Nasbe family!"

"We can't see anything either," Christyne reported.

So their entire assault force was gathering in the front of the building. Why would they do that?

"Hey, Big Guy?" Jonathan asked. "If you're the opfor commander, why would you assemble your entire force to the same side of a structure?"

"Got a lot of people out there, do you?" Boxers quipped. "They could just be stupid."

"Let's assume they're smart."

Boxers shook his head. "I can't get there. If they knew

what they were doing, they'd at least come in on two angles. Let's shoot at them and get them to disperse. Lord knows we've got the ammo and weapons."

It wasn't a bad idea. By firing into the gathering crowd, he could disrupt their assault even before it began. It was such a rookie mistake for them put all of their forces in such a small area that it almost seemed irresponsible not to capitalize on it.

Unless it wasn't a mistake. A piece of the puzzle fell into place for Jonathan.

"Hey, Big Guy—"

From a hundred yards away, the woods line came alive with muzzle flashes as the opposing force—the opfor—opened up with a torrent of small-arms fire. Their bullets hit with the sound of so many hammers pounding on the wall. Jonathan brought his weapon to his shoulder and slipped his finger in the guard.

For every muzzle flash, there was a shooter just two feet behind it.

Then he understood.

"Everybody away from the windows!" he yelled.

Boxers looked at him as if he'd just discovered a second nose on his face.

"Nobody return fire," Jonathan ordered. "They're trying to draw muzzle flashes. That's why they're being so obvious."

That didn't help Boxers. And then he got it. "The fifty cal," he said. It was the gun they'd heard being fired while surveilling Michael Copley's house. He pulled away from his window.

"Everybody come into the sanctuary," Jonathan said. "And everybody stay down."

Gail looked particularly confused. "But what about—"

An explosion cut her words—a startling double blast, followed by a fireball and stuff erupting on the altar just beside her. She dropped instantly.

Then the living nightmare began.

* * *

Brother Kendig could sense the soldiers' relief when he told them to open fire from way back here. That meant not exposing themselves to return fire. At least for now. There was something oddly beautiful about watching a building come apart a chunk at a time under the onslaught of bullets. Even in the relative darkness of the starlight, he could see chunks and crumbs flying away.

But those were distractions. He stayed focused on the front windows. Once he saw a flash of return fire, he'd know exactly where to put his Raufoss rounds, and once he started placing them, he wouldn't stop until there were no more to place.

Only the return fire didn't materialize.

"Could they be dead?" Brother Absalom shouted over the din.

Kendig couldn't see how. But he was tired of waiting. "Open fire," he said.

Ryan would never admit this, but he was relieved by the word to pull away from the windows. As tired as he was of this shit, and as cruel and awful as these Klansmen or whatever were, he didn't think he had it in him to kill them. Brother Stephen had been an accident. That was a whole world away from aiming at a human target and shooting it. He didn't even like first-person-shooter video games. Way too intense.

In the dark light of the candle wash from the sanctuary, he could see that his mom was relieved, too.

The urgency in Scorpion's voice was scary, though. Apparently there was danger in—

The front wall of the church erupted in splashes of white-hot silver and gold fire as thunder boomed through the sanctuary and huge holes were blown through the front and back walls. Pews erupted in fountains of splintering wood. It was too much to take in all at once. Whole chunks of their universe were exploding, one after another, with less than a second in between.

Ryan and his mom stood there, half crouched and frozen in the doorway between the vestry and the sanctuary. He'd never seen this kind of destruction. Off to his left, the altar turned to powder. To his right, the front wall was burning in half a dozen places, and spot fires flared throughout.

The noise was unbearable—off-the-charts loud, like Fourth of July times ten.

His mother was screaming. So was he, he thought, but all he could hear was the rapid-fire *boom-boom-boom* of whatever they were shooting at him.

The dim light of the room grew darker as the smoke from the fires billowed under the roof, and soon he found himself coughing from it.

Ryan and Christyne were both staring at the tableau of billowing destruction when Scorpion tackled them.

People never ceased to amaze Jonathan. Their capacity for self-endangerment—known in his world as simple stupidity—seemed limitless.

The Nasbes just stood there like human targets, out in the open, watching the damage caused by the world's most powerful sniper weapon as if it were a football game. He scrambled down the green side aisle as round after round sailed over his body to wreak havoc within the church.

"Get down!" he yelled. "Ryan! Christyne! Get down!" But they continued to stare.

If Jonathan was destined to lose this one, this was not how it was going down. He was not going to see them blown apart like pottery targets at a carnival shooting game. Throwing away countless years of experience and training, he rose to his feet under fire and took them both down with all the subtlety of a goal line tackle.

They hit hard, and Ryan howled in agony as Jonathan lay across both of them to protect them with his body.

"Ow!" Ryan yelled. "Oh, God, my arm!"

"You're hurting him!" Christyne yelled, and she pushed at Jonathan to get off of her.

"Stop!" Jonathan commanded. "Both of you, just stop!"

The command worked.

Jonathan felt for the kid. On the positive side, he was still breathing enough to yell, and he was not going to die as long as Jonathan was still alive.

In a minute or so, the punishing onslaught ended as abruptly as it has started. Dozens of spot fires had been ignited, and the entire front wall—what was left of it—was ablaze. Two-inch holes had been blasted through the armored masonry in dozens of places, and the shutters had been reduced to tatters.

"What the hell was *that*?" Gail yelled from the back of the sanctuary.

The sound of her voice answered half Jonathan's immediate question as he rose from the PCs. "Big Guy?"

"Whole and healthy," he said. "Here they come." Rising to one knee, Boxers brought his M4 to his shoulder and opened fire, sending twenty rounds downrange in one fully automatic string, and then he ducked for cover as a new fusillade of .50-caliber rounds consumed his corner of the world with debris and fire.

The punishing assault had just ended when Boxers' face appeared at the end of the nearest line of pews. "We can't stay here, Boss," he said.

"I concur," Gail said, appearing a few seconds later. "Who knew they had a cannon out there?"

Jonathan ran the options through his head and came up with nothing but bleak outcomes. If they stayed in here, they'd either get burned out or sniped out. If they tried to escape the building, they'd get torn apart; but even if they could make it to the woods, what then? Enemy evasion was a specialized enough skill for professionals. He had a mother and her son along for the ride.

His instincts said to stay put and fight it out, but that option, bravado aside, could only end badly for all of them.

His earpiece popped as someone broke squelch on the radio. Kendig Neen's voice said, "Last chance to surrender. That is, if you're still alive. In thirty seconds, we're coming for you."

Jonathan looked to Boxers. "We've had this discussion before," Big Guy said. "I don't surrender. You want to try to make a break with them in tow, I'll cover your six, but I don't surrender to nobody."

Christyne cried, "They're going to kill us all!"

He looked to Gail. "I don't see we have a chance either way," she said.

"I'll take that as a vote to fight," Jonathan said.

She shrugged.

Christyne whined, "Maybe they'll show mercy if we surrender?"

"No way," Ryan said. "I've seen their mercy. I'm not going through—" He paused. "I hear a helicopter."

"Fifteen seconds," Neen said.

Jonathan glanced past the fire and saw skirmish lines forming. With the shutters gone, that would be their entry point. He heard the helicopters, too. "Big Guy?"

Boxers cocked his head. He scowled. Then he smiled. "Little Birds?"

Then, as if in answer to his question, a new voice arrived in his ear. "Scorpion, this is Romeo Foxtrot Six."

The cavalry had arrived.

The sound of approaching helicopters startled Kendig. Aircraft never flew over this part of the world, unless they were ferrying Brother Michael from one place to another. Was it possible that he'd sent for his chopper to flee by air? If that were the case, then he must have been hiding from Sister Colleen when she went to his house to collect the weapons.

Then he heard the new voice on the radio. ". . . Romeo Foxtrot Six. We're on quarter-mile final, coming in hot, and recommending you stay inside with your heads down."

His stomach seized at the realization of what was happening. The sound of the rotors grew louder. The soldiers heard it, too, and shifted their gaze skyward, but there was nothing there. The sky remained black, free of any signs of approaching aircraft. All he saw were stars.

"There!" someone yelled, and he fired his rifle into the night sky.

Kendig saw the ink-stain silhouette against the stars just a second before the sky started returning fire. Muzzle flashes strobed like angry fireflies as the helicopter swooped to the ground with startling speed, and then, after only a second or two on the ground, swooped back into the sky.

Five seconds later, it happened again. The night roared with the sound of rotors and gunshots as the second chopper touched down and took off.

Now, though, the gunfire was louder. Black-clad killers moved out there among them, rending devastation.

Soldiers of the Army of God did their best to shoot, but no one knew for sure what the targets were, or where they were. Near Kendig, and all around him, people were dying in the darkness. He felt blood splash his face as one of the soldiers closest to him fell across the Barrett, rendering it momentarily useless.

Kendig looked to his left, to where Brother Absalom should be crouched with the other Barrett, but the young man had literally been blown in half at his navel.

Panic of the most malignant kind spread like floodwaters through a field, and in mere moments, the Army of God had been reduced to a fleeing mob. They pushed and jostled Kendig, who wasted precious seconds trying to reorganize them into something resembling a fighting force, but in the darkness and the confusion, that moment had passed.

With no one left to lead, he joined his fleeing troops.

CHAPTER THIRTY-THREE

Back in the sanctuary, Jonathan and his team had taken a position on the floor at the base of the stage that held the altar. They sat back-to-back in a circle around the Nasbes, weapons pointed out to address any threat that might materialize.

Jonathan could see nothing useful from their position, but the sounds told him everything. The crescendo of fire as the MH6 Little Bird choppers flared to land, and then the roar of the rotors as they took off two seconds later. In his mind, he could visualize Unit operators peeling off of the outboard benches to do what they did best.

The shooting peaked over the course of fifteen or twenty seconds, and then the shooting turned to the sounds of panic that always indicated the beginning of the end. The shooting slowed to singles, and then it stopped completely.

Jonathan's earbud popped. "Scorpion, Romeo Foxtrot Six. LZ is secure. Advise when you're ready for exfil."

This was too much. Could it really be this easy? He pressed his mike button. "Exfil in one." He stood, and along with Boxers and Gail, extended assisting hands to the Nasbes to help them rise.

Ryan looked terrible. The cumulative effect of fear and

exhaustion—and maybe blood loss—had turned his skin gray. His mom looked confused and terrified. "What now?" she said.

Jonathan loved this part. "It's over. You're going home."

Mother and son exchanged glances that betrayed their skepticism.

"Really," Gail said. Outside, the night filled again with the sound of an approaching chopper.

Despite the presence of friendlies, Jonathan and his team kept the Nasbes in the middle of a protective wedge as he walked quickly without running to the front doors. He threw the giant latch and pushed the heavy doors open—just a crack at first, as he double-checked against some kind of trap, and then all the way to allow everyone to pass.

Colonel Rollins met him just outside the door, where strewn bodies lay untouched and blood appeared black on the concrete. "I told you we monitor everything," he said, answering Jonathan's unasked question.

Actually, it answered only one; but the others could wait until the PCs were secure.

The Little Bird sat on the ground, its rotors cutting a windy disk in the frigid night. Jonathan counted eight black-clad operators surrounding the chopper, their weapons directed at every compass point. Rollins led the way to the tiny door in the chopper's side. He pulled it open and gestured for the PCs to enter.

Christyne looked stunned. Hesitant.

"It's all right," Rollins shouted over the roar of the engine. "With Boomer's compliments."

Ryan perked up at the name. "Dad's here?"

Rollins shook his head. "No, but you'll see him soon."

"Where?"

Rollins shot a look to Gail. "Soon," he said. "Time to climb aboard."

Gail understood the hesitation to mean that she wasn't cleared to know their final destination.

As Ryan scrambled aboard, Christyne looked first at Boxers, and then to the rest of the team. "Thank you," she said. She reached out for Big Guy, offering him a hug.

Entering rare territory for him, he allowed it to happen.

"You're very strong, you know," Christyne said.

Jonathan realized that he'd never seen Boxers blush before. At least not like that.

As she pushed away, Rollins put a hand at her back to urge her into the Little Bird. No one was safe until they were airborne.

Christyne braced herself against the door and turned one last time. "God bless you all," she said.

The instant she was clear of the door, Rollins slammed it closed, and the chopper was airborne, leaving them all to look away and close their eyes against the rotor wash.

Rollins said something into his radio that Jonathan couldn't hear, but soon the infil choppers were returning for exfil.

"What's next?" Jonathan asked the colonel as the birds got louder.

"I guess we all go home," Rollins said. "Mission accomplished."

Jonathan made a broad gesture with both arms. "What about all this?"

"All what?" Rollins said. "I don't see a thing. I couldn't. We've been on a training mission a hundred miles from here."

"We could use your help," Jonathan said. "These assholes dispatched execution teams across the country. We need to find out who and where."

Rollins shook his head. "Negative. We had one mission, and we accomplished it. You're welcome, by the way."

Jonathan felt a pang of embarrassment. "Appreciate the help."

The colonel shrugged as if it was nothing. The night started churning again as two more choppers dropped from the sky and flared to land. Rollins offered his hand, and Jonathan took it. "And we appreciate the loyalty. Sorry I can't offer you a ride. We're loaded to the max. I'll have a hell of a time explaining the hours and the fuel consumption as it is."

Translation: Roleplay Rollins had stuck out his neck as far as it would go.

"No problem," Jonathan said. "I've got a ride."

Rollins looked relieved. "Good luck, Digger."

The Little Birds were airborne again within seconds of landing. Then Jonathan and his team were alone again with the dead and the wounded.

"One-way asshole," Boxers growled. He shouldered his weapon and started scanning for targets. "This is a bad place to be, Boss. There's still a lot of people and weapons unaccounted for. I vote we start hiking."

"What about these people?" Gail asked. "They're wounded. Suffering. We can't just leave them."

"Watch me," Boxers said. He started moving away, ever vigilant.

Jonathan shouldered his weapon and followed.

"No!" Gail said. Her voice was firm, insistent. In different circumstances, petulant. "Look at what we've done. We can't just leave it this way."

Something snapped in Jonathan. He let his weapon fall against its sling, and he turned on her. "We cannot stay," he said. He felt blood pounding in his ears. "We didn't start this fight, we finished it. Everything that flows afterward is someone else's problem. We've got a long hike out of here, and I'm not endangering the team." Without NVGs to mask them, her eyes showed hurt and anger. "This is not negotiable," he said. "Now move."

"What about the ongoing threat?" Gail countered. "What about all the innocents who will die? Don't we owe the whole friggin' world a little intel gathering?"

"The whole friggin' world is pursuing their own leads. They chose *not* to pursue these. I'll make a call to Wolverine when we're back in the world. She can do with the information what she wants."

"You're going to tell her about this carnage?"

"Of course not. I won't have to. If I tell her to take a peek up here, I believe she'll put two and two together."

"And meanwhile, terrorist teams are free to roam, spreading random violence."

Jonathan took a step closer and lowered his voice. "Dammit, Gail, our mission was to save one family. It's done. Successful beyond any imagined outcome. Let's call it a day and leave saving the world to Batman and the Justice League."

"But we—"

"*Now*, Gail." He waited until she settled her hand on her weapon and moved to join Boxers.

The final look that she flashed at him before moving was one he hoped he'd never see again.

They moved through the night with combat stealth, staying in the cover of the woods. Weapons ever at the ready, they spread out, keeping twenty paces between them, with Boxers in the lead and Gail in the middle, due to the lack of night vision. They moved with agonizing slowness as they lifted their feet and brought them down in silence.

Five times in the first hour, Boxers signaled for the tiny column to stop and take a knee as movement in the trees raised an alarm. Twice it was a woodland creature of some sort, and once it was just nothing at all, but twice, Jonathan was pretty sure that it was Army of God Klansmen continuing their flight.

Without ever actually discussing it, Jonathan's team had tacitly agreed not to engage anyone who didn't engage them first. Jonathan found it counterinstinctive and a wide departure from any reasonable order of battle; but this opfor was so disorganized and traumatized that to do further damage just seemed cruel.

Jonathan considered walking back to Michael Copley's mansion and stealing a car to drive back to their command post, but the net gain didn't seem worth the net risk. All of those people who scattered into the night would be looking to regroup somewhere, and the leader's mansion would be as good a rallying point as any. It made no sense to unnecessarily engage anyone at this point.

So, they kept walking.

By five-thirty in the morning, they were on the edge of a familiar clearing. The sun was just turning the eastern sky orange when Sam Shockley's farm came into view.

Boxers stopped at the edge of the clearing and motioned for the others to join him. "I think we should move around this," Big Guy said. "I don't like wide open spaces."

"What, you think they've set up an ambush?" Jonathan asked. Hearing the words stated aloud made them sound ridiculous.

"Can you think of a better place?"

"That assumes a lot of advance notice," Jonathan said. "Even we didn't know we were coming here until forty minutes ago."

"It's on the straight line between where we were and where we're going."

Gail asked, "How would they know where we're going?"

Boxers made that growling sound that signified frustration. "I'm just sayin'," he said. "It's not a big leap if they track the truck we left back there."

Jonathan thought it through. He was as much about managing risk as the next guy, but it would add an hour to their trek if they skirted this huge plot of land, and there'd still be a lot of day left to be managed.

"She's good people," Jonathan said. "Her husband's on deployment, she lives there all by herself with her daughter. If there are bad guys in there, it'll be against her wishes. So I figure we owe her a security check."

Boxers gave him an impatient glare. "You know, Dig, sometimes I think you spend nights awake just thinkin' up more creative ways to get me killed." That was Boxers-speak for *Whatever you say*. He rose.

Jonathan rose with him and placed a hand on his shoulder. "But just in case I'm wrong, I'll go first. You and Gunslinger stay here."

"I want a new name," Gail said again. "And we're not staying anywhere. What is that, a hundred yards out in the open?"

Jonathan eyeballed the distance. "Maybe a hundred fifty. But she knows me. I think she trusts me. They don't know anything about you two."

"How do you want to handle it?" Boxers asked.

"I'm going to go to the front door and knock," he said. "I'm going to check to see if Sam's okay, and I'm going to give her a heads-up about her truck. When I get to the door, I'll give you the word to advance."

"Unless there are Army of God crazies in there and they cut you down before you get halfway," Gail said.

Jonathan considered it a good sign that she was still worried about him. He said, "If there are bad guys in the house waiting—which is a huge, steaming pile of *if*—then they'll know that I'm with others. If they see me approaching alone, they'll hold their fire so as not to draw more from you two."

Boxers put his hands on his hips. "You know that's utter bullshit, right?"

Jonathan beamed. "I thought it sounded good, though." He started toward the clearing. "Wait for my command."

He closed the distance casually, as before, not wanting to draw unnecessary suspicion. Of course, unlike the last time he approached the farmhouse, he looked far less like a lost hunter than a trained gunman.

He allowed the muzzle of his M4 to point harmlessly toward the ground, while his gloved hand remained on the grip, his finger close to the trigger guard. He kept his eyes planted on the windows of the little house, and on the corners, where snipers might lie in wait. He took comfort in the knowledge that Boxers and Gail would both be watching with digital magnification. If something looked bad, they would tell him. In fact, there was a better than average chance that they would shoot whatever looked bad.

A hundred fifty yards goes by fast at twenty-two hundred feet per second.

When Jonathan closed to within the last twenty yards, he became concerned that no one had yet appeared in the windows or on the porch. His only experience with the Shockley family to date was that they were early risers, and very attentive to their surroundings.

So, where were they?

He pressed his transmit button. "I can't tell you why, but I'm not liking this," he said. "Advise the instant you see any movement anywhere."

Jonathan climbed the three stairs to the front porch and walked to the door. He knocked.

No one answered, but scuffling sounds from the inside indicated that people were definitely at home. He radioed, "I hear people inside, but there's no answer."

He knocked again.

Jilly's voice shouted, "Mama, can we be home yet?"

Jonathan smiled. The stealthy, secret-keeping child had yet to be invented. He heard footsteps, and then the sound of a chain being stripped from its track on the door. It opened a few inches, and there was a very nervous Sam Shockley. She tried to smile, but she wasn't good enough at deception to get her eyes involved.

"Mr. Harris," she said. "What a pleasure to see you."

Bullshit. There was no reason for her to be anything but bothered to see him. She should be ragging his ass for coming by again at all after trying to steal her truck.

"Mrs. Shockley," he said. "I came by to make sure—"

"We've got a runner out the back door!" Boxers shouted in his hear.

"Shit!" He spun and headed for the stairs. He pressed the transmit button. "Gunslinger, clear the house."

"Don't hurt her!" Sam yelled. "She doesn't mean any harm!" She took off after him.

Jonathan cut to his left at the bottom of the steps and dashed around toward the back of the house. There he saw a woman in a plain woolen coat in a dead run across the scrubby harvested corn field.

"Target acquired," Boxers said in his ear.

"You!" Jonathan yelled. "Stop or we will shoot!"

She started running faster.

Jonathan took off after her, and he knew without looking that Sam Shockley was close behind. In his peripheral vision, he saw Gail sprinting across the field toward the house to clear it of any lingering bad guys. He pressed his mike button. "Give the runner a wide lead, Big Guy. I want to stop her, not hurt her."

Two, three-round bursts split the peace of the morning before Jonathan could even let up on his transmit button. Dirt kicked up in front of the fleeing girl, directly in her path. She slid to a stop, hesitated and started running again, prompting two more bursts from Boxers' weapon.

"Next time we hit you!" Jonathan yelled.

The woman stopped again. As Jonathan closed the distance that separated them, his weapon at the ready, she made to run again.

This time, Jonathan fired the warning shots. From this distance, the muzzle blasts would be near-deafening, and as he'd hoped, that was all the convincing she needed. From the back, he wouldn't have even known she was a she. Her hair had been cropped short, and she wore a stocking cap pulled low.

"Hands straight out to your sides," Jonathan commanded. "Fingers splayed wide."

Sam Shockley caught up with him and pulled on his vest. "Don't hurt her," she begged.

Jonathan pulled free and pointed his weapon inches from her nose. "Step back, Mrs. Shockley. Do not interfere."

She blanched and took two steps back. Behind her, Boxers was lumbering across the field to join them.

Jonathan returned his aim to the woman who'd fled. She stood as if crucified, her hands perpendicular to her body, elbows locked. "Our intent is not to hurt anyone," Jonathan said. "But if you make me, I will." He paused while Boxers arrived. "Now turn around."

His jaw dropped. It was her again: the one from the bridge and from the basement. All the toughness was gone now, entirely replaced by fear.

"Please don't hurt me," she said.

"Are you armed?"

"Please, I just want all of this to stop."

"Listen to me," Jonathan said. "Are you armed?"

She shook her head as her eyes brimmed with tears. "No, sir."

"Big Guy?"

"I've got her covered," he said.

Gail said, "House is clear."

"Copy, the house is clear," Jonathan said into the radio. He approached his captive. "What's your name?" he asked.

"Sis—" She stopped herself, and let out a little puff of breath as her head sagged. It was a look of resignation that could mean surrender or suicide bomb. He froze and watched her hands very carefully.

"Colleen," she said. "Colleen Devlin."

"Look at me, Colleen Devlin."

Her eyes came up to meet his.

"This is your come-clean moment, understand? For all I know, you could be loaded with explosives. If you twitch, my friends will kill you. If you have weapons on you, this is absolutely your only chance to tell me without harm coming to you."

"She wouldn't do that," Sam said.

Jonathan's hand shot up for silence.

"No bombs," Colleen said. "No weapons." She started to cry.

Looking back to make sure that both Sam and Colleen were covered by Boxers, Jonathan let his M4 fall against its sling and he frisked the young lady thoroughly. She in fact was unarmed. He zip-tied her hands behind her back.

He looked to Boxers and Big Guy broke his aim. "I think we need to go inside," Jonathan said. "There's a lot of explaining to be done."

CHAPTER THIRTY-FOUR

It felt good to be warm. Once inside the house, Jonathan asked for and was given the shotgun he'd encountered the previous day, and when he asked if there were any other weapons in the house, Sam willingly showed him the S&W .357 magnum revolver and Winchester .30-30, both of them unloaded with trigger locks installed. He allowed himself to relax. A little.

Jonathan sat at the kitchen table with Gail and Sam and Colleen, while Boxers stood in the archway, blocking any means of escape. Colleen sat awkwardly to keep the pressure off her wrists.

"Did the repo man ever show up?" Jonathan asked Sam. It was a friendly place to start the conversation.

Sam gave a wan smile. "No, not yet."

Colleen looked shocked. "You know these people?" Her tone was one of utter betrayal.

"It's not like that," Sam said. "I had no idea—"

"There's nothing to apologize for," Jonathan said, moving quickly to control the conversation. "Sam and I don't know each other any better than you and I do, Colleen." He let those words hang. "Do you remember me?"

"You killed my friends."

Sam recoiled at the words.

Jonathan placed a calming hand on her arm. "Not before you killed a lot of people yourself," he said. He tempered his words so they wouldn't sound accusatory.

More shock from Sam.

"I don't know what you're talking about," Colleen said, but the truth was written all over her denial.

"Don't you remember me shooting at you on the bridge that night?" he asked.

Her eyes grew huge.

"Yeah," he said. "That was me. And I was about half a trigger pull away from killing you when I got interrupted by that overzealous cop."

"Are you talking about the shootings in Washington the other night?" Sam said. From the look on her face, it was all bigger than she could process.

"Those are the ones," Jonathan said. He shifted his gaze and softened his voice. "Tell me why, Colleen."

"I was supposed to kill myself," she said, her voice barely audible. "I shouldn't have run."

Sam leaned in closer. "Your job was to kill yourself?"

Colleen nodded. "Yes." Then she shook her head. "No. Only if I was about to get caught."

Jonathan thought he understood. "I think she's saying she should have killed herself here. This morning. Is that right, Colleen?"

She bobbed her head yes but looked away again.

"But *why*?" Sam asked. "Why would you kill yourself?"

"Because it's the honorable way. It's the holy way."

Sam brought her hand to her mouth. "Oh, my God, what have they been teaching you?"

Jonathan looked to Sam. "Tell me about y'all's relationship," he said. "Why is she here tonight?"

"She came here terrified," Sam explained. "I never found out why. It was still dark. She was only here for less than an hour when you showed up and she took off running."

"But why here?" Gail asked. "You seem to know each other."

"We do," Sam said. "At least I thought we did. She came to visit me every week or so."

Jonathan sat a little taller and adjusted his rifle so the magazine quit poking him in the thigh. "What does *visit* mean?"

Gail shot him an annoyed look, but he ignored it.

"She would just come by. You know, to talk. And to play with Jilly. We'd have coffee or hot chocolate in the winter, Cokes or iced tea in the summer."

So this had been going on for a long time, Jonathan realized. "Colleen?"

She looked at her lap. "Why did you have to ruin everything?"

"Because you kidnapped my friend's family," he said.

Sam gasped again. "Oh, my God!"

"You forced my hand, Colleen. Why did you do it?"

She sighed and moaned. "What have I done?" she whispered.

"You killed a lot of people," Jonathan said. "What's done is done. Now tell me why you shot those people on the bridge."

"They're Users." She said it as if it were really an explanation. "We're at war with them."

"And the mall shootings in Kansas City?"

She nodded.

"The school bombing in Detroit?"

"It's war!" she yelled. "People die in war."

"And more are coming, aren't they?"

Colleen shut down and looked at the table.

"How many more, Colleen?"

"A lot," she said. "Brother Michael didn't trust me with all the details, but I know that there are many teams out there."

"I don't believe this!" Sam exclaimed.

Jonathan put his hand on her arm again. "Please," he said. "Just let us talk."

"I don't want to say any more," Colleen said.

"Why did you kidnap Ryan and Christyne Nasbe?" Jonathan pressed. "How did they figure in to your war?"

Colleen looked tired. "We needed symbols. We needed faces for the cameras."

"But why *them*?"

"Because they were Users and they were there." She clearly didn't understand why people didn't understand something so obvious. "I had orders to take prisoners and I followed them."

Gail looked shocked. "Just anybody?" she asked. "Random selection?"

"Users are Users," Colleen said. "This one or that one, it doesn't matter."

Sam stood, abruptly enough that Boxers moved to intervene. "I'm calling the police," she said.

"They're part of it," Jonathan said. "Kendig Neen is a leader, isn't he, Colleen?"

"*Sheriff* Kendig Neen? Is a terrorist?"

"A soldier," Colleen corrected reflexively.

Sam sat back down heavily. "Oh, my God. He comes by all the time, too. He's a nice man."

Jonathan turned his attention back to Colleen. "Where are the other attacks going to be?"

"I swear I don't know. What's going to happen to me?"

"This isn't about you anymore, sweetheart," Gail said. If anyone could pull off a nice tone under the circumstances, it was she. "This is about a lot of innocent people who are in danger."

"They're not innocent," Colleen said, kicking the table. "They're Users!"

Sam exploded, "That bomb at the school killed children, Colleen! Small, innocent children!"

"Children die in war all the time," Colleen said.

Jonathan's patience was thinning. "Tell me the end game, then," he said. "What does all of this killing accomplish?"

She snorted a laugh. "Same as in any war. We win."

"You win," Jonathan repeated. "And then what? What happens in victory?"

"The Users stop using," she said. "When people are afraid to leave their houses, when they can't shop or go to school, the economy will collapse."

"How?" Gail asked. "Tell me how one leads to the other."

"Users are weak," she said. "They frighten easily, and they're anxious to blame whoever they want to be guilty. When they get angry, they go to war, and their precious stock market falls. The Users lose their precious money, and when that happens, the poor will rise and get an even chance."

"It doesn't work that way," Jonathan said, but then he stopped himself. This wasn't the time for a civics lesson.

"You wait," Colleen said. "You wait until the head is cut off of the snake. You wait to see what happens then."

Gail scowled deeply. "Snake? What snake?"

A deep baritone voice rumbled from the living room, "Good morning everyone."

Jonathan jumped to his feet and Boxers spun on his axis, unblocking the doorway to reveal a haggard, exhausted Kendig Neen standing just inside the front door. With his ample belly and his handlebar mustache, he might have been Santa in civvies. Jilly sat in the crook of his elbow, one arm casually over his shoulder. His free hand held a cocked pistol.

"Good thing little Jilly knows how to call the police, huh, Sam?" he said. "Poor little thing saw people with guns and was scared to death."

"Nine-one-one is not for fun," Jilly said, obviously pleased at her own rhyme.

"Hands away from weapons, please," Kendig said. "I don't—"

Jonathan moved with lightning speed, dropping to his knee and drawing his .45 in the time it took the sheriff to bring his gun around. Jonathan fired two shots, hitting the sheriff in the ear and the eye as Neen fired off one of his own—by reflex, Jonathan imagined. Neen and Jilly fell together onto the floor of the foyer, where a river of gore instantly started to stain the wood.

Jilly screamed. And screamed.

Sam rushed to her and scooped her up in her arms. When she got a good look at the anatomical wreckage that was Kendig Neen's head, she started screaming, too.

"Holy shit, Boss," Boxers said, his admiration obvious to all. "I didn't know—" He paused and nodded to a spot behind Jonathan. "Uh-oh."

Colleen sat awkwardly in her chair, listing to the side. Bloody spittle formed at the corner of her mouth, then dripped like crimson thread onto the fabric of her coat.

"Ah, shit," Jonathan spat. He rushed to her, but Gail beat him to it. She opened the coat and revealed the rapidly spreading stain on her shirt.

"Get her on the floor," Boxers instructed from across the room.

In the hall, Jilly and Sam continued to wail.

Boxers whirled on them. "For God's sake, woman, will you shut up? You're safe now. Scream later." Not many people in the world can deliver a message like that and have it obeyed. Boxers was one of them.

Jonathan pulled the table out of the way to make room on the floor to lay Colleen down. An instant later, Boxers was with them, and he lifted Jonathan out of the way by his collar so that he could take his place. Boxers' combat medic skills had always been better than Jonathan's.

With her coat already spread wide, he stripped her shirt open, and there was the bullet wound: center-right chest. The froth at her lips told them the bullet had pierced her lung, but the location probably meant liver, too. The rate of blood loss said that it was fatal.

"Well?" Gail said expectantly.

"We got nothing for this."

Colleen reached out and grabbed Big Guy's sleeve. "What does that mean?"

Boxers pulled his arm away as if he'd touched a spider. He stood abruptly and turned to Jonathan. "She'll be dead in a couple of minutes," he said, and he walked out to the hallway where Sam and her daughter stood stunned.

"What's happening?" Sam asked. Her face showed desperation.

Boxers said, "Um, well, she's not going to make it."

"What have you brought to our house?" Sam shouted.

Boxers bent at the waist to look at her eye-to-eye. "A much better outcome for you and your little girl than if you'd been here alone with her when this asshole came by."

"Michael Copley's an asshole!" Jilly said.

In the kitchen, Jonathan and Gail kneeled next to the dying girl, Gail holding her hand. To Jonathan, she said, "There's nothing?"

"She needs a surgeon, and there's not enough time to get her one." Jonathan leaned closer and raised his voice. "Did you hear that, Colleen?"

Her face had turned gray, on its way to that pale blue that always meant the end. She shifted her eyes. "I'm dying?"

"Yes," Jonathan said. In his book, there weren't many worse sins than telling a lie to someone who's terminal. "And you're dying with a lot of sins on your soul. You know that means Hell, don't you?"

"Scorpion!" Gail hissed.

Jonathan shot her a glare that said, *Shut up*.

"It's true, Colleen. You know that, don't you?"

"Soldiers go to Heaven," she said. Her voice had a fraction of the strength it used to. "That's what Brother Michael said."

"Brother Michael's not here," Jonathan said. "You've been left alone to take the bullets."

"He had to leave us," Colleen said. "The snake."

Jonathan looked to Gail. "Did she say snake?"

"What snake?" Gail asked. She stroked the girl's hair. "Stay with us, Colleen. What snake?"

"Head off the . . . sna . . ." Her features went slack and her eyes dilated.

For a long moment, neither of them moved. Friend or enemy, Jonathan had never grown used to watching people die. He found the vulnerability of those last seconds between this world and the next to be . . . unnerving. But it was done.

He stood. "She's gone," he said.

"Who *are* you people?" Sam yelled.

"We're friends," Jonathan said. "Although I understand that you probably don't think so."

"And what am I supposed to do with *them*?" She spread her arms at the carnage.

"We'll take care of the bodies," Jonathan said.

"Oh, no, you won't," Sam said.

"What, you want to keep them?" Boxers said.

"No, I don't want to keep them. But when the police come—"

"The police are a bad idea," Jonathan said.

"Says the home invader."

"Says the home invader," Jilly repeated.

Something about the absurdity of it all made Jonathan laugh.

"This is *funny* to you?" Sam accused.

"No."

"You're still laughing."

Gail said, "Not at you, Mrs. Shockley, and certainly not at these poor people. It's just been a long night."

Jonathan showed his palms as a gesture of peace. "Mrs. Shockley, I apologize for all of this. My big friend is right that you're much better off for us being here when Sheriff Neen came around. He'd have killed you and your daughter because he'd have had to kill Colleen on the assumption that she'd shared secrets. But I don't expect you to understand or believe any of that."

"What the *hell* is going on?" Sam insisted.

"I'm afraid I can't make you understand that, either," Jonathan said. "I don't know that I understand it all that well myself."

"Who are you people?"

"Even more complicated, I'm afraid." To Boxers, he said, "Let's put the bodies into the trunk of the sheriff's car."

Clearly relieved to have something to do other than talking, Boxers went right to work. He effortlessly manhandled Neen's corpse into a textbook fireman's carry and headed out the door.

Jonathan reached out to touch Sam's shoulder, but withdrew his hand when she flinched. "Would you like to sit down?"

"No. I want you out of my house." As the shock drained from her features, fear invaded them.

"I understand," Jonathan said. "In five minutes, we will be. But there are a couple of logistical issues I need to discuss with you."

"I don't want—"

"Hush, Mrs. Shockley." Jonathan shot the command sharply, and it worked. "You need to listen to this. First of all, the quicker you wipe up the blood from the floor, the easier it will come up. In this case, it's good you don't have carpets."

Sam's jaw dropped. "Oh, my God. You're so cold."

"Whatever. It's your call, one way or the other. And bleach will not only get out whatever stain is left, it will also kill any blood-borne pathogens."

"Not to mention wipe away any DNA evidence," she said. It was a gotcha.

Jonathan shrugged it away. "Actually, that's not always true, but think what you want. Here's the rest: As soon as we're gone, you're going to want to call the police. I understand that. Remember, though, that Kendig Neen *was* the police. Something to think about. That, and the fact that he and another person were killed here. You're not going to like to hear this, but we're not traceable, so any efforts to catch us or punish us will be futile. Plus, we're the good guys."

Sam hugged Jilly more tightly and took a step backward. Apparently, the "good guys" comment frightened her.

"If you do want to roll the dice that way do yourself a favor and call the FBI, not the local police. When they tell you that murders are a local matter, you tell them that the local policeman was one of the killers."

"Except you're taking his body away."

Jonathan gave a commiserating wince. "Yes." He stepped aside as Boxers reentered the front door to head to the kitchen for Colleen's body. "Again, I'm sorry about all of this."

Sam looked to Gail for something, and got more or less the same look of apology.

As Boxers passed behind again, this time with Colleen's remains over his shoulder, Jonathan and Gail followed him out to the car. Both bodies fit easily into the trunk of the unmarked Ford.

The last they saw of Sam Shockley, she was standing in the doorway, with Jilly in her arms. The little girl waved good-bye.

CHAPTER THIRTY-FIVE

Jonathan had never given a lot of thought to the convenience of abandoned drift mines, but as they tied up loose ends in West Virginia, it became apparent. They left the bodies in the trunk of the Ford, dismantled the anti-trespasser mechanisms at the mouth of the mine shaft, and then Boxers drove the vehicle itself into the narrow passage as far as he could go and still be able to get out of the vehicle. When that was done, they replaced the wooden block and barricades and erased their tire tracks. By 8:45, they were back in the Agusta chopper and airborne again, on their way back to civilization.

Jonathan didn't like what he saw in Gail's expression. Not that long ago, she had sworn an oath to defend the Constitution against all enemies foreign and domestic, and to bear true faith and allegiance to the same. She had built a life around the rule of law, and now she was a player in an operation that broke every rule to achieve the intended goal. She sat quietly in her seat in the opulent executive helicopter, speaking to no one, visibly aging with every passing minute.

He left her with her thoughts, convinced that he could say nothing that would make anything any better.

When they were on the ground, a little before noon, and before climbing into the custom-designed Hummer that would take them back to Fisherman's Cove, Jonathan pulled her aside. "Are you going to be okay?" he asked.

She wouldn't make eye contact. "What choice do I have?"

Interesting point. "When we get back to the Cove, you should sit down with Father Dom," he said.

"I'm not Catholic."

"When he's got his psychologist hat on, he can be anything you need him to be. Mostly, he's a good listener." Jonathan knew whereof he spoke, having spent more hours than he could count in his counsel.

"I don't need a shrink to tell me right from wrong," she said. With that, she headed to the truck.

After a scalding shower and a shave, Jonathan felt mostly human again. He missed the long-gone days when occasional ten-minute naps could keep him functioning for days on end. Today he'd been up for a mere thirty-six hours and he felt like milled concrete.

One floor below, Boxers had chosen to crash in the guest room rather than drive back to the District, something he rarely did. He was always welcome, of course, but Jonathan did begrudge the loss in water pressure caused by competing showers.

Jonathan padded naked from his bathroom to his bed, where JoeDog had already staked her claim by lying crosswise on her back, as if to extort a tummy rub in exchange for surrendering her territory. On a different day, it would have worked. Today, though, he wolf-whistled and she scrambled to her feet, tail swinging, waiting to play. Or not.

Jonathan stripped the covers from one side of the king bed and climbed under. JoeDog read the signs and curled up on the spread at the foot of the bed on the opposite side. Jonathan stacked his pillows just so against the leather headboard, lay back, and closed his eyes.

Three minutes later, Jonathan realized that while exhausted, he was too spun up to sleep, so he lifted the television remote from the nightstand and thumbed the ON button. The thirty-inch TV mounted on the opposite wall jumped to life immediately, set, as always on his favorite cable news station.

He wasn't so much interested in the content of what was on as he was in the white noise of droning voices that rarely failed to lull him into unconsciousness. The current top story dealt with another machine-gun attack in middle America, this one killing over a dozen people at holiday street festival in Davenport, Iowa. The squeaky tenor newsreader reported that experts were considering the possibility that this incident might be linked to recent similar incidents in Washington and Kansas City, and the school bombing in Detroit.

"Gee, ya think?" Jonathan asked aloud.

"On a related story," the anchor continued, "administration officials are questioning the legitimacy of a sensational Web video that purported to show the execution of a young man by Islamic terrorists last night."

Jonathan shot upright, causing JoeDog to leap for cover on the floor. The television showed grainy images of Ryan Nasbe being prepared for execution. The images were blurry enough that faces were hard to discern.

"We warn you that this next part is rather graphic."

This by way of introducing Jonathan's nick-of-time marksmanship. Actually, there wasn't much graphic about it at all, just the sound of gunshots and the images of people falling down. An instant later, the webcam went black.

"That's all there was of the video," the anchor continued, "leading experts to suspect that the transmission was a prank intended to raise concerns among independent voters that the current administration is not up to the task of protecting the American people."

From there, they cut away to an interview with some K Street pundit who said exactly the words that were necessary to get him on television to prove the network's thesis.

Jonathan took that as his cue to lay back against his pillows again. "Okay, Joe," he said with his eyes closed. "It's safe now. You can come to bed."

Seconds later, the whole mattress shook as she resumed her spot.

The anchor closed his story with, "Despite increased violence across the country, Secret Service and administration spokesmen say that no extraordinary security measures are necessary to protect the president and other elected officials."

The screen switched to Presidential Press Secretary Rachel Pollack, who was speaking from the White House Press Room. "Come on, people," she said. "The president is the most carefully guarded human being on the planet. The Secret Service takes every precaution every day. If we start altering the president's schedule in response to random acts of violence, then the violent offenders win. The Marine Corps Anniversary celebration will go on as planned at the Iwo Jima Memorial. Be sure to dress warmly, because tomorrow's supposed to be even colder than today."

And so the newscast went, deeper and deeper into the possible ramifications of the ongoing terror killings across the country. Muslim clerics expressed outrage that Americans were so willing and ready to assign any acts of terrorism to them. Then there were the ongoing—

Jonathan's eyes snapped open. "Shit," he said aloud. The head of the snake was scheduled to speak at Iwo Jima Memorial tomorrow.

Venice already had the information he'd requested up on the big War Room screen when he arrived.

"This is everything I could find on the president's schedule," she said as he crossed the threshold. "At least what they make public. I could try to dig into the White House system, but that's a terminal course."

"The public schedule will be fine," Jonathan said. He

took his usual seat at the head of the teak conference table. "Michael Copley won't know what's not on the public schedule."

Venice froze. "What's going on, Digger?"

"I think that asshole is planning to assassinate the president."

"You say that as if it's easy to do."

"It is, if you plan well enough and you have the right weapon." He read through the list of scheduled appearances. The president would be attending a number of events over the next few days, including a lunch at the Capitol, a show at the Kennedy Center, and various bits of ceremonial bullshit at different federal building auditoriums.

"I was right," he said triumphantly, pointing with his finger to the second listing on the page. "The Marine Corps anniversary celebration is the only outdoor ceremony."

"Why is that important?" Venice asked. She was getting progressively more agitated with every moment.

Jonathan wasn't in the mood to explain just yet. "I need you to pull up everything you can find on Appalachian Acoustics again and tell me if the Secret Service is one of their customers."

"It doesn't work like that," she said. "For something like acoustic reflectors or whatever they call those things they make, the General Services Administration would make the purchase."

Jonathan shot her an impatient look. "Fine. Then go to the GSA site and see if the Secret Service is one of *their* customers."

"But I already know—" She saw the look. "Fine."

In his heart, Jonathan knew he was right—he felt it—but a little confirmation wouldn't hurt. It was just too on-the-nose not to be true.

Cut off the head of the snake.

That deathbed phrase, combined with Appalachian Acoustics' celebration of its government contracts, was just too convenient not to be connected. Something about those panels.

340   *John Gilstrap*

Jonathan pulled on a drawer just under his spot at the table and slid out a keyboard for the computer that controlled the War Room's main screen. He Googled Appalachian Acoustics and navigated to their website. The breadth and variety of their products was truly impressive. It took him a minute to find exactly the line of products he thought was applicable—"Major Outdoor Venues"—but once there, he took his time studying the photographs.

The common arrangement of the acoustic shells formed a semicircle around the speaker or performer. According to the specifications list, they could be designed as tall as twenty-five feet, or they could be as short as a standard office cubicle wall. Jonathan wondered what they'd use for a presidential speech. He imagined that taller was better.

In fact, he was certain that taller was better. He remembered from his early days in the Unit, back when their mission and capabilities hadn't quite settled out and they did a lot of executive protection for dignitaries in war zones overseas, that anything you could use to block vision from potential bad guys was a good thing. Protectees are routinely transferred from one place to another—say, from the front door of a building to a waiting limousine—under cover of tarpaulins of some sort.

He clicked deeper into the information on the taller models of acoustic shells. The Model 9000 Symphonic Reflector seemed to show the most versatility. It was modular in design and could be built in four-foot segments. Plus, it had an angled reflector at the top that would provide "the greatest degree of sound reflection available anywhere." If Jonathan were selecting the reflectors as a shield for his own protectee, that's the one he would use, and he'd max it out in height to block out any target that a sniper might try to scope.

They had access to Barrett rifles. Would aim even matter?

Aim always mattered. If you're going to risk everything on a shot at the most powerful human on the planet, you want to make sure it works. Or you name yourself Squeaky and become a punch line among your fellow terrorists for decades to come.

What about explosives? If Copley designed the panels with explosives embedded, an initiation in this configuration would create one hell of a blast wave. Explosions and sound were both mere variations in pressure, after all, so a configuration designed to focus sound would likewise focus a detonation. But how would that work?

"Okay," Jonathan said aloud, trying to pull up his EOD training from back in the day, "how much explosive would it take?"

There were a lot of variables, the most important of which was distance to target. The inverse square law of physics said that for every tripling of distance from the surface of the explosive—say from three feet to nine—the energy of the blast is reduced by a factor of nine. Assuming the president wasn't going to be sitting on the panels—in fact, assuming that the panels were going to be a good fifteen or twenty feet behind him, maybe more—Copley would need pounds of explosives to get the desired effect.

"How the hell would you do that?" Especially in a product whose primary selling feature is its light weight? Plus, he assumed that the Secret Service x-rayed and dog-sniffed every bit of equipment and organic matter that came that close to the president. Surely an explosive would be detected.

Or, maybe not. Jonathan wasn't an expert in state-of-the-art explosive compounds, so maybe if there was some non-nitrate formulation, the dogs wouldn't find it. Besides, the explosive would have been planted ages ago. Maybe once a purchase is made and the objects get into the warehouse, nobody pays much attention to them anymore.

He decided to assume that to be the case. So, how do you set it off?

Jonathan ruled out a standard detonator or fuse, simply because there'd be no opportunity to place it.

Again, he thought of the Barrett. He'd never believed in

coincidences, and he wasn't about to start believing in them
now. The Barrett was too specialized a weapon—and one
that had not been deployed in any of their previous terror
raids—not to have some momentous importance.

"I suppose he could shoot Marine One out of the sky," he
mumbled, referring to the president's helicopter. Certainly
the Barrett had enough wallop to pull it off. When he navigated back to POTUS's schedule, though, he saw that he was
scheduled to arrive by limousine, and it was back to square
one. Everyone in the Community knew that the presidential
limousine—not so affectionately referred to as The Beast—
was armored to the point where even the Raufoss would be
impotent.

Which again left him with the explosives, and with it the
whole weight ratio thing. Contrary to what many people
think, most popular explosives are not easy to detonate. You
can shoot at a block of C4 or PETN all day, and chances
were pretty good that it would never explode. They need the
hard hit of a primary explosive to really get going. Primary
explosives, on the other hand—the azides, picrates, and others—are so sensitive to impact, friction, and heat that they're
impractical for use in large quantities, and suicidal for use in
the explosive-laden panels that Jonathan had conjured in his
mind.

So what—

Venice appeared in the doorway. "Yes, the Secret Service
uses Appalachian Acoustic panels. Their most commonly
used model is—"

"The Model 9000 Acoustic Reflector," Jonathan interrupted, stealing her thunder.

She looked stunned. "How did you know?"

"I've been looking at their website," Jonathan explained.
"It's the one that made the most sense. Now I have to figure
out how he's going to use them to kill the president."

"What makes you think it has to be this event?" she
asked. "Or, even that it has to be this week or this month?"

"You know how I feel about coincidences," he said. "Plus,

they've got momentum going. This is the moment in time when they can do the most damage."

"And you think this guy planted explosives in the panels?" Venice pressed. Clearly, she wasn't buying.

Jonathan walked her through his analysis.

"Okay, if he's got such a special gun, why not just shoot through the panels?" Venice asked.

"Because the gun only has a ten-round magazine, and it doesn't go fully automatic. Even if he had a general idea, you've got to hit—" He stopped in midsentence. Could it really be that simple?

His hand shot to the mouse quickly enough to startle Venice.

"What?" she said.

He ignored her and navigated to the part of the Appalachian Acoustics' website that bragged about the attractiveness of the back of the Model 9000 Symphonic Reflector. *Perfect for outdoor venues where cosmetics matter*, said the site.

"Ho-ly shit," Jonathan breathed. He looked to Venice. "Box is at my place. Wake him up. Gail, too. Time to go back to work."

CHAPTER THIRTY-SIX

Jonathan laid out his theory. "You don't have to see the target to hit it," he finished. "The optimization instructions are very specific. 'For optimum quality when dealing with a single speaker, the podium and lectern should be situated fifteen to seventeen feet from the upstage panel, and equidistant from the center panels of the side walls.'"

"That sounded like math to me," Boxers growled. His bearlike qualities magnified significantly when he was awakened from hibernation.

"What it means," Gail said, her eyes wide, "is that the target is a fixed point in space. With a little trigonometry, by figuring your height relative to the target, and the angle of the side walls, you can be at any other fixed point and kill the target by shooting a point on the panel."

Boxers got it. "That's freaking brilliant," he said. "Son of a bitch has been planning for this forever."

Jonathan said, "The best terrorists are the most patient terrorists. What makes it particularly brilliant is that Secret Service protocol considers a protectee covered when he's out of view. He's got all the time in the world to settle into his sniper's nest and avoid the Secret Service sweeps."

"Doesn't even have to do that," Venice said. "From what you say, he'll probably be in an area where they wouldn't even be looking for a sniper."

"And that means no countersnipers," Gail said.

"I'm impressed," Boxers said. "This asshole's crazy as a freaking loon, but this is a great plan."

"You're not going to tell the Secret Service, are you?" Gail phrased the question as an accusation.

"Let's play that scenario out," Jonathan said, rising to the bait. "What exactly would you tell them that's not going to make you sound like one of the hundreds of crazies who call them every day?"

"There has to be a way," she said, though her face testified to the opposite. If they told the Secret Service that there was an imminent assassination plot, the agents would want to know details, and they couldn't talk about the details without confessing to all the nastiness in West Virginia. Not only would that get them all thrown in jail for the rest of their lives, it would also sully whatever case was ultimately built in court against the bad guys.

Plus, there was always the possibility that they were flat-out wrong—if not about the plot, then about the day.

"Suppose we just convince them to move the podium forward or backward a few feet," Venice said. "If he's shooting blind, wouldn't that make a difference?"

"That depends on the configuration of the stage and the lectern," Jonathan said. He tapped the keyboard and brought up a satellite photo of the Iwo Jima Memorial, the most prominent feature of which was the statue patterned after the famed Joe Rosenthal photo of six marines raising the American flag atop Mount Suribachi in February of 1945. The park was laid out as a rectangle that covered about an acre of land. The long sides of the rectangle ran north and south, with the statue situated on the eastern edge, facing west.

"Okay, Box," Jonathan said, "and Special Agent Bonneville. Pretend you're a sniper. Where do you want to be?"

"Zoom out a little," Boxers said.

Jonathan could tell that Venice was getting twitchy not being in command of the computer, so he intentionally clicked the wrong button, and the picture went away completely.

"Get out of my way," Venice said, elbowing him out of his chair. He stood, and she took charge. When the satellite image returned, she zoomed out to about a thousand feet.

"Hmm," Gail said. "There are a lot of options."

"Not really," Jonathan argued. He walked to the screen so he could point as he spoke. "We can write off any shots coming from the east," he said. "That's the Potomac River. He'd have to shoot from the roof of the Kennedy Center or Lincoln Memorial, and even then he wouldn't have enough elevation. Down south here, it's nothing but gravesites in Arlington. No elevation at all."

"But look north and west," Gail persisted. "Tall buildings everywhere."

"Look there on North Meade Street," Boxers said, pointing to the left-hand, or western, margin of the park. "You've got fancy townhouses right there. What is that, a hundred-yard shot? A ten-year-old who's never fired a gun could make that."

"Depends on how tall the trees are," Gail said, pointing to what appeared to be a copse of hardwoods along North Meade Street.

"Think it through, folks," Jonathan said. "We're looking for the back of the stage, not the front. The president is going to want the statue as his backdrop."

"Well, ain't nobody shooting through the statue," Boxers said.

"And I disagree that he needs the statue as the backdrop," Venice said. "This is the Marine Corps' birthday and it's just after Veteran's Day. The statue itself needs to be the star. With all the heat the president takes for putting himself before the military, he'd be nuts to block the view with a stage."

She had a point, Jonathan thought. Symbols mattered,

after all, and the incumbent was having a hard time with his media image.

"Is there anything on how many people are expected to attend?" Gail asked.

"I imagine it'll be huge," Jonathan said. "Certainly a lot of military. I'm guessing a lot of politicians, too. Security there on the ground will be really tight."

Gail stood and walked to the screen. "Look here," she said. "For that many people, wouldn't it be best to situate the president on either the north end or the south end, to allow more people to see him straight-on?"

"North end," Venice said. "He won't want the backdrop of Arlington Cemetery, either."

Jonathan liked that. "I think you're right," he said.

Boxers raised a finger in inquiry. "You know we're just wild guessing here, right? What we think doesn't matter. It's what we *know* that matters, and we don't *know* anything."

"You're right," Jonathan said. "So, fire up the Batmobile and let's take a ride to Arlington."

It wasn't easy finding a parking place in the Rosslyn area of Arlington under normal circumstances. Finding a spot for the Batmobile—the name Boxers had assigned to Jonathan's customized Hummer—was particularly daunting. They finally found a spot on a side street, seven blocks away from the Iwo Jima Memorial, and walked the rest of the way. They dressed as regular tourists walking in the cold. It was nearly four when they arrived, and what little warmth the sun had brought was quickly draining away.

At least their coats made it easier to conceal their weapons.

They approached the memorial from North Meade Street, and on first sight, Jonathan dismissed the townhouses across from the park as likely sniper locations. Indeed, the trees were too tall.

As they got closer to the park, Jonathan heard sounds of

construction, and when he stepped up onto the grass, he immediately saw why. "Looks like you were right, Gail," he said. Crews were already constructing the stage on the north end of the park, and laying out hundreds of folding chairs on the lawn.

"No acoustic panels," Gail observed.

"Specs say they're lightweight and easy to work with," Boxers said. "Maybe they go up last."

"Plus, there's a lot yet to be done. What did Venice say? The program starts at ten?"

"Right."

Jonathan ran calculations in his head. "Okay, the sun will have been up for about three and a half hours, which means it'll be pretty high."

"Piss-poor lighting on the monument," Boxers said.

"But perfect lighting for the crowd," Jonathan added. "Let's get a little closer to the stage."

They walked down what tomorrow would be the center aisle through the audience. The entire park was surrounded by trees, but most were hardwoods and fairly dormant now. He was disappointed by the complexity of the skyline on the distant north end, where sixties-vintage high-rises grew like so many bushes in a forest.

"Wow," Gail said, thinking his very thought. "That's a lot of potential sniper nests."

Of all the buildings, two stood higher than the others, and therefore impressed Jonathan as the most likely candidates. He pulled his phone from his pocket and snapped pictures of each. One of them, due north of the park, and directly in line with where the podium would be, was significantly taller than the other, and it gleamed silver in the afternoon sun. The second building, north-northwest of the park, appeared to be fairly new and constructed of red brick.

"I know what you're thinking, Dig," Boxers said. "But the ones you're looking at are both office buildings."

"So was the Texas School Book Depository," Gail said.

"And look how much good that did for Oswald. I'm just

wondering how he's going to get in and out in the middle of the day without being seen."

"Remember how much these guys don't like to surrender," Jonathan reminded them. "Maybe getting away isn't part of the long-range plan."

"It's always part of the plan," Boxers said. "Even for people who claim it's not."

"Tell that to suicide bombers," Gail quipped.

"Yeah, but they're crazy."

Jonathan laughed. "Do you remember last night? I could swear I saw you there."

A police officer in the telltale white-on-black of the Uniformed Division of the Secret Service approached from the direction of the statue. "Can I help you folks?" he said.

"What's going on here?" Gail said. "What are they building?"

"The president's speaking here tomorrow," the cop said. His name tag identified him as Greenwood. "I need to ask you to move on. We'll be buttoning it up soon."

"Buttoning it up?" Boxers asked, playing dumb tourist.

Greenwood reacted the way people often did the first time they spoke with Boxers, with a silent *Holy shit, you're big.* But he covered well. "That means we'll be securing the scene."

"But you said he's speaking tomorrow," Jonathan said, throwing his own hat into the thespian ring. "Why shut it down now?"

"In part so I don't have to answer questions like this." Greenwood said it with a smile to take the edge off, but there was no doubting his seriousness. Clearly, this was a guy who dealt with a lot of nosy tourists, and he knew how to walk the rope between friendly and official. "There's a lot more to be done. We gotta bring in mags and dogs. Screening of guests begins two hours before the speech. All of that is a lot easier to do when it's just the people who are supposed to be here."

"So, if we're in line by, say, seven, can we get in to hear him speak?"

The cop gave a tolerant chuckle. "Um, no. Invitation only, I'm afraid."

"Is that wise?" Jonathan asked. "I mean the whole thing? I know I probably shouldn't talk about this sort of thing—especially to a Secret Service agent—but with all the killings, should the president be staying inside?"

"First of all I'm not an agent—"

Jonathan knew that, but thought a little naïveté could play to his benefit.

"—and that's a call that the president makes. I just make sure that no one hurts him."

"Well, God bless you for that," Gail gushed.

Greenwood blushed.

"Can I get my picture taken with you?" Gail asked.

Now he was embarrassed. "Me? What for?"

"You're the very first Secret Service man I've ever talked to. We go back to Iowa in three days, and I want a remembrance."

Suddenly self-conscious, Greenwood glanced over his shoulders, then said, "Sure."

"Can we go to the stage?"

"Ah, no," he said.

"Well we can get closer, can't we?" She started leading the way up the aisle.

After about ten paces, Greenwood said, "That's close enough," and she stopped.

Jonathan thought this was brilliant. He used his cell phone camera to take the pictures, and when he was done, he had four photos he could use to judge the best firing lanes for the sniper to use.

Jonathan and his team got three rooms on the same floor at the Hilton Garden Inn in Arlington, about a mile from the Marine Corps War Memorial. After a cursory sweep for listening devices—Jonathan knew it was paranoia on his part, but it was well-earned paranoia—they got Venice on the phone and started stitching a plan together.

Venice used the pictures to find addresses for the two buildings Jonathan was most concerned about. The tallest one was indeed tall, clocking in at thirty-one floors. Located at 1101 Coolidge Avenue, just barely on the Virginia side of the river. "There was actually some controversy over building this one," she said. "It's so much taller than any other buildings that people objected."

"That's fascinating, Ven," Jonathan said, meaning exactly the opposite. He paced the room while Boxers sat perilously far back in a desk chair that clearly had not been designed with him in mind, and Gail sat propped against pillows, her legs crossed on the spread in front of her.

The other building, on North Loudoun Street, rose a paltry twelve stories, but it also sat atop a hill that gave it a commanding view of the kill zone. "Like the Coolidge Avenue building, this one is strictly commercial, and is home mostly to defense contractors."

"I still don't get why you're so quick to dismiss the apartment buildings," Gail said.

"I'm not dismissing them. They're just not the perches I would choose. Ven, you're cross-referencing the names of the apartment tenants with all things Copley, right?"

"Didn't you ask me to?" she said.

"Yes."

"Then what does that mean?"

Jonathan mouthed to Gail, *It means she's doing it.*

Over the course of the next hour, Jonathan piled more and more on Venice. As a practical matter, it was impossible to go door-to-door through multiple buildings surveying for a shooter that they weren't one-hundred-percent certain was even going to be there. They needed something—any bit of data—to winnow the list to a manageable size.

"You know this is going to take hours, right?" Venice said as the spitballing session ended.

"What, you want overtime?" Jonathan poked.

"Just appreciation," she said. "I have no life, after all. I live to serve."

She was being ironic, but Jonathan knew she was speaking the truth. "Can we be done for a while? I need rest."

"What time do we reconvene?" Venice asked.

"Not later than six, but right away if you get something hot."

"No," Boxers said. All heads turned to him. "I need to sleep. I don't need to get up again at two-freaking-thirty because you think there's an interesting tidbit I need to hear. Make it six o'clock. We're less than a mile from anyplace that can matter." He stood and when he got to the door, he turned and ostentatiously placed his hand on the grip of his Beretta. "I'm going to put the do-not-disturb sign on my door, and I'm going to shoot anyone who ignores it."

He left.

"Sounds like we're in recess," Venice said. "I'll use my best judgment in calling you, Dig. Get some rest."

The line when dead.

Jonathan shut down his computer and did his best seductive crawl across the bed toward Gail. When he arrived, he placed his head on her lap and gently stroked her leg. "What would you like to do?" he teased.

"Not what you're thinking," she said.

He rolled over to look at her face. "What, then?"

She stroked his hair from his forehead and gave a little smile. "You're such a little boy," she said. "It's all a game to you." Her teasing tone seemed dissonant with her very serious expression.

"What are we talking about?"

"All of it." She rolled her hips to eject his head from her lap and she stood. "Life. Your job. Everything's a game to you."

Jonathan sat up. "You say that as if it's a bad thing."

"Jon, we *killed* people last night. I *murdered* a young man in the woods just because he happened to walk into the wrong place."

"You killed him before he could kill you," Jonathan countered. "That's hardly murder."

She brought her hands to the top of her head, as if to keep it from exploding. "That's it for you," she said. "That's as complicated as the world is."

He shrugged. "It's not as if I haven't been around the block a few times. I know right from wrong, and I know life from death. Life is better."

"Is it?" she said. "Is living with this kind of guilt on my conscience really part of the good life?"

An alarm sounded in Jonathan's head. "Jeez, Gail, it was self-defense. We killed a lot of people last night, and they were *all* self-defense."

"Not according to the law."

"Oh, forget the law."

She looked stunned. "Really? That's all you've got? Forget the law?"

"We've met, right?" He extended his hand in greeting. "Hi, I'm Jonathan Grave. I save lives for a living."

"I don't need your sarcasm, Jon. You also kill people for a living."

"I've *always* killed people for a living."

"It's not the same, and you know it."

"It *is* the same," Jonathan countered. "That's the simplicity that you don't see. Ask Pablo Escobar's family if it makes a difference that the guy who pulled the trigger on him was operating with permission from Uncle Sam. Dead is dead."

"There's—" She cut herself off and paced a bit, gathering her thoughts. "In a nation of laws, individual citizens do not get to make the decision who lives and who dies."

"Wrong again. I spent nearly two decades of my life killing bad guys by order of the individual citizen who happened to be commander in chief."

"With the constitutional authority to do so."

Jonathan gaped. "So every bozo who's occupied the Oval Office is somehow endowed with more wisdom than you or me or the average guy on the street? I don't buy it."

"Presidents have the authority," she repeated.

"And I have the ability."

"So, what makes you different than a punk murderer on the street? The elements of the law are the elements of the law. I swore an *oath*, Digger."

He felt as if he'd been slapped. "I don't know what to say. I just know I'm on the side of the angels."

She walked to him and allowed herself to be enfolded in his arms. "Jon, I love you," she said.

A whole new warning bell clanged in his head. "Why do I feel there's a 'but' at the end of that statement?"

She released her arms, and took a step back. "But I don't know if I can keep doing this."

"You mean saving lives?" He said it with a wink.

"If everything we suspect turns out to be right, we're going to kill again tomorrow," she said.

He considered that. "Probably," he said.

She cocked her head. "Only probably?"

Jonathan inhaled deeply. "The asshole we're looking for has killed a lot of people. Dozens."

"So we'll be judge, jury, and executioner."

Jonathan thought it through for a long time. Finally: "Yes."

Gail grabbed his face gently with both hands and pulled his mouth to hers.

"Good night," she said. She closed the door to the adjoining room as she left.

CHAPTER THIRTY-SEVEN

"I've got nothing," Venice said, opening the telephone call at 06:01. "Of the three potential bad guys in the apartment buildings, all three have already been contacted by the Secret Service, according to ICIS, and all three are under intense observation. My guess is they're each going to spend their mornings somewhere else, or with their drapes closed. Here's the really bad news among the merely bad news: Michael Copley has nothing to do with anything."

"What about the office buildings?" Jonathan asked.

"A lot of security," Venice explained. She spent the better part of ten minutes delivering the minutiae of the various security systems, which, at the end of the day, were mostly dependent on the security guard in the lobby.

"I almost hesitate to tell you this," Venice said toward the end of her prepared presentation. "I know you, and I know how you obsess over coincidence; but the General Services Administration has an office at 1101 Coolidge."

Jonathan perked up. "This would be the same GSA that provides the Model 9000 Symphonic Reflector to the Secret Service?"

"Yes," Venice hedged, "but it's also the same GSA that

provides toilet paper to the Department of Commerce. It's a big agency."

Jonathan wasn't interested in the qualifiers. "That's the address," he said.

"Just like that?" Gail said.

"It's a place to start," Jonathan replied. The chill between them lowered the temperature in the room by ten degrees.

"Suppose it's the wrong place to start?" Boxers asked.

"What difference will it make? We can sit here and twiddle our thumbs, or we can go there and pretend that we're right. We will be or we won't be, but at least we'll be doing something."

Boxers gave him a funny look, then shrugged. "You're the boss, Boss. Load my gun, and I'll follow you anywhere." He gave him an air kiss from across the room.

Yep, it was official now. Everybody needed a good night's sleep.

Fifteen minutes later, they had a plan, and all the players had bought into it.

"You know," Boxers said, "we're gonna feel pretty stupid if Michael Copley just steps out of a crowd and blows him away at point-blank range."

"At least we'll have tried," Jonathan said. He rose from the desk chair. "Let's get going."

"I'm staying," Gail announced.

Boxers recoiled a step.

Jonathan said, "Fine. Suit yourself." Then he led the way to the door, and they left Gail alone in the hotel room.

"Say what's on your mind," Jonathan said after an awkwardly silent three minutes in the Batmobile.

"Do I really have to?" Boxers replied.

Actually, no, Jonathan thought.

Boxers let him off the hook. "I'm guessing she's still wrapped around the axle about the killing and the lawbreaking. Tell you the truth, I'm not surprised. So, how are you doing?"

"I'm mission capable," Jonathan said.

Boxers scoffed, "You'd be mission capable with two broken arms and your liver hanging out. I asked how you're doing. You and her were pretty tight."

"I'm fine," Jonathan said. "I don't want anybody doing anything they don't want to do. Not with the stakes this high." The answer didn't address the real question, but Jonathan wasn't in the mood to whine.

"Yeah, okay," Boxers said, and then he remained silent until they found a parking place—again on the street, but this time only six blocks from their target.

Jonathan checked his watch. Eight-thirty-five. "What are you carrying?" he asked the Big Guy.

"Not much," he replied. "I've got my Beretta on my hip, plus three spare mags. I got a Glock 23 in my shoulder rig plus another three spare mags, and I've got my backup three-eighty on my ankle."

Jonathan smiled. Boxers truly believed in the power of firepower. "Only a hundred rounds and change," he teased. "You must feel positively naked."

"I miss my tactical gear," Big Guy confirmed. "What about you?"

He had his Colt on his hip, along with four spare mags, and then his backup .38 on his ankle. "We're bringing a lot of firepower against one guy."

"That one guy has enough firepower for five. If he gets that Barrett turned around on us, the day will turn very, very bad."

Actually, *very, very bad* didn't touch it.

With the crowded sidewalks and the ridiculously long traffic lights on the crosswalks, it was almost nine before they made it to the entrance to 1101 Coolidge. They stopped a block short and Jonathan called Venice.

"We're in place," he said.

"Okey-dokey. Stand by one. Good luck."

* * *

Michael Copley sat casually in his La-Z-Boy, feet up, coffee mug in hand, scanning his five television screens for an image that would spark interest. He was shocked that the news was not filled with images of the attack on the Army of God compound and offended that the execution video was being so readily written off as the work of pranksters.

He recognized this as the tyrannical hand of the government. They were so anxious to portray themselves as the victors in any conflict that they would willingly twist and manipulate facts to form whatever preconceived conclusions they wanted to, and their media lapdogs would go right along with them.

Well, just wait another hour or so. He still had five active assault teams roving America, wreaking their havoc and shaking that precious sense of safety that Americans valued above all. They thought it was fine to throw principle to the wind and burn the Constitution as a nightlight, as long as Aunt Martha in breadbasket America didn't feel threatened.

Well, they should feel threatened now, because this was the day when two plus two would stop equaling four. In an hour and a half, within minutes of the time when he and Brother Franklin would tear apart the president in a cross fire, two bombs would detonate in Metro train cars under the Potomac River, causing the Orange Line to run red with the blood of shredded commuters. It was a shame that they couldn't target the height of the rush hour, but the president was notoriously inattentive to the timing of his own schedule, so there was no telling when he might actually show up for his own execution. Michael couldn't take the risk of the bomb detonating first, because that would likely cause the president to cancel his attendance altogether.

At eleven o'clock local time, a different bomb, this one placed three days ago, would detonate in the emergency department of Good Samaritan Hospital in Cincinnati, and throughout the day, his teams would exploit targets of opportunities in small towns throughout the Midwest.

And with the president dead—killed in color on live television—the vacuum of leadership would trigger the collapse of everything.

It will be a thing of beauty.

After repeated tries in the initial hours after the assault on the compound, he'd been able to make contact with Brother Coleman at the Farm, and what he'd heard disturbed him. Of the one hundred seventeen adults in residence at the compound, forty-four were dead and twenty-six were seriously wounded and likely to die. Another twenty were missing. Brother Coleman had begged to allow ambulances into the compound or, as an alternative, to transport the more grievously wounded down the mountain to a hospital, but Michael stood firm.

"We're a nation unto ourselves," he reminded him. "That means we live and die within our blessings and limitations. The Users have no role in our lives."

Brother Coleman ultimately came around, but it was a tough sell. He relayed that the members of the Army were scared, deep down to their very cores. Brother Coleman told stories of helicopters appearing out of nowhere to sweep the mother and her son to safety. He told stories of utter carnage.

"I don't know that there'll be room enough in the cemetery," Brother Coleman concluded. "You can't walk the compound for more than a few minutes without finding body parts. It's horrible."

Most concerning for Michael, in addition to the loss of so many fine warriors, was the fact the Brother Kendig had apparently chosen to run away with the deserters. With him gone, and Michael and Franklin both here for this mission of missions, the Army was left without leaders.

"Do your best to keep order," Michael said. "Stop the desertions at all costs."

"When will you be returning?"

"Soon," Michael said, and he clicked off realizing that had just told a lie.

Having the question asked so directly, and having to

a direct answer, he realized that he had seen the compound and his home and his business for the last time. He couldn't go back, not now that the secret of their existence had leaked out into the world. Somehow, the FBI and the rest of the jackals who denied liberty to the masses had neglected to raid the compound, but that would come in time. Would the soldiers fight, now that they had been beaten so terribly once before? He imagined no.

He wondered what would happen to those who were taken into custody, but he realized that it wouldn't matter. Their efforts had already had the desired effect. People were terrified, and soon their terror would be reflected in the collapse of everything. Perhaps he'd been naïve and overly ambitious to believe that his little Army could survive the war intact. He knew now that it would not, but he could imagine far worse outcomes. As it was, he was on track to make an indelible mark on history.

But first, he needed another cup of coffee. He kicked the footrest down and stood.

And then yelled out loud when his cozy little office erupted in the earsplitting sound of the fire alarm.

It was hard to believe that a building could hold so many people. Hundreds filed out into the cold as the fire alarm continued to screech. The first fire truck arrived after about a minute and a half, and within a minute after that, half a dozen more arrived.

Jonathan pressed a speed-dial number. "Jesus, Ven, what did you do? Every emergency responder in the world is coming."

"I've never triggered a fire alarm before," she said, instantly defensive. "I think I might have tricked a few too many smoke detectors."

At least a few too many, as it turned out. By the time they were able to reset the alarm and let people return, forty-five minutes had passed. Jonathan felt bad for the workers who hadn't thought to grab a coat on their way out. Then he remembered that this was Rosslyn, where coffee shops grew like clover, and he stopped pitying anyone who was too stupid to seek shelter if they were cold.

"Do you have any candidate offices?" Jonathan asked Venice on a second phone call. "It's inefficient as hell to go look at every southern-facing office."

"I'm working on it, Digger."

"It's nine-forty."

"I know that."

"The president speaks at ten."

"I'm hanging up." Then she did exactly that.

Once the all-clear was given, Jonathan and Boxers joined the crowd of returning workers who flowed through the doors like a human river. A phalanx of security guards had formed a gauntlet in the main lobby, and they made a show of checking identification cards. One of them, a short stocky guy who looked like he might be a moonlighting bouncer, zeroed in on Boxers and beckoned him over.

The Big Guy ignored him, but then the security guy pursued him and grabbed his shirtsleeve, adding himself to a very short list of people who had ever done that without spending the next six weeks eating through a straw.

"I need to see your ID," the guard said.

"I left it in my office," Boxers replied.

The guard turned to Jonathan.

"Ditto."

"Neither of you look familiar to me," the guard said. His name tag identified him as Mr. Farmer.

"So much for saying hello every morning," Jonathan bluffed. "I'm Dan Banks and this is Marlon Ford. We both work for the Handelsman Group on the third floor." Anticipating this moment, Venice had searched the rolls for the names of real tenants and employees. They had to roll the dice on the guard not knowing either.

"I need you to step aside while I check," Mr. Farmer said.

Boxers gave that smile that never led to good things and

Jonathan intervened. "Tell you what," Jonathan said. "I've got a conference call that I'm already late for—thanks to your malfunctioning building—and we're not staying anywhere. You go ahead and make your calls, and if it turns out we're bogus, you come on up and get us."

"I'd actually look forward to that," Boxers menaced.

Without waiting for an answer, they rejoined the crowd and headed for the elevators. Jonathan checked his watch. Nine-forty-three.

When it was finally their turn, Jonathan stepped onto the elevator and pressed the button for the third floor. With no place else to go, and on the off chance that the guard was watching on cameras, he decided that there'd be no harm in paying a visit to the Handelsman Group.

CHAPTER THIRTY-EIGHT

Unlike those of so many other high-rises, the architects of 1101 Coolidge Avenue had been thoughtful enough to include windows that could be opened for fresh air. They weren't big—God forbid that anyone might fall out—but they were a nod to those who needed to breathe unfiltered air from time to time. It probably never occurred to any of them that their thoughtful design feature would make a sniper's life so easy.

The folks at C-SPAN likewise probably never gave much thought to how live coverage of presidential goings-on eliminated the need for a spotter. Who needs conspirators when you have live television?

Michael Copley heard the motorcade before he saw it, and that fact alone told him that the wind was blowing from east to west. This would be important data very soon. He looked at the clock. Nine-forty-seven, and C-SPAN was still prattling about other things.

The office he'd rented two years before—actually, he'd sublet it from Beacon Accounting for a ridiculous amount of money—sat on the fourteenth floor, and was designed on a curve, with one window providing breathtaking views of the

Washington Monument, the Tidal Basin, and the Lincoln and Jefferson Memorials to the east, and a nearly unobstructed view of the Iwo Jima Memorial to the south.

Michael felt bad about what he had to do to the Beacon staff this morning. They were nice people, but they were Users. If they weren't doomed from the day they were born, they were certainly doomed from the day that Michael Copley was born.

He stayed well back from the windows as he watched the motorcycles lead the procession from Constitution Avenue across the Teddy Roosevelt Bridge. There must have been a dozen of them, looking from up here like so many red-flashing mosquitoes. Then came the D.C. Police cars, and behind them a couple of shiny black sedans with red and blue flashers behind the grille. Behind the sedans were the two presidential limousines—one of them a decoy, there specifically to frustrate people who might steal Michael's thunder. Behind the limousines, the flood of vehicles continued with all manner of vans and sedans, plus the ubiquitous black Suburbans, all hiding counterassault teams who soon would reassess everything. More vans followed the counterassault vehicles, and then a D.C. ambulance and more motorcycles and police cars brought up the rear.

The lead elements of the motorcade had already made it to the Virginia side of the bridge before the last of the trailing motorcycles had left the D.C. side. Michael didn't count exactly, but he estimated forty vehicles in all. Such wastefulness.

He didn't realize until the motorcade turned left onto Arlington Boulevard that it had traveled all the way across the river on the wrong side of the road in order to gain straighton access to the Iwo Jima Memorial grounds. He found his face getting hot. How was it possibly right—who would think it was okay—to shut down a main highway and inconvenience so many people just so that one man could give a speech that no one wanted to hear because everyone had heard it before?

His Barrett cannon sat poised on his desk, four feet inside the window, already pre-sighted for the spot he needed to hit. As the president's motorcade disappeared around the back side of the park, Michael settled himself into the hard-backed chair that would one day would be part of the museum dedicated to the day that the world changed. The muzzle bipod was extended, and sandbags were in place under the foregrip and the stock. When the time came, he'd need only to correct for wind and send his bullets down-range.

Settling in behind his scope, and taking care to keep his finger out of the trigger guard, he pantomimed the cross-shaped pattern he would fire. The first would nail the sweet spot, and the next nine—five on the vertical axis and four on the horizontal—would be placed within inches of each other. A kill shot was guaranteed.

Then, in the pandemonium that followed, he would run out of his office, just like everyone else, shouting, "What was that? Oh, my God, what was that noise?" By the time the truth was known, he'd already be out of the building and on his way to safety. If anyone confronted him, well, he had Mr. .45-Caliber Sig Sauer on his hip to do his talking for him.

On the television, C-SPAN switched to their reporter on the scene for the ceremonies. It wouldn't be long now.

Once on the third floor, Jonathan abandoned the plan to drop in on the Handelsman Group, and instead detoured to the stairwell. He pulled out his cell phone again.

"We're down to ten minutes, Ven."

"You think I don't know this? Nobody in the entire building has any known ties or connections to any of the parameters we set up. For heaven's sake, most of the businesses in there are defense contractors. They're huge, and they all have clearances. Even if Copley were among them, I don't know how he wouldn't be seen."

Venice's statement stirred something in Jonathan's mind.

Something about the businesses mostly being large. "Okay," he said. "Let's correct for the large businesses. What are the small ones?"

"Define small."

"Dammit, Ven, they're your statistics. Surprise me."

"Well, Digger, there are a total of seventy-two tenants in the building."

"The smallest, then."

"Hold one."

He heard tapping in the background.

Boxers said, "Hey, Dig? We don't need every small business. We only need the ones that face south."

Jonathan's eyes got big. "Ven, did you hear that?"

"I did," she said, "and I'm disappointed that I didn't think of it myself." More tapping. "I'm cross-referencing tax records with the tenant list," she explained. "It's sort of complicated."

"Talk less and type more, then."

"Maybe it's not even this building," she said. Her frustration flowed through the phone like electricity.

"Focus, Ven."

"Okay, here's one. Kendall and Associates. They're an investment firm with five employees, and they're on the south side of the building."

Jonathan's heart rate increased. "What floor?"

"Fourth."

Damn. "No. Higher floor." He looked to Boxers, who held up seven fingers. "Seventh floor or higher." There was no rationale to this, but much lower than that, and Copley would have a hard time sighting his shot.

More clacking from the other end of the phone.

Another look at his watch showed nine-fifty-five.

"I've got one," Venice said. "Fourteenth floor, south side. Beacon Accounting. Suite fourteen-twenty." Typing. "Oh, my God," she gasped. "Dig, I gotta go." The line went dead.

Jonathan didn't care. He had a target to shoot for. "Suite

fourteen-twenty," he said. He looked up at the endless stair-well. "Elevator."

He pulled open the stairwell door, and there was the guard from the lobby, Mr. Farmer. He stood with his hand resting casually on the butt of the .357 Magnum revolver in his holster. He'd brought a friend—a big fellow named Mr. Plano.

"Look, pal," Farmer said. "I don't know what you're doing here, but this is a secure building. You're going—"

Jonathan didn't have time for this. "Get out of my way," he said. He moved to the elevator and pushed the UP button.

"Stop where you are," Mr. Plano said. "Do not get on that elevator." When his hand got to his revolver, he curled his fingers around the grip.

"Be really careful, son," Boxers growled. "You're about two seconds away from a point of no return."

Fear more or less canceled out bravado in Plano's face.

The elevator dinged.

"You can shoot us," Jonathan said, "or you can come along on a great adventure."

"What the hell are you talking about?" Farmer asked.

"Yeah," Boxers said. "What are you talking about?"

The doors opened.

Jonathan and Boxers stepped in. "It's your call," he said. When the doors started to close, he placed his hand out to stop them. "Last chance," he said.

It's amazing what stupid things people will do when their curiosity is piqued. Mr. Farmer and Mr. Plano stepped onto the elevator with them. "You've got some explaining—"

"Hush," Jonathan said. "Please. We're here to stop a mur-der, okay? In fifty words or less, tell me everything you know about Beacon Accounting in suite fourteen-twenty."

Farmer retreated to a corner. "A murder? Who the hell are you?"

"Less relevant than my need for information," Jonathan said. They were passing the eighth floor. "Beacon Account-ing."

Farmer searched for words. "I don't . . . what do you need . . . who's going to be murdered?"

Jonathan looked to Boxers, who said, "Oh, you're gonna love this."

Jonathan steeled himself with a breath. "The president of the United States."

Gail had the television in her room tuned to C-SPAN, and she felt terrible for letting Jonathan down. While she prayed he could get there in time, she didn't know how it would be possible. They didn't even know where they were going. That meant either knocking blindly on doors, or simply breaking in—

Her cell phone rang, and she recognized the number at a glance. "Hi, Venice."

Venice's voice was nearly a scream. "Oh, thank God. Are you still at the hotel?"

Something happened to Digger, she thought. "What's—"

"Are you still at the hotel!"

She recoiled, not just from the tone, but from the volume. "Yes. You don't have to—"

"Get to ten-seventy-five North Loudoun Drive," Venice said. "Suite ten-thirteen. Right now. Hurry."

"Why?"

"Because I think there's a second shooter."

When the elevator door opened on the fourteenth floor, Boxers and Jonathan stepped out, but the security guards stayed behind.

So much for valor, Jonathan thought, as the doors closed. He drew his Colt, and Boxers shadowed him. A sign on the wall confirmed his internal compass, and showed Suites 1413 to 1420 to be down to the left. They started that way.

The elevator dinged behind them, and Farmer and Plano

both stepped out. "Really?" Farmer said. "The president of the United States?"

Even without an answer, they followed, walking fast to keep up. "Beacon Accounting has been here for as long as I've been here," Plano said quickly.

It took Jonathan a second to realize that he was answering the question from the elevator.

"They've only got about seven or eight employees, but they sublet one corner of their office to another guy. A one-man show with some kind of a church or something."

"God's Army," Farmer said.

Bingo.

"Let me guess," Boxers said as they arrived at the door. "He occupies the space on the far southern end."

"Incredible view," Plano said. He drew a .44 magnum horse pistol from his holster. "How does this work?"

"It starts by you putting that thing away," Boxers said. "And it finishes with you staying out of my way."

The television showed various military officers and political dignitaries being introduced. They were important enough for pictures, but clearly not important enough for sound. Or, maybe the reporter was too in love with his own voice to cede the airwaves to anyone else.

Michael Copley was surprised at how calm he felt. It was a moment about which he'd thought for so long, and for which he'd trained for so long, that now that it had arrived, it all felt nearly anticlimactic. He wished he could say the same for Brother Franklin. The man had never been as calm under pressure as Michael, but he'd trained every bit as hard.

Now, as they spoke on the phone, Michael could hear the stress in his voice. "You need to relax, Brother Franklin," he said.

"Yeah, relax. I'll be calm as a cucumber right before I blow away the leader of the free world."

"You're making history, Brother. And you're ridding the

free world of a leader who has destroyed far more than he's saved. It's been that way for forty presidencies. We can change everything."

For fifteen seconds, he heard only silence. "Brother Franklin?"

"I'm here."

"You need only stick to the plan. The program states that the president will begin speaking at ten-ten, and that his remarks will run around fifteen minutes."

"I know," Brother Franklin said. Nervousness aside, he clearly was tiring of reviewing the plan over and over again. "We wait precisely three minutes from the first word of his speech, and then we open up. Ten rounds, cross-shaped pattern. I already have my weapon sighted. I know what is expected of me."

"I know you do." Michael closed his eyes. In his mind, he could see the expression in the man's face. "Live or die, we'll likely not speak again, my brother."

"But what about the Army?"

"They're introducing the president now," Michael said, and he hung up the phone. He watched on television as the User-in-Chief walked in from the wings, passing in front of the tableau of American flags to downstage center, where he stopped and waved with both hands to the crowd, either in a gesture of jubilation or surrender.

The sound of the roaring crowd made it all the way across the road and into the window through which he would soon change the world.

The Marine Band—The President's Own—finished "Hail to the Chief," and then struck up the "Star-Spangled Banner."

Look at him, Michael thought. Not just a User, but a narcissistic one at that, preening for the cameras.

He could take him now. He could see nothing through his scope, but by sighting on the pattern of logos that he had so carefully designed, he knew precisely how to hit any point beyond his view.

How poetic would that be for history to record a president being blown in half in the middle of the national anthem?

It was a brilliant idea. An image even more horrifying than the Zapruder film, forever linking two of the great symbols of American greed in a single snippet of images and sound.

It wasn't the plan, of course, but as the architect, he got to change the plans at will. They were his to change, after all.

Michael Copley sat down in his chair, settled the buttstock of the rifle into his shoulder, and prepared to make history.

Gail remembered as the door slammed behind her that she'd left her key on the dresser. As if that mattered.

Ten seventy-five North Loudoun Drive was the second building they'd photographed last night, and Suite 1013 housed a consulting firm called Compliance Services Inc., which specialized in safety and environmental regulations. Somehow, according to Venice, that all equaled the most likely place for a sniper to perch. Something about small businesses among large, and the limited availability of southern exposures.

The details didn't matter because Venice didn't get this spun up over anything unless she was very, very sure that she was right. And the clock was ticking very, very fast. With her Glock on her hip and two spare mags in her coat pocket, Gail bypassed the elevators in the hotel and tore down the steps to the emergency exit. Her whole body still ached from the activities in West Virginia, her muscles still taut and bruised, but she forced them to work anyway.

Tomorrow, she was going to look for a Caribbean vacation package.

At ground level now, she crashed through the exit into the cold sunshine. The hotel fronted to the east, and the light blinded her. She hadn't had time to consult a map, so she processed her memory from last night, which told her that the North Loudoun Drive address was just a couple of blocks north. She turned to the left, and there it was, rising above all its neighbors.

She started running. Uphill, of course.

By the time Michael had made his decision to shoot, the moment had passed. The national anthem ended, and the president took his seat in the middle of the stage, behind the lectern, but in front of the wall of flags.

Michael knew the target spot for that location, too; but with the potential for true drama lost, it no longer made sense to vary from the plan. He could shoot and kill the president, but Brother Franklin would be caught off guard. Even a slight delay of a few seconds would ruin the effectiveness of a cross fire. After the first five seconds—and the fastest Michael had ever been able to fire the Barrett and reliably hit his target was one round per second, give or take—the Secret Service will have caught on, and people will have started to panic, meaning that the last five rounds of his ten-round magazine would be less deadly. The more concentrated the crowd, the more effective every shot fired.

On the television, a military chaplain droned out an invocation.

With Michael and Brother Franklin firing simultaneously, those first five seconds would put ten rounds on target while the crowd on the stage was still its thickest. To shoot early would squander that. It wasn't worth it.

Michael could wait. The chaplain sat, and another man stepped to the microphone. *Blah, blah, blah.* Then, "Ladies and gentlemen, the president of the United States."

Again, he could hear the roar of the crowd through the window. The User-in-chief stepped to the lectern and pressed down on the air with his hands as a gesture for silence that everyone knew he didn't want. "Thank you," he said. "Thank you. Please be seated."

Those words didn't count in the countdown. He and Brother Franklin had discussed this, anticipated it. Only when he got to the text of his speech—when he started lying in earnest—would they begin the count.

"Ladies and gentlemen, we are gathered at this hallowed place this morning . . ."

That was it. Michael pressed the START button on his digital timer.

Three minutes.

CHAPTER THIRTY-NINE

Gail was still a long block away when she heard the cheer erupt from the grounds of the Iwo Jima Memorial. Not polite applause, mind you, but a roar, the kind you'd expect from a football game. The kind that will travel across four lanes of a busy highway. The kind that would come when the president of the United States is introduced to a crowd of eight hundred.

The cold air had dried her nose and throat to the point of rawness. Her legs felt leaden on the long uphill slog, and she realized that she'd slowed. *Not now,* she thought. She could stroll on the beach after she arrived in the Caribbean. Now, she had to run.

Concentrate on the task, not the distance, she told herself, rekindling the mantra that got her through the endurance tests at the FBI Academy a thousand years ago. Sometimes, it helps to keep your eye on the goal when you're running a long distance, but that only worked for her on level ground. On a hill, she found it was better to watch her feet.

And when the sidewalk changed from gray concrete to red brick, she knew she was there.

She headed for the front door, pausing to control her breathing. Then she opened the door and strolled into the lobby. Approaching the security desk, she used her coyest smile in an effort to sneak past, but it didn't work.

"Excuse me," said the woman behind the desk. "Can I help you?"

"I'm going to ten-thirteen," Gail said. "Compliance Services."

"Not without signing in first, you ain't."

The door to the outer office of Beacon Accounting was locked, and the door looked to be of stout stuff. Jonathan pressed the doorbell.

"Really?" Boxers mocked. "I don't think I've ever seen you use a doorbell."

Jonathan smiled. He'd known some freakishly calm warriors in his time, but Boxers set the standard.

"Who are you, anyway?" Farmer asked.

After no one had answered the door in five seconds, Boxers elbowed his boss out of the way. "Stand back," he said. He took a step back and prepared to kick in the door.

"Wait!" Plano yelled. "I have a key."

Boxers fired a savage kick to the door that cracked the frame, but the door stayed in place. The second kick did the trick. The door exploded inward and rebounded off the parallel wall.

"I have a key, too," Jonathan said. Leading with their drawn pistols, he and Boxers squirted into the room, side by side, the Big Guy covering high and right, Digger covering low and left.

Farmer and Plano stayed in the hall. "Ah, shit," Farmer moaned. "Do you have a warrant for this?"

They were in the anteroom of a larger office outfitted in a colonial décor, with wingback guest chairs and a faux-mahogany receptionist's desk. An ugly splash of blood marred the papered wall behind the desk.

"Hey, Scorpion?" Boxers whispered. He nodded to the space on the floor behind the desk, where the body of a woman in her fifties lay in a heap, surrounded by a lake of blood.

Jonathan nodded toward the office door farthest to the right. "That's the one farthest south," he whispered.

"Oh, my God," Farmer yelped. "Oh, holy shit. She's dead."

Boxers said, "Mr. Farmer, Mr. Plano, you may draw your weapons now."

Michael Copley's ballistic computer told him everything he needed. He knew the drift and drop, and he held the spot perfectly still in the reticle of his telescopic sight. The sandbags gave him a rock-steady platform for the rifle. The weaknesses from this point on would all be man-made. At this range, every twitch mattered, every jolt of adrenaline. When the time came, he would squeeze the trigger between heartbeats.

With less than two minutes left, he felt a sense of calm settling over him. After so many years of dreaming and of practicing, now was not the time to seize up, either physically or mentally. It was just as he told his soldiers. Now, if he could keep only half the focus that they'd been able to display thus far in the war—

Someone rang the doorbell. What a ridiculous sound that was in a business environment. *Ding-dong, Avon calling.* He ignored it, of course. Whoever it was could come back or not; it wasn't as if the accountants at Beacon were going to be giving a lot of advice in the coming eternity. If it was a customer coming in for an appointment, they'd surely be upset, and then maybe they'd call to complain. So what?

Even if someone suspected that something was wrong, by the time—

Boom!

That was no knock. That sounded like a battering ram. Then it was followed by a huge bang that shook the entire office suite. Someone was invading.

No, no, no . . .

He lifted his cheek from the buttstock to look behind him at the locked door that separated him from his attackers, and then returned to his rifle.

Just take the shot! his mind screamed. He'd made snap shots before. He'd proved it just yesterday by blast-butchering a cow. He tucked his cheek to the buttstock again.

The clock read fifty-five seconds.

Behind him, he heard voices, and then someone yelled, "Holy shit! She's dead."

Forty-eight seconds.

Too many distractions. Even this little bit of time was plenty of time for him to resolve the threat and still finish the job.

Rising from the rifle, he spun away from the table and snatched up the Remington 1100 semiauto twelve-gauge from where it rested against the wall and brought it to his shoulder. Dropping to one knee, he took aim at the center of the door and fired.

The inner office door erupted as the double-ought buckshot punched a fist-size hole. Jonathan felt the breeze cut by ballistic path as a plug of nine .32-caliber pellets passed way too close at twelve hundred feet per second. He threw himself to the ground and yelled, "Down!" at the same instant that Boxers yelled, "Gun!" and likewise kissed the floor. From the corner of his eye, he saw a crimson spray as Plano pirouetted and fell, dead before the pellets exited his body.

A second shot followed a half second later, and then a third. The shattering bits of office all around him formed a cloud in the air.

Inexplicably, Farmer just stood there, stunned and staring.

"Farmer! Get down!"

A fourth shot caught the guard full-on in the belly, and then he was gone, too.

Jonathan rolled left, across the floor toward another office, but the shooter had anticipated the move and fired a fifth shot that pummeled the wooden filing cabinet over his head.

Jonathan looked to Boxers to check his status, and found the Big Guy trapped in the corner closest to the shooter's door, curled into a ball and trying unsuccessfully to look small.

Up and down the fourteenth floor, people had started to dial into the violence, and that's when the panicked screams started.

As Brother Franklin Demerest watched the digital clock tick down past thirty seconds, his heart hammered as if to break free of his rib cage. His palms were slick with sweat, and despite the open window and the frigid breeze, the room felt stifling—a hundred degrees and the air too thick to breathe.

This was fear, and it was the emotion that he dreaded most. His shot was eighty-three yards shorter than Brother Michael's, but in some ways required more precision. The bullets he fired would hit from the president's right side, catching the podium in a cross fire. Once his rounds passed through their initial target—which they would easily do—it looked from the pictures on the television as if they would threaten only the chaplain, and then whoever happened to be in the wings of the makeshift stage.

It was Brother Michael's bullets that would do the real damage, which was why he had chosen that perch for himself. From the position on Coolidge Avenue, whatever bullets passed through or missed their mark would drill on into the crowd. Every shot Brother Michael fired, then, would cause destruction. Franklin, by contrast, had to shift his aim a full thirty degrees to the right after his first five shots onto the stage to empty the remaining five shots into the crowd.

Thirteen seconds.

Despite the sandbags that wedged the giant Barrett rifle

into place, the reticle of his scope quivered and the sight picture danced from his pounding heart and trembling hands. His breathing chugged too fast. He inhaled deeply in a loud, throaty gasp and held it, the way he used to hold the pot smoke back when he was in college, and then he let it go. That should settle him down.

Seven seconds.

He reacquired his spot, though it still danced. He took another deep breath, let half of it go, and then held the rest as he settled his finger on the trigger and counted down in his head.

Four . . . three . . . two . . .

The pace of the shotgun blasts told Jonathan that the shooter had a semiautomatic—there were too many rounds for an over-and-under, and the cycle rate was faster than even the most skilled guys could shuck a shucker.

When the gun went silent after five rounds, Jonathan suspected that he was reloading, but there was no way to tell. One thing he was sure of was that cowering on the floor accomplished nothing.

He looked to Boxers and got an enthusiastic thumbs-up as the Big Guy rose to his haunches. Sometimes a warrior's greatest weakness was hesitation. He'd taught that at the Operator Training Course, and it was the mantra that guided Boxers' life.

Jonathan nodded his assent and rose to a crouch. Boxers kicked the door.

With the threat in the outer office neutralized—or at least distracted—Michael returned to his chair and his rifle. The clock no longer mattered. His time for martyrdom had arrived, and chances were good that he would die before the clock ticked to zero. That meant that he needed to abandon the plan to achieve the goal.

The Barrett settled into his shoulder like a familiar lover. He acquired his spot, and his finger found the trigger.

Before the door had exploded all the way open, Jonathan saw in a glance what was happening. From posture alone, he knew that Michael Copley was an instant away from letting fly with his cannon.

Jonathan's Colt bucked three times in his hand. He didn't aim so much as he pointed and shot; but the .45 read his thoughts. The three bullets stitched a straight line down Michael Copley's spine, from the base of his skull to the space between his shoulder blades.

As the leader of the Army of God died, he pitched forward onto his face like a drunk who had finally reached his limit.

With the echo of the shots still ringing, and gun smoke hanging in the air, Jonathan and Boxers squirted into the room and did a quick sweep for any other bad guys. "Clear," they said in unison.

"Nice shootin', boss," Boxers said with a grin. "Looks like we barely made it."

"Oh, shit," Jonathan said, pointing at the television. "I think we're too late."

The live television picture showed utter mayhem unfolding on the stage at the Marine War Memorial. The president appeared to be on the floor, and Secret Service agents swarmed the scene, weapons drawn. Agents and uniformed officers brandishing automatic weapons formed a tight perimeter around the spot where the podium used to be, and then a scrum of agents hurried the president off the stage on the far side.

"What the hell happened?" Boxers asked, agape. "I didn't hear him get a single round off."

"He must have had help," Jonathan said. Whatever triumph he'd felt ten seconds ago had all drained away. "Damn."

As the motorcade raced away, led and followed by the counterassault team, one with its roof hatch open and Dillon gun turret deployed, the sound of the sirens was piercing, even at this distance.

Gail made no pretense of stealth as she stormed down the hall toward Suite 1013. She vaguely noticed the Compliances Services logo on a brushed aluminum plate on the wall next to the frosted glass-paneled door. She pulled once, and when she found it was locked, she drew her .40-caliber Glock and fired a single shot at a spot on the floor on the far side of the glass. The panel became opaque for an instant, and then instantly transformed into a cascade of a million glass beads that tumbled in a neat pile.

A fraction of a second after she'd pulled her trigger, the entire floor shook from the massive explosion that had to be the .50-caliber Barrett. A second shot followed as she was ducking under the panic hardware on the door and scooting into the office space. The interior of the space was tiny, consisting of an abandoned ten-by-twelve-foot reception area and a single closed office door beyond it.

When she heard a third report from the Barrett, she took aim at the middle of the closed door and fired five shots through the wood panel, punching a near perfect horizontal line of bullet holes from left to right. Then she fired a sixth shot into the spot where the tongue of the lock met the jamb.

She kicked the door open, and the first thing she saw was the massive rifle poised on the top of the desk, its barrel still smoking. But there was no shooter. Her stomach seized when she realized just how perfect a target she had made of herself, literally framed in the doorway, and she dropped to a deep crouch, her weapon up and ready.

Then she saw the feet on the floor, oddly tangled with each other. She led with her weapon as she traced the feet to their owner, a man who was old enough to know better. He lay on his back with his eyes open, bloody bubbles forming around his nose and mouth.

His right hand moved in a slow, almost lazy motion to

draw a little five-shot .38 police special from the waistband of his trousers.

"Put it down!" Gail commanded. "Drop that weapon now!"

He didn't look at her, but he seemed to hear, because he laid the revolver across his chest.

"Put it on the floor!" she commanded.

Instead, his thumb found the hammer and pulled it all the way back.

"Don't make me shoot you again!"

Gail didn't want to kill him. She had killed too much, and she wanted it to stop. But she didn't want it enough to die for the cause.

Even by police standards, she now had just cause to blow the guy away. But she hesitated. He wasn't pointing the weapon at her. He wasn't pointing it at anything in particular, so far as she could tell.

"This doesn't have to end up with you dead," she said. "Put the weapon down. Please."

The man on the floor took a huge breath. It seemed to take all of his energy to say, "We won." Then in one startling spasm of movement, he brought the revolver up to the soft spot under his jaw and pulled the trigger.

"Oh, my God!" someone yelled from behind Gail.

She whirled, weapon still at the ready, and a young lady in a Polly professional black suit with a white blouse screamed, "No! Please don't shoot." She fell on the floor in the hallway and covered her head with her arms.

More office workers were swarming about now, and as the realization crystallized, panic started to spread. And Gail was the focus of it all.

It was time for her to go. Holstering her Glock, she hurried to the emergency stairs and took them all the way down to street level. From there, she tried her best to blend in with the fleeing crowd.

CHAPTER FORTY

Franklin Demerest had whiffed his shot, pure and simple. Whether it was nerves, or Gail's noisy sudden entry, they would never know, but that all-important first shot had hit six inches in front of the president's chest and disintegrated the lectern he was speaking from. The presidential seal medallion was found thirty feet away.

The president had been wounded—not by bullets, but by high-velocity fragments of splintered wood that penetrated both legs. According to the White House physician, the body armor that the president was wearing saved his life, but would have been useless against the size of bullet that was being used.

The investigation was ongoing, as it no doubt would be for many months to come, but the FBI had reportedly discovered a link between the assassination attempt and a West Virginian religious cult that called itself the Army of God. Early reports were indicating that there'd been some kind of rebellion among the ranks of the AOG, as the media was calling it, and the result had been an intense battle that resulted in many deaths and injuries.

In a last feat of unquestioned heroism, a late-morning

commuter named Tom Herod had thwarted a suicide bomber on the Metro's Orange Line by noticing him as he fumbled with the safety pin on the detonator and punching the bomber in the throat. That terrorist likewise was suspected of having ties to the group in West Virginia.

While pundits and talking heads pontificated on the intense dangers of religious cults, domestic terrorism, and the ready availability of firearms, the blogosphere and conspiracy theorists were abuzz with outrageous rumors of assault teams and a helicopter raid. If any of it were true, according to the nutty rumormongers it would mean that the government had overstepped its bounds, and the entire case against the Army of God soldiers would be suspect.

Lounging barefoot and in sweats in his living room, Jonathan watched a recording of Irene Rivers from earlier in the day as she addressed a crowd of reporters. "While we are following every lead, it is simply inappropriate at this time to reveal details of the investigation beyond those that we have already provided."

Off screen, someone asked something that Jonathan couldn't hear, and Irene smiled. "You know, after every incident like this, there are going to be kooks who make all kinds of claims. The only two facts that I can state without any hesitation are that the so-called government agents who shot the would-be assassins were not, in fact, a part of any government agency, and that whoever the heroes are who foiled this despicable plot are intent on remaining anonymous, and are very good at doing so."

Another unintelligible off-screen question.

"Of course I admire them. How can you not admire people who risk their lives to save the lives of others?"

With that, the network cut back to the anchor, and Jonathan got bored with it all. He drained the glass of the Lagavulin he'd been nursing for the last half hour and was considering another when the doorbell rang and JoeDog went nuts. She'd been sleeping under the coffee table, and she damn near tipped it over in her scramble to find her feet.

Jonathan rarely received visitors who rang the bell, and never received them after dark. The dog ran to the door and pretended to be ferocious while Jonathan casually lifted the pistol from the table next to the couch and hid it behind his leg. "Joe, hush," he commanded and the beast complied. Jonathan opened the door to reveal perhaps the last person he expected to see.

"Boomer," Jonathan said.

With his long hair and thick beard, the tall, heavily muscled man on the other side looked more like the Afghan he pretended to be than the Unit operator he was. Jonathan stepped aside to make room. "Come on in."

Boomer Nasbe shook his head. "No, thanks. I can only stay a minute."

"Then stay a minute and have a drink. When did they let you escape back to the World?"

"Officially, I'm on TDY to Quantico to brief the FBI," Boomer explained.

"And unofficially?"

Boomer's eyes reddened. "I know what you did for my family, Dig. I needed to tell you how grateful I am."

Jonathan blushed a little and smiled. "Officially, I don't know what you're talking about," he said. "But unofficially, how are they?"

Boomer gave a half shrug. "Physically, they're fine. The rest will take time."

"They seem strong to me," Jonathan said.

"It'll take time."

The moment drew out long enough to become awkward. "Are you sure you don't want to come in?"

"Listen, Dig," Boomer said. Jonathan sensed that he'd been preparing himself. "I owe you a debt I can't repay."

"You really don't—"

"Let me finish. I don't pretend to know all that you do, but I hear the rumors. If you ever need anything—and I mean *anything*—you get in touch with me, and it'll be there.

No limitations, no questions asked. That's true of anybody in the Unit. They wanted me to tell you that."

Jonathan knew that the man was stating fact, and then it was his turn to be speechless. "Thanks, Boomer," he said. "And you're welcome. I just wish it had gone easier for Ryan and Christyne."

"They're alive and they're home. The rest doesn't matter." Boomer extended his hand, and Jonathan shook it. "You take care," he said, and then he walked away.

Gail had no idea if she was doing the right thing. She hadn't had a meaningful chat with Jonathan since the night in the hotel, and with each passing day, the burden of what had happened—and of what might happen if the details were ever leaked—consumed her more.

She'd reached the point where doing anything was better than doing nothing, so here she was, literally about to pass through a door that could change everything. She pressed the doorbell, and fifteen seconds later, there he was.

At this hour, Father Dominic D'Angelo looked less like a priest than a guy who'd been lounging around watching television. His face morphed to mask of concern. "Gail," he said. "Are you all right?"

The tears came before she was ready for them, flowing freely and embarrassing her. "No," she choked. "I'm not okay at all. Have you got a minute?"

ACKNOWLEDGMENTS

Writing books can be a lonely pursuit. I spend long hours playing with my imaginary friends, and when things are going well, the reality of the story in my head can be more vivid than the reality of my chair and desk. (They call it psychosis if you do anything else for a living.) Were it not for the love and support of family and friends, and the diversions of a life outside of writing, I think the whole thing could become sort of overwhelming.

My wife, Joy, is the single best thing that has ever happened to me. I adore her, and she continues to love me even during the times when I can be not particularly loveable.

The best thing that Joy and I ever did together was make our son, Chris. He's fun and funny and handsome and smarter than anyone else in the family. He's also a great cook.

I'm honored beyond words that Christyne Nasbe made such a generous contribution to the American Heart Association to lend her name to a character in *Threat Warning*. Here it is for the record: I borrowed only her name. Whatever characteristics the real-life Christyne shares with my fictional creation is purely coincidental.

Writing books is a part-time endeavor for me. My real job at the Institute of Scrap Recycling Industries Inc.—my Big Boy Job, according to my wife—grants me the opportunity to work with a cadre of consummate professionals, and I want to express my gratitude for their friendship and counsel. I can't list every name here, but I'd be remiss if I didn't shine the spotlight on a few: Anne Marie Horvath, Tom Herod, Joe Bateman, Robin Wiener, Bob Garino, Kent Kiser, Chuck Carr, Tom Crane, Ed Szrom, Jerry Sjogren, Rick Hare, Cap Grossman, John Sacco, and Kendig Kneen.

Speaking of Kendig Kneen, rest assured that he is a far, far nicer man than the character to whom I lent his name in *Threat Warning*. And, Kendig, sorry about changing the spelling of your last name for the book. It seemed like the right thing to do at the time.

I'd put my publishing team at Kensington up against any other in the business. I've worked with a number of houses over the years, and I've never seen a more dedicated group of professionals. Michaela Hamilton is hands down the best editor I've ever worked with. She understands what I'm trying to say, sometimes better than I do. Publisher Laurie Parkin demonstrates the kind of excitement about the book business that you don't see anymore in today's world of product placement and profit and loss statements. At the very top of the pyramid sits Steve Zacharius, who exudes a love of the business. Thank you all for all you do.

Of course, nothing happens in a publishing career without the tireless efforts of a great agent. I have the best in the business in Anne Hawkins of John Hawkins and Associates. That she's also a dear friend makes it even better.

Don't miss John Gilstrap's next exciting thriller
starring Jonathan Grave . . .

DAMAGE CONTROL

More Books From Your Favorite Thriller Authors

Necessary Evil by David Dun	0-7860-1398-2	$6.99US/$8.99CAN
The Hanged Man by T.J. MacGregor	0-7860-0646-3	$5.99US/$7.50CAN
The Seventh Sense by T.J. MacGregor	0-7860-1083-5	$6.99US/$8.99CAN
Vanished by T.J. MacGregor	0-7860-1162-9	$6.99US/$8.99CAN
The Other Extreme by T.J. MacGregor	0-7860-1322-2	$6.99US/$8.99CAN
Dark of the Moon by P.J. Parrish	0-7860-1054-1	$6.99US/$8.99CAN
Dead of Winter by P.J. Parrish	0-7860-1189-0	$6.99US/$8.99CAN
All the Way Home by Wendy Corsi Staub	0-7860-1092-4	$6.99US/$8.99CAN
Fade to Black by Wendy Corsi Staub	0-7860-1488-1	$6.99US/$9.99CAN
The Last to Know by Wendy Corsi Staub	0-7860-1196-3	$6.99US/$8.99CAN

Available Wherever Books Are Sold!

Visit our website at **www.kensingtonbooks.com**